THE ICE AGE

The Ice Age

MARGARET DRABBLE

ALFRED A. KNOPF   NEW YORK   1977

Grateful acknowledgment is made to Levine and Brown
Music, Inc., for permission to reprint three lines of lyrics
from the song "Tie a Yellow Ribbon Round the Old Oak
Tree" (page 128). Copyright © 1973 by Levine and
Brown Music, Inc. All rights reserved. Used by per-
mission.

Library of Congress Cataloging in Publication Data
Drabble, Margaret [date]
   The ice age.
   I. Title.
PZ4.D7561c3   [PR6054.R25]   823'.9'14   77–3319
ISBN 0–394–41790–9

MANUFACTURED IN THE UNITED STATES OF AMERICA
FIRST AMERICAN EDITION

Methinks I see in my mind a noble and puissant Nation rousing herself like a strong man after sleep, and shaking her invincible locks. Methinks I see her as an eagle muing her mighty youth, and kindling her undazl'd eyes at the full midday beam; purging and unscaling her long abused sight at the fountain itself of heavenly radiance; while the whole noise of timorous and flocking birds, with those also that love the twilight, flutter about, amaz'd at what she means, and in their envious gabble would prognosticate a year of sects and schisms.

—John Milton, *Areopagitica*, 1644

Milton! Thou shouldst be living at this hour:
England hath need of thee . . .
             We are selfish men;
Oh! Raise us up, return to us again;
And give us manners, virtue, freedom, power.

—William Wordsworth, composed
September 1802

Part One

On a Wednesday in the second half of November, a pheasant, flying over Anthony Keating's pond, died of a heart attack, as birds sometimes do: it thudded down and fell into the water, where he discovered it some hours later. Anthony Keating, who had not died of his heart attack, stared at the dead bird, first with surprise—what was it doing there, floating in the duckweed?—and then with sympathy, as he guessed the cause of its death. There it floated, its fine winter plumage still iridescent, not unlike a duck's in brilliance, but nevertheless—unlike a duck's—quite out of place in the water. It gave rise to some solemn reflections, as most objects, with less cause, seemed to do, these solitary and inactive days. He fished the bird out of the pond with a garden fork and stared at it with interest. It was large, exotic, and dead, a member of a species artificially preserved. It had had the pleasure, at least, of dying a natural death.

Anthony's hand, in his pocket, closed over the letter from Kitty Friedmann, which had thudded onto his doormat that morning. He had opened it over his cholesterol-free breakfast, but had been unable to make himself read more than the first sentence. He would have to read it soon, but not now. Now, he would bury the pheasant: that would postpone Kitty for a while. And digging a grave would be good exercise. He was supposed to take a certain amount of exercise.

There were, at least, plenty of places one could bury a pheasant in, on the new Keating estate: indeed, one could easily have buried a large dog or even a sheep. In his London home, there had been few corners suitable for burials, and those that were suitable had been well stacked over the years with the small bones of mice and fish and gerbils. The sour London soil had been thick with bones and plastic beads and indestructible nuggets of silver paper. On the other hand, in London, pheasants did not fall from the air onto one's property.

As he dug the hole, he thought of the first sentence of Kitty Friedmann's letter. *These are terrible times we live in,* she said, with her loopy unused middle-aged script.

He heaved the pheasant into the hole. It occurred to him that perhaps he ought to have plucked and eaten it instead, but he did not much fancy a bird that had died in so tragic a manner. He buried it beneath a hawthorn bush, a windbeaten bush that leaned at an angle, in perpetual acknowledgment of its situation. He identified with the pheasant, and covered it gently with the dry chalky earth. A cock pheasant. He had been forbidden sex as well as butter, nicotine, and alcohol. Not that the prohibition, in present circumstances, had much relevance.

Kitty's letter, he knew, would be full of an unbearable goodness, in the face of a tragedy too horrible to think of, a tragedy that made his own problems look manageable and dull.

He kicked some dry leaves over the grave. Then he walked, slowly, up the garden, through the gate, and slowly up the hill to the view. Ah, the view. Was it worth it? Was it worth what? Anthony Keating, property developer, had paid a great deal for this most undeveloped view. A Yorkshire view, of a Yorkshire dale. From his hillside, if he looked down the valley instead of back toward the house and the village, he could see no buildings, no houses at all.

Surveying this empty space, in the bright blue autumn sunshine, he read the letter of Kitty Friedmann.

Kitty's husband, Max, had been killed by a bomb, as he sat eating his dinner in a Mayfair restaurant. Kitty had been injured, and had lost a foot. Amputation, at St. George's Hospital, Hyde Park Corner, where she still lay, in a private bed. Kitty wrote:

Dear Anthony,

These are terrible times we live in. It was kind of you to write. I am getting on fine you will be glad to hear, and all the family are being wonderful. Poor Max, he died instantly you will be relieved to know. I know that for a fact, not just what the doctors always say, some comfort! We were enjoying ourselves at the time, it was our Ruby wedding anniversary, and that seems a good way to go. We must all go one day. We had a good life and I am getting on as well as can be expected, and of course I am always thinking how lucky I am, I have a good family and they look after me. Max was sixty you know and I am fifty-eight, it still surprises me. Don't feel too sorry for me dear it is terrible as you said, and I don't know what Max ever did to deserve it, if he were alive he would be crying out for hanging and capital punishment, but I don't think that is the answer do you? You will be pleased to hear they say I will be able to get around quite well by myself in the end though of course the children say I will never have to!!! They are good children.

My writing is not what it was, I am sorry. Don't worry about me my dear, you have enough worries of your own. I see from the paper Alison is still in Wallacia. What a terrible year. Look after yourself, put yourself first, that is the only way.

Sincerely,

Kitty

Anthony Keating looked at the view and thought of Kitty Friedmann. Without a foot and without a husband, she lay in her bed at St. George's and thought herself a lucky woman. Put yourself first, said Kitty, who had never put herself first in her life. They are good children, she said: and so, perhaps, some of them were, though Anthony would never have trusted them. Kitty had dyed red hair, and wore a great deal of carelessly applied makeup, and diamond brooches, and fur coats that dwarfed her, and she saw no harm in anybody. She would be finding it hard now, as she lay there, to blame the I.R.A. She would be finding it hard to believe that they really meant it. How could they have intended to kill Max Friedmann, as he ate his smoked salmon? Perhaps it was a good thing that it had been an Irish bomb and not a Palestinian one. (Max had donated liberally to Israel.) Even Kitty, who had been heard to plead the Zionist and Palestinian causes in the same sentence, unaware of any contradiction, might have been forced to blame the Arabs, if she had been made to think they were really after Max. Which, of course, they had not been. The whole thing had been a ghastly, arbitrary accident. The bomb simply happened to have blown up Max and Kitty, a random target. This past year had been so full of accidents that they had begun to seem almost normal.

Terrible times. Still, I would rather have had a heart attack than lose a foot, thought Anthony. He remembered a foolish discussion he had once had at a party, years ago, about feet, during which several people claimed that they had so little interest in their own that they doubted if they would even recognize them, severed on a slab, presented after a rail crash in a policeman's plastic bag. Anthony had been surprised by this lack of sense of ownership. He would have known his own feet anywhere, attached or unattached. But his heart was another matter. It beat in his chest, soft and treacherous. It was invisible. Nobody had ever seen it. He had been unaware of it, most of the time, until it had reminded him of its existence, and now he thought of it often, he nursed it carefully, as though it were a baby or a bird, a delicate creature that must not be shocked or offended. Now that he was growing accustomed to its presence, he was learning to feel affection for it, as he felt for his hands, his feet. He would not like to have this new awareness removed. His own heart had complained, of neglect, perhaps. And now he paid it attention.

Nevertheless, it was puzzling that so many dreadful things had happened in so short a space of time. Why Kitty, why Max, why Anthony Keating? And why had the punishments been so unrelated to the offenses? Max and Kitty had nothing whatsoever to do with the Irish, and Kitty had never offended anybody in her life, unless there were some cynics who found her universal goodwill offensive. The maiming of Kitty seemed a particularly outrageous accident. It was like the maiming of a child. Kitty represented for Anthony everything that was generous, innocent, unsuspicious, trusting. He was particularly fond of her because she so little resembled the Christian patterns of virtue he had been reared to admire. She was a living proof of the possibility of good nature. There wasn't even any point in testing her good nature, if that had been God's plan, for, as her letter indicated, there was no possibility of her failing the test. God had wasted his time, maiming Kitty.

Anthony's own destruction was more logical: at least there was that to be said for it. He had the satisfaction of knowing that it was all his own fault. He had brought it on himself. Though that, in a way, simply made the general sense of accelerated doom more puzzling. He could rationalize his own misfortunes, but there was no rational explanation for the sense of alarm, panic, and despondency which seemed to flow loose in the atmosphere of England. There was no one common cause for all these terrible things. Or if there was, Anthony had not yet grasped it.

It was partly to escape panic and despondency that he had bought this house, this view. London was growing unpleasant, everyone agreed, and Anthony, like many others, had decided to leave the sinking ship. The view extended along the valley: harmonious, glittering, distant, dry, nature at its best. He gazed at it, at the pale greens and grays of the far limestone, the hard blue of the sky, the black trees in the lane, the gray-green roofs of the village beneath. The colors themselves spoke of an orderly composite life, slowly accumulated. It had seemed safe, a place where one could avoid the disagreeable intrusions of London life, the people, the garbage, the traffic. But they had not moved quickly enough. His timing had been wrong. He remembered the day when he and Alison Murray had stood here on this hillside, months ago, contemplating the promised land that they had just purchased: it now seemed that they had been aware then, in their bones, that they would never enter it. They had waited too long—for children to grow up, for ex-husbands and ex-wives to settle; they had waited to make enough money, to find the right house. And they had found the right house: even Alison, a Southerner, had agreed that it was a remarkable house. He looked down on it now: there it stood, as it had stood for nearly three centuries, High Rook House. Below it, the rooks which had provided its name cawed in the elm trees. Its roof was gray, covered with green moss, and on the barn grew house leeks for good luck. The windows were mullioned, and strange little fantastic finials topped its pediment. "Something of an architectural folly," Pevsner described it, and Anthony Keating's folly it had certainly proved to be. For, from the point of purchase onward, as though in revenge for his over-weening presumption, everything had started to slump and slide and crack. He had bought the house at the top of the market, and suddenly, overnight, the property market collapsed. It was almost as though it had been waiting for him to sign the contract.

The collapse had been dramatic, and had affected others more severely than Anthony Keating. He, a mere novice in property, watched events with dismay and mounting alarm. What had happened to those days of easy money in the early seventies, what had happened to the boom, to all those spectacular profits? Why had all the confident experts been so taken by surprise? Anthony had been seduced and corrupted by these confident experts into believing that profits would go on multiplying forever, unlikely though that had always seemed. Go for growth, had been the slogan, and everybody had gone for it. Now some were bankrupt, some were in jail, some had committed suicide, and only the biggest had survived unscathed. Casualties of slump and recession strewed the business pages of the newspapers, hit the front page headlines. Old men were convicted of corruption and hustled off to prison, banks collapsed and shares fell to nothing. Anthony could not quite believe that the whole slump had been caused by his own desire to buy himself an expensive country house, but was nevertheless aware that it could not have happened at a worse time, from his point of view. He was appalled. However had he got himself into this nightmare world, and however was he going to extricate himself? He was so far in that there was no way back to the safe little debts and overdrafts of earlier days. His imagined fortune, on the strength of which he had bought the new house, had dwindled into a tangled mess of unsaleable liabilities: at the time of reckoning, he and his two partners were the proud owners of an office block that nobody would rent, and of an undeveloped stretch of Riverside property that nobody wanted to buy, and which nobody could afford—with present building costs and interest rates—to develop. He himself owned two houses: High Rook House, and his old London house, which stood empty, squatted in, unsaleable. He was at last free to sell the latter, his first wife having finally been remarried, to a man with a proper job, and moved out, but it was too late, he had been too late getting it onto the market, had spent too much time with Alison messing about looking for somewhere else, and now it stood there, useless, incriminating, costing him four hundred a year in taxes, not to mention the price of the bridging loan. Nobody wanted it. Nobody wanted anything any more, the game had come to a full stop. And Anthony Keating, as he would have been the first to admit, was caught in a trap of his own making.

It was quite neat, in its own way. He could see the poetic justice of it, and wished at times that he could survey the disaster from a more detached position. But it is hard to be detached about one's own debts. (And anyway, what is the point of perceiving the poetic justice of the property crash when a man like Max, who had carefully put his eggs in many baskets, and had survived undamaged, survived only to die over dinner on his Ruby wedding anniversary?)

Anthony recognized that he himself had been particularly ill-placed. Not as ill-placed as Stern, or Lyons, or Poulson, or his good friend Len Wincobank, who was doing four years for fraud in Scratby Open Prison. But ill-placed, nevertheless, in that he had nothing behind him, no other strings to his bow. He thought of his partner, Giles Peters, who would doubtless survive the whole affair, unless a bomb got him too.

At times, Anthony thought it would have been far more appropriate for Giles to have had a heart attack. It would have served him right. It was his enthusiasm for adding the final touches to the Riverside site that had proved the fatal slip: Anthony himself would have been content with a more modest (though not particularly modest) scheme. But Giles had wanted those last few properties, and had bought them, and borrowed for them, against the swing of the tide, when the writing was already on the wall, when building costs were beginning to soar and interest rates to rise, when office rents were ceasing to soar. He had persuaded Anthony that it would be safe. And they had borrowed too much. Anthony had been weak, allowing himself to be persuaded, but it was Giles who had suffered from hubris, and it was Giles who ought to have had a heart attack. Anyway, physically, he was more the type: a fat man, a heavy man, a heavy drinker and a heavy smoker, a man who took no exercise of any sort. Whereas he himself, though admittedly once a drinker and a smoker, had been extremely fit, light, energetic, if anything underweight, a walker and a squash player: indeed, he had been so far from suspecting that he might ever have a heart attack that when he suffered one, late on a Friday night, he had persuaded himself that the peculiar pain in his left arm and shoulder and in his chest was tennis elbow, and that he had pulled a muscle playing squash. He had gone to bed, got up the next day, walked around all weekend in pain and perplexity, and finally visited a doctor some sixty hours later, when a suspicion that something might be wrong had begun to nag at his mind. The doctor's views had astonished him. A heart attack, at the age of thirty-eight?

After the event, he had rationalized it, unwilling to let anxiety take the blame. (Does anxiety give one a heart attack? Shock can kill, but what about incessant strain? Ulcers, surely, would have been more likely?) His mother had always had a bad heart: indeed, some years earlier she had had an operation, and a new plastic valve. His own must be hereditary.

It would have done Giles good to have a heart attack, re-flected Anthony. It had certainly taken the edge off most of Anthony's other anxieties. For a while at least, the fear of death had made his financial anxieties seem insignificant. There is no point, as many have observed, in being rich and dead. The desperate struggle to avoid smoking and drinking had proved an absorbing diversion: one's capacity for anxiety is not endless. There were times when Anthony would willingly have exchanged his entire prospects for a cigarette or a whisky. (At times he regretted that his debts were so enormous that these enforced economies would not make the slightest impression.)

But even the heart attack had not been the final blow aimed by fate at Anthony Keating. The heart attack had proved to have compensations, the chief of which was Alison, who stood by him, slept by him, diverted him, and paid him more attention than she usually thought his due, making him, for once, her first priority. Anthony enjoyed this, and began to imagine that there might be some agreeable future ahead for both of them, even without any money. Alison was very good at looking after him, when she chose to be. (His ex-wife, Barbara, had offered to return to him to look after him, but he had told her that she was more likely to kill him than cure him: humbly she had agreed, and relapsed into the prolific mess she created around her wherever she went. At thirty-eight, Babs was pregnant yet again, expecting her fifth baby. Anthony was glad it was not his. He felt sorry for Babs's new husband, a civil servant, previously unmarried, used to a quiet life. But at least he had a good, stable, decent government salary. Short of revolution, nothing too terrible can happen to a civil servant, unless, of course, he becomes greedy and accepts bribes. But Babs's new man didn't sound as though he was that kind of person at all.)

So, with Alison, the illness had been endurable, acceptable, and there had still been the hope that finances would improve, there had still been the house in the country. They planned to move after the summer, when Alison's younger daughter, Molly, went back to school. It was to be their first home together. Folly though it was, there it was. They had already sent up some furniture, when the coup de grâce was delivered. Like the bomb that killed Max Friedmann, it had no connection with Anthony's finances, so he did not feel responsible for it. But that was cold comfort.

The final blow was the arrest of Alison's elder daughter, Jane.

Jane, aged nineteen, was arrested and incarcerated on her way back from her summer holiday, in a Balkan country well behind the Iron Curtain and one not known for its tolerance of Western teenagers. Details of the charge were at first vague: dangerous driving, possession of drugs, both? Telegrams full of alarm and confusion arrived from the embassy, finally establishing that Jane had been involved in a fatal traffic accident, and that she was now in the prison hospital, lucky to have suffered no worse injury than a broken leg. Alison would have packed her bags and flown out at once, but it was difficult to obtain a visa: Wallacia had only recently started to issue traveling visas for tourists and was very cautious about visitors. But the Foreign Office had agitated, and the press, possibly counterproductively, had agitated, and after weeks of waiting she had received one and had gone out to see what was happening. She was still there. Anthony had offered to go with her, but he could tell that she did not want him there. It would be bad for his health, she said. Nor did he much want to be there. Secretly, he had never much liked Jane.

The British press had made much of Jane's imprisonment, portraying her as an innocent schoolgirl in the hands of vindictive Communists who had never heard of the concept of bail. They had pestered Alison before her departure for photographs and interviews: Alison was photogenic, and she could easily be made into a good news story. TRAGEDY STRIKES AGAIN, they declared. THE TRIALS OF A BRITISH MOTHER, they announced, and went into details about Alison's previous self-sacrifices. Others dwelled lovingly on the barbaric sentences passed on dangerous driving in Eastern Europe. None of this went down very well with Alison, who did not like the idea of her daughter being turned into a martyr for driving badly, whatever the consequences: journalists tried to persuade her that international support and protest would be the best hope for Jane's acquittal and return, but both Alison and the Foreign Office doubted this. Though, as Humphrey Clegg at the F.O. said, one can never be sure. Wallacia had not hitherto shown much sensitivity to world opinion on these matters, but it was changing, slightly. There was some hope.

Anthony did not like to imagine what it must be like for

Alison in Wallacia. She had written to him, saying that Jane looked very bruised, and that she was refusing to speak to anyone, including her mother, that two people had been killed in the crash, that the boyfriend with whom she had been traveling had simply disappeared. She said the best that could happen would be a speedy trial, but there were innumerable little delays and obstacles placed in their way, it seemed deliberately. She said the consul, Clyde Barstow, was very kind, but not optimistic. She said she was allowed, somewhat to his surprise, to see Jane twice a week, in the presence of witnesses. She said it was depressing, seeing Jane, because Jane would not speak.

So, there it was. A terrible year, a terrible world. Two of his acquaintance in prison, one dead by assassination, himself in debt by many thousands. It had all looked so different, four years ago, three years ago. So hopeful, so prosperous, so safe, so expansive. In those days, the worst injuries he had ever known had been a broken ankle, children's measles, Babs's cervical ulcer, a bout of flu that might have been pneumonia; the worst accidents had been a broken windshield, a flooded basement. The frequency and the intensity had changed. He had never thought of himself, when younger, as an optimist; now he realized that this was what he had been. It could not surely be the natural onset of middle age? It was too severe, too sudden, too dramatic. It was as though he had strayed into some charged field, where death and disaster became commonplace. Once, such things had happened to others. Now he was the person to whom they happened. They were attracted to him, they leaped toward him like iron filings to a magnet, they clustered eagerly around him.

There was no point in thinking these thoughts. They led nowhere, to no illumination. He stood up, and stretched. It was too cold to sit long, despite the bright sun. He would dig over the vegetable patch: the pheasant's grave had reminded him of his resolve. By digging, we stake our claim to the earth, and Anthony Keating felt that his claim needed some reinforcement. He doubted whether he would be able to hang on to the house for long enough to see the potatoes and leeks and carrots of next spring: unless there was a turn of fortune, a reversal, a remission, he would have to sell, when the creditors finally closed in—and for much less than he had paid, no doubt. Nobody could afford a house like his any more. He could not afford it himself: it was doubly mortgaged, offered as a security, tied up with a personal guarantee. When the final crunch came, if it came, High Rook House would be swallowed up as though it had never been, a mere crumb in the vast empty maw of debt. So it seemed an act of faith, a warding off of ill fortune, to dig the vegetable patch, to plan ahead. Also, there were no vegetables to be had in the village shop. One of the laws of country life is that one cannot buy fruit or vegetables in the country. So Anthony would grow his own. But first, he would walk along the footpath, along the edge of the scar, down by the nameless brook, into the valley, and back by the road. The water in the brook ran brown and clear and busy, sharp with its own newborn purity, uncontaminated, without a history. It collected on the high fell and rushed and bubbled downward, over moss and stones. The water from London taps has been through six pairs of kidneys. This had fallen straight from the sky. He liked it. He liked walking. It was a consoling pastime, monotonous, safe, unproductive. And the countryside, though riddled and mined with its own limestone secrets, with potholes and swallow holes, caves and underground rivers, was stability itself compared with the explosive terrain of the London property market.

It was, of course, his own fault that he had strayed into such a minefield. Whatever else had been accidental, this had been his own choice. He had rarely done the sensible thing in his life: his whole career had consisted of careless gambles and apostasies, most of them springing, no doubt, from the first—from the denial of his father and all his father had expected of him. The usual story. His father had been a churchman and a schoolmaster, teaching in the cathedral school in an ancient cathedral city: he had sent his three sons, on a special scholarship for clergymen's sons, to a more distinguished public school, and had expected them to do well for themselves. He was a worldly man, who despised the more obvious ways of making money: throughout his childhood Anthony had listened to his father and mother speaking slightingly of the lack of culture of businessmen, of the philistinism and ignorance of their sons, of commercial greed, expense accounts, business lunches. Under the massive yellow sandy shadow of the cathedral wall, the Keatings sat safely in their extremely attractive, well-maintained eighteenth-century house (it went with the job) and listened to good music, and laughed over funny mistakes in Latin proses, and bitched about the clergyman's wife who had a pronounced Lancashire accent and economized in small ways, for they were not well off, and had to appear better off than they were.

Mr. Keating had accepted Anthony's rejection of the church without a murmur, conceding that Christian faith was a rare blessing these days. He murmured slightly more at Anthony's premature marriage, while still an undergraduate, to Barbara Cockburn: muttered that it would be better if Anthony had waited to take his degree, made one or two nasty remarks about shotgun weddings and repenting at leisure, asked him whether Barbara knew about family planning (she didn't and wouldn't) and lent Anthony two hundred pounds. "At least she isn't a Catholic," he said, having met her, and having seen she was not as bad as he feared.

Two hundred pounds was not enough. Owing partly to Barbara's fecklessness, partly to the normal expenses of marriage and babies, and partly to Anthony's determination not to be completely subdued by that fecklessness, he was, from the earliest years, either in debt or just about to run into debt. He never had time to work out what he wanted to do for his living, in any serious sense: necessity obliged him to live on his wits to pay the bills. Luckily, he had plenty of wits, and soon discovered that there was not much future in being a hospital porter or a launderette attendant or a mortuary assistant: such jobs broadened one's vision, and were a short cut to paying the rent and the milk bill, but they had no prospects. So he tried to think of other possibilities, through his degree in history, and moodily stared at his own and other people's laundry, and listened to his baby crying in the small hours.

His parents had always assumed that he would become a professional man, of one sort or another: his two elder brothers were barristers. But to Anthony, with a baby and a large wife and another baby on the way, there did not seem to be enough time to train for a profession. He did not think he would get a good enough degree to enter the Civil Service; anyway, he did not much want to be a civil servant. So what was left? It must be said that it never once crossed Anthony Keating's mind that he might get a job in industry. Rebel he was, but not to such a degree: so deeply conditioned are some sections of the British nation that some thoughts are deeply inaccessible to them. Despite the fact that major companies were at that time appealing urgently for graduates in any field, despite the fact that the national press was full of seductive offers, the college notice boards plastered with them, Anthony Keating, child of the professional middle classes, reared in an anachronism as an anachronism, did not even see the offers: he walked past them daily, turned over pages daily, with as much indifference as if they had been written in Turkish or Hungarian. He thought himself superior to that kind of thing: that kind of advertisement was aimed at bores and sloggers, not at men of vision like Anthony Keating. His nearest approach to contemplating a proper job, at this stage, was to visit the Civil Service on an organized tour, an offer he accepted largely because it included two free nights in London, which he spent in a hotel on the Cromwell Road with a pregnant Babs. But he was so turned off, on his trip round the Home Office, by the queries about pensions and wives' pensions made by unmarried youths of nineteen that he decided that that kind of security was certainly not for him.

For despite the pregnant Babs, and then the crying babies, Anthony himself at this stage thought that there was something not very nice about money. One had to have some to live on, of course, but one ought not to concentrate too much upon the matter. His politics were left-wing, like those of most arts undergraduates: he disapproved of the Establishment (then a vague but fashionable catch phrase), deplored the fact that so much was owned by so few, would have liked to see public schools abolished, denounced the property-owning role of the church, and could not see why everybody did not agree that a radical redistribution of wealth was logical, desirable, and necessary. He thought that miners and garbage collectors and sewage workers and railway drivers should earn more, and that company directors should earn less. He would never have dreamed of voting Tory, although both his parents did. He worried about his fellow men, but, like many of his fellow worriers, could find no means of expressing his care. He was too busy caring for his own: for Babs and baby Mary, and then for baby Peter, and Stephen, and Ruth.

So, like so many, he stumbled into a career, rather than chose one. He had, in his first year at university, as yet unencumbered by Babs, shown a certain frivolous talent for writing revue sketches and lyrics and songs: he had always been fond of playing the piano, and had a small but useful gift, one in demand in undergraduate circles, for writing quickly and composing quickly—he could knock out a song in an hour or so, for any given occasion. He could sing quite pleasantly, too, and even after Babs and the baby enjoyed escaping to the college piano. Tired and penniless as he was, his friends found him rather dashing; to have a wife and baby so early in life seemed a form of one-upmanship. So he kept singing: in his second year, a show for which he had written the lyrics (they were vaguely satirical—this was just after his *Salad Days*, just before the satire boom) transferred to London, with some success. He didn't make any money, for he had signed no proper contracts, but for the first time it occurred to him that there might be money in the arts as well as in launderettes.

In his third year, his friend Giles Peters came to him with a proposition. Write a musical, said Giles Peters, and I will put up the money, and we will take it to the Student International Drama Festival in Chicago and win first prize.

Giles Peters, unlike most undergraduates, had a lot of money. At this stage, he had little else: indeed, Anthony tended to look down on him, from his tenuous but prominent position as fashionable witty young man. Giles was neither handsome nor witty: one of the hard lessons of the sixties was the spectacle of his frequent sexual successes (successes followed by disasters, it is true, but when has the maintenance of sexual happiness been rated as highly as the acquiring of it?). Giles was small and ungainly and already slightly overweight: he had reddish hair and a red complexion, whereas Anthony was tall and dark and pale of skin. As an under-graduate, Giles was interested in the arts, and hung around stage doors and exhibitions and got himself invited to the theater parties and literary parties: he gave lavish parties himself, which made him a welcome if not wholly popular guest. The clever set thought Giles was a bit odd but quite sweet: a bit of a bore, but not quite a bore. He had a kind of self-confidence and rudeness that made his social inadequacies appear deliberate and therefore acceptable. And he had one or two marked successes—for example, with the lovely Chloe Vickers, one of the most pursued girls in Oxford, who could have taken her pick of all the wealthy young men around. An-thony and his friends, bewildered by the incongruous liaison, tried to persuade themselves that Giles had simply bored and bought her into acquiescence, but they were guiltily aware that this hope sprang from a very deep desire to underrate Giles. And Anthony himself did not in fact find Giles at all boring, though he did not know why. He was not witty, he had no verbal elegance, indeed was rather slow of speech, and quickness was in others one of the qualities that Anthony most prized. But Giles had some other, indefinable, at this stage incomprehensible virtues that made him interesting company.

He also had a great deal of money.

His father had made a great deal of money, and his grand-father before him, out of bridges: they built bridges all over the world, over all kinds of chasms, and had diversified into roads and dams; work which those less snobbish and unrealistic and obtuse than Anthony and his friends might have found exciting. How-ever, Anthony and his friends thought bridges dull, and Giles, at this stage a third generation dilettante, tended to let them think what they chose about bridges, for he wanted to make his mark in other fields. And he wanted Anthony to write him a musical, to win a prize of five thousand dollars in Chicago. They discussed it, in Anthony's dank basement flat: it seemed like a fantasy, and, as Anthony poured Giles another glass of wine (then six shillings a bottle) he even said to Giles, "So you fancy yourself as an impresario, do you?" "No more than you fancy yourself as a composer," Giles had sagely replied.

Anthony had agreed to have a go: why not? He had abandoned, through sex, all hope of the good degree that might have been his. Why not write a musical instead? Giles had then spoken of money: better draw up a proper contract, he said, just in case. Anthony tried to conceal his surprise. A contract? He did not conceal his surprise effectively: Giles caught it, and, briefly, smiled. Anthony caught Giles's smile, and said—truly, for they were not beyond truth—"You know, Giles, I'm a lousy songwriter."

"Even lousy songwriters have a right to a contract," said Giles.

So Anthony wrote his musical, and Giles backed it and took it to Chicago. It did not win five thousand dollars, but it was favorably mentioned, and launched the career of Bill Wade, well-known star of cabaret. Bill Wade had a weakness for one of Anthony's not very good songs, and thanks to the contract and the Performing Rights Society the song is still sung, and even to this day Anthony Keating makes some money every year from it. In its best year, and his worst, it made three hundred pounds, which was very welcome.

Anthony was flown out to Chicago, to see the festival. He flew with Giles: the rest of the company had gone ahead, to rehearse. Side by side they sat, conspirators, drinking whisky, for now Giles was host. They discussed what they would do at the end of the year. Giles said: I think there are some interesting possibilities in commercial television.

So Anthony got a job with the BBC. They were looking for bright undergraduates: in those days, there were more jobs than people.

It was not at first a very well paid job, and in order to keep Babs and the (then) two children in London, which was even at that time expensive, he used to do other things on the side: sketches, reviews, a little journalism. He was quite successful.

Giles, meanwhile, like his father before him, diversified. Commercial television, a small publishing company, a radio station, a bookshop, a PR company. He was very successful. But also restless.

They met from time to time: Giles would call round for a drink and stay all evening, or they would meet by chance in town. Giles brought his wives round, one after the other: in return, Anthony would occasionally introduce Giles to the women friends with whom he would defend himself from Babs, her babies, and her infidelities; for Babs had proved to be the unfaithful type, a maternally spirited woman who could not resist a vulnerable face. Anthony did not like to reflect on how vulnerable he must once have looked himself. He put up with Babs's boys with a varying grace; Babs was the kind of person it was hard to dislike, impossible to be angry with for long, so desperate was her own need for affection. She knew her children loved her, which was why she wanted more and more children, to multiply and ensure the love: she was never sure of anyone else. Anthony felt guilty about his own infidelities, so he continued to be as kind to her as possible, but the whole life-style proved very expensive: he had to pay for wife and children, for his wife's lovers (who were usually non-self-supporting), and for his own lovers. His own women were usually girls from the BBC—research workers, actresses, editors; they could well have paid more for themselves, but this, in the early sixties, was not yet the vogue, and Anthony felt obliged to provide dinners, drinks, theater tickets (though luckily he could often get those free).

It was exhausting; there was little time to think, and when there was any time, he did not like his thoughts. After seven years at the BBC—producing, writing, editing—he too began to get restless. But what did he want? His work was interesting, he supposed: he was, by now, well paid, and it was certainly not the BBC's fault if he still had to worry about the mortgage. But it occurred to him more and more often that television, although not as dead-end a spot as a mortuary or a launderette, was not endlessly interesting: there was a limit to what could be done in it, and he himself seemed to have reached that limit, rather early in life, being quick-witted and hard-working. He did not want to move through the hierarchy to an administrative grade, for administration bored him, and there was nowhere else to go. Friends of his who had entered the parallel trade of journalism reported similar dissatisfaction: they had reached the top too early, some had even managed to earn startlingly high salaries too early, and from the age of thirty, what remained but a slow or rapid decline into hard drinking and ill health? Slight thoughts of envy were expressed, occasionally, for those who had entered professions with a proper career structure of proper incentives; but it was too late for those.

It had always been too late.

So Anthony Keating expressed his dissatisfaction with himself and his life in a predictable manner: he changed his job. He moved from the BBC to ITV, from arts to current affairs, accepting a similar job for marginally better pay. The change stimulated him for a while: new colleagues to impress, new offices, a new canteen, all these had the desired effect of raising morale and enthusiasm, and he had some good new ideas, and launched a successful new current affairs program. He set up some interesting investigations into current swindles and scandals, and was instrumental in the trial by television of some notorious crooks. This gave him a fleeting and superficial feeling that he was being useful to society, but he remained in some way unconvinced by himself, and decreasingly interested by the social evils he was engaged to expose. He would wake up in the middle of the night and think: Is this it? Is what what? In short, he was underemployed, bored, and not at all happy in his relation to his work, his country, or the society he lived in: ripe for conversion, to some new creed. A political creed, but there wasn't one; a religious creed, but he had had God, along with his father and life in the cathedral close. So what would happen to the vacant space in Anthony Keating? What would occupy it?

The vacant space was occupied by Len Wincobank; the conversion took place in 1968, while Anthony was watching unedited film of an interview with Len the property whiz kid. He had arranged the interview, had sent one of his own bright young men, Austin Jones, off to Northam to ask Len what he thought he was up to, raping the city centers of Britain and making millions. Austin, an aggressive enough interviewer, had asked all the right questions, and made all the right liberal noises about conservation, planning acts, small tenants, home ownership, and Len had made what seemed at first incriminating and predictable replies: as the film unwound, Anthony mechanically noted which phrases, which shots to cut, which to join together. But when the film had finished, he felt curiously uneasy. He walked up and down the corridor for a while, then went back into the studio and played the rushes again. And it struck him, suddenly, with a dazzling flash: how could he not have noticed it before? The truth was that Len Wincobank was a genius, about ten times as intelligent, ten times as perceptive, ten times as alive as Austin Jones. Austin Jones, in comparison, was a boring somnambulist, a ventriloquist's dummy, mouthing without conviction or information or even any intelligence the obligatory provocative questions—questions which were based on an utterly false premise, the premise that he and the viewers lived in a society which disapproved of the profit motive and which condemned private enterprise. No wonder, thought Anthony, no wonder I have been so bored and so half-hearted, for so long.

Elated, illuminated, he played the reels for a third time. Yes, there it all was. If you read the film correctly, with Wincobank as hero and Jones as villain, everything fell into place. He could not, of course, edit it that way: that was not his job. But he went home, thinking seriously for the first time for months. For three weeks, he thought hard, about money and incentive and private and public ownership: then he rang up Len Wincobank and invited him to lunch. Len, understandably a little huffy about the subtle way in which Anthony had contrived to make him look a greedy dishonest monster on the screen, refused.

Anthony waited another week, then rang again. "Look, I've got to talk to you," he said. "I'm thinking of doing a whole series, on the property boom, a serious series, not just a one-off job like that interview with you. I'm sorry about that, I know you didn't like it. But I must do the subject justice. I want you to tell me what I ought to do, who I should talk to. Please."

Len Wincobank consented. They had lunch. They talked. To

Anthony, it was a revelation. Whole vistas opened before him. In fact, the property business had interested him for some time, ever since he had read a gripping account of it in a book called *The Property Boom*, by Oliver Marriot, a book which had described the excitement and romance of the business in stirring terms, if not in wholly approving ones, and Anthony had noted in himself, while reading it, a certain envy for those who had the wit to prosper so spectacularly and so speculatively. He had not at the time taken his own envy very seriously, not connecting it in any way with himself, but with Len in front of him—Len, in his thirties, Len, with a new idea a minute and a vision of concrete millions, Len, who had not the slightest suspicion that it might be wicked to make money—his knowledge took on a new meaning. Len had borrowed his first thousand from the bank. Len had, like Anthony, lived off his wits, entirely: the difference was that Anthony had never even dreamed of the flights Len Wincobank had achieved. It had never occurred to him to ask himself, why not? On the way home, he asked himself, why not? There were some good solid sociological answers to the question, but none so solid that they could not be dissolved in the new sharp solvent spirit of free enterprise.

That night, he rang Giles Peters with a proposition. Hello, Giles, he said, rather drunkenly (for his new plans had gone to his head), I want to stop being a gentleman and become a businessman.

What a very sensible plan, said Giles Peters. How are you going to set about it?

With your help and your finance, said Anthony Keating.

And that was how Anthony Keating left a reasonably safe salaried job with a pension in television and became a property developer.

He and Giles and Rory Leggett, an estate agent friend of Giles's, started quite modestly. They bought a site in South London, conveniently near a projected new tube line. It cost them £70,000, of which they borrowed £65,000. Giles's name was good for credit, he had excellent contacts in the banking world, and anyway money was easy in those days. On the site stood a small sweets factory, a warehouse (disused), and a small publishing company which had printed travel books (bankrupt). The only going concern was the sweets company, and that was not going very well: it was a small, old-fashioned family firm, the old man wanted to retire, and neither of his sons was interested in the business—Giles, Rory, and Anthony did not have to feel pangs of guilt at removing them, though the old man did wax somewhat sentimental on his last tour of the place before signing the contract. "Confectionery's not what it was," he said, predictably. "We're the biggest sweet-eating nation in the world, did you know that? But people don't want hand-made sweets, these days. They want everything packaged. Everything American. They only want what they see on the television. They don't appreciate the individual sweet."

Anthony, following him, peered into bins and vats of sugar and treacle, gazed at weird antiquated pieces of machinery that cut slabs of jelly into fishes and stars, stared at trays of toffee, and watched a woman twisting strands of white and brown mint sugar into a long rope of humbug. It was not a highly automated factory. Nobody would want the equipment. "It's all out of date," said the old man. "They're museum pieces, some of these pieces. The end of an age, isn't it?"

He seemed surprised that they wanted the site, and accepted their offer without much trouble.

Anthony found the site inexpressibly romantic and exciting. When the last of the sweetmakers had gone, and all work had stopped forever, he walked around the eminently serious commercial property with immense pride. This, he said to himself, this is ours, this bit of the real world. He had felt only the slightest flicker of excitement at the purchase of his first house, in Shepherd's Bush, partly because the house itself was so shabby and undesirable, so remote from one's dream house, partly because the mortgage was so high, partly because he had had to borrow the down payment from his father and Babs's father, which removed any sense of independent achievement. How much better to owe a Merchant Bank than one's father-in-law.

The site was, in fact, very shabby and run-down, but the buildings (which would of course have to come down to make way for offices) were interesting, imposing, curious. The small publisher's still contained heaps of travel books lying on the floor: guides to Lapland, the Netherlands, the Pennine way. (It was while he was reading an unbound book on the Pennine way that Anthony, in the grip of powerful fantasy, said to himself that he would, when he had made his fortune, buy himself a house in Yorkshire.) The sweets manufacturer had left them his equipment, which had been included, at low cost, in the deal: he also left them various little heaps of sugar fishes and boiled sweets and pear drops. But it was in the warehouse that Anthony made his most interesting discovery. In one corner, in a crate, he found an enormous quantity of pots of anchovy paste, in perfectly good condition, anchovy paste being a more or less everlasting commodity, and a cardboard box full of large balls of string. All in all, these were the most desirable of the acquired assets, though the fishes went down well with the Leggett and Keating children at home.

There was a large, open, cobbled space in the center of the site, which had a strange look of the countryside about it. Weeds grew up between the stones. There were horseshoes, nailed on the warehouse wall. Once there must have been a stable: no doubt the sweetmaker's had distributed its sweets a hundred years ago by horsedrawn van. There was even a small tree: an elderberry had managed to root itself between the cobbles. It would be a pity, in a way, to remove this space, though nobody had seen it for decades, except for the handful of people who worked there, but it too would have to go. Anthony was quite relieved when Rory suggested that the local council might find their redevelopment plans more acceptable if they incorporated in them an open area for public use. "We could point out," said Rory, who knew many developers' architects and their ways with zoning boards, "that this present area hasn't been seen or used for years, and we're going to return to the community a nice patch of open space. With trees."

On the architect's model, the trees eventually appeared as neat little toy trees from toytown. They stood on a green patch. Anthony somehow felt that they would lack the charm of the cobbled yard and the secret elderberry, that the grass would be covered in dog shit, that the trees would be vandalized and killed off even inside their chicken wire protection. But that would not after all be his fault, or the fault of his property company. It would be the fault of the people.

The council liked Rory's architect's plans, granted them a variance, and the old buildings came down. Soon all that was left of the sweets factory was its name, which Anthony, Giles, and Rory inherited along with the empty sugar bins: they became the Imperial Delight Company. It was a satisfactory new identity. And the company prospered. They were easy days. Anthony picked up the business fast. It seemed that they could not fail, could not go wrong: as the site got under way, and the builders succeeded the demolition workers, Anthony scouted tirelessly around, looking for new suitable properties, revisiting Imperial Delight from time to time to reassure himself that the whole enterprise was real, not a mere fantasy. At times it did not seem possible that a mere idea could have become so concrete, that it could be employing so many men, so many cement mixers and bulldozers, so much cement, so many bricks. But there they all were, as evidence.

London became a changed place to Anthony. Before, he had seen it as a system of roads linking the houses of friends and the places of his employment, with a few restaurants and shops included in his personal map: now he began to see it as a dense and lively forest of possibilities. Whole areas, hitherto neglected, acquired significance. At first Anthony went around dazed by achievements that he had once taken for granted: what genius had assembled the land for Bowater House, for Eastbourne Terrace in Paddington, for soaring Millbank Tower and elegant Castrol House? And who could regret the forgotten buildings these giants had replaced? Even the much-maligned Centre Point of Harry

Hyams revealed itself to him in a new light: indeed, he began to remark casually to friends, he had always thought it rather a fine building. But what impressed him most about it was that it was there at all.

The I.D. Company did not think at once in terms of central properties of huge glamour: their success in Wandsworth led them to look at fringe areas, with potential. Anthony found himself doing most of the looking, for he enjoyed it. The activity made him immensely happy. He had never in his life been so fully committed, so deeply engaged, so deeply *interested* in what he was doing. He felt at times that he must have spent the rest of his life with a head in a bag, a bag which was taken off only when he got into some nice safe familiar middle-class intellectual interior.

His finest achievement was the purchase of a gas holding tank —a gasometer. It was not a very expensive gasometer, for the Gas Board had abandoned it some years earlier, on the advent of North Sea Gas, but it was a useful site, which would join very neatly onto a brewer's yard and an old bomb site, and possibly a whole stretch of river frontage. (There were still bomb sites to be found, amazingly, in Outer London.) It gave Anthony the most profound joy, to find himself in possession of a gasometer. He had always admired their delicate, airy, elaborately simple structures, and he would drive down to look at his own, for the pleasure of looking at it. It was painted a steely gray-blue, and it rose up against the sky like a part of the sky itself; iron air, a cloud, a mirage, a paradox, defining a space of sky, changing subtly in color as the color of the sky changed. It stood dark and cold, it would catch the pink wash of sunset, it would turn white like a sea gull, it would take upon itself the delicate palest blue against a slate-dark background. It was a work of art. It would have to come down, of course, for who wants an obsolete gasometer? But while it stood, while the I.D. Property Company negotiated for the other parts of the jig-saw, Anthony would gaze upon it with more pride and more wonder than he had ever, in childhood, regarded the cathedral outside his bedroom window, though that cathedral was thought by some to be the finest building in Britain. It thrilled him more to own it than it would have thrilled him to have a Velázquez, a Titian on his wall. A derelict gasometer, radiant with significance. One could see it from miles away, right across the Thames, from some directions. It lifted the heart. Up soared the heart like a bird in the chest, up through its light and airy metal shell, to the changing, so much before unnoticed sky.

Anthony was better at spotting things than he was at the financial details of transactions. But he trusted Giles and Rory to keep the accounts properly, and his financial grasp improved. It is so much easier to understand one's own debts than those of the Post Office, or Chrysler's, or the nation's. One has so much more reason for trying to understand. Motivation is all, as many a schoolteacher has remarked. In no time Anthony had picked up an impressive store of knowledge about rents and reversions and interest rates and debentures and mortgages. In his previous life, he had never quite grasped why the fluctuation of a quarter of a percent in the bank rate should cause such excitement, and merit such space in the press. Now, he wondered how he could have been so ignorant.

His friend Len Wincobank was much impressed and amused by Anthony's conversion. He watched his progress with protective benevolence, for Anthony was his protégé. He himself dealt on a scale that made Anthony feel slightly faint: he doubted if he would ever want to be involved with such vast transactions. Len took him on a tour of the Northern town centers that he had developed, showed him shops, offices, described deals with councils and triumphs over competitors, showed him failed monstrosities developed by others, took him to look at Park Hill in Sheffield. "I really wanted to go into housing," said Len, staring in admiration from the front seat of his Rolls at the massive block. "But there weren't the openings." Anthony continued to admire Len. He admired him because he was an articulate bloke, who knew all the arguments against what he was doing as well as those in favor of it: because he was self-made, had started from scratch, without a rich Oxbridge friend to back him; because he loved what he was doing, loved his buildings, believed in them, thought them beautiful, thought people ought to like them, was outraged when they didn't (and, of course, they didn't, as most people dislike anything new), and was determined, with a kind of blinkered faithful zeal, to *make* people like them. He was an enthusiast. Anthony liked Len's girl, Maureen, too. Occasionally he had misgivings about the appearance of some of the actual developments: the center in Northam looked to him, from outside, sinister and blank, but when Len explained to him that this was the new kind of architecture, that there was no need to have any windows at all in that kind of building, that most new buildings were going to be windowless, and what about the height, the fine expanse, and of course perhaps architects hadn't yet quite got the hang of building without windows, but they would, they would—well, Anthony began to see even the Northam center with new eyes.

Len Wincobank was not the only interesting new person that he met in his interesting, integrated new life. As well as a new London of buildings, he discovered a new world of people: stockbrokers, merchant bankers, town clerks, local councillors, commercial architects, contractors, accountants—all sorts of people now swam into his social ken, people who had once at best been fodder for social programs, usually cast as villains. Some perhaps were villains, but they were all of them very interesting, and none of them paid any attention to all those things that had previously drifted idly round Anthony's mind—they did not read novels, or go to good films, or read the arts pages of newspapers, or listen to music, or discuss the problems of the underprivileged. They "didn't much go" for that kind of thing. They were far, far too busy. He found them entrancing. The Other England. Where had they been, all this time?

Babs did not find them so entertaining. They had nothing to say to her, nor she to them: if they met her and thought of her at all, they thought her a Bohemian slut, which she was. She thought they were interested only in money, which they were. She accused Anthony of hypocrisy, of intellectual slumming, of folie de grandeur, of brain fever. They are all crooks, she wailed. They will do you, Anthony. Crap, said the new Anthony, his mind intent on some loophole in the Town and Country Planning Act, 1947.

Finally, she cooked up a satisfactory social explanation for his extraordinary aberration. "It's his Yorkshire blood coming out at last," she said. Anthony found this quite funny. It was true that the Keatings were original Yorkshire stock, and that Anthony himself had a yearning for the landscapes of his childhood holidays with his grandmother, those days of paradise by the River Wharfe. But the Keatings had hardly been of the tough, mill-owning, slave-driving, where-there's-muck-there's-money class that Babs's wild apology suggested. They had been quiet folk, farmers, school-masters, clergymen, doctors. It was they that, in this heroic stand, he rejected forever. Enough apology, enough politeness, enough self-seeking high-minded well-meaning well-respected idleness, enough of quite-well-paid middle-status gentlemen's jobs, enough of the Oxbridge Arts graduate. They had killed the country, sapped initiative, destroyed the economy. This was the new line of the new Anthony, Oxbridge Arts graduate turned property dealer.

In the early seventies, he no longer woke up in the small hours asking himself, What is it? What is what? He was usually too tired to wake, and when he did, he occasionally asked himself with horror, What on earth have I done? It seemed a better question. At least he had done something. He had made thousands of pounds, but had borrowed many thousands more. He had tackled the modern capitalist economy. He was a modern man, an operator, at one with the spirit of the age.

Babs was not the only person to suspect that Anthony's sense of empire was illusory. Alison Murray also suspected it, but unlike Babs she had a vested interest in believing it to be real. If Anthony became a rich man, Babs would lose him and Alison would get him. Babs, at this time, did not quite want to lose Anthony: she certainly did not want to risk the chilly winds of divorce, inadequate maintenance, quarreling over houses, looking singlehanded after four children, with a babyfaced man as her only support. (She had not yet met the civil servant.) Of course, if Anthony became rich, he would be able to support an ex-wife in style. But Babs regarded the whole thing as a bit of a gamble. And she liked Anthony.

Alison, on the other hand, invested a good deal of hope in it. She loved Anthony, and wanted to marry him, so she aided and abetted and morally supported his efforts to make this financially possible. She, like Anthony, had an unsatisfactory and feckless spouse, an actor of pathologically jealous and pathologically unfaithful temperament; like Anthony, she had been through a process of slow disillusion with her past life. She was an actress, but had abandoned the stage on the birth of her second daughter, who suffered quite severely from cerebral palsy: she started to work for the Society for Disabled Children, and devoted herself to fundraising, appealing, visiting, talking on radio, television, to the press. She was sufficiently well-known to be able to do this with some impact. The career she had given up had been highly promising, established, even, rather than doubtful, and most of her theatrical friends thought she was mad, though they did not like to say so to her face, because of their diffidence in face of her very evident tragedy; also, Alison's decision to stop acting removed a serious competitor from an overcrowded profession, and who could be unselfish enough to regret that? Nevertheless, behind her back, they speculated that it must have been some kind of guilt or self-punishment, rather than real goodness, that had made her relinquish so bright a future for one of such hard and, in their eyes, unsatisfying work. One or two of them guessed, shrewdly enough, that her husband, Donnell, might have had something to do with her decision, for Donnell's career, when the sick child was born, was not going nearly as well as Alison's, a fact which caused him a resentment which he was quite unable to conceal in public, and which, they felt, might well express itself somewhat violently in private. Like a good wife, perhaps Alison had chosen to retire rather than to compete.

Alison was thirty when she met Anthony, and on the verge of

turning from the good-natured friendly person she had once thought herself into a mean, embittered, angry, contemptuous woman. The transformation had surprised her, but she did not much blame herself for it. She blamed others. When she met Anthony Keating, at a party in the gay and prosperous party-giving sixties, she felt herself to be standing in the last ditch of pleasantness, smiling faintly and politely and hopelessly, resolving never to smile at another adult again, knee-deep in an intense dislike of almost everybody she had ever met, or might ever meet, including the good people of her professional life. Attracted by the nonsexual aroma of her unhappiness (for he thought he had had enough of sex, and making up to other people's disaffected wives), and provoked by her undisguised boredom, Anthony set out to interest her, and he succeeded. For he was a good talker, a good listener, a man of tact and feeling.

They had much in common, as well as feckless spouses. Both were tired of being good, or of pretending to be good. Both felt that they had encountered low standards of behavior in the outside world; both had tried, in their own ways, to behave better, and both felt defeated. Both were interested in money. Anthony was interested in it for the reasons already stated, Alison was interested in it in a more abstract sense. Years of fund-raising had taught her to read balance sheets and inquire knowledgeably about interest rates and investments and tax relief: she was able to listen to Anthony's financial problems and ambitions with some real understanding. She had also had to organize her domestic economy singlehanded, and had long been in charge of mortgage, bills, visits to the accountant, for her husband, Donnell, was a spendthrift and had, in the early years, often been out of work. By the time she met Anthony, Donnell was always working, for he was one of those whose natural stage or screen age is well over forty: he had been too young to play heavyweights in his twenties, but by his midthirties he was much in demand for businessmen, villains, chiefs of police, leaders of guerrilla groups. But Alison still had to watch the money; otherwise he spent it all on buying drinks and meals for friends, sending guests home on the minicab expense account, and staying in expensive hotels. So she was well aware of the shifting value of a pound note. She even knew what the *Financial Times* index was, from day to day. Anthony found this very companionable, for Babs had never been able to grasp the difference between debtors and creditors, and had to think very hard to work out the difference between net and gross, concepts she connected with cornflakes packets rather than incomes.

The alliance of Alison and Anthony was not as joyless or as mercenary as this summary might indicate. It had its pleasures, too. For instance, Alison happened to be a beautiful woman, whose chief weakness was for her own appearance. She dressed well, looked after herself, kept herself in excellent condition, and devoted much energy to preventing herself, successfully, from growing fat, gray, and wrinkled. As Babs had long been fat and never very stylish, Anthony naturally found Alison's appearance in itself good for morale. She was the kind of woman one could take anywhere. Merchant bankers treated her with respect. She was dark, with one of those pale, oval, sad, soft, expressive faces that are as typically English as the English rose: refined, delicate, slightly but not uneasily withdrawn. Her large, expressive dark eyes had once looked into the hearts of those sitting in the back rows of the stalls: when they turned their gaze upon Anthony, upon a merchant banker, upon a rich benefactor, their appeal could hardly be resisted. And she had remarkable legs. The clean, thin line of shin and ankle, the precision, the articulation, were a joy to behold, as she herself would have been the first to acknowledge. Her skin was also remarkable. It had a clear, pale, translucent smoothness, blue veins adorned her inner arm, her thighs, her breasts, her elegant neck. Even the touch of her hand had a dry, soft vitality: anybody who had ever so much as held your hand, Anthony said to her once, would surely never wish to touch another woman. She liked that kind of remark, naturally, and he was good at making them. He meant them, too.

And all these gifts she gave to Anthony. She was not in any conventional sense a vain woman, and certainly not a flirtatious one: she had by her prime received so much trivial sexual admiration that she had come to find it genuinely boring, thus offering to men a sincere rather than an assumed resistance. Anthony felt very pleased with himself for having overcome it.

Alison, for her part, found Anthony sweet. "Oh, Anthony, you *are* sweet," she would say. It was not quite clear to Anthony precisely what she meant by this, but he found the remark acceptable. She was not quite sure what she meant by it either, using the epithet actress-style to cover a wide range of possibilities: that Anthony was a spontaneously affectionate person, that he was generous with his praise and his money, that he often opened doors for her, that he frequently had a worried expression that stirred her maternal spirit. That he recognized that she was *the* beautiful woman, rather than *a* beautiful woman. He was also extremely sweet to her defective daughter, Molly. Molly spent the term in a special school, but she would emerge for holidays, and then Anthony would be very sweet to her indeed, driving her out into the country, taking her to the zoo, not minding when she messed up his car, playing dull games with her for hours. He did not at all mind the embarrassment of dealing with her in public, would wipe her nose, pick up the cups she knocked over in cafes, patiently cut up her meals and fasten her shoelaces, and read to her from her favorite comics. Once she was sick all over the back of his best suede jacket in the car, on the way to Whipsnade: Anthony had taken his jacket off, tossed it in the trunk, wiped up the rest of the mess, without the faintest discernible hint of any form of irritation. He had been upset that Molly was feeling bad, had been worried that her day might be spoiled. One cannot expect that kind of behavior of a man, but it is irresistible when one meets it.

Anthony was not quite so sweet to Jane. But nobody is perfect.

Anthony Keating, the pheasant buried, the vegetable patch dug, started at seven o'clock to cook himself a solitary early supper. He had spent more time alone in the last weeks, since Alison's departure, than he had done in the whole of the rest of his life. The doctor had told him to take things quietly, and so he was doing. He was also evading a fair assortment of problems, by removing himself from the London scene. He wondered how things were getting on without him. Giles spoke to him, daily, with a progress report on the Riverside scheme but there seemed to be little to report: the market could hardly be more inert. And Anthony had become a very inert partner. It was largely a question of hanging on. The night before, Giles had promised to visit: I might have business up North, he said, but he had said it in so uneasy a manner that Anthony, not much caring for his new role, almost took offense. He did not want Giles's sympathy; he could do without it. He could do without any human sympathy.

It was all very odd. Not only had the boom turned into a slump: his life, which had recently been far too full, had suddenly become extraordinarily empty. He would have to learn to cope with solitude. It had become the new problem. Occasionally he felt an urge to drive down to London, just to see what was happening, although he knew he could do nothing useful: part of him missed the anxiety, the tension, the racket. But he would train himself to stare at stones and trees. It was a longer-termed insurance. If he could afford to pay the premium. More frequently (for, in truth, the very thought of the London scene made him feel physically unwell), he felt an urge to drop in at the village pub, but this too he resisted. He would stick it out, alone. After a lifetime, or half a lifetime, of dissolute company, he would give solitude a fair trial. In a sense, he felt he owed it to Alison, who could not be finding much company in Wallacia.

Boredom had proved to be a problem, as one might have guessed. Anthony was a restless Londoner, tuned to the rhythm of ten new problems a day, ten different appointments; and even between appointments, sitting in his car waiting for a meal, he had in the old days been at times overwhelmed with boredom, as though eternity had suddenly set in and would never shift. A craving for excitement, for stimulus, was what had kept him on the move. Nothingness would yawn suddenly at him, worse than the prospect of a violent death. One of his most uncanny moments of self-knowledge had taken place once years earlier when he had by mistake locked himself into the lavatory in a seaside hotel in Normandy: the lock seemed to have jammed, fiddle as he would he could not shift it, and he feared to fiddle too much lest he damage it even more irretrievably. It was a gilt lock, a pretty French gilt lock, ornate, ill-made, useless. And there Anthony was, shut up in a small square box, without a window (it being a French lavatory, where the regulations are different) and with no prospect of deliverance for two or three hours, for Babs and the children had all gone down to the beach, and Anthony had said he would stay in the hotel room for the morning, working. The chambermaid would not pass: she had already done the room. Luckily he had a Michelin guide with him, which was better than nothing, so he sat quietly on the lavatory and tried to read, and to think of what to do, but waves of heat began to flow through him, at the prospect of imprisonment, and panic rose—not the panic of claustrophobia, for the lavatory was quite spacious, but deep panic at the prospect of deep, inert boredom. One Michelin guide could not possibly keep boredom from the door for a quarter of an hour, let alone the possibility of three hours. Desperately he looked around the rectangular prison: there was nothing to distract him, nothing at all to do. And then, on the wall, he spotted a hook. And ah, thought Anthony, without thinking at all, quite unconsciously —ah, if it gets *too* dull in here, I can always hang myself by my belt. The thought was so bizarre and so comforting and so alarming that it impelled him to a new, frenzied, violent assault on the lock, which suddenly and mysteriously yielded, and he emerged, pricking with sweat, horribly aware that at least a part of him would have preferred the action of death to the passivity of boredom.

And here he was, imprisoned in High Rook House, with nothing to do, no one to distract him. It seemed a challenge, which he would try to accept. He wondered why there was so little recognition in the world of the possibility of profound, disabling, terrifying boredom. One never heard people complain of it. It was not done, to complain of it. Like fear of death, it was supposed not to exist. Perhaps, because if one admitted it, one would never have the courage to live on at all. Perhaps people were ashamed of it. He was ashamed of it himself, ashamed of how often he looked at his watch, relieved if it was later than he had thought. Since moving to the country, he had found himself shifting his mealtimes earlier and earlier, going to bed earlier, and, by vicious consequence, being forced out of bed earlier, for he had not acquired the knack of sleeping more than seven hours a night. At his more optimistic moments, he thought that perhaps he was simply shifting his rhythm to a more natural time scheme: the rhythm of the night and the day. He hoped that that would prove to be so. There must be some way over the mountain of boredom that rose, ridge after ridge, before him.

There was a story in the valley of a heavy snowstorm one night many years ago. The snow had drifted against the windows of an old woman's cottage, a remote cottage, and she had been buried there alone for two days and two nights before neighbors dug their way to her. When they found her, she was still in bed and had not moved for forty-eight hours: she had been waiting patiently for the sun to rise. She said, That was the longest night I've ever known. Anthony smiled, remembering the story. How had she not died of boredom, trying to sleep, against nature, for so long? He tipped the pan, the fat sizzled ominously. What would one do in prison, like those poor buggers shut up for years alone by the Chinese? Would fear provide a sharp enough antidote to dullness? The fear of one's own death? We have come to need gross and violent stimulants. He wondered if it were possible to retrain the expectations of the spirit, to re-educate the palate.

He was cooking sausages for his supper, bought two days ago at the village shop. They were stuffed with cholesterol, but what was not? Very little, it appeared, and while he was prepared to believe in the anticholesterol lobby over a breakfast of Ryvita and honey, he had lost all interest in it by the evening. He didn't care if the sausages killed him. On the other hand, he did wish he could remember how to cook them properly. They were going to burst, he could tell, from the pinky brown way they were swelling up inside their skins, and oozing at the ends. He pricked them again, viciously, and turned down the gas, but one of them burst just the same: a nasty weal appeared along its side, its flesh gaped, lumpy, crumby.

They had bought the house thinking it would be big enough for all of them: for Anthony and any of his four children who wanted to visit, for Alison and her two daughters, for friends, for children's friends. Anthony had planned to commute to London, had talked in the good old days (albeit with a touch of astonished bravado) of getting a season ticket on the Executive Special from Leeds, for a mere £595 a year. And now, here he was, moodily turning four pork sausages, objects which seemed to recognize no state between the raw and the burned. So much for country house life.

He thought of Len Wincobank, whose company had gone so spectacularly bust. He wondered how he was getting on in prison. It was hard to imagine so energetic a man deprived of any possibility of private enterprise. He must surely have found some way of expressing himself, even in there. He had written to Anthony, twice, in reply to Anthony's letters, but he did not say very much. "It's just what I imagine public school is like, in here," Len had written. Anthony could dimly picture it: uniform, dormitories, playing fields, cold showers. A far cry from the bar at the Queen's Hotel, Leeds, with its dark brown bars and plum-jacketed bartenders, where they had shared so many gins and tonic, eaten so many small, pale, translucent onions. Though, geographically, not so far: Scratby Open Prison was in the North Riding, not forty miles away from Anthony's country house. He was due to visit Len, next week. He was going to drive Len's girlfriend, Maureen, over. The prospect made him rather nervous. He had been shocked by Len's sentence. It had seemed unreal, impossible. He had seen him several times while he was out on bail, had heard his stories of panic and collapse, had failed (like the jury) to follow some of the financial complexities, but had managed to persuade himself that Len would get off. But the tide had swung against such as Len. There had been too many scandals, too much corruption, and Len had served as an easy symbol. Down he had gone. How would he look, how would he behave, when they saw him?

The sausages were now burning on the outside. He cut one in half to see what it looked like on the inside. Rawish, still. God, he thought, I need a drink. But he had vowed, had promised himself not to.

Len would not be getting a drink in Scratby, either. Unless all those television series which showed prisoners secretly brewing liquor in the kitchen from yeast and old apple peelings were accurate documentaries rather than fantasies.

The jail in which Jane Murray had found herself did not sound as lenient as Scratby. Nor was the concept of bail much appreciated in Wallacia, according to Alison. Four weeks she had been there, without even a formal charge. Whereas Len, after the warrant had been issued, had had some months to rearrange his affairs, to sell this and buy that and transfer the other, before standing trial.

Anthony had never been very fond of Jane. Sultry, sulky, she had resented his existence, his relationship with her mother, and had been rude and offhand whenever he spoke to her. It was largely on her account that he had never tried to live with Alison: they had been going to wait, till Jane left school, left home, before setting up house together. Perhaps she had had the accident on purpose, to keep them both apart? He recalled with distaste meals in Alison's house, with Jane picking petulantly at her plate with a fork, making hostile comments on the cooking if ever she spoke at all, and often walking off, leaving the room without a word, as though Alison and Anthony's joint presence was too much for her to be expected to deal with. A petty, childish creature. Nothing ever satisfied her. She criticized everything; Alison never retaliated. She was a pretty girl, heavier in build than her mother, with a heavy, sulking, pre-Raphaelite mouth: when she was older, he guessed she would look rather like Janey Morris, and just as destructively dissatisfied. He wondered what kind of treatment she was getting in Krusograd jail. It would do her good to eat some disgusting meals, he unkindly reflected.

The sausages did not taste too bad. He had them with a tin of baked beans. Take it easy, the doctor had said. But it wasn't very easy to take it easy. Mustard helped. He covered everything in mustard, including a slice of Ryvita, then propped up a copy of the *Property Investment Review* against the radio, and read and ate. The *Property Investment Review* made interesting reading, these days. Its language had become curiously lurid. Every page was scattered with such mortal words as *death pangs, moratoria, fatal bleeding*: journalists spoke ominously of rocking foundations, and catalogued horrors, collapses, crashes, catastrophes—and chatted, more cheerily and colloquially, of skinned knees and burned fingers. The picture they ought to have evoked was of the end of the world, but it was strangely unconvincing, as though all the crashes were of cardboard skyscrapers or purpose-built film sets, as in a 1930s movie of the destruction of Nineveh. And, of course, most of the crashes were indeed metaphorical rather than physical. Only a few real buildings had really fallen. Ronan Point, Camden Girls' School ceiling, the roof of a swimming pool. Nothing much.

He finished the mustard meal, and sat there, gasping, eyes smarting, faintly cheered. Things were not as bad as the *Property Investment Review* might indicate, and mustard still really did the trick. The evening stretched ahead, long, dark and empty, but he was not wholly unhappy. This was so bad, some good was sure to come out of it. The darkest hour. He was not allowed to smoke or drink, but he could still think: the doctor had not told him not to think. And there were consolations, even in this long night. At least he did not have to worry too much about his own children, to feel guilty about them. They were a cheerful lot, not yet suffering from VD or schizophrenia or drug addiction or anorexia, as most people's children seemed to. Babs had done a good job with them. He missed them at times, but not, he had to admit, much. It was more fitting that he should brood by himself. He had been lucky with his children. Unlike poor Alison. He would not think about Alison.

He would think, instead, about Giles, and why he was slightly afraid of him, as though Giles had some undefined hold over him: and of Len, whom he did not fear at all, and whom, though a declared crook, he trusted: he would think of the problems of a mixed economy, state capitalism, the profit motive, corporate ownership, personal incentives. It would all make some sense in the end, if he worked on it. One cannot live alone for weeks in the country, untempted by any diversions, without coming to some useful conclusions. As yet, he had not the faintest sense of even the vaguest approach of understanding, but something would surely swim up out of the dark pool.

While Anthony cooked his sausages, Alison Murray was waiting in Krusograd, second largest city in Wallacia, to see a psychiatrist who might, the consul had suggested, be persuaded to visit her daughter in the prison hospital. Mr. Barstow was worried about Jane's behavior, and so was Alison, though—knowing Jane—she found it less surprising than he did. She sat on a hard chair in the waiting room and reflected that it was a good thing she was accustomed to doctors, hospitals, institutions, and the inevitable waiting they impose. It was a good thing, also, that she spoke enough German to make herself understood. She did not trust interpreters.

Dr. Gobian, the psychiatrist, spoke German. There were not many psychiatrists in Wallacia. It was not a country that much respected the revelations of Sigmund Freud. It regarded psychic problems as bourgeois luxuries, the idle tics of the underemployed. In her heart, Alison rather agreed with this view, but nevertheless considered it her maternal duty to do what she could for her own daughter. So there she sat, on a hard chair, hoping that the doctor might at least agree to look at Jane, and perhaps recommend that she should be released on bail, or be transferred from the prison hospital to a civilian one. Though maybe a hospital for the mentally ill would be as bad as prison, and even harder to get out of: she had read disturbing newspaper reports, about Jews and dissidents in Russia, that suggested that the Russians regarded psychi-

atric treatment as an alternative to punishment rather than as a
cure. How could one, in such a situation, know what to do for the
best? Clyde Barstow had himself been uncertain, and he knew the
country well. But he had thought it at least worth visiting Dr.
Gobian; it can do no harm, he said.

I suppose, he had cautiously added.

Jane could hardly have picked a worse country in which to
commit an offense. Wallacia was the most obscure and mysterious
of the Communist states, with the exception of Albania: it had
only recently allowed tourists to travel through its territory on
their way to the Black Sea, to Istanbul, to Greece, and then only
with severe and complex restrictions of visas and currency. Its
internal politics were highly secretive and little reported; its relations with its neighbors, and with the U.S.S.R., were shrouded in
ominous ill will. Like Albania, it flirted with China, though who
could guess with what intent. Its activities reached the English
headlines only when, as now, unfortunate foreigners found themselves incarcerated there on charges of espionage or dangerous
driving or drug smuggling. Alison had known nothing about it
before her arrival; now, she knew little more. The consul had said
there were signs of easing of tension and that hostility to the West
was diminishing: there was even talk of trade agreements. Alison
suspected, however, that he was trying, when he made these comments, to cheer her up.

She had been sitting there for an hour, waiting. It was nearly
eight in the evening. It seemed that people liked to make her wait,
these days. Instead of leaping to open doors for her, instead of
showering her with profuse if insincere flattery, the Wallacians
made it perfectly clear that she could not expect any kind of
preferential treatment. Although she recognized the justice and
propriety of this and had often complained of the obsequious way
she was treated back in England, she nevertheless found the contrast rather a shock, and would have been amused, had she been
cheerful enough to feel amusement, by her efforts to maintain her
own status in her own eyes.

After a while, she resorted to one of the most familiar of these efforts. She took her powder compact out of her bag, opened it, and looked at herself in the small oval mirror. There she still was. But Alison found, unlike Anthony with the mustard, that there was very little kick left in her own face. It was still there, but it didn't do much for her. She put the compact back in her bag, and went on waiting.

It would have been wrong to be bored, with one's daughter in such miserable danger. And Alison like Anthony was not, exactly, bored. She was too anxious. And she was also aware that some revelation was gradually shaping itself in her mind. But she did not much like the shape that it was slowly assuming: indeed, she wondered whether it was perhaps assuming a face of such unnatural monstrosity that it was no wonder that the pale small image of her own beauty had been unable to charm it. Alison Murray was beginning to have very bad thoughts about her daughter Jane.

It seemed an inappropriate time to be having them, but they would not go away. They waved, like Medusa's snakes, just beyond the edge of her vision, and she dared not confront them directly, though she knew they were there. She knew they were there because of the effort she was putting into not looking at them.

When the news of the accident had come through, Alison had been shocked, anxious, first for Jane's life, then for her safety: she had battled for the visa, waiting long hours in offices like this, and had set off to save, to rescue, to comfort, filled with savage maternal indignation. But somehow when she arrived and saw Jane's tight, hard face, her sullen impassivity, the sulking curve of her eighteen-year-old lip, her simple partisan sympathy had perished. For there was Jane, just Jane, as cross and perverse as she had ever been, the same girl with whom Alison had remonstrated, three years or so ago, for staying out all night without ringing home, for smoking pot in full view of the neighbors in the back garden, for leaving the bath taps running so that the water overflowed and brought down the dining room ceiling. Instead of feeling sorrow for her daughter, she had found many old irritations and resentments stirred and brought back to life. And, as the days dragged on, she dwelled more and more on these things, for which she had tried not to judge Jane; for after all the child had had a difficult childhood, poor girl, with Molly spoiling everything—embarrassing, pampered, messy, expensive, time-consuming Molly, eating up maternal attention and affection. She had tried not to judge Jane. But how could one not?

Sitting there, she remembered the scene last year at her parents' home when her father had been dying. The family had assembled, dutifully, for his last days: he was in the hospital dying rapidly of cirrhosis of the liver, and Alison, her mother, and her sister, Rosemary, reunited for the first time for some years, had found themselves, to their surprise, shame, and horror, spending most of their evenings complaining about what a dreadful nuisance he had been in his later years, how cantankerous, how selfish, how foul-tempered, how demanding. And with him dying painfully, not two miles up the road. They had been ashamed of themselves, but they had not been able to stop.

When he had died, then they had stopped. They had spoken of him no more to one another, though occasionally, now, Alison found herself able to remember the good things.

Maybe, she thought, my bad thoughts of Jane will disappear after the trial? It is the not knowing, the suspense.

She crossed her legs, neatly, looked for comfort at her neat ankle, her Milanese shoe. She tried not to think of Jane's stubborn, rejecting face. She thought instead of Molly and her jerking, ungainly, relieved surprise whenever one went to collect her from school.

On this same evening, while Anthony was brooding over the *Investment Review* and Alison over her daughter, Len Wincobank was lying on his dormitory bed in Block D and listening to the radio. On the walls around him, naked girls in various rude attitudes winked at him and offered themselves to him, thrusting out handsome bums and eccentrically large tits; they mingled oddly with a few sober snapshots of quiet-looking wives and ordinary children in jerseys and track suits. There were some children's drawings on the walls too, fresh from primary school: My Mum, A Space Ship, A Jumbo Jet. One man had a picture of Loch Lomond painted by himself in art class. Len Wincobank, over his bed, had a photograph of the Chicago skyline in a lurid sunset, a picture of the Chay Bank development in Northam, and a picture of the undeveloped town center of Porcaster: Porcaster, pig town, which had been his undoing.

He had been surprised that he was allowed to stick these subversive mementos on the walls, but nobody had commented, and there they stayed, along with a nude portrait from a Pirelli calendar, put up largely as a sop to his companions, for Len was a diplomatic fellow unless provoked and did not like to provoke hostility unnecessarily: if nudes were the scene, he would have nudes. He had not stuck his girlfriend, ex-secretary, and fellow conspirator, Maureen, on the wall, next to the Pirelli, because he did not want the other men to peer at her. Also, he didn't have a good picture of her, one that did her justice. And unlike many of his fellow inmates, Len was a man who liked to turn his fantasies into realities; he did not accept the gap between the nude pin-up and the homely wife. When he got out, if she had waited for him and was still willing to co-operate with him, he would have a nice nude portrait done of Maureen. On a white fur rug. With her socks on. For private viewing only. She wouldn't mind: she was an easygoing girl, Maureen.

Meanwhile, the radio was informing him that there was to be a twenty-five percent increase in the price of gas, that another prestige car manufacturing firm was going into liquidation, that a local councillor in Dexted had been charged with corruption, and that three more soldiers had been killed in Ulster. He could understand the view, sometimes expressed in his present residence, that one was better off inside than out. He didn't share it, but he could see its point. Particularly, he could understand the fear in the eyes of the ineffectual bumbling lazy dishonest old men who formed a recognizable section of the community: what would the world be like, by the time they were let out into it again? There was one old boy in particular, for whom Len felt sorry: he was due for release in a few months, and the prospect terrified him. He was an ex-primary-school headmaster, from a village in County Durham: he had been put away for nicking, quite pointlessly, five hundred toilet rolls, two gross of pencils, seven hundred reams of paper, and a hundred electric light bulbs, all school property. He was not the kind of person to cope buoyantly with a twenty-five percent rate of inflation and a lost pension.

Len switched off the radio: he'd hoped there would be a discussion of the Community Land Bill, but evidently not.

He thought about land. And buildings. Unlike most property men, Len had a genuine passion for buildings. He loved them. He loved modern architecture, brutal architecture, concrete and cement; he liked the buildings of ten, twenty years ago too, glass, steel, elegant, airy. But he liked cement better, being a man of the moment; or rather, a man of the last moment but one, a man of six months ago. He had friends in the business who didn't give a damn what they bought, what they put up, as long as they made money out of it, others who enjoyed collecting sites and fitting them together like expensive jigsaw puzzles, others who thought big enough, but only in terms of square feet and high rents, others whose sense of power seemed to want to force people to go and live where they didn't want to live, shop where they didn't want to shop, work where they didn't want to work. Len had a little of all these impulses in him, but his strongest impulse was a love of the grand. This had gone out of fashion: nowadays, conservationists wrangled over unattractive little Victorian tobacconists' shops on dingy corners, architects had abandoned high-rise, and even in America, the home of the grand, they were blowing up their largest blocks of flats. He had seen one of these explosions on television. The explosion itself had been grand enough, in its way: the whole block, hundreds and hundreds of homes, thousands of tons of concrete, had shaken and curved elegantly and collapsed forever. People like blowing things up these days, thought Len. They prefer blowing up to building.

Len's love of the grand had been nurtured in the industrial

North. The landscape had seemed to him magnificent: huge hillsides, slag heaps, cooling towers, furnaces. But the civic buildings were so petty, so ugly, so horribly out of scale, so grimly undistinguished. He did not notice this at first, of course: he was content to play football on the willow-herb-blossoming bomb sites, without asking himself what could be done with those bomb sites. Nor did he ask himself until it was nearly too late: many of them had gone, in the tardy piecemeal postwar rebuilding schemes of the late forties and fifties. He had started life in a real estate agent's office, collecting rents—a bright boy, with no A Levels, who left school at sixteen to help pay the bills. In his twenties, after ten years in the trade, he saw the light. He saw the light on an evening visit to Sheffield from his hometown of Northam, and it was gleaming on the block of flats at Park Hill, built by Lynn, Smith and Nicklin: pink in the smokeless sunset, the huge building rose, like an outcrop, like a part of nature, a massive cliff with every window glinting in a pale golden pink, dazzling, beautiful, inspired. Len Wincobank fell in love with Park Hill. What did he care if the families in it went to the bad, pestered by bugs in the heating ducts, by sociologists and research workers and visiting foreign architects; what did it matter if they went mad like animals too constantly displayed in their cages in a zoo? The building was beautiful; it sang out.

And so now did Chay Bank, his own inspiration. It too sang. It was built just before the architects decided that back-to-back tenement housing was really a perfectly decent way of accommodating people, and that all one needed to do was to put in bathrooms, so that old ladies dying of cancer did not have to shuffle two hundred yards to the lav on a dark wet night, or piss into a stinking chamber pot. The theory behind this, Len Wincobank was occasionally prepared to concede, might be right, but if everyone obeyed it, what would happen to the grand, the huge, the magnificent? What would England *look* like? He did not care all that much about people. When he thought about them he thought them petty, to prefer convenience to grandeur. He had wanted to wipe away all those squalid little strips of houses and make them into something big, something significant. It upset him, born in a back-to-back, to hear slum housing praised. "They'll be slapping preservation orders on Victoria Buildings and Ballard Dwellings next," he would yell aggressively when people stood in his way or argued with him. "Anything that's old and nasty, people want to keep. Why do you think this country's in the shit? Because people think small, they live in the past, they've got no vision," he would yell: quite effectively, until the country's downward slide into the shit became too pronounced for a one-man resistance.

He left his mark before he too slid, and got his four years. Chay Bank, built by the council but largely through his persuasion, still stood, and was a noted success: remarkably few of its inhabitants had as yet gone mad, jumped out of high windows, murdered and mugged each other's grandmothers, or wantonly destroyed the children's adventure playground. A gleaming office tower, with at least half the office space let, was another monument to Wincobank. Many lesser enterprises—small shopping developments, a conversion of Nutley's old covered market into an air-conditioned paradise, a department store on an overlooked bomb site in that laziest and ugliest of towns, Bonsett—bore witness still to his successful activities. But, of course, people had turned on him. They even criticized Chay Bank, an acknowledged masterpiece.

He could not really understand it. Did they really like their shabby nonconformist co-ops, their mucky little alleyways, their dull unadventurous little spread of suburban streets? Couldn't they see what he had been offering them? All right, he had made (and largely lost) a fortune out of it, but that wasn't the point. Out of sheer disinterest, they ought to have seen his visions. Look at Bonsett—Bonsett, the ugliest dump you could ever hope to find, stuck down in the middle of the moor, littered about with little miserable mine adits and yellow clay pits, and the best buildings in it, before his company put up Weightman's Store, had been a mock-Gothic Wesleyan chapel and a nineteen-thirties Essoldo cinema. Or look at Porcaster—he groaned, to think of Porcaster. It had had, unlike Bonsett, some advantages: an old market town, it had a market square with a cross, a church, a bridge. But they were swamped in such miserable squalor, surrounded by such chilly grimy incompetent unplanned silly little developments—and none of them very new, for Porcaster's Borough architect seemed to have been dead in his chair for twenty years. Three minutes' walk from the main square, there were neglected back alleys, cobbled, weed-filled, passing among houses with broken and boarded windows, like something out of the depression (the last depression) where old ladies in curlers and slippers still shuffled. Three minutes from the town square. Len had nearly passed out with excitement, had leaped into a phone box to ring Maureen, then leaped out again, overcome by the strong stink of urine—Christ, what a dump—had taken refuge in the main hotel, the town's main hotel, which stank of dog and stale beer, which was full of old men playing billiards at three thirty in the afternoon—and had rung Maureen. "Get in the car, love," he said. "Come over, come and have a look at this, it'll knock you over."

It had finished him, Porcaster. He had borrowed too much money, bought too many properties at fancy prices, and then been obstructed, at a vital moment, by the evidently malicious planning authorities. They didn't want to be developed by Wincobank: they wanted to stink and rot in their own manner. They ruined him. He tried to rescue himself, injudiciously, with funds from another company: injudiciously, and, as a jury decided on a fine spring afternoon in 1975, criminally.

He thought of them with hatred.

England. What was the matter with it? Shabby, lazy, unambitious, complacently high-minded when it so chose.

He thought of America. New York, the most beautiful city in the world, the apotheosis of aspiration. What buildings there, what inspiration, what vision, what glory, steel, glass, concrete, Art Nouveau, Art Deco, Brutality, fountains, spires, windows, avenues, intersections, passion, and desire. Or Chicago, with the glittering lakefront, the water that flowed backward, the highest building in the world, the largest multicolored fountain in the world, a paradise of invention and felicity. They said that Sydney was beautiful, too. When he got out he would go and have a look at Sydney and pick up a few ideas.

Meanwhile, he sat here on his bed in a drafty Nissen hut. Soon he would go and while away an hour or so at Twenty-one with

that clever young ex-copper in Bed Eleven. He had learned a lot
from the clever young ex-copper, who, like Len, was undismayed
by the rate of inflation and speed of collapse in the world outside.
He saw these problems as a challenge to his ingenuity. He had
some interesting plans. There are some interesting people to be
found among Category D prisoners in open prisons, as well as some
very dull ones. Len felt that he was not entirely wasting his time.

While Len Wincobank was thinking about New York and Sydney, Maureen Kirby was thinking about Len Wincobank, although that was, she knew, a waste of time. There was nothing
one could do about Len. The exciting dance he had led her and
himself had come to an end, at least for the present. There was no
way one could profitably think about Len in prison. She went to
see him every month, but that was not much fun. And now she sat
here alone, in her tiny shabby Sheffield flat, idly cutting her toenails in front of the gas fire. Unlike Len, she was free to go out.
But she did not much want to go out. There was nowhere to go,
no one to go with. And she had a toothache. She ran her tongue
experimentally around the tooth with the missing filling. It didn't
ache badly, but it was sensitive, and of course she couldn't stop
herself from giving it a feel, which made it worse. She knew she
ought to go to the dentist. But she couldn't afford to go to the
dentist. She was hard up. She'd got a new job as soon as Len was
put away, but there'd been a lot of debts lying around. Luckily she
wasn't responsible for Len's, but her own were bad enough. She'd
had to sell the car. And she couldn't afford to go and see Eric
Hargreaves about her filling. He charged at least eight quid a go,
and it just wasn't worth it. She'd have to get herself back on the
National Health. But she'd got so used to sinister Eric, with his big
Jaguar and his smooth talk and his dubious innuendoes. He was a
good dentist; he knew her teeth. She didn't want to risk an unknown dentist with an unknown out-of-date drill and no reassuring patter.

It's a bit of a laugh, really, thought Maureen Kirby glumly, not laughing at all, that I've ended up here worrying about private dentists. Me, of all people.

Maureen Kirby had been born in Attercliffe, Sheffield, in 1946, nine months after her father was discharged. She was the youngest of six and slept three to a bed through most of her childhood. Her first idea of bettering herself was via hair dressing, the glamour of which appealed to her and most of her school friends, so she started cutting hair at the age of fifteen. She was quite happy for two or three years, cutting, shampooing, back combing, trying to make eighteen-year-old girls look thirty, as was then the vogue, and looking about thirty herself, in her cheap-smart two-piece suits with her brown bouffant hair. She was a friendly girl, happy to titivate the thinning locks of old-age pensioners as well as the sticky, pungent beehives of her contemporaries. But even she could see she wasn't going to get anywhere, from the back salon of Suzanne's. The area was going downhill, too, if that was possible. Too many Indians and blacks. Not that she had anything against them. But she could see there was no future in Suzanne's. The glamour was fading.

So at the age of twenty she took a secretarial course. Secretaries were glamorous, thought Maureen. She had seen many sexy advertisements for them, had read stories in which they married the boss, had even seen rude pictures of them being groped by the boss. That side of the business appealed to her, after five years of the female world of hair and a boring boyfriend. So she left boyfriend and salon, learned shorthand and typing, started work in a seedy solicitor's office, and found herself, somewhat to her own surprise, very good at the job. She didn't stay long with the seedy solicitor, who sealed his own fate by groping her, much as she had expected: she didn't mind him putting his hand up her skirt, in fact she quite liked it, but she recognized that if he did that, just like in the pictures, then so might someone better. So she worked hard, and after a couple of years' experience found herself with a very good post, as secretary to a director of a company that sold air-conditioners and ventilation. He was called Stanley Flood, but she soon learned to call him Stan. Life was fun with Stan, in its own way. The pay was good, the work was interesting and involved quite a bit of travel and staying in smart hotels for sales conferences. It also involved quite a bit of groping, and much of the lighter side of business, for Stan, as he willingly admitted, was a dirty old man, who didn't mind a little harmless fun, and didn't mind putting it in the way of his clients, either. Maureen did not object to this for it was all done, as Stan said, in good spirit and no harm meant: she would have sworn in a court of law that Stan was more interested in fun for its own sake than in bribing or corrupting potential clients. She didn't let him go too far with her, because he was after all old enough to be her father, but she certainly didn't mind his dirty jokes and dirty postcards, his souvenirs from Copenhagen, his sex diary and his Danish playing cards, and she didn't mind him putting his hand down her blouse in the summer or up her skirt in the winter for a quick feel. Why not? It didn't hurt her, she didn't mind a squeeze. This was the age of the mini-skirt, the swinging sixties, the days of liberation, and dirty old men like Stan felt that the golden age had arrived at last: they had waited long enough for it, had worked away for Ventex in the repressed provinces with repressed and aging wives, through a World War and through years of austerity, and suddenly here it all was, the world of *Penthouse* and the Beatles, the world of large steaks and double cream on real *gâteaux*, the world of girls and nightclubs and expense account champagne. No wonder Stan was in such high good humor most of the time, and no wonder his clients enjoyed themselves so much, and handed him such healthy contracts. Maureen couldn't see much wrong with that. She would have been astonished if anyone had described Stan to her as corrupt, corrupting, calculating: to her, he was a nice old boy with very vulgar tastes, and no harm in him. It was his vulgarity that helped to refine Maureen a little, though she never became very refined: when he showed her, for instance, a joke rubber toy of a nude lady which, when filled with water and squeezed, performed certain natural functions, she laughed rather feebly, and said, "Stan, you do go too far sometimes." And she hadn't much cared for the extraordinary object he had once produced, with a flourish, from his briefcase; it looked harmless enough at first sight, and she had allowed herself to be tricked into inspecting it quite closely. It looked like a rubber sea anemone with all kinds of little flaps and fringes; it was called Happy End, Stan said, and when Maureen realized what it was she screamed and dropped it, as she had as a child dropped rubber spiders. Stan was amused, but Maureen had turned quite pale, and he had to put it away and comfort her and promise never to show her anything like that again.

But some of his jokes she thought quite funny. For instance, she sympathized with his urgent desire to purchase a car number plate that he had spotted in a multistory car park in Rotherham: SO SEXY, it said, though one could see on closer inspection that it in fact read 50 5EXY. It was much smarter than Stan's own, which simply read SF 2001. Maureen spent much company time and money advertising for the owner of this car, and when she finally contacted him was as disappointed as Stan when he refused to sell.

Maureen's mum for some reason took against Stan, and all she heard of Stan. Although by no means a puritan herself, she was offended by Maureen's stories about him, and kept asking Maureen when she was going to settle down, staring critically meanwhile at Maureen's new trendy gear, her Dolly dresses and silver tights and Mary Quant eyelashes. You shouldn't show your arse to all the world like that, you'll wear it out, she would say, then wheeze at her own wit. Oh, piss off, Mum, Maureen would reply, amiably, explaining that although Stan was no gent, he was a good boss, and the money was good, and that she was learning a lot about the way the world goes. Anyway, she'd say, I'm young yet, who wants to get stuck with a lot of snotty kids, like our Mavis? I want to see a bit of life: I don't want to waste myself like you did, Ma. You girls these days, it's self self self, money money money, said Maureen's mum, who had always put herself first and money second, but had unfortunately put family planning rather lower down on her list of priorities.

She saw even more of life when she met Len Wincobank. She

met him at a sales conference in Wakefield. She and Stan were staying the weekend, selling (one of Stan's jokes) a lot of hot air. Stan introduced her to Len in the smart modern anonymous hotel foyer. "This is my perfect secretary," said Stan, giving Maureen a friendly thump. "We don't know where Ventex would be without our Maureen. The temperature would certainly drop without our Maureen." Maureen smiled and wriggled in an appropriate manner and stared at Len, who stared back at her. Len was a new man, the new businessman of the sixties, she could see that at a glance. He was of a completely different breed from the jovial Stan, though he and Stan were clearly on good terms. For one thing, he was of another generation: Stan was in his fifties (he was coy about the precise date), whereas Len was nearer her own age, surely not more than thirty, and dressed in a trendy style. Stan's hair was silver, short back and sides, but Len's was black and curly and too long for a businessman. He had sideburns.

"Never recommend your secretary to anyone," said Len, still giving Maureen the eye, "or they get stolen, didn't you know? We'll have her off you, if you don't keep an eye on her."

And that was how it happened. They met up in the bar that night, spent the night in one of the twin beds in Len's room, and had arranged their plot by the morning. Stan was sad, but philosophic. Maureen was delighted. It wasn't till she started sleeping with Len that she realized what a relief it was to be able to do all those wicked amusing things with someone she was really keen on, someone more in her own age group. She and Len got on fine. She liked working for him, and after a few weeks she moved into his flat and lived with him. Nobody minded that kind of irregularity, in the swinging sixties. Len's style made Stan's innuendoes and dirty weekends seem very dated. She got more and more fond of him: I love you, she'd say, and he'd reply, of course you do, but both of them were in fact rather surprised by this unexpected extra bonus that life had suddenly handed them.

Though life was full of handouts in those good days. Those were the days when it seemed that Len couldn't go wrong. Money for jam, money for old rope. He worked hard enough, and so did

Maureen, but they were still surprised by their good luck. It's a joke, isn't it, Len would say, as deal succeeded deal. And it was. That was why they got on so well: born from the same kind of background, motivated by the same wish to get on, they understood one another perfectly, and they agreed that their success was, really, a bit of a giggle. So they giggled together, over the oddities and pomposities of their elders, over the lack of nerve of their rivals, over the joke of finding themselves drinking large drinks in four-star hotels and driving a large car and bouncing about in a large soft bed. Maureen proved so good at business, so quick off the mark, that at one point Len suggested making her a partner, but she declined: it's more fun pretending to be a secretary, she said, and he agreed. For the truth was that both of them found the idea of the boss-secretary relationship extremely stimulating, and variations on the theme afforded them much innocent amusement, during the prosperous late sixties and early seventies.

Maureen stared at the clippings of her toenails, neatly piled up on the *Daily Mail*. If Len had made her a partner, maybe she would have been in jail herself by now, instead of sitting here bored and irritable. As it was, there had been some talk of charging her with collusion, but luckily she'd been able to appear as simple secretary, a mere slave to orders. And, in fact, she hadn't known much about Len's last suicidal financial panics and misdealings until it was too late, because he'd been too embarrassed to let her in on them. So she hadn't really been party to the fraud at all, only to the aftermath of it. She'd been able to appear in the witness box, looking very honest, in defense of Len's character. She's a good little actress, Len's counsel had thought, watching her performance, but Maureen was not acting: she believed in Len, she was on Len's side, against all the old buffers who had tried to trap him simply because they couldn't make as much money as him.

Now she was beginning to wonder about herself and Len. After all, she thought, things have come to a sorry state, when a girl like me daren't go and see an ordinary dentist. We were corrupted, Len and me. We lost our sense of reality. All that fine living. It's true, it's like a train, once you get on it and it starts moving, you can't get off. You can't go back. You can't undo what you've done to yourself. Once you've started wanting more, you've got to go on, you can't stop and you can't go back.

Although Maureen had, in fact, been forced to go back. Not as far as the house in Attercliffe, but into this tiny flat, little better than a bed-sit really, with its two-ring electric cooker and its wheezy gas fire. The flat she'd lived in with Len had had the lot: de luxe washing machine, dishwasher, six-ring automatically timed cooker, deep freeze, lights that dimmed on a knob rather than blinked crudely off and on with a switch, underfloor central heating, two bathrooms, shower, remote control color television. The lot. And here she was, back with a little portable black-and-white set that she couldn't even be bothered to watch.

Still, it could have been worse. At least I've got myself a decent job, thought Maureen. She was working for an architect, the most respectable employer she'd ever had. Though he, too, had shown a slight tendency over the last week or two to brush against her in corridors.

She spared a thought for Stan. Stan had got himself into trouble, at last. He'd been had up for offering bribes to council employees: the whole story had been ridiculous, a farce, tales of nightclub outings and wild nights in hotels, of call girls and twenty-pound notes, of tax evasion and pornomovies. Most of those involved had been over sixty, call girls excepted.

Poor old Stan. Perhaps he was a bit of a crook after all, thought Maureen. Perhaps *I'm* a bit of a crook, and that's why I end up working for people who end up in jail.

Outside, appropriately, a police siren wailed.

I wonder if Len will guess, if I sleep with my architect, thought Maureen.

Kitty Friedmann lay in her hospital bed. She was surrounded by flowers, enormous bouquets of many colors: her bedside table was heaped high with gifts, letters, telegrams, chocolates, candies, grapes.

She was thinking about her grandson, Jonathan. It wasn't right, the way Daniel went on at that poor boy. Nag, nag, poor little lad. They'd popped in to see her after school, and very nice he had looked, in his little pink and gray cap and blazer, but all Daniel had done had been to nag at him and about him—"Don't touch this, Jonathan, no you can't have that, Jonathan, don't bang on Grandma's bed, Jonathan,"—and when she'd tried to change the subject by asking how he was getting on at school, all she'd had was a long lecture from Daniel about how he couldn't keep up with the maths and was having to have special coaching for his Latin, and how he didn't like rugger but would have to learn. The poor little lad hadn't been allowed to open his mouth. She'd managed to slip a box of chocs into his pocket when his dad wasn't looking, but maybe that wasn't the right thing to do, he *was* a bit plump, still, it wasn't fair to keep on at a child like that, who cares if he isn't a genius? Better have a word with Miriam. But then, Miriam herself was getting a bit odd these days, maybe she'd better keep her big mouth shut, never interfere between husband and wife. That hat she'd come round in, she must have picked it up at a jumble sale.

Perhaps Daniel had money worries. But how could he have, now poor Max was dead? Of course, times were hard, everyone's business was in a bad way, and Daniel was not the greatest businessman in the world, she suspected—but still, Max must have left enough. Come his way long before he could have expected it. Max had always insisted on fair shares: however they're doing, leave them all equal, then there'll be no fighting after I've gone, that had been Max's motto.

Miriam was getting·skinny. But Daniel and Jonathan were getting fat. She must ask Miriam's sister Evie if there was anything the matter with Miriam.

No, she mustn't. She must mind her own business.

She heaved, uncomfortably. She felt uncomfortable, her leg was strapped and she couldn't move it, and her bottom both itched and ached. The nurses had said to ring if she felt poorly, but she didn't like to disturb them, poor overworked girls.

I hope Rachel will come in, she said to herself. I must remember to ask Rachel to call round on Mrs. Boxer the cleaning lady, and make sure she gets paid properly for all the time I'm in here. And to bring me another clean nightie. I couldn't half do with a bath.

She picked up the *Evening Standard*, which Daniel had brought round, and turned to her favorite bit, the Londoner's Diary. Who was up to what? Albert Finney was going to appear in a new play by Christopher Hampton. She'd be out in time to get to that, she hoped; she liked Finney, though the language in some of these plays was shocking. She smiled to herself, remembering what Miriam's sister-in-law Zelda had said when they took her to see Harry Secombe in that new musical. "I never thought he'd sink so *low*," she'd said, with inimitable outrage.

What else? A sculptor had left three million pounds. Now that was a nice sum to make with your own two hands. She wondered how much Max had left: nobody'd been tactless enough to tell her yet. Max always called me an extravagant woman, but I wasn't really: look, here's a story about a man who bought a house for half a million pounds. I'd never have let Max do a thing like that, would I? And it was only in Hampstead, the house. Can't have been up to much. An Arab. Arabs are buying up all the London property market, Daniel says. But that's just Daniel. Why shouldn't they spend their money? It's theirs, isn't it?

On another page of the *Standard*, there was an article about a baby who was suffering from a rare bone disease: his mother was appealing for a donor, for new bone marrow. Kitty Friedmann's eyes filled with tears. Poor little lad. Poor woman. Beneath the article about the baby was a brief report of an old man who had been kicked to death and robbed of forty pence on Wimbledon Common. She read this too. She continued to cry. She had always had the greatest difficulty in believing in the existence of ill luck, let alone of ill will. One of the many survivors of a family that had fled the pogroms of Russia in the 1880s, she had always refused to contemplate the possibility of evil: she had utterly suppressed all knowledge of the wickedness of history, had spent all her conscious life in atonement, in cheerfulness, in redressing the balance, in proving that such terrors could never have taken place. The Second World War had tried but not defeated her. Occasionally, faint shadows of doubt reached her: how, in this day and age, could a child die, slowly, publicly, foredoomed, of an incurable disease, how could an old man be kicked to death? Still crying, she turned to the cookery column, which she always enjoyed. She was blowing her nose vigorously, and reminding herself to remember to remind Rachel to remind Mrs. Boxer to tell Mr. Harris not to deliver the usual fish next week, when a nurse entered, on a routine visit, and noticed Kitty Friedmann's red eyes. "Feeling sorry for ourselves, are we?" she said, in pointless nurselike jargon. Kitty Friedmann smiled, guiltily, at the poor overworked underpaid bitch of a nurse.

Not everybody in Britain on that night in November was alone, incapacitated, or in jail. Nevertheless, over the country depression lay like fog, which was just about all that was missing to lower spirits even further, and there was even a little of that in East Anglia. All over the nation, families who had listened to the news looked at one another and said, "Goodness me," or "Whatever next," or "I give up," or "Well, fuck that," before embarking on an evening's viewing of color television, or a large hot meal, or a trip to the pub, or a choral society evening. All over the country, people blamed other people for all the things that were going wrong—the trades unions, the present government, the miners, the car workers, the seamen, the Arabs, the Irish, their own husbands, their own wives, their own idle good-for-nothing offspring, comprehensive education. Nobody knew whose fault it really was, but most people managed to complain fairly forcefully about somebody: only a few were stunned into honorable silence. Those who had been complaining for the last twenty years about the negligible rise in the cost of living did not, of course, have the grace to wish that they had saved their breath to cool their porridge, because once a complainer always a complainer, so those who had complained most when there was nothing to complain about were having a really wonderful time now.

Expansionist plans were, it is true, here and there being checked: for a second holiday, a three-piece living room set, a new car. But very few people were having to work out how to do without what they already had, though they were puzzled by the way their hard-fought wage increases had got them nowhere at all. The old headline phrases of freeze and squeeze had for the first time become for everyone, not merely for the old and unemployed, a living image, a reality: millions who had groaned over them in steadily increasing prosperity were now obliged to think again. A huge icy fist, with large cold fingers, was squeezing and chilling the people of Britain, that great and puissant nation, slowing down their blood, locking them into immobility, fixing them in a solid stasis, like fish in a frozen river: there they all were in their large houses and their small houses, with their first mortgages and second mortgages, in their rented flats and council flats and basement bed-sits and their caravans: stuck, congealed, among possessions, in attitudes, in achievements they had hoped next month to shed, and with which they were now condemned to live. The flow had ceased to flow; the ball had stopped rolling; the game of musical chairs was over. *Rien ne va plus*, the croupier had shouted.

Some, who had thought they understood, were more bewildered than others. An economist who had just received a salary increase of £2,000 in expectation of next year's inflation pondered the problem of growth over a supper of macaroni cheese. He was one of those who had tried to work out an antigrowth policy. He had signally failed to communicate his enthusiasm for this concept to others, and, indeed, recognizing his sigh of relief at the salary increase, to himself. Man needs a prospect of increase. Only static, stagnant, hopeless communities can live without it. The poor must get rich, the rich must get richer. He prodded his static macaroni cheese, a satisfying but fattening dish in pleasant tones of cream, yellow, and brown, in pleasantly graded, smooth, affiliated, doughy textures: one of the favorite dishes of his childhood, as of his manhood. His real tastes had changed little with the years. Why then the elation at an extra £2,000 a year when he of all people knew how little that could mean?

There were, of course, a few perverse souls who enjoyed the prospect of a little austerity. They had been happiest during the war, and had returned to a life of cheese-rind-paring and carrot-growing with alacrity. To them, affluence had always been an unreal delusion: there was nothing in it against which one could pit one's wits. And now once more, with a sense of virtue, they could go around switching off heat and lowering the power of electric light bulbs, bathing in water three inches deep, using up old crusts, and thinning sauces in the bottoms of old bottles with vinegar. Some of them even wanted to reintroduce rationing and were disappointed when first sugar, then petrol, then salt, then lavatory rolls dropped off the economic hook. According to their enemies, their philosophy was: *it is wrong to enjoy oneself, it is right to sit in the cold by a candle end.* But they, in fact, enjoyed sitting by a candle end.

This generation had produced another minority group, their spiritual and often their physical offspring: the war babies. They had accepted recession with a balanced cheerfulness, for they had always been astonished at their own purchasing power each time they bought a pound of bananas or a small pot of double cream. Hearing the gusts of anguish that shook the country, they shook their heads in mild amusement. Early childhood had solved for these lucky few the economic problem of growth: they would never be able to regard growth, or indeed survival, as anything other than an astonishing blessing.

Others enjoyed the crisis for more indirect reasons. Odd new groups of the far left hoped that each rise in the bank rate and each strike in a car factory heralded the final collapse of capitalism. Sociologists expressed approval of the rate of social change, the radicalizing influence of increasing confrontations of worker and management. Out of this, some sincerely believed, would rise a new order, of selfless, social, greedless beings. So they applauded disruptive strikes for more pay and illogically snapped crossly at their children when their children told them that, yes, it really did cost 15 pence to get to the football match on the bus, and, yes, that really did make 30 pence there and back, and, yes, there were three of them, and yes, 3 times 30 was 90, and could they also have at least 50 pence each for a hamburger and 20 pence each for a Coke?

There were also the real poor: the old, the unemployed, the undesirable immigrants. They were better off than they would have been in the thirties, for Britain is, after all, a welfare state, and not many slip through its net. Let us not think of them. Their rewards will be in heaven.

Finally, there was the small communion of saints, who truly hoped that from this crisis would come a better sharing among the nations of the earth; who truly in their hearts applauded the rise in price of raw materials from the poorer countries of the earth; who thought of the poor, and of themselves rarely, and included themselves among the rich—which most of them, by Western European standards, were not. They tried now to repress their horror and their satisfaction at the unedifying spectacle of the death-throes of greed in their own so-privileged nation. Among these, one might record an elderly Quaker in Keighley who sent every spare penny of her small income to a school in Africa where she had once worked; a one-time Member of Parliament who had lost his job through lack of charisma and was prepared to spend the rest of his life working, ill-paid, for the Child Poverty Action group; a bishop who had taken in his youth a vow of poverty and celibacy, in fear of his own too great charisma, and who prayed nightly for the country of his birth, where most people were so much richer than he, where the needs of others, compared to his own, seemed to be so great.

There are not many people like the bishop, the ex-M.P., and the elderly Quaker. It is just as well that there are not more. Self-sacrifice is all very well, in the eyes of God, but where would the country be without self-interest? Two and a half centuries ago the poet Pope expressed the optimistic view, which maybe he believed, that God ordained self-love and love of society should be the same. But which self, which society? The population of Britain then was only five and a half million: now it is sixty million.

Pity the bishop, on his knees on the cold linoleum. His love is strained, dilute, insufficient. Could even God's love suffice this multitude?

It must be said that even the bishop cannot find it in his heart to regret that Britain has struck oil.

This is the state of the nation.

By half past eight, on this same long November evening, Anthony Keating had finished his sausages, idled away half an hour with a cup of coffee, switched the radio on and off several times, and done some thinking. He had thought about the nature of property, and why it was that some people considered the owning of property particularly wicked: why was it more wicked to own a strip of land with a house on it than to own a sausage, a bicycle, a secondhand fur coat, or a color television set? Then he wondered why it was that the British, unlike some other nations, had traditionally considered it a good thing to own one's own house and one's own little garden. Then he wondered how much space there would be left if everybody did in fact own a little house and a little garden. Then he tried to imagine a situation in which there might be free housing, as there is free education and free medicine, and, in some districts, free contraception. And failed.

He remembered the Diggers, who had dug up Richmond Hill. He thought of the enclosure of the Commons. He thought of Shelter, and the homeless, and vandalized council property, and large houses with burglar alarms and guard dogs and barbed wire around them, and of the beaches of the Riviera, parceled out and cordoned off and sold. Public and private. Locke—he thought it was Locke—had said that we make our stake to the land by working it: was that why he, guilty, owning far more than his fair share, tried ineptly to grow woody carrots? The stake is the labor. And those who do not labor, who do not dig and redecorate and plug up the holes in their leaking roofs, shall be evicted? He did not think that such a view would be very popular with his left-wing friends of the old days. But then, it was hard to know what they did think, what they did want. He had visited, some years earlier, a twenty-story council block in his own London neighborhood to collect one of his children from a schoolfriend's party: the lift had been broken, the walls covered with graffiti, there was dog shit on the stairs (was it dog shit?) and broken bottles dumped in corners, the trees uprooted in the communal strip of garden, the communal flowerbeds trampled. Verminous one-legged cross-beaked pigeons scrabbled in the dirt and hung like thick bats or rats in the one surviving tree. Inside his daughter's friend's flat, it was cozy, neat, compact, bright, with spectacular views across London and the canal and the river. A question of perspective. At home, he discussed with Babs the contrast between the outside and the inside: ever-liberal, she blamed the oppressive architecture rather than the people, but a friend who had called by, a one-time progressive like himself, had said: "We must recognize that what belongs to everybody belongs to nobody. And nobody will care for it."

And so it was. It had not always been so. Surely?

He thought of a Wellsian paradise, a Welwyn Garden City, with neat boxes. But people did not like that kind of thing. What did they want? It was not surprising that neither political party had a coherent housing policy. HOMES, NOT OFFICES, declared placards all over London, accusing property developers like Anthony Keating of the wrong priorities. And he could see that to be homeless must indeed be unpleasant. But why, he had once tentatively asked a friend who was complaining of the cost of bed-sitters in Kentish Town, why do so many of the homeless want to live in London, where there are neither houses nor jobs? What is the attraction? You live here yourself, his friend, a sour and stubborn writer, had replied. Yes, but I no longer much like it, said Anthony, who was already contemplating the luxury of removal.

It seemed that his dislike was not shared by those who chose to inhabit, rancorously, decaying terraces, and to squat in derelict slums.

But other friends, in the past few years, had moved to the country, some driven by prosperity, others by failure. Most had acquired properties within reach of London: in Kent and Sussex, in Suffolk and Norfolk, in Oxfordshire, the Cotswolds, Wiltshire, even, by motorway, Wales. Some claimed they wanted to grow vegetables, others that they could not take the pace of London life. Anthony and Babs, then later, Anthony and Alison had been to stay with some of these emigrants and had contemplated the country life. What were they seeking, what were they fleeing? Were they fleeing a London that was going the way of New York—garbage-strewn, transport-choked, dirty, violent? Or were they simply seeking every Englishman's dream: his own plot, his own castle, his own estate? The most successful had undoubtedly been those who had moved farthest: a journalist who had removed himself and his family to a house on a cliff in Cornwall, an ex-secretary who had gone with husband and child to live up a mountain in Wales, without electricity, gas, or running water, with a sheep, a goat, and hens. They had really moved themselves: they had not tried to compromise. Impressed by their success, Anthony himself had decided to move far afield, and had persuaded Alison to try the North, despite the problems of traveling.

There are not, after all, unlimited ways of spending one's money, and Anthony, when he bought High Rook House, had thought that he had money. He did not want a Rolls or a yacht, he did not want an airplane, he did not even want to ski or to water-ski. So a country house had seemed a natural stage in his natural progression. In it, he would drink, eat, smoke, and sleep with Alison; from it, he would go for walks, perhaps with a dog. Or that had been the plan, the plan of expansion.

Luckily he had not bought the dog. He had not had time to get around to buying an expansive expensive meat-eating dog.

Unexpected illnesses often strike their victims as punishments for known or unknown crimes.

I wonder what mine was, thought Anthony. He really did not know. Getting out of his depth, perhaps? Trying to be a heavyweight, when he was by nature a lightweight? (The reverse journey of Donnell Murray, Alison's husband.) Not recognizing his own limitations? Biting off more than he could chew? These variations on the same theme were the only thoughts that occurred to him. Would it have been better, would he have been happier, if he had stayed on in his old frivolous job, messing about, reading novels and gossip about old friends in *The New Statesman* and the Sunday papers, getting older, more ironic, more cynical, more amused by more things and less touched by anything, apparently successful, drinking too much and trying to eat sensibly? He had thought so, at times, during those sickening months when the interest rate soared, when rents were frozen, when politicians were declaring open war on property developers, denouncing them as the scourge of Britain: he had wished himself back on the sidelines, wished himself free to smile ironically as yet another secondary bank collapsed, yet another solid-seeming empire was transferred into the hands of the receivers. And yet, all in all, he did not yet repent. It had, at the very least, been interesting. And even now, even at this late day, it might all work out for the best. And why, anyway, fear the worst so much? The worst was what had happened to Len Wincobank, and Len Wincobank seemed to be surviving well enough. It would be interesting to see what had happened to Len. Anthony had never visited a prison. He did not like to admit it to himself, but he was secretly curious to see what it was like. It is not every clergyman's son who has an opportunity to visit a good friend in jail. The wider horizons he had sought were wide indeed.

Meanwhile, his own fortress, so dearly purchased, was to him not unlike a prison, he reflected, and as though to prove the point a mouse, well-known haunter of dungeons, ran over his hearth rug. It appeared not to notice him, as he was sitting so still. He was not much afraid of mice, but was momentarily glad that he did not have anyone with him, to whom he would have to pretend not to be at all afraid. Odd creatures invaded a country house. One night there had been a bat in the bedroom curtains. And the bath was always full of spiders. At first he had taken them as bad omens, and had feared to wash them down the plug, but there were so many of them that they had deprived themselves by their multiplicity of any special significance, and now found themselves heartlessly washed away.

When he and Babs had first got together all those years ago, he had discovered that she shared his greatest private fear: a fear of moths around the bedside lamp. Screaming, her head under the pillow, she had implored him to do away with them. He would retort, in cowardly fashion, by turning off the lamp, hoping the moth would fly off to the moon, or into a lighted corridor. But although he never screamed as she did, he knew that she had found him out, and had ceased to respect him, because he was afraid of moths.

The most depressing country-dweller that Anthony could think of was his old friend Linton Hancox. He thought of him to cheer himself up. He had been at school with Linton, and also at college. Twenty years or so ago, it looked as though Linton was going to do well for himself in life: he had been a bright boy, a pretty boy, a scholar, a poet and classicist, had done well for himself with scholarships and prizes, had had poems published young in distinguished journals, had embarked on research, had seemed sure of a readership, a lectureship, a professorship, a slim volume, a fat volume, translations, collected works. He had married a pretty girl, had produced pretty children. For years, he seemed to be about to be doing well, safe in his academic world, with his good degree: it had been years before Anthony had begun to realize how unmistakably the water was running out of that particular pond. How could one go wrong, he had thought to himself when he thought of Linton, with a good degree and a good post at Oxford? So he had thought, from the shifting rapids of the BBC.

It was in the late sixties, when everyone else was beginning to do better, that Anthony began to notice that Linton was doing worse. They did not meet often: at the infrequent parties of a friend who kept up with both, accidentally on a train or at a theater, by design, once or twice, at each other's house, for a drink or a meal. Babs had a soft spot for Linton because he was—or, as they learned to say, had been—a pretty boy. But even Babs began to remark that Linton was becoming rather sour. His sourness took a common—but to Babs and Anthony (unworldly innocents), a rather surprising—course: he began to complain about falling standards in education, about the menace of trendy schoolteachers who couldn't even teach children to read, about the dangers of assuming that all learning could and should be fun—odd remarks from one who had always been rather confident and casual in his own life-style. These remarks about education were paralleled by remarks about the state of poetry. Linton's own poetry was, naturally, academic, intelligent, structured, delicate, evasive, perceptive, full of verbal ambiguities and traditional qualifications; his reaction to the wave of beat poets, Liverpool poets, pub poets, popular poets was one of amusement, then of hostility, then of contempt tinged with fear. Anthony and Babs could not sympathize with this, for they were themselves vaguely and carelessly progressive, and any creative or literary talents that Anthony had ever had had been for the popular low-middle-brow, rather than for the élitist genres. They simply could not believe, either, that Linton's fear of an anticlerical conspiracy, an anti-intellectual lobby in high and low places in the educational world, had much justification. And if it had, they didn't care: their children jostled their way easily through state primary schools and into a disparate mixture of comprehensives, dying grammar schools, colleges of further education.

But Linton, no doubt about it, was a changing man. In 1970, when Anthony was already an apprentice property developer, the two of them met accidentally in a pub in Covent Garden. Linton said that he had just moved with his family to the country: would Anthony and his family like to come for a weekend? It was one of those casual invitations which become, through some strange shift of power, impossible to refuse, so, three weeks later, Anthony and Babs and two of their children set off for Oxfordshire, to the Hancoxes' place in the country.

It was very depressing. The cottage was in a small, straggling, insignificant, not unattractive village, and it was old and should have been picturesque: it had a garden sloping backward onto a wet field with cows, it had a low roof, and an old stable door, and old walls made of wattle and daub, and a large open fireplace with a chimney corner in the main living room. It was picturesque enough for both Anthony and Babs to be able to cry, without implausibility, "Oh, how pretty, how charming," but each could feel the other's heart sink. It was old, but it was shabby, cramped, and ill-organized: there was enough room for the four adults and their four children, but only just. Unfortunately, the weather was poor, and the cottage was bitterly cold, full of an icy damp: being old, none of its doors or windows fitted, and the chill oozed in from the fields and the garden. The dining room was so cold that Anthony could see the backs of his hands turning blue as he ate the exceedingly tough partridge that seemed aptly enough to represent country comfort.

Linton's wife, Harriet, was depressed. Anybody could see that. Linton was more angry than depressed. The next morning, after a freezing night in a sloping bed beneath a sloping ceiling, which Anthony spent in his socks and a jersey, Linton took Anthony on a country walk—one of those walks which ends badly, in mud, at the end of a plowed field from which there is no egress save into another plowed field occupied by long-horned and hostile cattle: there is always something lowering about being forced to retrace one's steps, and on the way back to the bridle path, which they had lost, a man on a tractor shouted at them that they were walking on private property, and to keep off.

As they walked, Linton talked about his students. Or undergraduates, as he unfashionably persisted in labeling them. They were very, very dim, he told Anthony. They had been appallingly badly taught: Cambridge Latin was in his view a disaster. None of them had any solid grounding in grammar, none of them could write a prose even to old O Level standards, they had all been corrupted by vague "classical studies" and thought that if they knew a few Greek myths and could recognize a piece of Ovid or Homer and make some approximate sense of it, that would do.

It sounds depressing, said Anthony, politely, trying to pull his borrowed wellington boot out of a deep puddle of mud, in which he had accidentally stepped. Rooks and seagulls rose, cawing, from a brown expanse, as they approached.

"Why do seagulls get so far from the sea?" asked Anthony.

But Linton was not to be deflected from his grievances by country lore. As they trudged coldly back to the cottage, he continued to berate society, which had thrown away its cherished values for a myth of egalitarianism, for a nonsensical fantasy of a popular culture. His views seemed to have aged ten years, rather abruptly. And although Anthony himself had abandoned the television world in a state of disillusion and dissatisfaction, he found that he felt even further away from Linton's curious nostalgia than he had felt from the liberal good intentions of a progressive popular institution peddling progressive popular views. The golden age of solid education which Linton evoked, to the mocking cries of bleak rooks, had not been like that at all, as he recalled. Linton himself had complained bitterly—surely it had been Linton—sitting up late one night over a bottle of cheap wine in Balliol, describing his walking holiday in Greece, twenty years ago: Linton himself had complained that the trouble with conventional teaching of classics was that it gave one no feeling that Greek and Latin were real languages, with a real literature—that the most important thing of all was to realize the *beauty*, the *significance*, the *intelligence*, the *message*, of Plato, of Thucydides, of Lucretius, that there was more to the classics than grammar, what a pity it was that so many schoolchildren were turned off the classics by too much insistence on grammar. . . . Yes, that had been Linton.

Linton's views had aged; so had his appearance. Without consulting Babs, Anthony could tell that this upset Babs even more than the cold bed. Linton had grown fat. It seemed impossible, for he had been a slender young man, with hair like curling tendrils of vine around his classic forehead; but now he was fat. He had a pot belly, and a double chin, and his hair was thin and cut short; yet he did not look comfortably plump, as do those who have grown fat by cheerfulness. Rather, he looked as though the thin man were still hovering inside him, anxiously: misery rather than happiness had inflated him, and it did not suit him, he had not the natural build, the natural weight, to carry this excess. It sat on him uncomfortably, like a sad growth.

Anthony found himself hoping, as they walked up the back drive through fitfully cultivated and dying pallid yellow seeding lettuces, that there would be a large stiff drink waiting for him. But he somehow knew there was not. And there was not. Though Linton had once been one of the lively lads, the likely lads, far from averse to a bottle or two. Instead, there was a glass of beer, a drink Anthony found decreasingly adequate, and a meal of overgrown sprouts, Walls sausages, and baked potatoes. The potatoes had been excellent, though Anthony could hardly bring himself to eat his, so well did they serve as handwarmers, as they sat at the polished spread of country-auction-late-Victorian-gateleg table, shivering, as the air sighed its way in through the cracked windows.

Country life. In the evening, Anthony insisted on going down to the pub, somewhat against his host's inclinations, and managed to buy half a bottle of Scotch, discreetly, while Linton was parking his car: he felt safer with a bottle in his pocket, and managed to get a much more comfortable night's sleep, despite the fact that he had inflicted a nasty wound on his leg while trying to help Linton to fill the coal scuttle for the stove from the coal shed in the pitch dark.

On the way home to London, after listening to their children's complaints about how mean and awful the Hancox children had been, he and Babs vowed, with a shiver of horror, that they would never be seduced into trying to go and live in the country— or if we do, Anthony had added as a proviso, if we do, at least we'll do it in some *style*.

Brooding, now, over his stylish country house hearth, Anthony thought about Linton. He realized clearly now, as he had not perhaps then, that Linton had been delivering an unfair attack on the quality of education. What had happened to Linton had been part of some much larger trend. Poor Linton had had the historical misfortune to be gifted in a dying skill, and to have been insufficiently aware of the shrinking domain of his own subject. Nobody wanted to do classics any more: there were no promotions possible in his field. He had come to a dead end, having chosen what seemed, initially, a well-structured and secure career. No wonder he defended himself by carping about the state of education as a whole, by blaming his undergraduates. And, no doubt, his undergraduates were less gifted than his own generation had been, for nowadays the bright and gifted ones chose on the whole to do other things. There were empty places, Anthony had read, in most universities, for classics scholars, because nobody applied: those who applied were those who had little hope of getting in on a more popular course. So no wonder Linton found his pupils unsatisfactory. Most were duds.

A pond, out of which the water had slowly drained, leaving Linton stranded, beached, useless. Unable to adapt, unable to learn new skills, obstinately committed to justifying the old ones—and, alas, as so often happens, ruining quite unnecessary and disconnected parts of himself in his willed, forced, unnatural, retrogressive justifications. For there was no reason in nature why Linton should not teach classics to a lot of second-rate students, and yet continue to write first-rate poetry. Why should the whole man grow sour, because one part of him was no longer vital? But it was so. It was as though Linton, in his rejection of the modern world in education, had resolved to reject the modern world altogether, and his poetry too had become sour, petty, carping, reactionary, lightened only by the odd flash of fairly useless and despicable nostalgia, which was more distressing to a reader than the carping itself. Linton had had a real gift, but he had ruined it by ignobly blaming the wrong people for the wrong things. He had started to complain almost as a joke—Anthony could remember those first, tentative complaints about Nuffield physics and concrete poetry— and the joke had obscured reality, had detached him from it, had become the reality. And now Linton sat there in his cottage, depressed on his low salary, with few prospects of promotion, writing cross letters to the papers about the falling standard of literacy, and sneering, if anyone cared to listen, about the inflated reputations of Ted Hughes, Philip Larkin, Sylvia Plath, Seamus Heaney —for it was not simply the popular who now attracted his fire, it was enough that a poet was successful for Linton to resent his work. He had lost, in bitterness, the power to distinguish.

Success may corrupt, but failure also corrupts.

So thought Anthony Keating, who had tasted something of both. And as he sat reflecting that the fate of classical studies might, like the fate of the property market, indicate something of a watershed in British history—for who, in a recession, can afford the luxury of Greek, who can afford the luxury of a civil service staffed by those who have first class degrees in classics?—the telephone rang.

He was quite pleased. He had had enough thinking, for one day. A chat would be a diversion. But it was not merely a chat that was offered: it was Giles in person. He was ringing from a call box in a service station on the motorway, going North, ten miles away, wanting to visit, wondering if he could stay the night. Anthony said, yes, of course, but he hadn't got much to eat. We'll pick something up on the way, said Giles.

Giles had never visited Anthony's new house, although he had heard a great deal about it. Anthony looked around himself, slightly flustered, wondering what he could do to make it look more homey, uncomfortably aware that it had a touch of Linton Hancox discomfort about it. Not very handy with a dustpan and brush or vacuum cleaner, he had let dust and rubbish accumulate; he had not even bothered to unpack some of the articles that had arrived from London, and boxes of books and clothes and crockery stood around the large drawing room and the long stone corridor. But at least it was not freezing: the central heating worked, and he had boosted it with an electric fire, albeit a temperamental electric fire, which needed the occasional kick. And the structure was good. In fact, fine. Beautiful. It was a fine house, he was proud of it. It was a house to be proud of; even Giles would see that it was a house to be proud of.

Anthony was slightly afraid of Giles. Although Giles had many weaknesses, and some characteristics which could even be called ridiculous, Anthony could not recover from his primal impression: that Giles knew what he was about, that he was a man of the real world, a man of substance. And I, thought Anthony, am I a man of straw? In the intense silence, an owl hooted, a dry leaf rustled in the drafty corridor. I want to impress Giles, thought Anthony. As though he were my superior, my employer. Perhaps I bought this house not for myself and Alison, but to impress Giles? Though there was little point in trying to impress Giles on such a level. He had visited the Peters family home, an enormous Victorian pile in Dorset; he had made passing acquaintance with Giles's many passing residences—Mews cottages in Belgravia, little houses in Chelsea, a large house in Canonbury, a flat behind Marble Arch, a cottage in Sussex, a house in Sussex, a whole island with a house on it in an Essex estuary . . . no, there was little point in competing with Giles. But perhaps his own house did manage to make the point that Anthony was not completely frivolous, that he had at least to be taken seriously?

The car approached, up the long steep uneven drive. Giles had brought a girl and a chauffeur, and the girl had brought a small dog. The chauffeur Anthony had met before: he was a taciturn and eccentric Scot, who seemed content to sit for long hours in a corner, and who, when he spoke, was often very rude, like his employer. He had convinced Anthony long ago that it was a bad idea to have a chauffeur, no matter how wealthy one became: one might get on with one's own chauffeur, but one could not expect everybody else to do the same. Giles, however, had to have a chauffeur, for he had been banned from driving.

The girl was called Pamela. She was carrying a bottle of whisky and some cartons full of chicken and chips, and a small miserable old dog trailed from her wrist on a lead. She stood in the doorway, clutching her parcels, in a full-length fur coat, and said to Anthony in a voice so thin and upper-class that it at once set his teeth on edge, "It is too kind of you to invite us, really."

"I didn't invite you, you invited yourselves," said Anthony, determined not to allow himself to be cast in the role of host, a role in which he would inevitably prove inadequate; but, being polite, added, "I do hope you won't be too uncomfortable."

Pamela looked around, sniffed the air expertly. "Oh, I'm *sure* we shan't," she said, with evident reservations.

Giles, meanwhile, was already inspecting the property: turning the key in the huge Jacobean lock, testing the thickness of the walls and window embrasures, padding into the enormous kitchen, peering at the central heating thermostat, opening the door to the butler's pantry, testing knobs, tapping wood, ending up, with

Pamela and Anthony and the chauffeur, in the packing-case-filled drawing room.

"Oil-fired central heating, I see," was more or less his first audible remark, after a few preliminary grunts. "That was a mistake."

"Not my mistake," said Anthony. "It was here already."

"Oh well," said Giles, placing himself firmly in front of the bar of the electric fire, his hands in his pockets, standing stockily, occupying space. The electric fire did not like him, and went out. Anthony crossed to it and kicked it, with some satisfaction: odd, how much pleasure kicking that fire had given him, in the last few weeks. The fading bar blushed and brightened. The two men stood there. It was always slow, socially, with Giles, for all that they had known each other for so long. Slow, but for the time unworried: for Anthony had been able to tell, from the nature of his inspection, that Giles was impressed by the house.

Pamela stood, pulling off her gloves, looking at the paintings. "Are these yours?" she said, nodding at them. She pulled off her coat, and Anthony took it from her and laid it on a chair. She was wearing a long Oriental embroidered dress, and had black hair, done up in a bun, and a white, pinched, little girl's face, uneasily gracing a woman of thirty.

"Guess," said Anthony.

"I don't like guessing games," she said. "In fact, I don't like games at all, before supper. Shall we eat, before that chicken gets cold?"

"It's cold already," said Giles. "We bought it in Leeds. Go and put it in the oven for half an hour, Pam. We'll have a drink. Where are your glasses, Anthony?"

Pamela went into the kitchen with the boxes of chicken, in a curious bidden way, quite in keeping with her hard and sprightly self-possession. Anthony nearly called after her, to say that he had already had his supper, but he didn't for he was hungry again. He did not care either for her smartness, nor for her submission. She was exactly the kind of girl that one could expect from Giles. He thought with longing of messy Babs, with more longing of unhappy unlucky lovely Alison.

The glasses were in one of the unpacked crates. Anthony removed a layer of newspaper, unwrapped one from its newspaper twist. It was his favorite: a glass with a twisted stem, and a rose engraved on it. He had been wondering where it was, but had not bothered to look. He gave it to Giles, unwrapped two more.

"You'll have to drink your own drink," he said to Giles. "I haven't got any."

"That's not like you," said Giles.

Anthony, playing host, unscrewed the top of the bottle of Teacher's, feeling with a pang the thread unlock under the tough plastic integument. The familiar smell assailed him, through senses no longer dulled by smoke.

"I'm not allowed to drink," said Anthony. "I must have told you that."

He poured a glass each for the two guests, put the bottle down by the third glass on the card table.

"However long for?" said Giles.

"I don't know," said Anthony. "Forever, who knows?"

"Who says you can't drink?"

"My doctor."

"Then why don't you find a doctor who says you can drink?"

Anthony laughed. The possibility had occurred to him.

"I decided to see how long I could stick it out," he said.

Pamela had come back into the room. She asked him what it had felt like, having a heart attack so unexpectedly; he told her. Then she had a drink, and guessed, not very accurately, which pictures were his and which had been left in the house. Listening to her, Anthony felt his craving for a drink increase almost beyond bearing: his eyes kept straying back to the bottle, to the crate of unpacked glasses, he imagined in detail the taste, the sensation, the concept of the liquid running along his arteries and veins, coursing through his body. His blood felt strange even at the thought, and his head swam. He longed for it. And yet, at the end of the drinking, what had one got? Just drink, in one's bloodstream.

Worth dying for? Surely not. He did not know. Surely not?

They ate the chicken and chips. Giles, unlocking, became talkative, told Anthony the latest property gossip, the latest rumors and scandals, who was up, who was down, who, like themselves, was still hanging on. Nothing was happening at all, in their own affairs, said Giles: not a flicker from anywhere. But there were signs that the situation might ease, in the end: there were straws in the wind. These two statements seemed to Anthony to be contradictory, but he did not bother to query them. He felt out of touch, slightly guilty that he had escaped and left Rory and Giles to do all the work and all the worrying, reluctant to be drawn back into the feverish atmosphere of doom and speculation, the big talk about money, money that did not exist except on paper. It seemed so long ago, though in reality it was only a matter of weeks, since he had spent every night discussing the situation, mesmerized by the bleeding and draining and seeping away of profits in bank charges and interest, paralyzed by prospects of disaster. It had been so gripping, so absorbing, and clearly Giles still found it so, but to Anthony it seemed like news from another planet. He listened, asked questions from time to time, tried to revive the passionate paternal interest he had felt in the Imperial Property Company, the pride he had felt in Imperial House, the hopes he had had for the Riverside, but he felt remote, geographically remote, detached, unwilling to get caught up in their powers of reasoning, their sense of self-preservation. They had *known* they were making mistakes at the end, but that had not stopped them. Why not?

And why, he wondered after a while, had Giles come to see him? He said that he was on his way to Newcastle to have a look at a new office development, which might or might not have been true: Giles was a notorious liar, who it sometimes seemed would induce mystification for its own sake. Maybe Pamela was the real reason for the excursion, Anthony and Newcastle merely pretexts. Giles made one or two remarks about Anthony's geographical distance from the flagging pulse of the Imperial Property Company, and inquired when he planned to return; but without, Anthony felt, much enthusiasm. On the contrary, he seemed pleased to find Anthony so well installed, in such peaceful and beautiful surroundings. He approved of the house, and said so several times. You were very wise to snap it up, he said. Anthony did not point out that the price he had paid for High Rook House hardly suggested a snapping up: that he had to strain open the jaws of his bank account somewhat brutally in order to introduce this large new expense, and was naturally now extremely doubtful as to whether in the new depressing financial situation the bank account would ever digest and absorb it. Giles Peters might well have been able to open his pikelike jaw and suck in a country house or two, without gulping, but Anthony, as Giles knew perfectly well, was hardly in the same league. As Giles Peters knew perfectly well, Anthony Keating's fortunes were entirely dependent on the fortunes of the I.D. Property Company.

It grew late, and Giles and Pamela and the chauffeur finished the bottle: Anthony, sober, watched the level drop, and began to hope that it would drop so far that his guests would not notice the deficiencies of their accommodation. For, he now realized, he did not think he had any extra sheets; or, if he had, did not know where they were, and did not feel up to a search. There was one pair on his bed, one at the laundry in Blickley, and where the others had got to, God alone knew, or possibly God and Alison, but Alison was a thousand miles away. He himself had not made his bed for weeks. He would crawl into it at night, like a hamster into its ball of straw, and pull everything around him. Alison would have hated that. She liked the sheets clean and smooth and well tucked in, at least to begin with.

Pamela looked as though she would like clean smooth sheets too. Was she drunk enough to bed down happily in the rough, in the woollen? There were plenty of blankets, plenty of bedrooms. Princess Pamela, with her white face and white fingers, looked as though she might well be the type to complain about a pea under the twentieth mattress. Her voice was intolerable. She was the kind of person who makes greengrocers wince behind their stock, who attracts the sneers of taxi drivers and the covert insults of all but the most servile and cowardly of those engaged in the services. He wondered what she was like in bed. The thought of her and Giles in bed together was peculiarly unattractive. Perhaps they weren't sleeping together after all; perhaps she was merely there for the ride.

It was two o'clock before they staggered upstairs. Pamela wanted a room to herself. He had an uncomfortable feeling, as he showed her into it, showed her the heap of blankets in the large mahogany wardrobe, apologized for the lack of sheets, that she was expecting him to make some kind of pass at her—possibly only for the pleasure of rejecting it, but expecting it, nevertheless. He could not bring himself to push chivalry so far. But, when she commented on the lack of a bedside light, was weak enough to offer her his own. "And you wouldn't have such a thing as a hot-water bottle?" she asked, when he returned with the lamp, standing there, expectant, in her long embroidered dress, dangling her fur coat. "I'm afraid not," he said.

She shivered, ostentatiously. "I'm afraid I'm very cold-blooded," she said; an unfortunate remark, for indeed she did look cold, and slightly reptilian—a cold, ancient little creature, determined, bloodless. Surprising, in a way, that her species had not become extinct long ago.

"I'll get you the electric fire from downstairs," he said, and went down and fetched it. The bar did not wish to illumine itself at all for Pamela's benefit, and he kicked it till the sparks flew before the connection magically connected. He stared at the reluctant angry glow.

"It might go off, I'm afraid, in the middle of the night," he said. "It's very temperamental. I don't know why it behaves like this. Sometimes, when I'm sitting quite quietly, not moving at all, it will go off. For no reason."

"If it goes off in the middle of the night," said Pamela, "and if I'm freezing to death, I'll come and get you to kick it for me, shall I?" She stared at him, rather rudely. He found her most unattractive. And yet there was something in him that felt as though he had been issued an order, to which he ought to respond: as she had responded, with docility, to Giles's order to warm up the chicken and chips.

He had no intention of responding. He smiled, with more charm perhaps than he intended—or perhaps he intended to demonstrate that it was he, after all, that had the charm—and said, "Oh, do please try not to do that. I'd *much* rather you didn't do that," and walked off, leaving her standing there.

The chauffeur had disappeared into his room as into a burrow, not to re-emerge, and Giles, by the time Anthony had got around to seeing what had happened to him, was asleep, in most of his clothes, under an eiderdown.

Anthony went to his own room. He looked out the window at the brilliant sky. There is so much sky in the country, and there rode the pale moon, high over the valley, shedding so much light that the trees with their few leaves glimmered and shone: the moon, the pale bride of death, the still, the chosen one. She shook and stirred him. Her shadowy silver face leaned toward him. Radiant, luminous, enigmatic, attendant. Three quarters full and on the wane. Soon, the bright and savage sickle. The soft, unshapely shape, the unfinished circle swam in the clear sky. What has she to do with profit and loss? Something, perhaps. She too waxes and wanes.

Len Wincobank, in Scratby Open Prison, lay awake and stared through a flimsy bit of curtain at the same moon. In a closed prison, one of the things that men suffer from is their inability to see the sky. In his weeks in Northam jail, before his transfer to this relatively lenient spot, he had heard stories from other inmates of the famous strike, when the men had refused to return to their cells from exercise: all night they had stood in the grim nineteenth-century yard, surrounded by high walls and barbed wire, on strike, for a better parole system, or at least to be given reasons for the refusal of parole; and the night had begun in anger and fear of violence and had ended with two hundred men standing, squatting, staring with awe at the night sky that some of them had not seen for years, would not see again for more years. "It was uncanny," one of them said to novice Len. "Uncanny, that's what it was. It was a clear night, see, and there was this bloody great full moon, and stars so thick it was like daytime. I'd never seen anything like it. I'd never looked at the sky before."

There was plenty of sky at Scratby. High on the Yorkshire moors, exposed, cold, flat, and high, the prison was a disused air-base, near enough to another, well-used RAF base: as the men worked in the grounds, they could see aircraft, fighter jets, scream-ing across the heavens in formations, singly, looping, swooping, cutting, and slicing, a free display of free movement. Len worked in the open air; he had asked to work in the forestry department. One of the prison's main industries was forestry: the men grew, from seed, trees for the Department of the Environment and Scots pine for the wood and timber of the future. So much of prison labor is dull, repetitive, wasteful, and most of the men hated the forestry too; they hated digging, bedding out, messing around with little seedlings in little Japanese egg boxes. Len did not much like it either, but it was better than taking apart old radios and washing machines, or cutting up strips of plastic weatherstrip-ping, or watching the washing machines in the laundry. And Len was aware that forestry was a major industry of the future: he had followed with interest accounts of paper shortages and wood shortages, of difficulties over imports from Sweden and Norway, of new schemes for recycling shredded newspaper into animal protein for poultry. Trees were a growth industry, and that ob-scurely pleased him. Perhaps he would expand into forestry, when he got out? But perhaps not. The growth was so slow, the returns so slow. Buildings were better.

But something in him was touched by the tiny trees, shivering under the cold wind on the hard earth. Odd that so many of them survived, for conditions were far from ideal, and they could at-tempt only the hardiest species, although they had expensive mod-ern greenhouses, sheltered nursery gardens with high walls. He liked the trees to take. It saddened him to see those that died, those that withered in their infancy, turning yellow, then brown, then drying into thin twigs. Oh yes, he tried to take an interest in trees.

The work was tiring, but nevertheless he lay awake. His system could not adjust to bed at ten; without a drink. In the days of extreme strain before the collapse, in the months between the warrant and the trial, Len had hit the bottle, and had suffered for weeks after his conviction from withdrawal symptoms. A kindly prison officer and a sanctimonious, tedious, and obsequious fellow prisoner had tried to persuade Len to attend the monthly meetings of Alcoholics Anonymous, but he had refused, for he had no intention either of admitting that he was an alcoholic or of seeking a cure if he was one. He would stick it out, and the day he got out he would have a bottle or two to celebrate. He had been discussing the subject that evening, with the copper, over Twenty-one: the copper told him the sad story of Alfred Collins, who had lost all his remission because one night he had said to himself, fuck it all, and had walked out of the prison (quite an easy thing to do) and walked the three miles down to the village, and into the pub, and drunk himself into a paralytic stupor, before he was picked up. "Poor sod," said Len with feeling. "Poor sod."

"Yeah, I can imagine how it came over him, though, can't you?" said the copper, dealing Len an eight and a seven.

"I guess I can stick it out," said Len, although a faint sweat was breaking out on his forehead and in his armpits at the very thought. He told the copper about Anthony Keating, who had had a heart attack at the age of thirty-eight, and who had been told to lay off sex, drink, and smoking. "It doesn't leave much," said Len. He felt sorry for Anthony: almost, in a sense, responsible. His gamble had so nearly paid off. There was a Gamblers Anonymous group in the prison too: Len sometimes wondered if that wouldn't be more relevant to him and his problems than the Alcoholics. Gambling was a much more serious vice than drinking, and one he would never be able to kick.

After the story of Anthony's enforced abstinence, Len and the copper moved on to talk about food, a favorite theme in prisons. Both agreed that the prison bread, baked on the premises, was fine, but that nothing else would bear inspection—apart, perhaps, from the doughnuts, also prison-baked. The copper worked in the bakery and had learned much about bread. He even toyed from time to time with the thought of earning a decent living by taking up baking seriously. But he knew he wouldn't: he was too ambitious.

The copper described to Anthony the best meal he had ever had. It had been eaten in the company of his wife, his brother, his sister-in-law, and a mate and his wife. They were celebrating his brother's promotion. He had taken them all out, to a newly opened roadhouse restaurant outside Manchester: his brother knew the manager, and they had put on a good show for them. First of all, drinks at the bar. He had a whisky and dry ginger. Then, at the table (with real roses on it, not plastic ones, and a real tablecloth), pâté for starters, though the girls had all had prawn cocktails, and Jim had the soup. After the pâté, a steak, the like of which you never saw in your life—it just melted in the mouth, said the copper lyrically. Accompanied by? Mushrooms, French fries, French beans, and garden peas. All perfect. Just so. For dessert, chocolate *gâteau*, with cream and cherries in it, and some kind of liqueur flavoring. Then the girls had knocked off, but he and Jim and Dave had had a slice of Stilton each, and a couple of brandies. Lizzie (that's my wife) drove home, we were all past it. That was a meal to remember, all right. Lizzie was wearing her blue dress.

Lovely shoulders, my Lizzie has. She's not a bad cook herself, either. But you can't buy steak like that in the shops. The restaurants get it all. You've got to be like *that* with the butcher, to get a piece of steak like that.

Len had seen Lizzie on visiting day. She was a big woman, a blonde, who treated the whole shaming occasion in high style, marching into the dismal canteen as though she were the Queen of Sheba, and talking in a loud Lancashire voice, not to be put down, not to be silenced. He had not seen her shoulders, for they were concealed by a large fluffy coat, but he could imagine that her husband's praise of them was justified.

Len had not been able to reciprocate with the best meal he had ever had: he'd had so many good meals in his time. The Christmas dinners of childhood had been hard to beat, but he'd tried to beat them, with business lunches and business dinners at the Carlton Towers, the Mirabelle, Stone's Chop House, Simpson's in the Strand. He thought of Simpson's. The beef off the trolley was quite something. Red slices, off a great slab. Red gravy, red blood. And the silver fifty-pence piece that Len (an astute observer) had learned to lay on the edge of the silver trolley, for the man who carved. The niceties of wealth, the finer points of ostentation.

Their supper that night had been tinned soup, hamburger, mash and swede, and rhubarb and custard. The thin green-pink strands of rhubarb had floated like weed, like scum, acidic, sinister, in the watery juice, nudging uneasily, like a jellyfish against a rock, against the great solid dob of custard. Custard, the poor man's cream. Len, like many of his generation, did not taste fresh cream until he was a man: for a year or more he had surreptitiously preferred condensed milk, before weaning himself onto the real thing. Now he was back on condensed milk again: the prisoner's treat. The men would buy it from the store, with their £1 of earnings a week, some of them preferring it, in their craving for sweetness, to tobacco.

In bed, looking at the moon, Len decided that the best meal of all had been that meal he'd had with Maureen in the Palmer House hotel in Chicago. He hadn't wanted to describe it to Jim, but now he recalled it, in loving detail. It was her first visit to the States, his first to Chicago, to visit an architect who specialized in multistory car parks: they arrived late, a delayed flight, and went straight from the airport to the hotel, finding themselves, at two o'clock in the morning, almost alone in the huge Edwardian foyer, with its trees and its chandeliers, its enormous carpet, its myriad lost armchairs. They checked in, were shown up to their room, in a lift with brass doors twice as high as doors could ever need to be; their room had a carpet so thick that one's shoes sank into it, a thick green carpet like deep grass, and a bed large enough for four, and a color television set, which was demonstrated for them at once, before they were left alone together, to stare at one another, to hug one another, to laugh in astonishment.

"*What* a place!" said Maureen, sitting on the edge of the bed, tugging off her high-heeled boots, flinging off her coat. "This really is quite something!"

And she prowled around in her stockings, opening doors, turning on taps, swishing the heavy curtains, opening them on a stunning but rather frightening view of a brightly lit, faraway street, too far below to watch with ease. Len fiddled with the television, and found a late-night movie: *Gentlemen Prefer Blondes*. It seemed singularly appropriate. Enraptured, they sat on the edge of the bed and watched for five minutes, then, at the sight of the people on the screen eating, decided they were hungry. So Len, keen to impress Maureen, who was so delightfully impressionable, reached for the telephone, with more calm than he felt, and ordered two de luxe turkey sandwiches, and a bottle of whisky, and some fruit.

"I think you're wonderful," said Maureen, with deep sincerity. "I hope they hurry up. I want to take my clothes off."

So did Len. But it would never have occurred to either of these children of the North of England to take their clothes off before the arrival of their dinner.

It arrived, in ten minutes, on a clinking silver trolley wheeled by a black man in a picturesque uniform. Len, who had been impressed on previous visits more by the evidently unoppressed blacks of America than by the oppressed, wondered briefly why so large and imposing a man allowed himself to be dressed up in so ludicrous a manner, and nervously offered him a few dollar bills, which were, somewhat to his relief, accepted with the merest formal gesture toward gratitude.

The turkey sandwiches were many-layered and filled with mayonnaise; they were garnished with gherkins and olives and onions and pieces of tomato. The fruit was arranged in a basket, the kind of basket one sees in the movies, the kind that was now flitting before their greedy eyes on the TV on the *Queen Mary* of the 1930s. And there was ice in buckets, and soda in siphons, and an array of glasses, and a bottle of Dewar's. He poured Maureen a generous tumbler, splashed in some soda. She pulled off her red jersey, revealing her black lace brassière, her cream shoulders, her lovely thick neck. She drank, he watched the liquid travel down. She unfastened her skirt, took a huge bite of turkey sandwich, and, mayonnaise oozing, giggling, wriggled her bottom till the skirt dropped off. Her pants were floral, Marks and Sparks: she had once confided in him that she had had this pair since she was fourteen, but as they were as good as new, why throw them away? She was wearing black knee socks. "When I was little," she said, taking another huge bite, "I used to *hate* mayonnaise."

She took her pants off. "I'm getting into bed," she said. "Shove the trolley over, there's a love."

And there she sat, in her socks and bra, eating and drinking and watching the television. "I think this is paradise," she said.

And so did he.

While Len Wincobank was lying in his prison bed thinking about Maureen in a king-sized bed in Chicago, Maureen was trying to write her weekly letter to Len. It was heavy going; you can't say much in a letter, and Maureen had never been much of a one for personal correspondence. Business letters she was good at, but there wasn't any more business, and if she tried to give him the latest on the fates of subsidiary companies and old enemies in property, they'd only cut it out. And she couldn't think of any sexy or encouraging jokes. She didn't want to tell him about her new job, because it would annoy him to think she was going on living when he wasn't. And she couldn't tell him about what was uppermost in her mind, which was the fate of Auntie Evie.

I had supper at Marlene's yesterday, she wrote. *Those kids don't half make a row, and the walls in that flat are like paper. The plaster is full of cracks.*

She stared at the typewriter. That would please Len: he disapproved of the architect who had designed the block that her sister-in-law Marlene lived in. She didn't like the flat much herself: it was poky and the lift was always broken, and it was no fun walking up six flights of stairs with shopping carts and strollers and two kids under three. No wonder Marlene was foul-tempered and kept clobbering them all the time. Yes, Len would be pleased to hear about Marlene's flat. *The lift is always broken too*, she added, then came to a full stop.

The truth was that Auntie Evie was weighing on her mind, and thinking about her made her feel irritable with the absent Len, which wasn't fair, but there it was. Maureen knew quite well that it was hardly Len's fault that Evie's slum was to be redeveloped, and that Evie had been given notice and was furious, but she couldn't help imagining how unsympathetic Len would be, if she were rash enough to force the story on him. For Len too was grossly inconsistent. Much as he disapproved of some individual council developments, and much as he despised many city architects (particularly those of Porcaster), in principle he was always in favor of rebuilding, and nothing annoyed him more than stories about pathetic old ladies fighting lone battles to preserve their cherished crumbling homes. He was all for more ruthless powers of eviction. Conservationists and litigious obstructionists annoyed him equally, and poor old ladies touched not a chord in his black heart. Auntie Evie's case would get no sympathy from Len. He had forced his reluctant mum out of her decaying terrace cottage into a nice suburban semi, where she had moped briefly behind lace curtains, despised by her suburban neighbors, and then died: of loneliness, Maureen was sure. "Balls," Len would snarl, when Maureen raised this possibility. "She never had a friend in the world anyway, nobody was ever allowed to cross our threshold, when I was a kid."

So Len would not be interested in Maureen's feelings about Auntie Evie's house, which were quite strong, for Maureen had spent much of her childhood there, and she too did not want to see it go. She could see why it would have to go: it was in very poor condition, the middle of a sloping hillside terrace, hit by bomb damage and subsidence. The roof sloped, the windows would not shut by four or five inches, every door was out of true, the steps were crumbling, and the floor of the front room was buckled as though by an earthquake. But Evie paid only a pound a week for it, and she had lived there all her married life, and she had made it very nice, as everyone agreed. Evie was much the most respectable member of Maureen's feckless family, but had had a tough life: as, again, everyone agreed. Her husband had died of cancer when she was only thirty, leaving her with three kids and one on the way. She had worked all her life, charring, washing up in the Korner Kafe, cleaning at the Children's Home, and she had brought the children up a treat, a credit to her—two of them were printers, earning good money, one a draftsman, and the fourth worked as a nurse at the Children's Home. And she had kept her house a treat, too, with little bits and bobs from here and there, from jumble sales, castoffs from employers. Maureen knew every corner, every item: the tea caddy with the wooden lid, the willow pattern plate on the wall, the china dog on the mantelpiece, the old Singer sewing machine, the lacquered button box, the old armchair from Dr. David's, the firescreen with the brass rail. It was no good saying you could move all that to a council flat: you couldn't, there'd never be room, and anyway, it would never look right.

Auntie Evie had spent thirty years making herself one of the most respectable women in the neighborhood. Wherever she went —to the butcher, to the launderette, to the fish shop, to the Indian emporium—she received her due, the courtesy due to years of toil. And how had she done it? Through cleaning and washing dishes. It was a triumph, a careful slow laborious victory, over circumstance. Maureen would not have liked Auntie Evie's life at all, and would have found its rewards meager, being a child of affluence and expectation, a postwar baby, but she could see it for what it was, and she shared her aunt's helpless indignation. To have so much undone, by a council decision: all those patient years, all the rewards of old age—honor, love, civility, streets of friends. But what else could happen? The house was falling down. "I hoped it would last me out," said Evie, "but it seems it won't." Maureen had tried to cheer her, with stories of nice new flats with views and central heating, but her cheer had rung hollow.

I don't know, thought Maureen. It's funny, I wouldn't want to live on that shabby little terrace for anything in the world, I wouldn't go back to that part for anything, to be honest, it stinks, around there; every time I go back, I think what a filthy hole it's turning into, garbage and muck everywhere and the shops seem to get dirtier and dirtier and cheaper and cheaper. But then, when I think of Auntie Evie, it's as though I was thinking about a different place. Seeing it through her eyes.

She tried to look at it through Len's eyes. A run-down, seedy, neglected area, an eyesore, a disgrace. A monument to lousy housing policy, bad planning, council ineptitude.

She wrote to Len: *You will be glad to hear that the council has at last decided to do something about Whitethorn Road and Ambleside Road, Auntie Evie got a note from the council last week. Naturally she is not very pleased at the moment, but . . .*

Maureen stopped. But what? She could not think of anything else to say about Auntie Evie.

There was nothing else to say about Auntie Evie.

Maureen scrubbed out her remarks about Auntie Evie, and began a sentence about her new hairdo, trying hard not to think about all the old ladies whom she and Len had dislodged, by fair means or foul, to make way for wonderful new shopping centers and office blocks. Len had been fond of a phrase that had always puzzled her: "You can't make an omelette without breaking eggs," he used to say. But that was nonsense. She tried to work it out. Of course an omelette *is* broken eggs. That was the point about an omelette. There's nothing accidental about breaking eggs for omelettes. Whereas nobody could pretend that an office block *was* angry evicted old ladies. Could they? One didn't have to crunch them up and pound them in a cement mixer, did one?

I had my hair tinted at Suzanne's, Maureen wrote. *The old place has gone downhill a bit since the last time I was there. They never seem to sweep the floor between the customers these days. The highlights have come out a bit funny too. Perhaps I'd better get rid of them before I see you again next month, Len darling.*

Alison Murray, far away in the Balkans, sat up late, long after Len Wincobank and Maureen Kirby and even Anthony Keating had fallen asleep. She could not sleep, these days. She sat at her hotel window, and stared out into the darkness, trying to write a letter to Anthony, thinking. Inactivity and sleeplessness and impotence were driving her insane. Her hotel room was small, and bleak. On her arrival, before the hotel manager had worked out who she was, mistaking her perhaps for the film star she still dimly resembled, she had been given a splendid apartment, with vast rubber plants, a bedroom, a drawing room, a luxurious bathroom with crystal vases of the district in a glass cupboard and Balkan icons on the walls and picture books of the country's attractions by the bedside: doubtless one of their new specially rigged specially bugged suites for visiting businessmen and diplomats. When they had discovered that she was of no importance whatsoever, indeed more of an embarrassment, she had been moved to the back of the hotel, to a small, square, prisonlike room with a bed, a table, a hard-backed chair, and no hot water. Its chief advantage was that by Western European standards it was amazingly cheap. The British community of Wallacia, such as it was, had made various offers of half-hearted hospitality, but Alison had declined them: she preferred to be independent, she did not like to be an encumbrance, and she did not want to have to talk when she had nothing to say. At times, as now, she regretted this decision, particularly on account of the consul Clyde Barstow, who was a nice and interesting man. But Mrs. Barstow would not have liked it, she had known instinctively, and she did not want to be more of a nuisance than she anyway was.

Things were not going well. The psychiatrist had agreed to see Jane, but held out no hope that his word would be of any use. He had not been amiable. When told that Jane refused to speak to her mother, he had looked at Alison with undisguised hostility. He had not been impressed by Alison's statement that she could not herself say what had caused the accident, as she had not been there: he seemed more impressed by the fact that two people had been killed.

As, indeed, was Alison herself. Jane had refused to speak at all about the event, beyond a curt remark—"It wasn't my fault"—but as Jane had been saying that things were not her fault, in precisely that tone of voice, since early childhood, when they very evidently were, Alison could not place too much reliance on this statement. Maybe the shock had silenced her: who could say? Whichever way, a man and his son were now dead, who had been alive and driving themselves home from work, whereas Jane was alive, and her boyfriend and fellow traveler had disappeared. It was not even clear whether or not he had been in the car at the time of the accident. It had occurred on an empty stretch of road: there were no witnesses.

It was all too clear that the Wallacian police considered Jane Murray an irresponsible fool who should never have been allowed into their country in the first place. There were some unfortunate precedents. An English student who was driving a tourist coach for his vacation job the year before had been involved in an incident with a truck, and had been sentenced to ten years in prison. Three years earlier, an English businessman had suffered the same penalty. Students were now regularly jailed if caught carrying drugs. Some had been imprisoned, albeit for short stretches, for having insufficient currency on them.

Alison, who felt herself to be a thoroughly English person, reflected on the way in which other nations had turned against England in the last few years. England was a safe, shabby, mangy old lion now: anyone could tweak her tail. So the Indians imprisoned schoolteachers and writers, the Ugandans threatened to execute British offenders, schoolgirls were tried for currency offenses in Kenya, a mere child was jailed for drug smuggling in Turkey. Malice and justice united to persecute the once so prosperous, once so arrogant, once so powerful of nations, the nation on whose empire the sun had never set. Powerless, teased, angry, impotent, the old country muttered and protested and let itself be mocked. And it served it right, Alison could not but think, in many ways. For too long, the English had assumed they had a monopoly not only of money but of morals: who could blame the new nations of the world for wishing to take their revenge? Alison herself did not approve of dirty, idle, parasitic British teenagers who thought they could smoke and strum their way around the world on their grass and their appalling guitars, preaching freedom and idleness to those who believed in work: no wonder they found themselves unwelcome from time to time. The vagaries of the rich and powerful are permitted; the vagaries of the poor are not. If her daughter Jane had, in fact, through careless driving, killed two innocent men, Alison would be the last person to say that she should not pay the penalty for it.

But a vindictive penalty, an anti-British penalty? This was clearly what the British consul feared, although he tried to conceal his foreboding.

Whatever was England going to do? Alison, far from home, thought of home with sorrow and yearning, but also with a deep dismay. She did not see what could be done to salvage so much that had been so good, and sometimes she felt herself to be one of the last generation that could remember what the good had been; it would all be forgotten. She would not like to trust the future to people like Jane. And she herself was too old: weak, ineffective, impotent. So was Anthony. They had planned to retire, early, from the scene, because they no longer had the energy to deal with daily life. Had that been it?

England, sliding, sinking, shabby, dirty, lazy, inefficient, dangerous, in its death-throes, worn out, clapped out, occasionally lashing out.

She thought, at last, of Kitty Friedmann. News was slow to reach Wallacia on the whole, but anti-British news always seemed to arrive with unnatural speed: the *Times* was only delivered to Alison's room when the headlines were spectacularly bad. Fortunately or unfortunately, these days that was quite often, so Alison had read of the bomb that killed Max and wounded Kitty Friedmann only two days after it had gone off. The pleasure which the Wallacians took in the Irish problem, coupled with their refusal to believe that it had anything to do with religion, had for weeks been causing Alison acute spasms of patriotic despair, and now it had come home to her, in so violent, so gruesome a way. She tried hard not to think of Kitty, but now, in the small hours, there was no way of getting away from it. She lit herself a cigarette: she had moved onto local cigarettes, and, like the local wine, they were good.

Kitty Friedmann had lost her foot.

I think, thought Alison, that I would rather die than lose my foot.

But of course, she could not die yet, because of Molly, who was still only ten, and whom nobody else would ever love.

Her horror of physical injury had always been extreme. To die a violent death seemed to her the worst of all things, except perhaps the survival of a violent death.

How had Max died? What parts of him had been blown up? With what? Had he died instantly? Of a recent bomb explosion an eyewitness had said, in a large headline, "I SAW A WOMAN BLOWN TO PIECES." Horrified, compelled, Alison, like a million others, gripped by the poetry and language of violence, read on: the same witness had carried the blown-to-pieces woman into the airport lounge. How? Which pieces? How, if blown to pieces, could a woman be carried?

How had the two men hit by Jane's car died? Nastily?

She had never seen a dead person.

There are those who rush to the sites of air disasters, bomb disasters, to catch sight of a corpse, of a piece of corpse. Why?

And what had happened to Kitty's foot? Where was it? Incinerated? And had it been blown off, or cut off? And if cut off, what with? A knife? Leaving what? A stump? And what did one cut through? Bone, tendon? Or did one find the joint, as in a chicken?

I would sooner be dead, thought Alison. But I know why. It is because I am a vain, a wicked woman, who thinks too much of this world, and of her own body. I am not humble, I cannot face old age, I cannot face ugliness and decay.

She shivered. She was afraid. A large, a terrible fear gripped her. Of death? No, not of death. To die in one's sleep, to fade away, seemed easy enough, as a prospect.

Of mutilation? Why, of mutilation? Nobody had ever threatened her with it, so why, so unnaturally, so wastefully, at least so prematurely, face it, fear it?

Slowly, Alison Murray rose to her feet, and shut the curtains, and crossed to the wardrobe mirror. Slowly, she inclined her face toward her face. The harsh unshaded light fell without mercy. Yes, there were wrinkles. At last, after years of grace, there were wrinkles. There would be more. There was strain around the eye, the mouth, the nose. The neck was slightly ringed. Rings, dark and grave, lay also beneath her eyes: dark red, weary. She bared her teeth at herself: yes, her gums were receding, slightly, they were creeping back in distaste from her too-large, too-old, nicotine-stained teeth. Her face felt stiff; it woke stiff, took all day to soften, then stiffened again each evening. Her hair was touched with gray: she had always admired young women with gray hair, with white streaks in the black, had not minded her genetic inheritance. But a young woman with gray hair was one thing, an old woman with gray hair another. Meditatively, she untied her wrap and stared at her body. There it was, source of so much pleasure, so much self-congratulation. And still lovely: hardly a mark upon it, hardly a sign of wear, the body of a young woman. But for how long, she said to herself, panic beating noisily in her ears; for how much longer? When will it collapse? Will it collapse overnight, like Dorian Gray? It is unnaturally preserved already, as it was unnaturally endowed in the first place. When will I cease to be able to look at myself naked in the mirror? And God, oh God, what then, what then will I do? What will I do, in five years, in ten?

For Alison Murray, beauty had for years been identity. She had no other. How could she ever make another, for the second half of her necessary life?

She sat down again, at her chair by the window: lit another cigarette. Watched her hands, holding it. She had pretty hands, long fingers, two of them adorned by rings: an engagement ring, a cluster of pearls and tiny rubies, and a huge topaz which Anthony had given her, when things were going well. But the veins showed, and would show more. The knuckles were wrinkled, would wrinkle more. She remembered an evening with friends, years ago: laughing, mercilessly, over a touched-up press photograph of a fifty-year-old actress of their acquaintance; laughing, unkindly, because she claimed in the interview to be only forty, and could have been, from the face, but that clever bitch Helen had said, "Look at her hands, though, you can always tell from the hands"—and it was true, the photographer, courteous though he had been, had forgotten to touch up the hands, and there they lay, on the elegant actress's elegant little coffee table, the hands of a woman of fifty. Ribbed, veined, corded. Alison raised one of her hands into the air, let the blood run down out of it, leaving it thin, pale, pretty. How long can one stave off death and ugliness with these ancient little tricks?

Alison Murray had an elder sister. Her sister was called Rosemary. A year ago, Rosemary had gone into the hospital, with a lump in her breast, and had woken to find the breast removed, for the lump had been malignant. The night after this news had reached her had been one of the worst of Alison's life. She had been unable to sleep for fear. Her own breasts had felt ill with terror: for months afterward, she had not dared to look at them, to touch them. The knife slice through the soft innocent tissue haunted her nights for weeks.

Alison and Rosemary had not been particularly close, saw one another rarely, so why should the news have upset her so much?

Rosemary had always been jealous of Alison. Because Alison was admired and beautiful. Rosemary was good-looking herself, but did not think so. Rosemary's ill will had made Alison feel guilty, sick. And when she herself produced two daughters, one beautiful, one remarkably not so, she had insisted that Jane should love Molly, had insisted that Jane should be kind, affectionate, loving. She knew too well what jealousy and ill will do to the jealous one and to the object of jealousy.

At the same moment, at the birth of Molly, she had retired from her profession, she had ceased forever to compete, had ceased to contend, had withdrawn herself and put herself away.

Jane had never been unkind to Molly, in any evident way. **But** she had no feeling for her. And she expressed her resentment in a hundred other devious ways: by complaining about her own trivial illnesses, by rude remarks about cripples and the deformed, by an excessive revulsion from any sight of physical malady or infirmity, by a stubborn refusal to engage in any physically unpleasant activity—scraping plates, cleaning shoes, emptying dustbins. Guilty, confused, Alison had let her get away with it; as long as the resentment was not expressed directly against Molly, let Jane abuse the wretched and maimed of the earth as much as she liked. Unfortunately, Jane was reared in an age and an environment where black humor was considered chic, where defects, long tenderly exempt from mockery, had become legitimate targets, where clever young men cracked jokes about the blind, the deaf, the limbless, the speechless: she was a child of the times.

Alison, sitting alone thinking, thought: I should have told her that it was wrong. Whatever she thought of me, however she hated me for telling her, I should have told her she was wrong, and that such jokes must not, must never be made. Such thoughts must not be thought. There is nothing healthy about their expression. They must not be thought.

I loved Molly too much, Jane too little. God knows what that effort cost me.

Anthony had said to Alison, after the property crisis and his heart attack—poor Alison, poor darling, what a bad choice you made again in me.

She had not, at the time, thought it in any way a relevant remark. But maybe it was? Choice was not a simple matter. Was it a matter of choice that Jane, who could drive perfectly well, had chosen to kill two men in the country which possessed the most stringent penalties for traffic offenses in Europe? Choice. Bad luck. For years, for ten years, Alison had striven to believe in accidents, in the possibility of bad luck, for that would exonerate herself, her husband, Jane, Rosemary, her parents—they would all be exonerated by such a belief from the guilt of Molly's sacrifice. But if it were not so? She glimpsed for a moment, in the dark night, a primitive causality so shocking, so uncanny, that she shivered and froze. A world where the will was potent, not impotent: where it made, indeed, bad choices and killed others by them, killed them, deformed them, destroyed them.

I gave Rosemary cancer of the breast, said Alison to herself, aloud, to see how the words sounded. They did not sound very foolish. She held her hands over her own breasts. Shivering. Well, they would get her in the end. Age and Death would catch her, if their forerunners did not.

Part Two

On Thursday the nineteenth of November, Anthony Keating's guests rose in good spirits, for it was a fine pink morning, with a mauve blush over the hills: shepherd's warning, said Anthony, but nobody could believe it. How could so lovely a color foretell bad weather? Giles was more impressed by the house in daylight than he had been in the dark, and Anthony and Giles strolled around the grounds together, leaving Pamela to wash up the breakfast dishes. Anthony pointed out the features: the finials, the small rose window, the pond with its little gray rim, its modest little dolphin. "I always wanted a pond with a statue in it," said Anthony. "It's not exactly a Bernini, but it's pretty enough, don't you think?" Giles nodded, staring, without seeing, at the gray stone, the iron-red and yellow lichen, the little cups and plates and velvet cushions of the green moss.

They wandered on, and paused by an overgrown bed of persistent yellow roses.

"Well," said Giles, "what do you think?"

"About what?"

"What are you going to do?"

Anthony shrugged.

"What can I do? Wait for you to pull off some new coup, I suppose. There's nothing much I can do. You don't need me, in town, do you? I'd come, if you did."

Giles felt in his pocket, opened his cigarette case, took out a cigarette, lit it, stared at the damp grass.

"I was thinking," said Giles. "Rory and I were thinking—maybe you'd be happier if you could get out of this whole business?" He looked around. "You've got such a fine place here, it seems a pity to risk it." He stared, innocently, at the house, at the great gray barn with its overgrown roof. "And you've had a bad time. Being ill. And then, Alison. It can't be doing you much good, worrying about the Riverside debacle."

"I don't worry myself to death, you know," said Anthony, staring also at the grass, at Giles's square brown polished city shoes, at his own unpolished city shoes.

"No, I daresay not. You're looking fit. But Rory and I were thinking . . ." And, slowly, Giles expounded what he and Rory had been thinking. They had been thinking of offering Anthony a get-out, a release from the company. Of course, he said, the company being in such a sorry state, they couldn't offer much money, but they could release Anthony from all of the company's liabilities, and perhaps arrange for a capital sum to be transferred, in exchange for Anthony's share.

He was too delicate to mention a sum, and Anthony too delicate to inquire, but he hinted that they could come to some agreement in the light of Anthony's personal finances, with regard to his old house, his new house. "It would be nice, for instance," said Giles, "if you could feel that this house was your own, wouldn't it? I'm not saying we'd ever be able to cover all you borrowed on it, but we could go some way to making sure you didn't lose it. If anything happened to the company."

"That's very considerate of you," said Anthony. "And what about you and Rory? If anything happens to the company?"

"Oh, we aren't in the same predicament as you," said Giles. "We haven't got your commitments. And we've both of us got other interests, as well. . . . I've been worrying about you, Anthony. I feel responsible. I'd like to feel you weren't going to come out of this too badly."

Anthony bent down, pulled up a fibrous sprig of plantain, considered. Giles was a shocking liar, but he is also, Anthony thought, one of my oldest friends. Why should I suspect him of behaving worse than I would behave myself? And whatever Giles's motives, what a relief it would indeed be, to get rid of one's liabilities, to stop thinking about those bloodsucking monstrous properties squatting down in London, to forget the whole business, to get rid of one's second mortgage, to return to being a private person, only a few thousand pounds overdrawn. To begin again.

"I must say," said Anthony, carefully, staring up at the pink glow, "that it's a very attractive idea."

A rook cawed, sardonically.

A little too quickly, Giles said, "If you were interested, we've already looked up the details of our original agreement, when we set up the company."

"Have you got the papers with you?" said Anthony. "I don't think I've got my copy of the agreement here, or if I have, I wouldn't know where it is."

Giles hesitated.

"No, I haven't got them here," he said. Anthony knew he was lying.

"I'd have to ring you, when I get back," said Giles.

"I'd better think about it," said Anthony, who was already thinking hard. "It's very generous of you, to worry about me so much. Don't let it get you down, I'm all right."

"It's a bad business, about Alison," said Giles, changing the subject. "What a country to get stuck in, of all the countries in Europe."

And they talked of Alison, and the politics of Wallacia, and of the pruning of roses, about which neither knew much.

"You make a good country gentleman," said Giles to Anthony, as they strolled back to the house.

Giles and Pamela left at twelve. The weather was already darkening, and it had turned cold. Anthony went down with them in the car to the village, where they dropped him off. I'll think about it, I'll ring you, said Anthony. Thank you for your hospitality, said Pamela. They drove off: he waved, from the little bridge over the river. He was glad to see them go. He stood for a while, staring into the water, watching the weed flow and turn like hair, watching the brown stones and the surface shimmer. He would go back and look at the terms of the original agreement that he and Rory and Giles had made; he had a copy in his desk, and knew which drawer it lay in. It was obvious enough that Giles and Rory were trying to get rid of him, for reasons of their own: but what reasons? There had been, he was sure, a clause allowing for the release of any one of the three partners, but he could not recall the precise conditions. Why, if the company was losing as badly as it seemed, should they want to release him from his share of the liabilities? Did they have expectations they had not revealed—bites, nibbles, even the sight of fish in the water?

It was starting to rain: the sky had clouded over with extraordinary speed and thoroughness. He felt pleased that his weather forecast was vindicated, went into the village shop to buy a couple of tins of soup, and started to walk back up the lane to the house. Great wet drops fell like pennies on the pale dusty road. A bird sang in the hedge, a song of warning, a liquid song. He did not trust Giles, trusted Rory even less, knowing him less, yet what would he lose, if he accepted their offer, except a constant sense of hideous anxiety?

I might, of course, lose the possibility of my share of profits. But how could there be profits, the way things are going? And would I care, if there were? Would I care, if I opted out, and then had to watch while Giles and Rory made a killing?

They have ganged up on me, he reflected. They have conspired behind my back, while I was away. Like Caesar and Lepidus, while Antony was lolling about with Cleopatra. A triumvirate cannot work. It was my mistake, to leave London.

He did not much care. He wondered what Alison would say if she were here. She was far too far away to consult. She would, he thought, be likely to advise him to get out while he could: she had had enough of the strain. She had been game enough at the beginning, but the last few months had worn her out.

But I don't think I will. I think I'm too stubborn. I think I'll hang on, thought Anthony. If they can gamble, so can I.

When he got back to the house, he was met at the door by Pamela's ancient little dog. She had left it behind. It looked up at him, with an expression of anxiety on its wizened face. It seemed to expect rejection, hostility. He wondered how often it had been forgotten before. He stared at it, with some irritation. He did not want a dog, least of all this kind of dog. But there it was. He bent down, patted its wiry hard skull. It wagged its tail. "Oh, all right," said Anthony, aloud. But resolved, in the same instant, to refuse Giles's offer of release.

On the morning of the nineteenth, two letters, conveyed in the diplomatic bag, were delivered by hand at Alison's hotel. The ordinary post from England to Wallacia was erratic. One letter was from Molly's house mistress, Judy Channing. She said that Molly had noticed that Alison had not been to visit recently, and was growing disturbed: they had had to increase her daily dose of Oblivine and hoped Alison would approve. She had had a slight tantrum the night before and had attacked Diane Harwood, fortunately not seriously. Had Alison any idea when she would be back? They didn't like to make promises that weren't true, as Alison knew, but it was a difficult time, and it would be nice to be able to say that Mummy would definitely be back for Christmas. It would give Molly something to look forward to. Meanwhile, if Alison could write, Molly did so enjoy getting letters.

Judy Channing, a brisk, sensible girl, ended with her best wishes and her hopes that all would go well in Wallacia; she managed to imply, in her good wishes, that Jane Murray was not deserving of so much time or attention. Judy Channing lived in a small world of sick people. She had no sympathy with the problems of health.

Alison had written regularly to Molly, in fact. Perhaps her letters were not reaching England? It was easy to write to Molly, for one knew exactly what to say to her. What one had for lunch, what for supper. Whether one saw a horse, a cow, a dog. But one of the problems with Molly, tentatively articulated by an anxious Judy Channing, was that she did not understand about time. She seemed to accept the rhythm of her mother's weekly visits, the alternation of term time and holiday, but it was impossible to explain to her a necessary absence: she could not grasp the concept of "next weekend." And she was becoming fretful, in Alison's prolonged disappearance, and had attacked Diane Harwood. Not seriously? It must have been serious, or Judy Channing, by no means a scaremonger, would not have mentioned it.

Judy Channing was a tall girl, with blond hair and a large chin. She looked after thirty children suffering from cerebral palsy, day and night. The children had a wide and alarming range of disabilities: some had severe motor defects, some had visual defects, most had speech defects, most had eating problems, some were incontinent, and some suffered from time to time from akinetic seizures and convulsions. Judy Channing appeared to have no private life, though she would occasionally speak of a distant boyfriend who worked in a juvenile offenders' home and whom she hoped one day to marry. The day, Alison felt, would never come, for Miss Channing was too subdued to the demands of her children. She took an interest and a pride in them, though she did not claim to love them: she was too sensible for such an excess. Alison liked her better than Mrs. Newsome, the house mistress of last year, who had simulated affection, unconvincingly. Alison knew how difficult it was to feel affection for a clumsy, perverse, and dribbling child, and did not see the point of pretense. Judy Channing preferred to talk about case histories and prognoses and new experiments in therapy.

Molly was one of her more agreeable charges. Alison had, naturally, debated long over the wisdom of sending Molly away to school at all, and longer over which school, but it had seemed better for everybody that she should go, and they had achieved a great deal with her: she had learned to dress herself quite competently, to wash herself, to speak more clearly, to eat quite tidily. She had learned songs, a few letters, a few simple games. She could play percussion instruments, and follow the plots of stories. She did better than some of her schoolmates; she was one of the more able, which was good for morale. But at what a cost, Alison would think, on her weekly visits, as she greeted the tragic instances of God's inhumanity to man: to be so surrounded, to shine in so dim a night.

Judy Channing found Molly's case history interesting. She had turned out so much better than had been expected. She had been born prematurely, and for the first year of her life had lain like a doll, hardly moving, responding to nothing, watched over by a desperate Alison, who would smile and talk and sing to this nonbaby as though believing that faith alone would bring her to life. And Alison had succeeded, for at a year the baby had begun to kick, to notice, to reach for objects, to smile back, stirred from her deep damaged trance. When she was two, she began to suffer from convulsions, and cerebral palsy was diagnosed. The convulsions were terrifying. This was the stage at which Alison, at her wit's end, started to contact other parents, groups that dealt with such problems, and began to work for the Foundation for Disabled Children.

At the age of four, Molly began to speak; single, disconnected, hardly comprehensible words. But speech, nevertheless.

It was hard to assess her I.Q. The school did not approve of subjecting children to constant tests. On the other hand, it did not accept children who were severely subnormal, mentally. One or two of them were thought to be very bright: one sixteen-year-old boy had mastered an electric typewriter and had started to write poetry. Alison had found journals to publish it. Molly would never reach such heights. She would never learn to read, although she could recognize symbols and even one or two words. Her own ignorance frustrated her. She wanted to learn, but could not. Sometimes Alison looked back to the days when she had lain immobile in her cradle, her placid eyes gazing at nothing, and wondered whether she had been criminal to nag and tease and catch at her with maternal love, to drag her into the land of the conscious, only to find herself one of the helpless of the earth. Judy Channing said that she would probably have surfaced anyway, without Alison's attention, but Alison, remembering those hours of tears and imploring by the cot side, took leave to doubt this. She felt that she herself had summoned up this stumbling ghost. And she loved her, hopelessly, tenderly. At times it seemed worthwhile. At other times, not so. Either way, there was no choice. It was so.

If only Molly could understand, that she was not staying away on purpose, out of malice or neglect. If only one could write and say, I would come back tomorrow, if I could. But Molly was like a perpetual infant, suffering an everlasting repetition of separation trauma. There was no reassurance one could offer. One could not say, I cannot come because your sister Jane is a bloody fool and is sitting in a prison hospital with her leg in plaster and I must stay here to be with her, even though I am wasting my time.

Molly had adored Jane, once. But she had learned to be cautious, the hard way. She had learned to keep out of Jane's way.

I don't know what I ought to be doing, thought Alison. I don't know where I should be, or what I ought to be doing.

She opened her next letter. It was from Kitty Friedmann. Kitty said that she had not really much to say, she just wanted to tell Alison that she was thinking about her, and what a brave good girl Alison was, what a wonderful woman and a wonderful mother, and she was sure Alison and Jane too would both be home again safely soon. P.S. I am getting on fine, and will be home myself next week, I hope, said Kitty.

A wonderful woman and a wonderful mother. Yes. Alison stared at the two airmail letters. People were always describing her as a wonderful woman and a wonderful mother. Why? Because she let Molly come home for the holidays, instead of dumping her all the year round, as so many did? Or in the hope that, if so described, she would continue so to behave?

Alison had known Kitty for years; she had known her before she had met Anthony, before Molly had been born. An elderly aunt of hers had married Kitty's widower cousin: it had been a mixed marriage, a scandal, and Kitty had been, of course, the mediating angel between the two angry families. Kitty could not see why people could not be friendly and sensible, in this day and age. And so, bowed by necessity, and bribed by hospitality, they had all become sensible and friendly and Kitty and Alison had become and remained good friends.

Kitty was a keen theater-goer. She had been upset when Alison gave up the stage. But had admired her for it, or so she said.

I wonder why I did stop working, thought Alison, for the first time for years. She folded the two letters up and put them back in their envelopes. It was not wholly on account of Molly. Even at the beginning, I did not imagine that the Foundation couldn't do without me. Or that it would do much good with me.

She had done it because she did not want to compete with her husband, Donnell. Competition had made him angry. So she had withdrawn, and he had still been angry. One cannot win.

Alison stood up, and walked around her hotel room. It was small, and she felt caged. Though, of course, she was not. She could go out, and would go out. She had nothing to do until the afternoon, when she was due to have tea with the consul, to discuss what, if anything, to do next. The consul seemed to think that the authorities were about to fix a date for the trial. She hoped that that was true. She wondered if she would dare to ask him more about conditions in the prison camps he had visited. The chief problem, he said, was that the camps were remote, and that prisoners would be moved from one to another without warning, apparently to inconvenience any visitors. There had been few British subjects held in the jails of Wallacia, and none of those had been women. "If she is sentenced," Mr. Barstow had said, on their last meeting, smiling apologetically at the very idea, "she will probably be sent to the Maritza Camp. It's up in the mountains. It's very beautiful scenery there," he had said. "Quite Alpine."

Alison shivered. The thought of Jane, living on fishbone stew and cabbage, and sewing mailbags in an Alpine prison, was not heart-warming. She would forget it. She would go out. It was a fine morning, frosty and blue. Mrs. Bourlatos, the American wife of a Greek businessman, and one of the few English-speaking people in Krusograd, had advised her to try the museum, as an outing. "It's surprisingly undull," she had said. So Alison Murray put on her fur coat and her fur hat and her kid gloves and picked up her lizard-skin handbag, and marched off to look at the museum. What else was there to do? One could not even window shop in Krusograd, for there were so few shop windows, and in those that there were, the stock did not change: no new arrangements tempted the eye or the purse. The same objects sat, dumped, undisplayed. Even the greengrocers and butchers seemed to have caught the prevailing esthetic apathy: the fruit and vegetables were plentiful, but arranged to look meager and dull and as unattractive as possible, and from the butchers' shops, with their great hairy sides of meat, their messy heaps of entrails, their untidily severed heads, one had to avert one's eyes. No, this was not a country for the window shopper, and Alison was rather glad she did not have to do any other kind of shopping in it. She had been obliged, on one occasion, to look for a drugstore to buy herself some Tampax, but the word Tampax, which she had thought as universal as Coca-Cola, produced no response at all from the shop assistant, and she had been obliged to walk out empty handed. She had visited the town's only sizeable department store, in search of the same product, hoping to be able to point rather than to speak, but the store, which resembled nothing so much as a wartime Woolworth's in Croydon (the nearest hometown of her childhood), did not seem to stock Tampax either, and she had been forced for the first time since her last pregnancy to buy old-fashioned cotton sanitary towels. Inspecting them, in the privacy of her hotel room, she was not at all sure that they were not even so old-fashioned as to be washable. Walking down the street she thanked God that she lived in a consumer throw-away flush-away advertising society, and wondered idly what the dynamic Len, whose enthusiasm for trade and advertisement and shop frontages bordered on the comic, would have made of this fine display of apathy. How he would have longed to develop the High Street of Krusograd. What opportunities, what undiscovered riches.

The museum, however, was far from shabby. An imposing modern building, it stood confidently, a tribute to the superiority of culture to commerce. A proper sense of values, it no doubt considered itself to manifest. Alison entered. It was, of course, free, even to capitalist foreigners. (But then so, thought Alison defensively, is the British Museum.)

Alison Murray was not a very well educated person, so she looked for the striking objects on display, rather than those of historical importance: she would have been hard pushed to find anything less undull than old flints, of which there was a copious supply. The descriptions were anyway incomprehensible, written in Wallacian, a language which remained for her a cluttered splutter of unusual consonants. So it was inevitable that she would find herself staring at the glass case containing the most spectacular exhibits. And they were spectacular. For one thing, they were golden. Made of gold. One does not often see gold in such quantities. There was a huge golden bowl, with two handles: plain, solid, vast. There was another golden bowl, of the finest fragility, beaten thin, papery, delicate, slightly crumpled after centuries of concealment (the dates at least she could read: they dated from the fourth century B.C., and had been found in 1960). There were more ornate gold objects—buttons, rings, bracelets, vials. And, most beautiful of all, there was a wreath, shimmering and quivering, golden, perfect, light, bright, insubstantial. She had never seen anything so lovely. The perfect adornment. It was made of laurel twigs, with thin beaten leaves; one could see the delicate markings of the twig. The leaves shivered in the artificial light; they quaked as she moved nearer the case to look, responding to her slightest movement on the marble floor. Hanging from the twigs, on neat little golden loops, were golden berries. The wreath stood, poised on its stand in the dark air, between the two bowls. She gazed into the bowl. It was filled with yellow light, filled with lightness, not shining like the wreath in its glinting, but still, absorbent, deep, dull.

The wreath must surely have been a queen's possession. How on earth had it survived burial?

She had been to see the Crown Jewels once, as a child, on a school outing. She remembered them as heavy things, lumpish, solid. Not the kind of jewels to wear lightly. Crowns, scepters, miters. And modern jewelry was not much better. Bond Street was full of gold and silver and precious stones, but how lumpishly assembled, on the whole: thousands of pounds' worth of diamonds assembled into the shape of a Scottie dog, a pheasant, a poodle.

Kitty Friedmann had a diamond peacock. Diamonds and emeralds.

Gold. The gold standard. It was not perhaps surprising that the Egyptians, the Greeks, the Indians, the Americans, the British had chosen gold. It seemed to speak of something. Of the sun under the earth, so long concealed.

Gold. Money. Ambition. Alison walked up and down the empty marble corridors, her hands in her pockets, thinking. The gold rush. Property speculation had become a kind of gold rush: easy money, but not only easy money—enormous money. Until she had met Anthony, she had never thought much about making money. She and Donnell had never been desperately hard up; there had always been work, always enough, and latterly, as Donnell began to have more and more film work, there had been more than enough. And always the possibility of a lucky break, a windfall, a repeat fee. There had been nothing much that she had wanted; she ate well, she dressed well, what more could one want? She had never understood what it was that drove people on to want more: had not understood, that is, until she had met Anthony, and his new friends. And then, suddenly, the glamour of the whole business had enraptured her, as it had enraptured Anthony. She too had been thrilled, corrupted, by the prospect of large risks, large profits. The victor's crown of gold. How on earth had she and Anthony, two perfectly unambitious, ordinary, middle-of-the-road people, got themselves caught up in such a ludicrous world?

It was easy enough to see how someone like Len Wincobank had got into it. Len's mother, as he had described to her one evening over a large steak, had worked in a laundry. He had shared a bed with his brother. From rags to riches. Max Friedmann was another sort: he had been born into the world of commerce, was expected to make his mark, had a textile business anyway, had started on property as a sideline. Making money was natural to him, he had been brought up to it, as Anthony had been brought up to expect to go to Oxbridge. Giles was one of the same, and as for Rory Leggett—Rory lived, ate, drank, breathed property, he cared for nothing else, he loved it so much that he even found the dangers and potential collapse of his own company quite, quite fascinating.

One of the problems was that she didn't see how they were going to get out of it: not only practically speaking, but also emotionally. It was like an addiction, a fever. After so much excitement, how could Anthony go quietly back and become anybody's employee? How dull her own old life seemed to her now: how dull, and how unnecessary.

She went back and stood in front of the wreath, and stared at it once more. A fine piece of costume jewelry. She had worn some fine fake gear herself, in her early days on the stage: princesses she had played, in those old days. But she had turned from gold, and chosen the leaden casket. How had she allowed herself to be tempted back to the gold again?

The safe choice. The bad choice. The good choice. The dangerous choice.

Poor Anthony. The heart attack had warned him that he was not of the mettle to make dangerous choices. Failure of some kind was written into him.

What will we do? she wondered. There was the house. She had liked the idea of living in the country, with Anthony: watching the seasons change, walking, reading, drinking less, smoking less. Growing old gracefully. It seemed this would not be. What if they had to sell the house, before she had even taken possession of it? She had so loved the idea of the house. How could they sell it? And how much would they lose on it if they were forced to sell?

Perhaps Anthony would actually be declared bankrupt. She did not know what bankruptcy was. It seemed that when Len Wincobank came out of prison, he might still be a rich man. On the other hand, if Anthony lost everything, he would not go to prison. But what would he do, where at his age begin again? She did not think she wanted to live with a failed man. She wanted to turn back the clock, to six months ago, when all had been well: to wipe out the last six months, bombs, heart attacks, traffic accidents, property slump, the lot. She wanted it so badly, standing there staring at a golden laurel wreath in a remote Iron Curtain museum, that a small tic started up in her right temple: Oh Christ, she thought, perhaps I'm about to have a cerebral hemorrhage, from too much of the wrong kind of thinking.

But she didn't. Instead, she went out into the cold refreshing air, pulled herself together, and set off for the consulate. She was getting to know this small town as well as if it had been her birthplace.

Jane Murray could not understand why the Wallacian authorities were not more friendly toward her. She could not understand a word they said, but she could see that they were not friendly. They must surely see that she was a victim of Western Europe, that she like them despised possession, that she was a real person, an individual person, politically on their side if anything, and that she had an absolutely gruesome mother. How could anyone not forgive anything to a person who has a mother like mine, thought Jane Murray, sick with resentment, as she sat and waited for Alison to turn up, in her capitalist furs, with her anticonservationist handbag. How does she think she's going to get anywhere, if she comes along looking like that? And how can they not see, thought Jane Murray, that it's all her fault?

The weather changed during the night before Anthony's visit to Len Wincobank. He woke feeling cold, wondering if the central heating had failed, if he had lost his blankets in the night, but when he opened the bedroom curtain he saw the cause, indeed saw it as he approached the window, in the strange gray pallid glare that beat against the fabric. Outside, everything was different. The sky was hard and iron-gray, and a thick frost, the thickest Anthony had ever seen, had appeared; the yard and drive and lawn were white as with snow, and the trees were encased in a thick crystalline fur, a jeweled coating, as though they had been dipped into some strange chemical, as though some mysterious transformation had changed their very substance. It was beautiful, but sinister.

Just outside the window, a few leaves still clung to the creeper: he looked at them curiously, noting the iced veins, the spiked frost, the odd heightened pattern of the leaves that looked now more like carvings of leaves than leaves themselves. And, looking up to the distance, he could see that the hills had disappeared into a blue white blur. Another kingdom. He wondered if the winters were truly so much harder here than in the South. He had been warned, but had disbelieved, dismissing stories of snowdrifts and blizzards as instances of idle Northern folklore. He had been a Londoner so long, a Southerner so long, he had lost touch with the extremes of the weather.

Shivering, he went downstairs, and turned up the thermostat to 70, and switched on a few extra radiators. Pamela's miserable dog was standing bleakly in the kitchen, its teeth bared with suffering, shaking with cold, more offensively frail than ever. It looked up at Anthony with such pain and helpless indignation that he bent down and patted it. It was not a bad dog. It was not its fault that it was so ugly and so old.

He had to drive carefully down the valley to Leeds to meet Maureen; the roads were icy to begin with and, as he reached more traveled regions, muddy. The hedgerows had never looked so unattractive: bare stalks and withered plants, mud-spattered, hung desolately on to a dirty life, tattered, bent, spent, spattered. The trees retained their beauty and their icy, mineral excrescence, but they looked unnatural, watchful. Like the beginning of a science fiction film, thought Anthony. Oh God, thought Anthony, I hope it isn't a bad omen, about the rendezvous with Maureen and Len.

He hadn't seen Maureen since Len was put away. The last time he had seen the two of them together had been while Len was on bail. They'd had supper together, in London, in Anthony's empty London ghost house. Take-away curry, some bottles of wine. Maureen had been subdued and anxious, but Len had been in good form, in high spirits, aggressively optimistic, eating the hottest curry and talking as the sweat leaped up in beads on his forehead about lawyers and loans and bank managers. He had asked Anthony about his own affairs, listened with interest, advised him over his comparatively puny dangers, as curious as ever. After dinner, discussing the trial, due to begin next week, Maureen had said, "You know, Len, you really ought to get your hair cut, make yourself look respectable." Len, whose hair was thick and black and curly and indeed overlong for a respectable businessman, had said, "Why don't you cut it for me then, love?" And Maureen had found a pair of kitchen scissors, and wrapped a towel round Len's shoulders, and snipped away: and as she snipped, she and Anthony looked at one another in growing alarm, for it was clear that the haircut (and she did it very neatly, an ex-professional), far from making Len look meek and proper and law-abiding as had been intended, revealed instead the man beneath, dangerous, aggressive, threatening, the kind of man that a timid jury would surely put away. Safer behind bars. Poor Maureen, standing there with the large scissors and the black curls of Len's hair in her little hand, perplexed. Delilah revealing her man as one of the enemy. Len had leaped up from the chair, the barbering over, to look at himself, and had noted at once the change for the worse in his plausibility as an honest mistaken man. She had shorn away his disguise: he had been pretending successfully, for years, to be a charming new man of the seventies, pleasant, informal, easygoing, but underneath all the time there had been this man of iron purpose, with a head like a rock and a lowering brow.

All he had said was, "It's a prison haircut you've given me in advance, duck." And had poured himself another drink, and re-turned to the subject of the wickedness and folly of those bloody small-time fools who think they can make money out of shares without running risks, without imagination, without suffering for it, without sweating for it. As he spoke, the sweat leaped back to his brow. Len's contempt for the squealing of small investors had inspired much impassioned rhetoric of late.

Anthony, driving through the icy landscape, wondered what Len was making of the investment scene, from his retired position in prison. Were prisoners allowed to play the stock exchange?

He was nervous about the encounter. It seemed sordid, to visit a prison, as though one were a morbid voyeur. It seemed mean to be free, when Len was put away. But it would be even more mean not to visit. Think of others, not yourself, said Anthony to himself, as his mother had said to him when he complained about visiting senile elderly relatives, the sick in hospital. Think of the pleasure you bring. Anthony, as a boy, had been sure that he had taken no pleasure to old Auntie Grace or to Mrs. Nicholson, the dean's mother, but now realized he had probably been wrong. And anyway, it was ridiculous to compare Len Wincobank to old Auntie Grace or Mrs. Nicholson. Len would surely have survived prison with some aplomb. And Anthony was looking forward to asking Len's advice about Giles's offer. It is very easy to stall over two hundred miles. It is very easy not to answer the telephone, to pretend to be cut off, to pretend to have a bad line. He had promised Giles a decision, but had deliberately waited until this visit to Len. His distrust of Giles had been growing, over the past days, and it was not entirely related to the abandoning of the wretched little dog. He had not told Giles that he would visit Len. He too could be devious.

He met Maureen at the barrier off the train from Sheffield: she came bouncing along toward him, trailing scarves and packages; little, overburdened, smiling.

"Anthony, this *is* nice," she said, dropping her parcels to throw her arms around his neck. "You *are* a duck," she said, kissing him firmly on the cheek. Her lips felt warm: he had not touched a person for weeks, he remembered. "What a day," she said, picking up her parcels, brushing her hair out of her eyes. "Incredible weather, isn't it? Do you think we'll make it? It might be all snowy up on the moors. Poor old Len, in that hut. I bet the poor love is frozen to death. They can't be planting trees in this weather, can they? The ground must be like stone."

They had lunch, before they set off, in the Queen's Hotel. Maureen looked around the old place with affection. She did not mind that it was growing more American, with its sauna and its coffee shop: to her it was still the height of luxury, the height of style. She was too young to remember the old days, when English hotels were English hotels. They had a gin and tonic in the Linton Bar, then entrecôte steak and French fries in the dining room. She ate with gusto, though sighing guiltily every now and then as she thought of Len. She looked around at the groups of businessmen in their well-polished shoes, and wondered what dirty secrets some of them might be concealing; she stared at the few prosperous trouser-suited Northern women drinking pink wine. "It doesn't seem right," she said to Anthony, on her return from a visit to the powder room. "All that space, even in the ladies', and to think of those poor buggers locked up over there, and shivering to death, I bet you." The powder room impressed Maureen. It had velvet curtains, of deep red and pale apple-green: it had a pink flowered wallpaper, and a pink geometric-patterned carpet. She liked it, connoisseur of conferences and hotels and business lunches. Over lunch, she expressed to Anthony her disapproval of the London Hilton, which she had had cause to visit recently in the company of her new boss: It's a real *dump*, she said warmly to Anthony, you've never seen such a mess. I mean, I know they've had a bomb in it, but that's no excuse for letting it get quite so shabby, is it? The whole place was full of *sawdust*. And with that bomb damage, you can see it's all made of plywood anyway.

On the way over the moors, she continued to talk: about Anthony's health, about Alison's absence, about Maureen's new job, about her last visit to Len, about how difficult all the men's wives found it to visit. Maureen, not naturally a public-spirited person, although a kindly one, had been shocked by some of the stories she'd heard from the other women, last time: long journeys, no money, no public transport, nowhere to leave the kids while one talked. "What do they want to put a prison in a place like this for?" she said, shivering ostentatiously as she looked out at the countryside, which grew higher and bleaker with every mile, then laughed in response to her own question. "I brought Len a few Mars bars," she said. "And half a bottle of Scotch. But I don't suppose I'll get a chance to slip it to him. Do you think they'd stop me coming, if they caught me at it? Perhaps we'll have it ourselves, shall we? We'll need it, after this lot."

She seemed cheerful: overdoing it a bit perhaps, but still, genuinely cheerful. She told him about her new job, and Derek Ashby, her architect employer; she liked him, he didn't at all mind her taking a long weekend off to see Len. She told him about the kind of houses he designed. Expensive, modern, private houses for business executives: expensive conversions of old barns, mills, Methodist chapels. Once he had even done a water tower. He was successful, and, because successful, amiable—a friendly, easygoing, kindly person, doing work he enjoyed, in his own good time, only occasionally frustrated by the lack of taste and vision of his clients. Maureen sighed. "I envy him, really," she said. "He's got no worries. He earns a good living, and he likes doing it. You wouldn't think a man could make such a good living, just designing private houses, would you? I'd got so used to thinking big, with Len. Thinking in millions. But who needs millions?" Anthony knew what she meant.

"Still," he said, "he's lucky, your architect, to have found a job that satisfies him. A creative job. A self-employed job."

She told him about the house they were working on at the moment: an old stone farmhouse for a steel man, off the Glossop Road. They were building a cottage in the grounds, for the elderly parents. She rattled on, describing features, describing her employer's theories of the blending of old and new. Anthony listened. He liked her, she was no trouble, she liked to please.

"I'm looking forward to seeing *your* house, Anthony," she said. "It sounds great. Derek knows it, he went to have a look at it once. He says it's very unusual, but I can't remember why, now. You mustn't sell it, you know. You'd never find another one like it. Think how you'd kick yourself, in ten years' time, when you're rolling in money, looking for somewhere to buy. You'd never forgive yourself. You hang on to it."

The prison lay open to the cold sky, covering acres: an open prison, highly exposed. High walls surrounded it, but the public road ran through it. One could imagine that in summer the position might be pleasant; to Anthony, the whole thing looked at first sight like something in Siberia. But as they approached, showed their permits, parked, he noticed that perhaps it was, after all, more as Len had remarked, like public school. There was a lodge, there were playing fields where men were even, despite the weather, playing: men in uniform, gray trousers, striped shirts, gray jackets, were sweeping paths, like overgrown sixth formers. Seagulls from the North Sea sat on the rooftops. At any moment, one felt the bell might toll for Maths, for History, for Greek. A physical pang, of mixed horror and nostalgia, shot through Anthony's chest, as memories of cold, humiliation, close bored companionship swept back through him. Did any of them like it here? As some had liked even the miseries of public school, where one had to break the ice in the washbowl, where one could not sleep without three pairs of wool socks and three jerseys? Did some of them feel safe in here? And how am I coping? thought Anthony: how am I coping with my freedom, now I am freed from every institution, from school, from Oxford, from the BBC, from ITV, from all those restricting reassuring wombs?

The prisoners and their visitors met in a canteen. They could have cups of tea. There was an anteroom where children were left: it contained some battered wooden toys and a chewed teddy bear or two, and looked not unlike the waiting room in an East End children's hospital where Anthony had once had to sit with a girlfriend and her sick toddler. Desolate, defeated, ill. Each prisoner was allowed only one visitor at a time, so Anthony waited while Maureen went in: he waited with a row of other relatives and friends, some of whom were smoking nervously, some of whom stared at the floor, some of whom chatted, old hands, old friends, used to the pilgrimage. Overhearing, Anthony learned that a new bus service had been laid on by the social services from the nearest town; that the wife of a man named Darren had had non-identical twins; that the wife of a man named George had shacked up with another fellow and that nobody was to let George know or there'd be trouble. Only the women talked, he noticed. As in a hospital, the visiting men—fathers, brothers, sons?—sat silently, grim, depressed, a strange array of physical types: small working-men, bent old men, raw big young men. But the women had made a little home for themselves, even here, even in a waiting room. Some had brought their knitting, and they gossiped and exchanged the small coins of living, making something out of nothing, making a little company even out of this grim sojourn.

Anthony had never felt very much at ease visiting the sick. Maybe he was as bad at it as these miserable-looking men, in their caps and scarves, with their cheap tobacco. What can one say to a person in a hospital bed, to a person in a prison? What can one tell them of the outside world that they will not bitterly resent? And how can one enter their own inner world? Two memories nudged at him, uneasily: a day at school, a Sunday, when his parents had come for the weekend to visit, to take him out for lunch, and he had sat in the local hotel eating Sunday lunch, beef and horse-radish, trying desperately to think of something, anything, to say to these estranged parents, while his mind returned incessantly to the only thing that interested him, which was his never-to-be de-clared passion for his French master's wife; a visit to Babs in hos-pital, after a D and C, when she had lain there still gray from the anesthesia and had talked to him with immense animation about fibroids and hysterectomies and mastectomies and all the other gynecological dramas of the ward, and he had been so grateful to dear sweet Babs for doing all the talking, for he had not the faint-est idea of what he ought to say, what could one say, amongst those long white rows of suffering women? He must see Kitty Friedmann one day, he supposed.

But now, Len Wincobank. He need not have worried about Len. He took Maureen's place at the small table, and there Len was, himself still, not mysteriously transformed into a beaten-look-ing cloth-capped Northerner, as Anthony had irrationally feared. He looked fit, even lively. They shook hands, warmly, smiled, stared, smiled again. "Well, how is it?" said Len. "How are things?" And before Anthony knew where he was, he was telling Len the whole story of the Riverside deal, of Giles's offer, of his own precarious finances, about his anxiety about the Erikson bank calling in its loan.

Len listened, nodded, calculated, asked questions, added up in his head. Then he stopped and thought. Then he said—and as he spoke, Anthony knew exactly what he was going to say, but knew it only because he had, in some way, participated in Len's silent additions, his silent assessments—he said, "Don't touch it. Don't touch it, man. Hang on. Don't touch it. What would he make you an offer like that for, if he didn't have something better for himself up his sleeve?"

"But he was," said Anthony feebly, a last throw, "he is an old friend."

Len smiled. "I'm not saying he isn't," he said. "But there are friends and friends in this world, aren't there?"

And there it was. It was so. Giles was trying to doublecross him. It was, of course, perfectly obvious. That was the kind of man Giles was. He had never claimed to be anything else.

"All right, then," said Anthony. "I'll hang on."

"You trust my word," said Len. "You wait and see. You've got to be a good judge of character in this business. You can't afford to make mistakes. You can't afford to remember that people are your friends. If they're not."

Then Len lowered his voice, dramatically. "See that guy over there?" he said, nodding toward an elderly silver-haired gentleman, of strikingly different demeanor from most of the rest of the room's occupants—for even Len, well though he looked, did not look exactly a gentleman, and never had. "Do you know who that is?"

Anthony stared, as politely as possible. The man did indeed look familiar, but he could not place him.

"That's Callander," said Len, in the same conspiratorial whisper. Anthony stared with renewed curiosity. So that was Callander: corrupted city architect.

"What fascinating people you meet in here," said Anthony. "What's he like?"

Len shook his head, pitying. "Can't adapt, poor fellow. Too old. Can't really believe it happened to him. Goes on and on about the dinners at the Rotary Club. Poor old boy. A terrible bore."

"You seem to have adapted all right," said Anthony, risking a personal comment.

"Oh, I'm all right, I get by. But I'm more at home in this kind of company, aren't I? I'll tell you what, I'm thinking of organizing a strike. About the heating. Bloody freezing it's been in here this last week, we'll all die of hypothermia if it goes on like this, and then what a scandal that would be. Do you know, there's ice on the inside of the windows every morning? It's a scandal. I've made suggestions, if they double glazed they'd halve the fuel bills, if they installed a Stafford heating system they'd save themselves thousands of pounds a year, and a lot of fuel. But they're an unpatriotic lot, the officers. Don't care about the energy crisis." Len grinned. "So I'm thinking of organizing a little protest."

"Would people co-operate?"

"Some of them would. Of course, there's always those who are afraid of losing remission, or being refused parole, but there's a lot of feeling about the cold at the moment. The time is ripe. Strike while the iron is hot. Or cold, as it might be." He grinned, confident, ambivalent, amused by the image of himself, apostle of free enterprise, as union organizer.

"We used to have ice on the inside of our bedroom windows at school," said Anthony. "And we paid several hundred pounds a year for the privilege."

Len laughed. "They're paying more than a few hundred a year to keep each one of us in here," he said. "It's a very uneconomic system. Perhaps I'll go into prison building when I get out. I could give them a bit of really valuable advice, if only they'd listen."

"It's a relief to see you looking so well," said Anthony.

"Christ, man," said Len, "one's got to keep going. And it's not so bad. Nothing's as bad as you think it's going to be. And how's Maureen? Keeping all right, would you say?"

"She's a good girl," said Anthony. "She's all right. She seems all right."

"When I get out," said Len, "we'll have a party. You hang on to that site, and see what happens in the next few months. And then, when I get out, we'll have the best party you ever went to in your life. And then, I'll begin again. I did it once, I'll do it again. It's the first time that's difficult."

"You're a confident man," said Anthony. "I'm beginning to think I can't have been cut out for this kind of life. I can't stand the strain."

Len looked at him curiously. "I don't know about that," he

said. "I wouldn't be able to say, about you. I'd have thought you'd got better nerves than you think you have."

Anthony was flattered. No doubt about it, he admired Len Wincobank. Len had quite cheered him up, although that wasn't what he was supposed to have come for.

Len, returning to the dull routine after the excitement of visitors, writing labels for small trees in the well-heated greenhouse; working out a few telling phrases about the fact that it was warmer in the greenhouse than in the prison canteen, why put trees before men; thinking of Maureen, wondering if she'd stay with him, stick by him, wondering how much he'd mind if she didn't, you couldn't expect a woman to lay off for two years, thinking of her round bottom and her oddly sexy fondness for knee socks: even in this bitter weather she had bare thighs, from the top of her boots up under her skirt to that other place he'd managed to grab under the table; thinking of Anthony, Giles Peters, the I.D. Company, trying to rationalize his certainty that Giles was up to no good—if he thought about it enough, the answer would come to him, even in here he could still think, his instinct was still sound, he would guess right because he knew he was right—sweating, even in the cold, with frustration at his distance from the action; picturing Maureen and Anthony driving back together, alone, alone together, across the lonely moor. Absconding prisoners had been known to die of exposure on the lonely moor. There were gruesome prison stories, some true, some legendary. But Anthony and Maureen were going back to a house, a house with heating, and drinks, and double beds, and stairs (how one missed stairs), and doors that one could open and shut at will, and a television (he supposed wrongly that they had a television) that one could switch from channel to channel at will. Still, no point in complaining, as some did, that one should have appreciated these blessings more while one had access to them. It would have been impossible to have appreciated them more than Len Wincobank had done. A war baby, an adolescent of the years of austerity, with an invalid father and a mother who worked in the municipal washhouse in one of the worst paid jobs known to woman, he had certainly appreciated every blessing of the material life. The day they had electricity installed. He could actually remember it. The addition of bathroom and lav by the council. The day that his mum had bought a new table lamp, with a base like a dancing woman, and a plastic rippled shade: how Len had loved that lamp, the elegant glow of it, the discreet pool of warm light, the intense homely charm, the safety, the beauty. The turkey at Christmas, the extravagant Sunday roasts and Yorkshire pudding, the odd bar of scented soap, the trip to Scunthorpe, the piece of stair carpet—secondhand, but good as new—the whipped Carnation milk, as a treat, on the tinned fruit, for Sunday tea. Every little luxury Len had enjoyed, admired, and as he and his brothers started to work, began to bring home pay packets, how miraculously easy and warm life had become, with a hired television set, a new radiogram, and even, finally, a telephone, which had frightened his mother at first so much that whenever it rang she would jump up in her seat, rigid with alarm, and say imploringly, "You go, Len—or you, Kev, or you, Arthur." How Len had loved the slow easing of the fifties, the glories of the sixties. And now here he sat, writing labels, as though back at school, his hands warm enough to write because too much frost would kill the little trees.

Anthony and Maureen. They had had lunch, they said, somewhat guiltily, in the Queen's Hotel. He thought of Leeds station. The fast train to London. He thought of Alison Murray, stranded in a foreign town, unable to speak a word of the language. Now that was a situation in which he, capable though he was, would never be able to cope.

Trains. Airplanes. The modern world. Concorde, a beautiful glittering white angel of our time. Park Hill. The Hancock building. His mind worked. Leeds station. Northam station. Color supplements rhapsodizing about Broad Street and Marylebone Station, both obsolete spots, useless beyond anything. Yes. Suddenly he had it. Stations. Northam station. Building. All that waste space plashed into his head, like a whole three-dimensional map, ripe with possibility. That was it. If only nobody touched it till he got out. But they wouldn't, they couldn't, not with a recession like this, not with money as tight as this. No, no, nobody but himself would ever have thought of what should be done. How extraordinarily slow other people are. How slow he had been till this instant. Nobody would ever see it. Blocks rose and glittered in his mind. Look what a balls-up they had made, not building offices over Euston. How could he have missed it? Northam station. There were two stations in Northam, the old L.N.E.R., and the old L.M.S., one of which was now obsolete and disused, except for the occasional shunted goods train. The whole lump needed developing, desperately needed rebuilding. And a lot of that space didn't even belong to the notoriously difficult (but surely desperately hard up?) British Rail. Some of it belonged to Batleys, the brewers, who also owned the old station hotel which looked like a BR hotel but wasn't one—the old Royal Northern, stranded now by the disuse of the L.N.E.R. station, for it was too far to walk with a suitcase to the trains, too near to get a cab—oh yes, down would come the Royal Northern, up would go a new complex. He could see it all. He knew exactly what they wanted there. Hotel, shops (covered center?) office accommodation. Car park. Cinema? By 1978, when he was out again, the money would be on the move again, and they would be begging for him to come back and tell them what to do.

Cupressus, he wrote on a little label. Prison labor is uneconomic, designed partly to waste time, he suspected. But he was damned if he was going to apply himself to a useful trade, and join the queue of those respectable prisoners who wanted to learn carpentry, printing, electronics. He had a trade already. He was a man of vision. Meanwhile, he would write little labels.

It would be a pity to pull down the Royal Northern. It had been in its day, before the line was closed, the finest hotel in Northam. And it was still fine, fine and faded. High rooms, flowered wallpaper, an enormous staircase, some real marble and some fake marble, ancient waiters of great servility and gentility, chambermaids of fifty in black dresses with white aprons, high beds, white sheets, and those huge white dense old-fashioned pillows that one never finds except in such places. All that would have to go. England had undoubtedly been great in the days when the Royal Northern prospered. Len had worked there for a month, in the school holidays: laying carpet, putting up trestle tables for municipal functions, then dressing himself up like a monkey in a damnfool red jacket with brass buttons and collecting tips from drunken old aldermen and town councillors and freemasons. They would all have to go, too. The catering trade, the laundry business, and hair dressing are three of the worst paid jobs in Britain, and he, Maureen, and his mum had had a go at all three. Who would spend a life at that? He regretted nothing. He had had a go, he would do it again. Nobody would stop him. The material paradise. Find me a better one, thought Len Wincobank, and I'll pursue it. But meanwhile, this one will keep me busy.

The labels were finished. Soya bean shepherd's pie for supper, very nourishing. The automatic sprinklers started up, spreading a fine warm spray over the tiny plants, over the working men. Len walked down the aisle to tell the officer he had finished, pausing to glance at the little *cupressi*. They had taken nicely. Little exiles, from a warmer clime, unnaturalized, little green-gray sprigs, branching bravely, like dry seaweed, delicate survivors, blue and gray and green, no leaves, but dry tight curled sprigs and needles, tough as well as delicate. Evergreen. Outside, the thick frost lay on the moor, on the brown heather and the bog cotton and the long dry reeds. Maureen and Anthony would be home by now. I can't stand asking this mean-minded bugger permission to leave and go to the hut. I want just to walk out, without asking. I want to be my own man.

But it's not much worse, he said to himself, than National Service. What if it were for life?

Anthony and Maureen got back after dark. She was to stay the night: it was Friday, no work in the morning. I'll cook you a supper, she had announced cheerily, so they had stopped in Blickley for her to do some shopping. She had disappeared into the International Home Stores (part of a complex built, Anthony remembered, by Max Friedmann's company in 1959, and very flourishing it looked, though not very esthetic) and came out again with a lot of plastic bags, sniffing hard; when she had shoved the bags in the back seat she sat down again by Anthony and sniffed and blew her nose and cried. Her nose tended to turn red in the cold at the best of times, and after a good cry it looked quite raw. "Oh, I *do* look a fright," said Maureen, getting out her powder compact and miraculously restoring the whole thing to a fairly normal color.

"Sorry," she said. "Poor old Len. It was so fucking cold. Wasn't it?"

"He'll survive. He's very tough."

"Some of them looked a bit weedy, though, didn't they? And I bet they get a rotten supper. And just think of us, with that nice steak, and then this lovely frozen chicken."

"Never mind, love," he said, and reached for her hand: they held hands, crossing the dark moor.

"What a funny place to end up," said Maureen, laughing uneasily as they wound their way up the last stretch of very frosty, very minor road.

"I haven't ended up *yet*," said Anthony, who was afraid he might have done just that.

And to cheer them up, he switched on the car radio. By some unpleasant trick of fate, an American singer was belting out with heartfelt passion the song about tying yellow ribbons on the old oak tree:

> I'm coming home, I've done my time,
> I've learned to know what is and isn't mine . . .
> It's been three long years, do you still want me?

he groaned, and they sat it out, to the end, where the whole damn bus was cheering at the hundred yellow ribbons round the old oak tree, and Anthony found himself near tears also, and Maureen naturally began to overflow again.

"Oh *fuck*," she said emphatically, as Anthony switched off radio and car engine in the courtyard. "Oh fuck it all. I'll never stick it out, he knows it. The whole damn bus, indeed. Do you know what the fool was on about today, when he wasn't trying to get his hand inside my knickers? He says when he gets out, he's going to charter a private airplane, and take off from that prison airstrip in style. There's nothing against it in the rules, he says."

They both began to laugh. Len was, after all, mad enough to survive, in his own way. And the house cheered Maureen up even more. Like Giles, she loved it. "I *say*, Anthony," she said, as she looked around. "Stables and all. What a place." An owl hooted. "Owls too," she said.

"It's a tape-recorded owl, just for you," said Anthony. She was even quite nice about Pamela's frightful little dog. "*What* a pathetic creature," she said, patting it tenderly. She busied herself about the supper, finding cooking things that Anthony didn't even know he'd got. How much nicer she is than Pamela, thought Anthony. And how odd that she and Len should be so very much easier to get on with than Giles and Pamela. It made the possibility of a future of some kind seem momentarily more probable, to see Maureen swamped in a large apron, filling a frozen chicken (rapidly dethawed under the hot tap) with packet stuffing.

They enjoyed the meal, reminisced over it about the good old days, wondered if they would ever come again, for themselves, or for the country. "I don't really understand inflation," said Maureen, gnawing at the wishbone, holding it neatly in her greasy fingers. "I mean, what will happen when it stops? Will there just be a standstill, or will there be another boom?" She took another swig of her Spanish white wine. "And I don't understand about the Arabs and oil, either. Why didn't they think of putting the price up earlier? There was nothing to stop them, was there? Was it just that they didn't think of it?"

"I don't know," said Anthony, who did not know.

Later in the evening, their mood became more somber. It was cold, despite the central heating: they huddled together on the old settee, in front of the erratic electric fire, Maureen with her feet curled up under her and her head on Anthony's shoulder. "I really miss Len, you know," she said, sighing heavily. "I don't know if I'll be able to wait. You know what I mean?"

This time he did know, but the declaration, unlike Pamela's covert invitation, did not disturb him: it was an appeal for sympathy, not sex. "It's not so long," he said. "Two years is a hell of a long time, at my age," said Maureen. "I'll be all fat and wrinkled when he gets out. But I'll stick it out a bit longer, I suppose. The funny thing is, we didn't get down to much in the way of sex in those last few months, anyway. Even though I suppose we knew he might get put away, and by rights we ought to have got on with it while the going was good. But we didn't feel up to it. Anxiety puts one off that kind of thing, don't you find?" She sighed, then laughed. "Len used to say he couldn't keep his mind on it, he said his brain had turned into an enormous balance sheet, and his head was so full of figures he couldn't concentrate on the job at all."

"I suppose I know what he meant," said Anthony, who had not himself suffered from the same disability; but then, his financial problems had been so much smaller than Len's, and until his heart attack, he had found sex with Alison much the best way of forgetting his worries. "I suppose it depends what kind of anxiety one is suffering from. And how bad it is. They do say that whenever war breaks out, everybody leaps into bed with everybody. To keep the human race going. Destroy, and procreate."

"Well," said Maureen, "I can mark the exact point at which old Len started to lose interest. It was when Rosewood Securities called in that loan. That night . . ."

And she proceeded to describe, in some detail, what had happened that night. She was very amusing. They both laughed a lot. Anthony suggested that chronic debt might have the reverse effect on some characters: there were those who found it stimulating. "I can't have been one of them," he concluded. "Or I wouldn't have had this heart thing, would I? I didn't feel all *that* worried, I mean I always thought there must be some way out—but then, wham, there I was. Funny, really. It happened just as I'd worked out that even if the worst came to the worst, there'd still be Max Friedmann, who would help me out—mind you, I'd have hated to have asked him, but I could have asked him. Perhaps the body worries more than the mind."

"Must do," said Maureen. "During the trial, I came out in these awful spots. All over my chest, would you believe it? I mean to say, what a place to get spots. I'd never had such a thing in my life before. I'm not saying I never had *any* spots, when I was a girl I had my fair share, but they were in proper places, like all over my face—but on my chest, I ask you? The doc said it was anxiety."

"Have they gone away now?"

"Mostly. Look, I'll show you. I bet you wouldn't fancy sitting so close to a really spotty person, would you, but it's not so bad. Look."

And she pulled up her jersey, and displayed her midriff, and her breasts, encased in a black bra. There were indeed a few small spots, and a quality in the skin that suggested the departure of more.

"I wouldn't call those *spots*," said Anthony gallantly. "More a kind of rash, really."

"You're sweet, Anthony," said Maureen, and resumed her place on his shoulder. They sat, companionably, in silence, for a while. And then the phone rang. Anthony at once assumed it was Giles, about to repeat his villainous offer to buy Anthony out: he rose to his feet and strode to the phone, determined to reject the offer, and moreover to insist that Pamela remove her wretched dog. But it was not Giles, it was Donnell Murray, Alison's husband.

Donnell was in a bit of a fix, he said. He wondered if Anthony could help. If it's money you want, you've come to the wrong person, said Anthony, hollowly; it was astonishing how many people had come to him with pleas for financial assistance since they had heard he was really in the shit, as though working on the principle that Anthony might as well be hung for a sheep as for a lamb. In vain did he protest that he simply hadn't got any money any more: they clearly did not believe him. But Donnell did not want money. He wanted Anthony to look after Molly for a fortnight while he himself went off filming in the Caribbean.

"I thought Molly was at school," said Anthony. So she ought to be, Donnell agreed, but unfortunately she had become so disturbed by Alison's prolonged absence that the school was finding her too difficult to manage. He had an urgent appeal from the school that morning, had tried to ring Anthony but Anthony was out, was sorry to ring so late . . .

He was pissed. Anthony, now himself always sober, was very much aware of the drunken condition of others.

The thing is, said Donnell, she needs to be with somebody who knows her. And I can't very well take her to the Caribbean with me, can I? And she likes you so much, she's always so good with you.

What an unbelievable cheek, thought Anthony. He did not know what to say. He said: "I don't honestly know if I could cope, on my own, Donnell. I'm supposed to be taking life easy, you know."

That took the wind out of Donnell's sails slightly; he hesitated, then started on a new tack. "I'd send a girl up with her. To cook for you both. I'd pay. I'd get someone from an agency. It's just that she needs to be with someone she knows. And Alison's always done so much for her herself, she doesn't really *know* anyone else."

Anthony knew that he would consent. He was, even, flattered to be asked. He saw himself turning into a full-time dog-minder and child-minder. He consented. Donnell was relieved, delighted, could not thank Anthony enough. He would drive Molly up the next day, picking her up straight from school. He would see Anthony in the afternoon. How ever could he thank Anthony enough.

"What's this film you're doing in the Caribbean?" asked Anthony. Donnell said that it was a piece of commercial crap, about gun running, and he himself was playing a double agent who got shot in the first reel. It seemed appropriate.

He went back to Maureen. She had fallen asleep, was snoring slightly. He wondered if he dared ask her to stay on and help with Molly. He didn't want a strange girl from an agency. But he didn't suppose she could. She'd have to get back to her architect employer. He sat down by her, joggled her, woke her, told her about Molly. "Poor old you," said Maureen sleepily. "You do get put upon."

"Do you think I'm some kind of fall guy?" asked Anthony. He was not quite sure what the phrase meant.

"No, I just think you're nice," said Maureen.

"It's probably the same thing," said Anthony glumly.

They went to bed, got into the same bed, for warmth. It was bitterly cold upstairs. He was somewhat ashamed of the sheets, but she promised not to look. She turned away from him, and he held her. The temptation of St. Anthony, he thought, and stirred slightly. But he was not much tempted. She was Len's girl. He held her breasts: she moaned slightly and appreciatively, then shifted around a little restlessly, then said, "Go on, give them a squeeze." He squeezed them, obligingly. They were firm and squashy at the same time, under her striped nightie. "They really need squeezing," said Maureen. "They miss it. Poor old Len." She giggled, sadly. "What a life," she said.

Within five minutes, both were asleep. But at three in the morning, Maureen woke again, as she often did these days, shaking slightly, her heart beating loudly with panic, only slightly reassured to find herself by the sleeping Anthony: she had been dreaming of those last days, which she had tried to describe in amusing terms to Anthony, but the reality had not been amusing, it had been terrifying, to see Len's stubbornness, to see his determination to justify himself, to see the mad energetic streak in him that had created his success harnessed to precipitate his failure. For Len was no good at half measures: he was a man who threw himself wholly into everything, and he had thrown his whole self into self-justification, in and out of the witness box. It had been frightening to watch, frightening to live with. He was a bad witness, unlike Maureen; he was rude, passionate, impatient, and the prosecution had

found it easy to rile him into contemptuous remarks about share-
holders and colleagues. It had been horrible, sitting there loyally
watching, while they baited him, and then going back to the luxury flat to listen to his imprecations, to watch him pace about, to
watch him drink himself into a frenzy. She could tell that he was
saying all the wrong things, in court: he should have kept calm,
but instead he lost his temper. Then, guilty at having lost his
temper, he would lose it again every evening, not at but for Maureen, who, he clearly felt, might be judging him for his behavior on
many counts. Maureen had not felt herself to be a judge; she was
on his side. Nevertheless, it was hard to listen to him without
becoming aware that so much passion could only indicate, on his
part, a bitter sense of failure, if not of guilt.

The day of the verdict, they had driven to court, knowing
that unless there was a miracle of obstinacy on the jury's part, they
would not drive back again together. Len drove: Maureen had not
fancied driving the Rolls back alone, it was too big, it frightened
her, and when she drove it people whistled and leered at her,
which she did not mind as a pedestrian, but which distracted her as
a driver. She had taken Len's toothbrush and razor and socks and
things in a briefcase, as though packing for him to go on a business
trip. Neither of them had been able to believe that this was the
end. The trial had dragged on so many weeks, the preparation for
the trial for so many months, it seemed unreal, to find themselves
at the end of the road. But that was how it had been. She had
driven back alone, paced alone around the empty flat, watched the
television news alone, while Len, alone, served the first night of his
four years.

Anthony heaved in his sleep: he had his arms around her still,
holding from behind. She could feel his cock, heavy against her
inner thigh. It would be easy to wake Anthony, to rouse Anthony.
For comfort. But she didn't want to. It wasn't that she didn't fancy
Anthony, exactly, because she did and always had. But she couldn't
really imagine sex with him. She didn't have that kind of relationship with him. Maureen's views of sex were not very proper, and
Anthony seemed to her a proper person. Of late, she had to admit
it, she'd been thinking more and more about the architect who

employed her. It was impossible not to. He, like Anthony, was quite a proper person, but their relationship made any personal remarks improper, and he had been making a few of late. About her wasting her life while Len was put away, a young woman like her, and about how his wife had started going to evening classes because she thought the children had destroyed her identity. Maureen knew where that kind of chat led, and indeed last Tuesday Derek had kissed her—not very forwardly, and with the pretext of saying good night, but nevertheless full on the mouth, and holding her against him at the same time, with a bit of pressing of the leg. "You're a good girl, Maureen," he had said, and she had smiled back, excited by the contact. It was true, she was still a young woman, and if she wasn't going to wait for Len to get out, what was the point of waiting at all? It wasn't even as though she was married to him.

Still, it would be shabby, to do it so soon. It would be more decent to wait a while. I wonder if Len could tell that Derek's trying it on, she wondered. He never asked about Derek, so she never mentioned him, but Len knew as well as anyone what kind of life she'd been used to before she jumped into bed with Len. It would be different if we'd got married, had kids, she thought. But it's so easy not to have kids, these days. I've probably ruined my chances of having any ever, with all those pills I've swallowed. And then, if you did have one, what if it turned out like poor old Alison's? Maureen had kept on taking the pill, even after Len had been put away. It seemed a bad sign, as though she was expecting the worst. Giving in well in advance, throwing in the sponge. I've got a rotten character, thought Maureen, philosophically.

She wondered what it would be like if they ever introduced these conjugal prison visits the papers sometimes talked about. Fucking to order didn't somehow appeal, and although men were different, maybe even some of them would feel a bit embarrassed to be told to get on with it, as it were, by order, at the Queen's pleasure. She couldn't imagine herself and Len getting down to it, seriously, on prison property. It had been hard enough, as she'd described to Anthony, to work up much interest even when Len was out on bail. Sex isn't the most important thing in life, she decided, wriggling her bottom slightly to see if her movement would affect Anthony. It did: he stiffened slightly, but slept on. But if sex isn't the most important, what is?

Several things happened during the first week of Molly's stay with Anthony. Kitty Friedmann was released from the hospital, and went home to her house in St. John's Wood, and tried to learn to walk on one leg. She was embarrassed about her own clumsiness, and did not like to practice in front of other people, but as she was never left alone by her affectionate family, she did not get much practice, except late at night, in the privacy of her own bedroom, and even then she was frightened of banging and making a noise and making other people anxious.

A date was fixed for Jane Murray's trial. It was to be held in three weeks' time. Clyde Barstow, the consul, thought this remarkably prompt, and seemed to expect Alison's gratitude. He was a large, agreeable, and erudite man who had during the war been obliged to walk across a large section of the North African desert, with two companions, both of whom died on the journey. He confessed to Alison, over a bottle of mellow Wallacian wine, that he had never been able to take anything very seriously after that. He liked Wallacia: he had actually requested the post. Alison, who had assumed that such a posting would be insignificant and undesirable, and that a man who had walked for ten days across a burning desert ought to have found a more comfortable niche, asked him why, and he said that he had always been interested in the Iron Age, and Wallacia contained some fine sites; also, that he was something of a linguist, and was enjoying learning Wallacian, a notoriously difficult language. She found these reasons for liking Wallacia inhumanly pure. Were people really motivated by such fine considerations? Perhaps they were. Or perhaps the consul was a diplomatic liar, concealing intrigue.

During this same week, the intrigue over the Riverside site thickened. The local authority met, planned, considered, and considered again. There was a lot of money at stake. They could not afford to make any more mistakes.

Giles Peters, who was more privy to their deliberations than he had chosen to inform his partner Anthony Keating, waited in something more like real agitation than he was accustomed to experience. From his point of view, also, there was a lot of money at stake; and even more, in his case, of that priceless commodity, self-respect. It would be hard to exaggerate the degree to which Giles Peters wished not to look a fool in the eyes of the financial world. Maybe he was even prepared to deceive his oldest friend Anthony in order to preserve his reputation as a sharp dealer. Or maybe, as he occasionally said to Rory Leggett, he felt it his duty to preserve poor Anthony from any more anxiety and uncertainty.

He need not have worried so much about Anthony. Anthony, after three days of Molly, rang up to reassure Giles: I'm quite prepared to hang on with you, said Anthony, don't you worry about me. I couldn't dream of accepting your kind offer.

Giles's first thought was that somebody had been talking to Anthony. Who? Rory? Friedmann? No, of course, Friedmann was dead. The boys of the Merchant Bank? His second thought was that Anthony was fool enough to believe that the offer had been made for his own good, and quixotic enough to wish to go down with the ship, if the ship went down. His third thought was perhaps the most perceptive: that Anthony, like himself, had more to lose than money, and that his attachment to the Riverside scheme was even more emotional than his own attachment to his own self-respect.

He knew Anthony well enough to realize that there would not be much point in trying to put any pressure on him. So all he could do was to wait, while the Twyford Authority deliberated and did sums on their calculating machines. He did not like waiting. The strain encouraged him to eat too much, and he developed a light but irritating rash on his face, put on weight, and suffered from sleeplessness and indigestion. Pamela left him and went off with a stockbroker. Uneasy lies the head that is waiting to see whether or not it has lost its share of twelve million pounds.

Anthony, meanwhile, back in West Gonnersall, was feeling amazingly much better. For several reasons. One was that he could tell, from Giles's response to his telephone call, that Giles, as Len had predicted, had got something up his sleeve, and for the first time in his life he felt, however irrationally, one up on Giles. This so pleased him that he even forgot to mention Pamela's dog. It was not much trouble, after all. He was also pleased by the notion that maybe the Riverside scheme might after all be salvaged: it even began to cross his mind at optimistic moments that it might even *pay off?* Supposing it paid off, supposing, instead of being in terrible trouble, he and Giles and Rory remade their lost fortune after all? It no longer seemed impossible. What a laugh that would be. If it all worked out all right. If it works out all right, Anthony promised himself, touching wood superstitiously, crossing and uncrossing his fingers childishly—if it works out, I will quit. I will dabble no more. I will retire, I will get a proper job, I will go and travel with contraceptives in India, with sanitary tampons in China, I will find a useful social role.

But what a laugh it would be, he thought to himself, if it paid off. There was something about the end-of-the-year light, the dark evenings, the iron frosts, that had turned from despair to hope, and his body had revived too: he could feel his body thinking of the spring. The tiredness of doing nothing had left him; he was sure that his heart tissue had mended itself. He could feel that it had. It had been a warning, a portent, not a final blow. I will listen, he promised. Let me just pull this one off, and I will listen.

One of the reasons for his renewed cheerfulness was, of course, Molly. Ill-fitted as she was to play the part of Pollyanna or Anne of Green Gables, Molly undoubtedly brought with her to him a new sense of purpose, and her pleasure at seeing him was very flattering. It reassured him that Alison would surely come back soon, and that at least some of their dreams might be made real. Private happiness might, after all, exist, despite the public woes of Britain.

Donnell had arrived with a very thick large spade-shaped black beard. A gun-running beard. He seemed in good spirits and did not talk much about Jane, though he hoped for everybody's sake that Alison would be home by the time he himself got back from the Caribbean. Anthony found that he did not envy the Caribbean trip at all. "No," he said to Donnell, as he forced him to stroll around the grounds. "No, I don't envy you at all. I'm really into the English winter, myself. Don't you think it's beautiful?" And he waved, vaguely, expressively, at the bare shaking trees, the colony of rooks down the lane, the yellowing roses, the frosted lawns, the gray-green stone of the house, the leafless gnarled trunk of wisteria. But Donnell, unlike Giles, was not remotely interested in property; the extreme beauty of Anthony's only stake seemed to leave him quite cold. Literally cold. He shivered, constantly, during the two hours he was there; a big hairy man, he shivered and blew on his hands and said, "It's a big place you've got to keep warm here, isn't it? Whatever will your heating bills be?" Donnell was interested in people, and, only by association, money. He was not interested in things. Or places. He had always been unacquisitive, haphazard, vagrant. Anthony liked him, and could never quite sympathize with Alison's occasional outbursts against him.

Donnell had not brought an au pair girl, he had brought an au pair boy. "I forgot it was the weekend, when I rang; the agency was shut. So I brought Tim instead. You don't mind, do you?"

Anthony stared at Tim. Tim stared nervously back. He was a pale, tall, thin youth, with large dangling hands, lank black hair, and several layers of jersey. And a strange accent, which Anthony could not place, though he discovered later that it was a heavily overlaid and distorted Lancashire. He was obviously queer. You could tell he was queer from the look of the top of his pullover. It had stripes, and was too narrow in the shoulder. He looked like a boy who had outgrown his garments in the last year at school.

Out of earshot, Donnell explained that Tim was an out of work actor, who worked most of the time as a dresser at the Regent: Donnell had met him around in pubs for years ("He's older than he looks"), had bought him meals, got him bit parts in films. But Tim still drifted. "Doesn't really seem to want to make a go of it," said Donnell, rather surprised by the subtlety of his own analysis. "Self-destructive type, you know? Can't come to terms. But he's very capable. Oh yes, he's very capable. He works for the Morrices sometimes, babysits, cooks dinners, cleans, that kind of thing. That's why I thought of him. They've got a baby with muscular dystrophy and Tim's marvelous with him. He's a good cook, too. You'll be surprised. And he won't get in your way, I don't think." Donnell's confidence wavered slightly. "Well, I don't expect he will. If he talks too much, tell him you've got work to do. That's what I do. Anyway"—brightening, the lure of the Caribbean glowing in Technicolor, the memory of dull chats with Tim about hopeless aspirations fading—"anyway, it's not for long, is it? And now"—looking at his watch—"now, I'll just explain to you about Molly's pills and things, and then I'd better be off."

The first evening with Molly went all right. Maureen stayed on, and supper with Tim, Molly, and Maureen was not bad at all. Maureen cooked it, and Molly enjoyed it, and Anthony and Maureen and Molly listened with some interest while Tim told them about how he'd walked on with Richardson, and how he'd understudied Alec McCowen and had nearly had to go on one night for him because his car had been held up in a bomb scare, and how he'd run away from home when he was fifteen. As he talked, Anthony realized that he wasn't so obviously queer after all: he certainly didn't assume that Maureen and Anthony would assume that he was, and any references he made to sex were conventional heterosexual ones, and very polite, at that. A mixed-up boy, Anthony decided; or that was what he would have been called twenty years ago. There was doubtless some new offensive bit of slang for such a predicament these days.

After supper, Molly wanted to watch the telly. But there wasn't any telly. Never mind, I'll get one tomorrow, promised Anthony, wondering if she understood. Then he remembered that tomorrow was Sunday, but it wasn't worth explaining that to Molly.

Luckily, Molly took to Pamela's dog. Although not as good as a telly, it proved a diversion, and sat on her lap. He wished she would not kiss it, it seemed unhygienic, but did not like to stop her.

In bed that night, he wondered if perhaps Donnell, despite the plausibility of his excuses, had not brought an au pair boy instead of an au pair girl out of some misdirected sense of jealousy about Alison. He had lost Alison himself, and had been exceedingly unfaithful to her, but nevertheless did not want her new man to sleep with an au pair girl. And as Donnell was clearly the kind of person who would judge another's morals by his own, he would find it inconceivable that a man of Anthony's age could share a house with an eligible girl without attempting sexual intercourse. Indeed, on being introduced to Maureen, he had given Maureen some funny looks, but Maureen, a bright girl, had made her status in Anthony's life exceedingly clear: she was very good at making blunt points. And had gone off to a bed on her own tonight, aware that it would be unwise to provide Tim with gossip. A large house did have advantages.

Anthony thought about girls. Perhaps he was relieved, after all, that Tim was not one, although he threatened to have some nuisance value. But girls were always a nuisance. His mind ranged back over the strange selection of au pair girls, mother's helpers, student lodgers, and sheer parasites that he and Babs had looked after in the old days: Babs, a real sucker if ever there was one, had let the lazy slobs lie in bed all day if they wanted, would even make them breakfast and run errands for them in town, and entertain their boyfriends, and their mothers, and their sisters and cousins. One or two had responded with kindness to kindness: a six-foot blond Austrian girl, who had proved ten times more efficient than her employers and had made the children enchanting Christmas decorations, and who had visited evening classes and learned impeccable English and French, as well as photography and ancient history. She was a very good photographer: she sent them, still, samples of her work from Graz. And there had been Eloise, not as clever or as ambitious as the heroic Margrit, but just as enthusiastic about the Keating household, and no trouble at all, because she had a permanent fiancé, who shared her room and occupied all her free time in a very harmless way. She married him too, when he finished his degree at the London School of Economics.

But most of the rest of them had been pains in the neck. Tearful, self-absorbed, inept, promiscuous, morose, garrulous—and nearly all of them bone idle. "It's your fault they're so lazy," Anthony would say to Babs. "You *encourage* them to be lazy. You're always offering to do things for them. You make them feel they're doing you a favor by breathing. You corrupt them." "You're just as bad," Babs would say. "You never ask them to do anything either. And as for telling them—I'd like to hear you *tell* anyone to do anything."

She was right, of course. It was so nice when they all went away. Poor old Babs, would she have to start on all that again, when she got the new baby?

Meanwhile, it would be interesting to see how Tim shaped up. I have learned nothing in life, thought Anthony. Nothing. I have had four children and several jobs, I have made and lost half a million pounds, I have loved two women properly and several more not too badly, I have a friend I visit in prison, I have found and bought one of the finest houses I've ever seen, I have even had a mild heart attack, and yet I know that I am completely at the mercy of that boy. I am just going to wait, to see how he behaves. I know it. And what if he is one of those that takes advantage? I have learned nothing.

But it was not so bad. It was cheering, distracting. On Sunday Maureen left, on Monday Anthony replaced her with a color television, hired from the electrical store in Blickley. Then he and Tim and Molly settled down together in their ménage à trois. Molly could play simple games, like Snap with picture cards (she could not count), and could follow if Tim and Anthony played Ludo, though she could not work out how to move her own pieces. Her I.Q., Anthony thought, was somewhere in the sixties, though it was difficult to tell, because she had such physical difficulties with manipulating objects, and in speaking: he found he could understand most of what she said, except when she became very excited or agitated. He had on occasion suspected that Alison underestimated Molly's abilities, for at times she expressed herself very clearly, and with great feeling: "It's annoying," she would say, when she dropped her spoon for the fifth time over a meal, "it's very annoying, not to be able to put it where I want, when *I* know *where* it ought to go—" and such remarks seemed to indicate an area of awareness, frustration, inexpressible understandings that could find no normal outlet. One did not need a psychiatrist to explain that Molly's fits of rage were fits of intense frustration at her own inability to do the things she felt she ought to be able to do. And if she felt this about physical problems, might she not also suffer the same rages about other skills, like reading and counting? It was a delicate area, and Anthony respected the fact that Alison had been for many years familiar with the problem in a way he could never be; nevertheless, he felt quite strongly that she had the misfortune to be intelligent enough to experience, acutely, her own disabilities. Snap and Ludo did not satisfy her, as they would have satisfied a very small child: they amused her for a while, but there was an element of rage in the way she tipped over the board at the end of a game, or scattered the cards on the table, as though she knew that there were more interesting games, from which she was excluded.

In other ways, she was like a small child: she enjoyed talking to the dog, she enjoyed being taken for walks, although it was bitterly cold, and she liked being driven in the car, to look at things. She even liked looking at the scenery: he wondered what she saw in it. Being with her reminded him of the old days, when his own children were still small: he and Babs, driven to exert themselves by the boredom and irritation of staying in, had undertaken many dull weekend expeditions to distant parks, to fairs and playgrounds. There was more to see in the country, or more that Anthony himself enjoyed seeing. They went to look at the pig farm, at the river, at the horse in the field, at the strange mountain of horseshoes that some eccentric villager had erected in his front garden, at the ship in a bottle in Mrs. Appleyard's front window, at the cows in the barn, with numbers stamped on their rumps. She liked to stand on the little bridge over the river that flowed through the village, dropping in sticks and leaves, watching them appear on the other side. She liked, too, the village shop, with its archaic bacon slicer, its dotty and confused array of packaged foods, its postcards and plimsolls and paper handkerchiefs. The woman who ran the shop, a middle-aged and confused person called Mrs. Lightfoot, was patient and unperturbed, as Molly made her mind up between Dolly Mixtures and Smarties: she was the worst saleswoman in the world, much given to pointing out what was wrong with her own wares (I wouldn't have the oranges, Mr. Keating, they're squashy in the middle, going off a bit, you know), apologizing for her produce (I don't know what's the matter with these eggs, Mr. Keating, they look like bantams to me, I'll charge you a penny less, shall I?). She never hurried: nobody in the shop ever hurried. It suited Molly well. She could stare and poke about without fear of reprimand. Mrs. Lightfoot had herself a fat simpleminded youngest son of much the same age, who would run in from the back to steal sweeties when his mother was not looking. After a few visits, Anthony began to think that Mrs. Lightfoot had probably not even noticed that Molly was in any way odd. Or, if odd, no odder than Anthony himself.

In the evenings, there was always the television. She enjoyed the television greatly. Undoubtedly, thought Anthony, as he sat through hitherto unheard-of programs, undoubtedly the television is a great invention. It took care of the evenings entirely.

Tim, as Donnell had promised, was a good cook—almost too good a cook, for he liked composing rich and complicated dishes that made Anthony worry about his diet, and which Molly reasonably enough rejected from time to time, preferring, in a normal childish way, hamburgers and fish fingers and fried eggs. But Tim would not let her eat them all the time. He bullied Anthony into driving him in to the delicatessen in Blickley, where he stocked up with herbs and spices, rice and cheeses, olive oil and pasta, salami and Polish chorizos, dried beans and frozen prawns.

But Tim was, also, a bore. As Donnell had ineffectively tried to conceal. At first Anthony could not work out quite why he found him boring: it was not so much that he talked too much, although he did, it was more that one could not quite believe anything he said. His stories were too interesting to be interesting. At first Anthony did not think of suspecting his veracity, for the stories seemed plausible enough—theatrical anecdotes of a familiar variety, tales of an impoverished childhood, adventures experienced on running away from home. Strange encounters, strokes of good or ill luck. Perhaps, thought Anthony at first, this is what life is really like in that particular kind of underworld: mad landladies, beneficent old Etonians, narrow escapes from the fuzz, wild weekends in country houses, propositions from famous film stars, betrayals and little acts of violence. But if it really was like that, why did such strange narratives arouse in him so little curiosity? Why did he have to work so hard to bring himself to say, every now and then, over the yellow paella or the Greek salad, "How astonishing," "Goodness me," "He didn't *really*, did he?" It was oddly hard work, responding to Tim. The explanation did not occur to him for some days. One evening, Tim embarked on a story for which he unfortunately chose as protagonist an actress whom Anthony, through Alison, knew quite well. Anthony listened politely to an account of her career and marital adventures which culminated in a scene, alleged to have taken place at a party given by Lord Kinarth in Eaton Square. The party had indeed taken place, for Anthony had been to it, but it did not at all resemble Tim's description; nor was it possible that Laura's antics could have taken place after Anthony and Alison's departure, in some strange surreal postscript to the real party, for he had on that occasion driven Laura home, and she and Alison had complained all the way back to Laura's house in Kensington about the dullness of the occasion, the drunkenness of Kinarth's butler, and the inadequacy of the food. "Call that a *buffet supper*," he distinctly remembered Laura remarking, in her high camp tone of exaggerated horror. "More like a nursery tea." And she had invited them in for eggs and bacon, and several slices of toast and Marmite.

So it simply was not possible that at the same time she was taking off her blouse and bra and dancing on Kinarth's four-poster bed, watched by Tim and others, was it? No, it was not.

Nevertheless, it was hard to interrupt or to contradict a storyteller in full flight. So Anthony listened politely, and at the end said mildly, "Well, that is surprising. I've met Laura Blakely several times, and that's not the kind of impression she made on me at all." At which Tim looked at him, sharply, but without real suspicion.

After that, Anthony found Tim's stories increasingly dull and increasingly unreal. He had never gone much for the theory that good storytellers never have any respect for the truth; on the contrary he tended to think that only the truth could possibly be interesting. However dull the truth, it was more interesting than a fantasy. Anthony began to evolve for himself, while listening to Tim, a new theory: that bores are not necessarily people who talk too much, or who talk too much about themselves, they are people who do not tell the truth, either about others or about themselves. Perhaps because they do not know it? Tim was such a strange boy, it would be hard to convict him of a genuine desire to deceive: it seemed more likely that he was a fantasist, who found it hard to unravel his own stories, once he had invented them. Why don't I just sit back and listen and enjoy it, Anthony said to himself. But he found it difficult, it was not in his nature. Tim disturbed him too much. A strange desire to protect him from his own lies came over him: he had entered into connivance. He began to agree more easily, nod more eagerly, to steer him off dangerous ground. Tim was quick: he picked up quickly the areas of social life of which Anthony had first-class knowledge and avoided them, confining himself to unexplored fringes where Anthony and Alison had never strayed.

He was not, of course, at all interested in Anthony. Anthony did not expect him to be, although from time to time he wondered why he accepted this lack of curiosity so naturally. For, after all, there was a sense in which Anthony could be seen in a romantic light: a failed adventurer, alone in his country castle, brooding amongst the rooks and mice over the collapse of his immense aspirations. Maybe, thought Anthony, I will feature, transformed, translated, in Tim's future fairy stories: "You know Anthony Keating?" Tim would say to future audiences, "you remember

Anthony Keating? I stayed with him once, in his country house, High Rook House—a fantastic place it was, you'd never believe it, these beautiful old windows, and an amazing view, and a tower . . . and do you know what Anthony used to spend his time doing?" There Anthony's own imagination boggled: he could not conceive of the activities that Tim would invent for him. But certainly Tim would not tell the truth, which was that Anthony had spent most of his time listening to Tim's stories. That would be far too dull.

From finding Tim a bore, Anthony began, partly through necessity, to find him a very absorbing case. He speculated constantly on how Tim saw himself, and lived with himself. And, most of all, somewhat crudely, on whether or not he saw himself as—or, indeed, was—a homosexual. It was impossible to tell. Anthony knew so many well-adjusted homosexuals that he found it hard to believe that Tim had not yet come to terms with the problem. But it seemed that perhaps he had not. A boy from St. Helen's, who had run away from school and home at fifteen— maybe he really didn't know what to do about himself, what he was, at all? Occasionally, when he could get a word in edgeways, Anthony would try to draw the conversation toward Tim's own sexual experiences, and away from the voyeuristic elaborations that seemed to intrigue him so much, but Tim would not be drawn: a fact which in itself seemed revealing. Anthony found himself thinking from time to time very simple thoughts, such as: he needs a psychiatrist; he needs to join a gay group.

Tim's presence forced Anthony into a course of action on which he would not otherwise have embarked. At first to escape from Tim and, later, to give Tim a break and an evening out, Anthony started to go to the village pub. Still committed to a course of nondrinking, he did not find the forced abstinence as painful as he had expected. He did not count half a pint of beer as drink, and as everyone else drank beer too, he did not feel himself as much of an outcast as he would have done in the BBC bar, on Fleet Street, or in the Queen's Hotel. Nor did he feel himself an outcast in other ways. He had speculated on the villagers' attitude to their new resident, but in fact they all seemed remarkably incurious about him. The regulars nodded when he entered for the first time, exchanged a few words, even asked him if he played darts. They were, of course, used to visitors: from Easter to October the village was filled with tourists, some in cars, some walkers doing the Pennine way. This was the dead season, but they nevertheless made him welcome. They knew who he was: on his second visit, the manager's wife asked him how he was getting on with the central heating. Her son-in-law from Blickley had helped to install it, so he was happy to be able to give it a good report. Nobody minded Anthony; he was an inconspicuous, inoffensive man, when he chose, good at taking on protective coloring. A neutral-looking man.

He even struck up a friendship, in the pub. With the warden of the local Youth Hostel, which was in a village five miles away. The warden was a handsome, weatherbeaten young chap in his late twenties or early thirties, and he had been in Alverwick for five years. He preferred the West Gonnersall pub, he said, because whenever he went to any of the three pubs in Alverwick he had to spend his time listening to complaints about the behavior of delinquent Youth Hostelers. And some of the things they got up to did indeed sound rather alarming. Drinking, gambling, fighting, suicide attempts. "It's the school parties that cause the trouble," said Ned Buckton glumly. "They get dead bored in the evenings, and most of them are under age, and the pubs won't have them, and the teachers forget to organize anything for them, so they just muck about, seeing who can cause most trouble." The YHA was thinking of banning school parties, he said.

On their second meeting, Anthony asked Ned what had made him become a warden. Ned found it hard to explain. "I liked the place," he said, several times. "I walked through this way once, when I was a kid, and I liked it. So when we saw the job advertised, my wife and I applied. And here we are."

"And do you like it?"

"We love it," said Ned Buckton.

He had been a teacher of geography. Like Anthony, he liked the limestone scenery. They compared their feelings about it with their feelings about the Lake District. "I like this better," said Ned. "I know some people find it a bit bleak. And it hasn't got the variety of colors you get in the Lakes. Nor the real mountains. But I think that's what I like about it."

"It's more secret," said Anthony.

"And I like the stone walls," said Ned.

So did Anthony. He liked the way they marched across the contours, and up the steep slopes. He liked their gray whitenesses, their persistence, their human scale, their mathematical parceling out of the infinite. They squared it off and captured it, as his gasometer had caught and enmeshed the sky.

On their third meeting, Anthony told Ned about Molly. "You should bring her down here for a drink," said Ned. "I'm good with kids."

"She's under age," said Anthony. Ned said that Mrs. Bunney wouldn't mind. So Anthony went off and collected Tim and Molly, and Molly had a pineapple juice, and Tim had a vermouth, and Ned showed Molly the interesting objects in his pockets: a snail shell, some stones, an elaborate penknife, a pheasant's feather. Then he built her a house from the pub dominoes. She tried to build one herself, but lacked, of course, the manual control. Anthony was afraid that she might cry with rage, but Ned diverted her by taking her to see the goldfish in the public bar. He was, as he had said, good with kids. A harmless man, leading a harmless life. The good shepherd. Sometimes, he said, he and his wife, Sally, had to cook forty suppers in an evening. Mind you, he said, it was only simple stuff, packet soup, eggs, beans, sausages. Anthony reflected with shame on the struggle he had had to cook himself four sausages.

He reflected, also with shame, that he had disowned Molly. He had told Ned that she was Alison's child, his stepchild. Why had he not accepted her, introduced her, as his own? It would have cost him nothing.

Ned and Sally Buckton had two children. They were still at the village school.

He thought of Alison, as he watched Ned, Molly, and Tim. I

have ended up in some strange company, he thought. He thought of Alison, who had owned Molly and disowned Jane. She too had led a hard life. His own had been, was, an indulgence.

At the end of Molly's first week, Anthony received a telegram from Alison. It said: ON WAY HOME. WILL BE WITH YOU BOTH SOONEST. LOVE. To his surprise, as he put down the phone after receiving the message, he could feel tears starting up in his nose and eyes. He had not dared to hope that she would come so soon. Then, looking at the words again that he had taken down, he saw that she was coming for Molly, not for him. He did not blame her. And anyway, it was for him, also. For both. Will be with you both.

He tried to tell Molly. She smiled. One could never tell with Molly. Anthony sat down and cried. He had not cried for years.

Alison decided to return to England as soon as she heard that Donnell had dumped Molly on Anthony. She heard this from Miss Channing, whom she had rung at school in an unusually acute fit of anxiety. The warmth of feeling for both child and man that invaded her as soon as she heard the news was decisive: she would go back where she was wanted, to those who loved and needed her, instead of hanging around pointlessly in an alien place with an alienated daughter.

She told the consul. She told the hotel. She booked a flight. Then she went to tell Jane. They let her see Jane alone. She and Jane met in a little office. There sat Jane on a chair, pale, upright, tight, angry. My flesh and blood, thought Alison. There she is, one hundred and twenty-five pounds of my flesh and blood. There was no need to harden her heart. Her heart had hardened itself.

"Jane," she said. "I'm sorry, I'm going back to England."

Jane stared at her.

"There's nothing more I can do for you here. I've done all I can. I'll come back, as soon as anything happens."

Jane stared. Will she ask, thought Alison, will she bring herself to ask me to come back for the trial?

"Suit yourself," said Jane. "Not that you don't always suit yourself."

A hardened heart is as painful as a soft one, thought Alison. Intense waves of emotion poured through her. It was the kind of confrontation she had tried, for years, to avoid.

"I can't split myself in two," she said.

"You never tried," said Jane, speaking almost reasonably. "You always put her first, didn't you? You never gave a fuck about me."

"Don't you use bad language to me," said Alison, stalling; and then suddenly heard herself begin to speak, very fast, very quietly, as though she had been storing it up for years and years. "Yes, I did give a fuck about you," she said, "yes, I did, I worried myself sick about you, I saw what a raw deal you got, don't think I didn't notice, I'm not blind, you know, I saw the whole thing. I saw it happen, and do you know what I think? I think I don't think much of you. There you are, eighteen years old, with everything going for you, good looks, brains, money, the lot, and what do you do, you sulk and feel sorry for yourself and sleep with halfwits who run away when there's any trouble, and you're all eaten up with meanness and jealousy, and Christ, Jane, what do you think you're jealous of? A poor lump, who doesn't know what's happening to her, who hasn't a hope of a decent life—and she suffers too, you always tried to pretend she didn't have any feelings, but you know as well as I do that rages like that don't happen out of nothing, out of unfeeling—and you, you have the weakness, the feebleness, the lack of—the lack of dignity, the lack of proportion, to let yourself—well, it doesn't bear describing, what you've let yourself do. I daresay what you need is a psychoanalyst who will let you think Donnell and I treated you rottenly, but just you remember, child, if ever you get near an analyst or anyone willing to listen to you, and before you try to start their tears jerking, just you remember that you had seven solid years before Molly was born. Seven years. You had all those years. And at the age of seven, you decided you weren't going to help. *You were old enough to know better.* There, I've said it now. *You were old enough to know better.* I'm sorry for you, Jane, you've got yourself in an awful mess, but just you remember that *you* got *yourself* in it. There's no appeal, you know. There's no way you can be excused. You have to pay your own penalty. I can't pay it for you. Do you know what I mean? Are you listening? Do you understand what I mean? I daresay I'm the worst mother in the world, to speak to you like this, in the mess you're in, but what else can I do? I don't care. I've done what I can. You're grown up now. You can vote, you can marry, you can kill yourself if you want, I don't care. All right, so a terrible accident ruined your life. Yes, it was bad luck, we all know that, and my God didn't you let us know it, make us know it. But just you remember this. Whatever happens to you, it can't be as bad as what happened before birth to Molly. Have a sense of proportion. Have a little honor. I wash my hands of you."

Jane, throughout this, looked at the floor. Her feet were encased in woollen socks and institution shoes. She looked up, as Alison finished. She had a satisfied expression on her face.

"You see," she said. "You've ruined us both. I don't know how *you* can go around thinking yourself such a wonderful mother. Look what you've done to us both."

Alison stood up. She was shaking.

"No," she said. "No. What I am saying is, *you* look at what *you* have done to yourself. I will worry about myself. There is no need for you to worry about me."

A slight flicker of something like anxiety appeared to enter Jane's spirit.

"Are you going, now?" she said.

"Yes," said Alison. "I'll write, I'll keep in touch. But now, I must go."

Jane stood up. She was taller than her mother. "Good-bye, then," she said. And approached. They stared at one another, a quick screen of many possibilities running no doubt through both their minds: a silence, a kiss, a slap, a collapse, tears, repentance, hardening, turning away. They stared, and Alison could see on Jane's clear forehead the faint tiny pocks of a bad adolescent bout of spots and blackheads, tiny pores and stars accentuating the otherwise unblemished surface—yet not unblemished, for there, over Jane's right eye, was the scar of her first bicycle accident, a clean white strike below the eyebrow, a miraculous escape, for at first they had thought she must surely lose the eye. Alison remembered the incident, of which she had not thought for years, the small child tottering in from the street, her face covered in blood, her skin embedded and scraped with grit, her filthy sleeve clamped into her eye, and Alison, faint, sick, scooping her up, rushing her into the bathroom, forcing away the arm, forcing herself to look, looking as it were with her eyes shut, calling to Donnell to get the car out to take her to Emergency, trying hard not to see what she was seeing as she laid the cotton wool on the bleeding eye—and there, after all, was the eye, escaped, preserved, miraculously intact, though the brow and lid were torn. Mopping, soothing, wondering, doctor, hospital, ambulance, the smell of TCP, the child screaming at the stinging antiseptic, not knowing whether or not to pry out with one's fingers the larger lumps of grit, the relief of arriving at the hospital and finding a clean white-coated calm doctor, smiling, patient, mopping and swabbing, stitching, reassuring, as Jane relapsed—oh yes, then as now—into a shocked and alarmed silence, her tears and terror controlled, her lifted brow stoic. How old had she been? Six? Seven? Before Molly? No, of course not: just after Molly. Seven years old. And the doctor, saying, "Well, well, you *are* a lucky girl. You'll have nothing to show for this in a few weeks' time, I bet."

But there was something to show. There was a scar. A permanent white memorial. The flesh, sometimes, graciously consents to record for a lifetime.

Alison, gazing at her daughter's face, overcome by recollection, suffered, for she did not know what to do. Let this be taken away from me, she said, in her head. Let it be over. And as though in response, Jane, who had too, it must be said, noted in this brief gaze the tired skin around her mother's eyes, a skin wrinkled and papery and oddly vulnerable, unresilient, tired and stretched, as she finally guessed, by Alison's ceaseless watching, by her long sleepless hours of waiting—Jane took a step toward her mother, and politely kissed her tired cheek. A courteous, distant, social kiss. Alison returned the gesture.

"Good-bye," said Jane.

"I'll be back," said Alison. "As soon as there's anything I can do."

"Don't worry about me," said Jane. And added, with something that almost resembled a smile, however malicious, "And do give my love to Molly and Anthony, won't you?"

"Oh, grow up," said Alison crossly, suddenly too worn out by the drama to bear it a moment longer. "Just grow up, won't you?" And she turned and left, pausing at the window to look back, wave. Across a safe distance, Jane smiled properly: probably because she's got rid of me at last, Alison reflected, as she went back to the hotel to pick up her bags.

As she settled herself on the airplane, she thought of the West, London, shops, Harrods, Kitty Friedmann, familiar faces. It would be good to get back. Or would it? Was England still that dangerous, violent place she had left, where each step could mean death? She could not help hoping that everything would have changed, during her brief absence, for the better. It was too much to hope that all the problems hanging around the neck of the government —Ireland, unemployment, inflation—would have sorted themselves out, but surely things could not be quite as bad as they had been when she had left. She wondered what would have happened to Anthony's Riverside scheme. She hoped, for the sake of his pride, that he and Giles would devise some way of justifying their terrible errors to themselves. That, she supposed, was the best one could hope for.

She felt unbelievably tired. She had slept badly for weeks, had run out of sleeping pills, and was now suffering from a very heavy period, brought on perhaps by anxiety. But perhaps not? Maybe it was fibroids, cancer. Certainly the sight of the dark red clots of blood had been far from reassuring. It would be a kind of poetic justice, if she too, like Anthony, were to contract some serious ailment.

She had been so scornful, when younger, of those who thought all illnesses psychosomatic, those who talked of "cancer types," those who believed one could bring on quite clearly definable physical symptoms by either fearing or wishing them. Nowadays, she was not so sure. As one grows older, as one explores, slowly, the responses of mind and body, one learns a respect for their intimate connections.

There is no such thing as an accident. We are all marked down. We choose what our own ill thoughts chose for us. Jane fell off her bicycle because of Molly, for attention. Or for equality? Had she lost her eye, as she so nearly managed to do, that would indeed have evened the score between Molly and Jane. An eye for an eye. A sacrificial gesture, rather than a gesture of spite.

She shivered, uneasily, in her seat. What, in ill thoughts again? As somebody said in *Lear*. Was it *Lear*? She had once played Cordelia. Of course.

No, one must continue to behave as though one believed in the accidental. That shows our greatest faith. Molly's fate is an accident, not a retribution. So I must see it.

There was no point in thinking about these things too much. But how to prevent one's mind going round the old wheels? In a less advanced age, Molly might well not have survived; nowadays, most families have a physical victim, alive, surviving. But with a morality so punitive, so primitive, that we do not give these people the means to live. We make them scrabble for money, we make their relatives scrape.

Oh God, I am so tired, thought Alison, and shut her eyes. She would sleep. The plane got in at six in the evening: three hours to sleep. I will not think about any of them, she told herself, not about Molly, not about Jane down there, I will empty my mind.

But she could not sleep. The plane was comfortable, old-fashioned, she lay back with her head on the white antimacassar, quaintly embroidered: a first-class ticket that nice man Clyde Barstow had given her, with deprecating mumbles about its being a personal gift. She was back in the world of gallantry and service, of bells to push and telephones that answered, of stewardesses with trays. The seat was upholstered in dark red plush: the whole interior more resembled her notion of a Russian train than of a modern plane. A halfway house.

She could feel the heavy blood flowing from her, and got up, and went to the lavatory: there, for the first time for weeks, she found a Tampax machine. A promise of civilization. And when she got back to her seat, an American businessman leaned over to her and asked her politely whether she would like to look at his copy of *Time* magazine, another promise of civilization. She accepted, politely, and leafed through it, marveling as ever at her own ignorance about world affairs: perhaps it had been good for her, after all, to be forced, even so brutally, to acknowledge the existence of Eastern Europe. There was, of course, no mention of Wallacia. Not even a footnote. But there was a page and a half on Britain's economic decline, and the sinking pound, and the dismal state of British industry, and the failure of British firms to deliver goods, and the folly of trying to support workers' co-operatives with state money, and the inevitability of cutback in public spending, particularly in the Health Service. Reading, Alison felt the usual surge of British patriotism: things were not as bad as that, surely? She glanced across at the businessman: there he sat, pleasant, solid, confident, eccentrically dressed by British standards, but civilized indeed, doubtless well informed, well traveled, well read. (He was reading a novel by Norman Mailer, she could see.) She wondered what he thought about the British National Health Service. Did he think it rotted the spirit of enterprise and self-help, that it demoralized doctors and patients alike? She wondered what she herself thought about the National Health Service. She was herself no socialist, she did not even consider herself to have any political views, but she felt very strongly indeed about the Health Service, and the Social Services.

Because of Molly. She was lucky, she could pay for Molly to

go to an expensive private school, where she could learn, from experts, what little she would ever learn. But she was bitterly, painfully aware of the less fortunate, of those that even the Health Service shuffled off into the cellars and garbage dumps of survival, to sprout in the dark like unplanted potatoes, to spring up astonishingly every now and then like indestructible rhubarb, to rot, to decay, to die. She could not understand society. She could not understand how normal people, with their eyes, and their ears, and their limbs all functioning, could refuse to the less well-endowed an excess, a largesse, a sumptuous recompense. To haggle over invalid cars, over paying for night nurses, when it was obvious that out of sheer gratitude for our own health we should give more than we give ourselves to those that lack this elementary blessing. In some areas, society and the law do recognize this: they award to those who lose faculties and limbs enormous sums of damages, hundreds of thousands of pounds, when human error can be convicted. But when the error is God's, we have no mercy, we are selfish, we are mean.

Maybe it is true that we cannot afford to be generous any more, as a nation? If so, thought Alison, then life is not worth living. And she shut the magazine, firmly, and shut her eyes resolutely, and waited for the plane to land. If Britain went down, she would go down with it. At least it had tried.

When the filthy little train reached filthy Victoria Station, it was eight thirty. She had not really decided where she should go: to Donnell's empty flat; to Anthony's empty house to see if there were any more squatters; to friends, even? She stood on the platform, amidst the garbage and the pigeons. After Krusograd, London seemed very large, very frightening, very noisy, very dirty. She wanted to ring Anthony, to say she was safely back, but it seemed better to do it from some safe place, rather than from a noisy call box. Now she was back, she felt, obscurely, frightened. The West did not seem reassuring after all. Could this be home?

Yet she felt Anthony's house might be even more alarming, in its emptiness, and its lingering echoes of Babs. And what if there were squatters, broken pipes, bottles, broken windows, cats?

She rang Kitty Friedmann. Kitty, of all the world, could be guaranteed to ask her round at once and mean it, which she did. "Dear girl, dear girl," she kept saying, "you're back again, thank the Lord, you're back." It wasn't until she was in the taxi that the full realization of what she had done entered Alison's mind: now, suddenly, in ten minutes, unprepared with things to say, she was going to have to look at Kitty Friedmann's leg. Her ears began to sing and hum with panic.

The door of the neat white house in St. John's Wood was opened by Sadie, one of the seemingly numberless Friedmann family circle. She was a cousin, or a second cousin, a large woman from Manchester, and she greeted Alison with effusive warmth, grabbing her case, grabbing her coat, ushering Alison, before she had time to think, into the lounge, where Kitty lay on the settee, surrounded by several other Friedmanns. Kitty cried out gaily from her couch, "Oh, Alison, what a treat, how *nice* of you to come and see us, it *is* kind of you to think of us—isn't she looking lovely, Danny?"—for it was one of Kitty's principles that all women needed to be told constantly that they looked lovely.

"I can't possibly be looking lovely," said Alison, stooping to kiss Kitty's well-powdered cheek, "I've had such a long day, I feel filthy. But you"—it suddenly seemed very easy to say, being true —"you really look remarkably well, Kitty."

She pulled up a stool, sat herself down by Kitty's elbow.

"I *am* well," said Kitty. "I'm fine, aren't I, boys? Now, my dear, let Sadie go and find you something to eat, you must be starving"—for another of Kitty's principles required her to offer food to any visitor at least once every half hour.

"I'd love something to eat," said Alison, "but don't hurry, there's no rush. I'll go and help myself to something soon."

"No, no, you sit there, you must be exhausted. What a terrible time you must have had, dear. Tell us all about it. Just you sit back and relax and tell us all about it."

So Alison found herself an armchair and sat back, and kicked off her tight shoes, and looked around her, and talked, and ate. Sadie brought her a tray full of chicken soup and chopped liver and cold chicken and cold salmon and salad and fruit and gherkins and water biscuits, and Alison made her way through it, for it seemed the healthiest food she had encountered in months, infinitely digestible, infinitely reassuring, like the room itself, with its thick white Chinese carpet, and its velvet braided curtains, and its gilt mirrors, and its deep chairs, and its profound bourgeois peace, which not even death and mutilation had been able to disrupt. The Friedmann clan sat around, loyal, cohesive, a united front: behind Kitty's back they might bicker and squabble, but in her lounge they behaved themselves, at least for a stranger. Alison was always rather surprised by how much she liked Kitty's house. It was not her own taste, there was not an item in it she would herself have chosen, but it was unmistakably pleasant, put together by a loving eye. Whereas Kitty's clothes, alas there was no doubt about it, were on the whole rather frightful. Perhaps the explanation was that Kitty cared a great deal about her home, and not at all about her personal appearance? Her makeup was often applied in so random a manner that one wondered whether she had bothered to look at herself in the mirror while applying it. Perhaps, when buying clothes, she simply bought whatever the saleswoman recommended, not caring enough to have any notions of her own.

When Alison had eaten her supper, and finished her saga, she tried to ring Anthony, but his telephone was out of order. The operator on the Blickley exchange said it was a terrible night up there, terrible winds, perhaps the lines were down. Alison returned to the lounge and reported this news, and the gathering fell silent, and behold, there was a strong wind in London too, but they had been too absorbed, too cocooned in their double-glazed interior to notice it: but when they listened, they could hear it in the trees in the garden, rattling the lids of dustbins in the street. Outside, a long way off.

At ten, the Friedmanns began to leave. They did not keep late nights. Sadie was staying; so was a nurse, who had taken the eve-

ning off, and who came in as the others left. Kitty did not approve
of the nurse, but the family had bullied her into having her. "What
do I need a nurse for?" said Kitty, heaving herself up, reaching for
her crutches, bidding Alison good night, begging her to stay
longer—"Stay a few days, dear, have a good rest"—and finally
hobbling off, up the stairs, with the nurse's arm to support her.
Sadie, switching off lights and fires on her departure, shook her
head, said, "She's very stubborn, you know. You wouldn't think it,
would you? We wanted to make a bedroom for her downstairs,
but she wouldn't have it. She wanted her own room. Stubborn,
that's what she is."

"She seems so well," said Alison.

Sadie snorted. "Well! She's as well as can be, I expect." She
stood, with her finger on the last light switch. "We always said of
Kitty, if anyone spat in her eye she'd say, sorry. And now, look at
her." She snorted again, and Alison could not tell if it was with
admiration, or impatience. As she went upstairs to her guest bedroom, and ran herself a bath, she thought about Kitty: was it
unnatural, to adapt so well to such a double loss?

She lay in the guest bath, looking through the open door into
the bedroom, the bed with its satin cover, the white wardrobe
with gilt knobs, the Utrillo reproduction on the wall. (Downstairs,
there was a large Keith Vaughan, bought by Max in a spasm of
cultural benevolence; everybody hated it and derided it, but there
it hung, because Max had bought it, and Max had said, with increasing defiance, that it was good. Now it would no doubt hang
forever, in deference to the dead.) She thought of Jane, in prison;
of Len Wincobank, in prison; of poor Anthony, imprisoned with
Molly in his remote eyrie.

The family is a good, multiple, reparable fortification against
death: when one member dies, the gap is filled by another. A
communal survival. But the individuals die, nevertheless: Max
Friedmann was dead, although his relatives contrived to cluster so
thickly that his absence was not noticeable.

Alison's family had not been like that at all. She clambered out
of the bath, thinking of them, noting with dismay that she was still

bleeding heavily, onto the thick blue towel and the white tiled floor. They had been separate, distinct, alone.

I must do something, Alison said to herself, as she climbed into the wide soft bed, I must do something to bring to an end this terrible fear. It would be better to be dead than to suffer such terrible fear. How long can I go on pretending not to feel it?

Kitty Friedmann was getting quite good at unstrapping her artificial limb. She had been clumsy to begin with, but one can learn anything, if one puts one's mind to it. She sat on the edge of the bed, neatly folding the straps. She would have liked to have spent some time practicing walking, as she usually did when she went to bed: there were also exercises she was supposed to do, given her by the physiotherapist. But she was afraid she would make a noise if she did them, and disturb or alarm Alison. She would hate to upset poor Alison. She looked pale and tired, and no wonder. I don't know how I would bear it, thought Kitty, if such things had happened to my children. First Molly, and then this terrible thing with Jane. I simply wouldn't be able to bear it, if such things happened to my children. Thank God that mine are all healthy, all well.

She heaved herself into the wide double bed, and took a sleeping pill, and thought of her children, and her grandchildren. She did not think of Max. She did not dare to think of Max. Max had been exiled to the black outer wastes of incomprehension and impossibility: he lived out there now, with the six million Jews, and those who died in the Soviet labor camps, and those who were languishing now in camps and prisons. The black wastes, where the winds of hell perpetually howled.

In here, it was warm, and safe, and comfortable. The wallpaper had a pattern of roses and honeysuckle, the carpet was thick and white, the dressing table was white and gilt, and on it lay the silver-backed brushes of her wedding day, the little powder jars, the scent bottles, the little china ring tree. Her artificial leg and crutches leaned incongruously, crudely, against the rose-colored button-backed chair. She wished she had remembered to drape them with her dressing gown, as she usually did. They were not pretty objects. But it was not worth getting out of bed. She looked the other way.

The house was solid and quiet. The walls were thick. Outside, the wind blew, and for a moment, before she fell asleep, Kitty imagined that the spirit of Max was pouring in the gale and streaming against her outer windows, beseeching entrance. But the house was well insulated, and she would not, could not admit him. If she admitted him, she could not survive, and she had to survive. For the children, the grandchildren.

Anthony lay in bed listening to the howling of the wind, wondering what damage it would do next, wondering where Alison had got to, telling himself that there was little likelihood that this gale had tossed her airplane into the high mountains or the fields of France. She had no doubt arrived, tried to ring, been frustrated.

The telephone wires and the electricity had all gone at once, while he and Tim and Molly were watching an old Peter Sellers movie on the television. Complete darkness descended. Molly screamed, understandably, and Anthony comforted her, and found some candles, and a flashlight, before setting off to see what had caused the damage. He switched on his car headlights, and could see at once that the wires had been pulled down by a fallen tree: the big elm in the lane that had for generations housed the rooks. The gale whipped through the fallen branches: he could see, in the light of the flashlight, savage white splinters, a gaping wound. It was too cold and, he felt, too dangerous to stay out for long, for who could tell what might go next? All the trees were straining and groaning; he was anxious about the roof, the outbuildings. But what could he do? He went back in, and persuaded Tim and Molly that it was time for bed: then he wondered whether he ought to drive down to the village to report, but of course he could not, for the lane was blocked by the elm. It would have to wait till the morning.

Somewhere in the kitchen there was a little paraffin lamp. It had been left by the previous owners, or more likely their predecessors, for precisely such emergencies, he guessed. He looked for it, by candle, found it, filled it, lit it. A quiet glow emanated from the lamp like a spirit. He took it up to bed with him, and watched it for some time, then read for a while by its unambitious gleam. Outside, the storm raged. He liked the lamp. But the truth is, he said to himself, that one cannot turn the clock back. What on earth am I playing at, lying here in the middle of nowhere, by a paraffin lamp? Playing, yet again?

As most of the buildings of Scratby Open Prison were only one story high, the storm raged safely over them, despite the site's exposed position. Len, playing a game of snooker, found himself wondering, somewhat to his surprise, about the fate of his little trees in their greenhouses. He enjoyed the howling of the wind: it added variety. Not everybody, however, seemed to appreciate the free show of the elements as much as he did; one or two who ought to have known better were looking rather jumpy, and one even admitted that nothing in the world frightened him as much as thunder and lightning. Len, in a helpful spirit, pointed out that one's chances of being struck by lightning were exceedingly remote. Others produced stories of rare coincidences and unlikely deaths. Len, as often, marveled at the superstition which surrounded him. It was astonishing.

The man who seemed most deeply disturbed was old Callander. Usually Callander kept himself to himself, spending his spare time alone reading, but the storm had upset him: he hung around the common room, evidently in search of reassuring company. Every time the thunder crashed, he started. Len watched him for some time: nobody spoke to him, naturally enough, as he had never bothered to speak to anybody. Most of the men regarded him with mingled awe and contempt: awe, for he was an educated man, a man of standing, once of authority; and contempt, for he had been weak, had blamed others at his trial, had groveled and wriggled. And could not mix, could not say the right nothing, find the right small change. He looked remote, broken, stunned. The men resented his withdrawal. They suspected that he considered himself as a member of a class apart. As, indeed, he was. So now, none of them would speak to him.

Len knew he would have to. He somewhat resented the duty: it would do him no good with his mates. But he had known Callander in his former, brighter days, had visited him in the luxury mansion which had proved part of his undoing, and he could not now let him twitch grayly in a corner. He had never much cared for him, as a man: he had always even in his days of success had a peculiar air of ingratiating superiority which had not been much Len's style. Nobody had liked him much: maybe it was an awareness of this that had made him willing to purchase friendship at the cost of bribery. Though he and old Jackson had been real friends, it seemed, as well as fellow conspirators. Jackson (now serving his five years in the South) had said at Callander's trial that any offers he had made to Callander had been made not with a desire to corrupt, but in a true spirit of friendship and goodwill. "He was my closest friend," Jackson had said, and then, looking at the colorless figure slumped in the dock, had added, as though to give substance to his evidence, "You may not be able to imagine it when you see him today, but when I first knew Tom, he was a wonderful man, a kind and lively and generous friend, a man of real stature. I looked up to Tom. I still do." Callander had wept in the dock. How could anyone ever see what two men see in one another? It is as obscure as the bonds of marriage, thought Len. Feeble Callander, and Giant Jackson. Maybe they had really liked each other, maybe the money had, as they claimed, been a secondary issue.

The house that Callander had got out of his corrupt friendship had been impressive. Worth a tidy sum. Architect-built, swimming pool, tennis court, sauna, the lot. Len wondered if he dared go across and ask what had happened to it. Why not? He finished the game, laid down his cue, crossed, took the next seat. Callander looked up from his paper, nodded.

"Evening, Len," he said. His voice sounded croaky from disuse.

"Not a very fine one," said Len, as another clap shook the room.

Callander nodded gravely, lowered his voice, leaned across to Len confidentially. "It's not the thunder I mind," he said. "But you know what the problem is, don't you?"

"What?" asked Len. He's gone dotty, he thought. Not surprising.

"It's those airplanes," he said. "They take them out specially, in this weather, you know. To test them."

"Surely not."

"Oh yes. Certainly they do. I have my information. *And*"—he leaned across still farther, portentously—"and just you tell me what would happen if one of them got struck by lightning, and came down *in these grounds?*"

Len laughed.

"What chance is there of that? It's a chance in ten million."

"It's a chance in ten million that I found myself in here. But here I am. No, you mark my words, they're fooling about up there—" He gestured nervously, with his pipe, toward the ceiling. "There'll be one of them down before the night is over, I've a feeling. And tell me, have you ever seen any notices in here about fire? What do we do, if there's a fire?"

"I can't see what you're worried about. There could hardly be a building easier to evacuate than this one. It's all on the ground floor, practically. Anyway, there won't *be* a fire."

"That's what you think."

"Yes, that is what I think. A chance in ten million."

"I suppose you think it was a chance in ten million that killed Max Friedmann, do you?"

Len stared at Tom Callander. He looked serious, even intent.

"Yes, I do. Something like that."

"You listen to me," said Callander. "You listen to me, and I'll tell you something very interesting. Keep it to yourself, though, won't you?"

Len nodded. What else could he do?

"Something has gone wrong," said Callander, "with the laws of chance." He said it with the portentous authority that such a statement required, and sat back, relighting his pipe with an air of doom and satisfaction.

He's as nutty as a fruitcake, thought Len.

Nevertheless, the idea was quite striking, and worth pursuit.

"How do you make that out?" he inquired, in a tone of careful neutrality.

Callander proceeded to tell him how he made it out. His reasons were confused but interesting. He had been reading, he said, Arthur Koestler's *The Roots of Coincidence*, which had shown him the light. His first suspicion had been roused by the remarkable number of disasters in his own immediate acquaintance: "You wouldn't believe," he said earnestly, "the number of people *known to me personally* who have suffered the most unexpected reverses." (Len could well believe it: if jail was an unexpected reverse, Jackson and Callander between them must have been directly responsible for landing a few of their friends there.) Then, he said, there was the question of inflation: that, too, was surely an unpredictable phenomenon, unrelated to any previous known monetary laws. Len tried to suggest that this was not quite so, that they had all simply been a little slow off the mark about inflation in the building and property business, but Callander would not accept this. He added, as further proof, an account of some bridge hands that he had held on the night before he received the warrant for his arrest: they too had defied all known laws. With this, Len, who was no bridge player, could not argue.

"And what do you think is the cause of this extraordinary situation?" Len asked, when the evidence had been presented.

Callander thought it might be something to do with nuclear waste, though he was not sure. "I'm not a physicist," he admitted, to Len's relief.

"Well, I find that very fascinating," Len said, rising to his feet. Callander looked better, more cheerful, for having imparted his anxiety.

And in bed, in the dark, he thought about it. It was obvious enough that old Tom was trying to find some way of explaining his own dramatic reversal which would exculpate him from all personal blame, and the idea was pretty ingenious. Indeed, it even had certain attractions. Len himself, like Anthony, had had a sense of late that things were going unnaturally, excessively wrong, and Max Friedmann's death, administered from so unconnected a source, with such arbitrariness, had puzzled him too. But it was madness to think that way. Utter madness. Poor old Tom had gone mad. Why, there were more murders a day still in Detroit than in the whole of the U.K. in a year, including Northern Ireland. Or something like that. Did that mean that something had gone wrong with the law of averages in Detroit? It was all rubbish.

Old Callander's house had had a patio with a marble floor, and a fountain, and around it in marble niches had stood busts of Roman emperors. That had not been Len's style. For all his energy, Len had never quite got around to acquiring a house. Or a wife to put in it. Just as well. He had been lucky, really. Let off lightly.

Maureen Kirby watched the storm from a window of the Hallam Tower Hotel in Sheffield. She was dining with her employer; they had just got back from a visit to Thirsk, and Derek had insisted that she should eat with him. They sat over their kidneys flambé and watched the steep hillsides and valleys laid bare by the flashes of the lightning. The white blocks arose on the distant slopes like marble statues, like the pillars of Stonehenge, like resurrected souls, standing palely, elegantly, lifting their heads against the noisy wrath of the elements. "It's a wonderful sight," said Derek. "Wonderful," agreed Maureen. The reclaimed hills, lit a lurid green, rose up to the sky's edge. The dark satanic smoke had gone forever, and Sheffield lay purified by the apocalyptic flames of a new Jerusalem. The white sisters stood, bearing witness to the shining urban dream of the sixties and early seventies. How forlornly they might stand there in the new darkness, who could say. They looked, now, wonderful.

It is a good thing Auntie Evie moved out last week, thought Maureen. Her roof will surely come down in this.

The storm died down, the bright flares vanished, and rain streamed down the huge plate-glass windows, obscuring the spectacular view. The whole dining room was sobered, hushed with admiration. Derek thought, I was lucky to have been born in such a time, in such a city, when there was still energy, when men could still build views and windows. Already windowless buildings were rearing themselves up, buildings with arrow slits like medieval fortresses, conserving heat, repelling invaders. The world has changed forever, thought Derek, and this is a moment of grace.

Alison tried to ring Anthony again in the morning, and again failed, though this time she received confirmation that the wires were, in fact, down. Kitty tried to persuade her to stay another day, but she was determined to go, though not at first sure how she would get there. There was a little branch line train that went from Northam to Blickley: perhaps she should try that? And ring Anthony from Blickley, in case the wires were back (she had no idea how long such a job might take), or take a bus or a taxi. I must go, she told Kitty: it's been so long since I saw Anthony, and he's been so good, looking after Molly. . . .

The Northam trains went from St. Pancras. As Victoria had appalled her the night before, so this morning the station appalled her. She told herself: it is the storm that has produced this vast quantity of garbage and newspaper and plastic bags, this sea of rubbish. But she had to pick her way. And she thought to herself: in Wallacia, it was clean. The streets were clean. There was no garbage. Cows' heads with hair on in the butchers', but no garbage.

She looked up, at the crazy Gothic façade, at the impressive iron arches. Victorian England had produced them. She had so loved England. A fear and sadness in tune with her own breathed out of the station's shifting population: old ladies with bags, a black man with a brush and bin, pallid girls in jeans, an Indian with a tea trolley, a big fat man with a carrier bag, they all looked around themselves shiftily, uneasily, eyeing abandoned packages, kicking dirty blowing plastic bags from their ankles, expecting explosions. It can't be like this, thought Alison: how can it have got to be like this? Who has so undermined, so terrified, so threatened and subdued us? How petty, how perky, how irrelevant, the few signs of improvement: the Shires Bar, the Buffet signs.

The train was less dispiriting than the station: Inter-City, new stock, coffee brought round, albeit in plastic cups. But Alison had the misfortune to be sitting opposite a garrulous South African, an elderly man with a Hemingway beard, who ignored all her icy indications of reserved hostility, and insisted on pointing out to her that although the train was new and the seats not uncomfortable, there were no waste-disposal bins, so that one had no option but to nurse one's plastic cup and paper plate for several hundred miles, or to throw them upon the floor. From this, he launched into an attack on the filth and porn of Soho, the wickedness of a musical called *Let My People Come*, which he had seen the night before, and the poor quality of council housing, particularly in the North of England, which they were by then approaching. Alison tried not to listen, tried to read her paper.

Nevertheless, she could not help but recognize that some of his remarks echoed her own reflections. But it was for her, an Englishwoman, to voice them, she felt, not for him, a foreigner. She toyed with the idea of commenting on his own country's political situation, but contented herself with remarking mildly that nobody had coerced him into going to see a pornographic musical, and that such musicals catered, as far as she could see, largely to the taste of tourists. "There was nothing to stop you going to the Royal Shakespeare instead, was there?" she said: to which he replied, "Shakespeare's been dead for hundreds of years, it's the here and now that interests me." She thought of moving to another seat, but instead kept silence. Why argue? And it was true that Shakespeare was dead.

The scenery outside the window altered, slowly, to the derelict Northern wastes and dump sites that nobody could now afford to landscape: was it true that the English had ransacked their riches for two centuries, had spent like lords, and were now bankrupt, living in the ruins of their own past grandiose excesses? Perhaps it was so. Fear constrained her. The spirit had gone out of the country, or so its hostile critics claimed: denunciations thundered from Uganda, from Russian exiles, from Australia, from men like this bearded South African. She did not respect their judgments, but she had to listen to them. The country was growing old. Like herself. The scars on the hillsides were the wrinkles around her own eyes: irremovable. How could one learn to grow old? Neither a country nor a person can stay young forever.

The North of England, in itself, frightened her. She was a Southerner, brought up in Hampshire. These perspectives alarmed her. She had tried to love them for Anthony's sake, but her nerve was failing her, ebbing away. The train made its way through a blackened cutting: the sheer stone slices on either side of her wept black, dank, perpetual tears. It emerged, in a wasteland—a canal, cinder-strewn patches of grass, slate-colored rubble. In a field full of heaps of bricks and rusted metal stood two dirty piebald ponies. To the right stood a strange stranded terrace of houses, oddly elevated, in the middle of nowhere, workmen's houses with blue doors and steep stone steps, built of gray stone, unbelievably gray. Who could have built such human habitations? Those great Victorians, perhaps. Anthony and Len Wincobank must see something in these slopes and angles, this man-made dereliction, that she could neither see nor feel for.

Though at times she suspected that even Anthony's enthusiasm was a little forced: how could anyone like Anthony possibly like so raw, so ugly, so foul a prospect? True, it was no longer as filthy as it had once been; the air was cleaner than it had been for a century. But the pits, the buildings, the slag. Len Wincobank was another matter: she could believe that his passion was genuine enough, for to him this wasteland had spelled not muck but money. Len had had energy, ambition, vision, like those Englishmen of the past, who had shaken an armed fist at the insults of lesser nations. He had also been a crook. It was all too complicated for her. She sighed. It was unkind of history, to force a lightweight person like herself, who had surely suffered enough, in personal terms, to think of these weighty matters.

The train arrived at Northam in the early afternoon. There was three quarters of an hour to wait before the first little diesel out to Blickley. She decided to leave the station, go to a bank, to a drugstore, stock up with bits and pieces, buy a present for Molly. (There had been no possible presents to purchase in Wallacia.) She tried to leave her suitcase at the Left Luggage place, but the man refused to accept it: because of bombs, he said. So she had to lug it with her. She did not know Northam well, but thought she remembered that there were shops near enough to the station entrance, but when she went out they had all disappeared. The developers had been at Northam since her last visit, and she was confronted by an enormous traffic circle, the beginning of an overpass, a road leading to a multistory car park, and an underpass. They had even pulled down the façade of the station: it had once been rather an imposing pile, but it had gone, and in its place were hardboard hoardings, advertisements for builders and contractors, huge flapping sheets of polyethelene, scaffolding. And no activity; nobody was doing any building. She could see some shops, far away, over the traffic circle, on the beginning of a shopping street that led into town: less than five minutes' walk, as the crow flies, and easy enough to manage, even with a suitcase. But although accessible to cars and crows, the street seemed quite impossible to approach for a pedestrian. Maybe if one plunged under the underpass one would come up somewhere near it? It was impossible to tell. She would have abandoned the project, and bought Molly a rubbish object from the station bookstall, but she needed some more Tampax, and had a feeling that it was Blickley's half day closing. The combination of obstacles was almost too much for her: she put her suitcase down, wondering if she dared leave it, then decided that if she left it in a corner the police would surely pick it up, even if a thief didn't, so she set off with it, down the unpromising concrete tunnel.

By the time she had struggled along for a few hundred yards, in the stink of exhaust fumes, shuffling through litter, walled in by high elephantine walls, deafened and sickened, she was feeling extremely cross with both Len and, alas, by association, Anthony. So this was what people complained about when they complained about the ruination of city centers. How right they were. It was monstrous, inhuman, ludicrous. It was just as well that the country had gone bankrupt, that property development had collapsed and that Len was in jail, and that fewer monstrous offenses of this nature could be perpetrated. This was no improvement: this was an environmental offense as bad as a slag heap. She would give Anthony a piece of her mind when she got home; she would tell him what she thought of his flirtation with these dangerous lunatics. Riverside walks, indeed! She must remember to ask him if their architects had considered the question of how the walkers were to reach the wonderful planning gain of a walk. They had probably made it inaccessible except to cars, sealed off from pedestrians at either end. Maybe, with any luck, one would be allowed to park one's car at one end of the walk, sprint down, and rush back before one got a parking ticket. If it ever got built at all.

The tunnel did not go on forever: it finally sloped upward, and Alison emerged. She could have wept. She was, in geographical terms, nearer the shops, but they were as inaccessible as ever, for the tunnel emerged on a kind of traffic island: she had four streams of traffic to cross, and a railing prevented her from stepping into the road at all. She put her suitcase down, and stared. She could backtrack, for several hundred yards, until the railings stopped; there were no traffic lights, but there was a gap, as though it had crossed somebody's mind that a person might want to cross the road. Had she been younger, and without a suitcase, she might have risked jumping over and making a dash for it, between cars, but that seemed out of the question. Her arm ached so much that she could hardly face the extra walk. She stood, and rested, staring at the distant promised land: there was a drugstore, she could see, and a bank. Was it worth it? She looked around her, back at the plastic-fronted station: to her right, on another traffic island, an isolated church reared up, abandoned, a strange relic, a survivor from another age, another world. Piety had left it there, but what congregation could now ever gather in it? How could it be approached? It seemed a meaningless and ironic gesture, to have left it there, solitary, anachronistic, a pointing finger of ignored reproach.

She would, she thought, climb over the railings. She was fortified in this resolve by the sight of a middle-aged workman calmly doing the same thing: he swung his leg over, waited for a pause in the traffic, lifted his hand confidently to stop the oncoming flow, and marched across. There was still some initiative, some free enterprise left in the land. She picked up her case, swung it over, balanced it on the perilously narrow verge, and was just about to follow it, when she saw a sight that made her pause.

It was a dog, an Alsatian dog, plodding down the middle of the four-lane road. Its nose was down, it ignored the cars, it walked resolutely on, nose low, tail low, with a plodding, determined, dedicated gait. And she could see that the whole of one side of the dog had been ripped away. She could see its red flesh. Its fur had been scooped and flayed backward: a wad of it hung rumpled. It must, she thought, be dying, but on it walked, without a glance to either side, contemptuous, indifferent. It was a wolf walking to its lair to die. Its red flank was the red flank of death. But where would it go? It had collided with a car, evidently: the cars now parted for it, too late. Where would it go? There was nothing but concrete, as far as the eye could see. There was no cave, no hole, no retreat, no lair. But it walked as though it had some purpose. It was going somewhere, if only to death. Maybe, thought Alison, it has a sense of some place to which it is walking, and it will walk until it drops and dies. The steppes, the forests, the mountains. On it went, out of her vision, padding on the hard surface of the hard road. No forest awaited it, no pond, no stream. Its fur had been scooped back like an old jumble sale coat. Rucked and rumpled, from the living side.

If the traffic will part for a dog, it will part for me, thought

Alison, illogically, and climbed over the railings, as strange a sight in her own way and as displaced as the dog: a well-dressed woman, in a well-cut coat and Italian shoes, forced like the dog to pursue her own ends in a hostile environment, swinging her shapely legs smartly over the rail, elegantly collecting herself.

The shops, fortunately, had what she wanted, and the return journey to the station seemed easier, as return journeys do. Nevertheless, her knees were trembling, as she collapsed into her seat in the small Pay Train. She could have well done without the concrete tunnel and the dying dog. Anxiety about Anthony and Molly gripped her: perhaps the storm had killed them, perhaps the roof had come off, perhaps they were dead. She would not know until she got there. Rigid, trembling, she sat there, willing the train to move, yet afraid of what might await her at the other end of the journey.

Anthony, meanwhile, was feeling good. He was helping two men from the village to clear the shattered elm from the road. They were all enjoying the emergency. The entire village had lost its electricity the night before, as Anthony learned when he walked down in the morning to buy paraffin for the lamp: most of the village was gathered on the same errand, thrilled by the disaster, comparing notes, discussing what they had been doing, precisely, when the lights went out over West Gonnersall. He learned at the post office that the council would send an electrician to cut him off, as his cable, drooped and festooned like a liana over the crashed elm and the courtyard, was alive, sparking, and dangerous: "We can cut you off all right," the man from the council promised, "but we can't promise when we'll put you back on again. You're the end of the line, at High Rook."

Anthony hacked and sawed. The men had a tractor; when they had severed the crown they would hitch it up and drag it to one side, and he would be able to get the car out again. The wood was living: it was a shame the tree was gone. In it were the skeletal remains of the nests of the rowdy stiff-legged rooks, which they patched up from year to year. Next year, they would have to find a new property. After centuries. "It was quite a landmark, that tree," said one of the men. But Anthony, looking around, could not but reflect on how well everything else had stood up to the violence of the elements. Elms are notoriously dangerous, and it had been an old tree. It was an interesting job, a good initiative test, moving the tree. He was feeling exceptionally well: country life was suiting him. And it reassured him, that all this landscape had stood up so well to the onslaughts. England. It would never shake to the roots, surely. An old tree might crash, but the rest endured. It was a fine morning: the clouds had blown away, the air was clear and blue and damp, fresh, unending. A glittering calm lay over the valley.

He wondered where Alison would be, if she were on her way, if she had tried to ring, and, if so, if she had guessed why there was no reply. He felt confident that all would be well. He was pleased with himself, pleased with his own total lack of anxiety about the absence of electricity and the prawns that must perish in the re-frigerator or be eaten in a final feast, pleased with how well he felt—perhaps all the abstinence had really been worthwhile. And he was pleased with his little ménage. Molly was happy, even Tim was happy, Anthony had learned to deal with them both. Tim, with a captive audience, had become more confiding, less garish, and therefore more interesting in his stories; Molly seemed content: she said from time to time that she was glad it was the holidays, glad not to be at school. The place suited her. The pace of life suited her. And it was beginning to suit Anthony, too. For the first time, he began to imagine that he could perhaps lead a real life away from London, a peaceful life with a peaceful rhythm. As he hacked, his mind turned vaguely toward projects—if there was any money left after the Riverside scheme's final stand, he would stay in Yorkshire, he would dig and grow his own vegetables, he would let people like Molly and Tim hang around year in, year out, he would struggle no more to do, he would learn to be—and if there wasn't any money left, if he had to sell High Rook, he would get a job, in a school. He would teach. Why not? A country school. A school for the handicapped. Vague idealistic notions drifted very pleasantly around his mind: fantasies of peace and virtue. He would opt out. Surely, after the unpleasant experiences he had suffered during his attempts to opt in, he would have a right to make such a decision? And anyway, what was there wrong in a quiet life, digging one's own garden, being pleasant to those that need pleasantness. It would not have suited him when he was younger, but whyever should one's life show any consistency?

The thought pleased him. The last dry splinter gave; the broken piece was loose. It took them some time to attach it to the tractor: Anthony had hoped that Jim Eaves and Michael Eyam would know how to do it, but of course they didn't, for the tree presented a unique problem. They had to apply their minds. Tim brought Molly out to watch, as they worked out which angle, where to drag it. "Where will the rooks go, next year?" said Tim. The tractor and chains creaked, the great branches heaved. Molly laughed. It was better than the television. It was a fascinating spectacle. A real event. They all enjoyed it.

Alison, in Blickley, found that there was only one bus a week to West Gonnersall, and that it went in three days' time. It would be possible, the man at the station told her, to get within two miles, by changing buses twice, but it would take over two hours. She asked if there was a taxi. Not strictly speaking, he said, but he had a number she could ring, if she wanted. He said this with the kind of Northern ill will that makes a sensitive stranger wilt. Alison, feeling rather ill, rang the number. An equally reluctant man answered, and said that he supposed he could drive her out to West Gonnersall. The prospect did not seem to arouse much enthusiasm in him.

Alison arrived just as the elm was being dragged into the courtyard: they had decided that the courtyard was the safest place to put it. Anthony rather enjoyed the idea of chopping it up, slowly, day by day, for firewood. His own small contribution to the energy crisis.

They were all so absorbed, in the gathering winter afternoon, with the job of freeing the tractor from the tree, that they did not at first notice Alison's arrival: she was unloading her case, and listening to her driver grumbling about having to reverse down the lane, when they spotted her. Anthony, covered in tractor grease and sawdust, rushed to embrace her, in a moment so long awaited. He put his arms around her, kissed her, held her. But she stood there, hardly returning his attentions. She was watching Molly. Molly was still watching the tractor: she turned around, saw Alison, smiled vaguely, then went on watching the tractor. Alison stood very stiff, inside Anthony's arm. She was pale, and icy cold. She said nothing.

"What is it, darling?" said Anthony, picking up her case, making toward the door, imagining disasters—as the memory of Jane, for whom he had not spared a thought for days, suddenly returned to him. Alison sighed, shook her head, dumbly followed him. She was struck dumb.

Over a cup of tea she revived slightly, gave her present to Molly, chatted to Molly, listened to the story of the storm and the tree. But she looked remote, unattached. Anthony, watching her, was anxious for her; she did not seem to hear what they said to her, gazed at Molly with a kind of suspicion, though as far as Anthony could see the child looked perfectly clean and well, rather better than usual in fact. "You must be tired," he said to her gently, every now and then, to excuse her silences and her heavy sighs.

"Oh yes, I'm tired," she said, and sighed again.

"Go and have a lie-down, till supper," said Anthony. "We'll look after everything. We'll cook you a nice supper on the paraffin stove. We're good at looking after ourselves. I bet you haven't had a proper meal all day. You go and lie down, we'll look after ourselves."

"I can see you will," said Alison, and rose to her feet, and went upstairs.

"I'll call you when supper's ready," said Anthony. She did not reply.

She must be tired out, said Anthony to himself, again, as he lit the lamps, inspected the central heating (which, despite electric thermostat and time switch, was still working), and tried to tidy up downstairs for her descent. It was not the homecoming he had expected, but perhaps homecomings are never what one hopes. But had he not noticed on her face a look of something like hostility? He could not be mistaken, he was never mistaken about these things. But he willed himself to be so. It had not been hostility, it had been fatigue.

She made an effort to be pleasant, over supper: to take an interest in their affairs. But she seemed still like a stranger from another world, and Molly appealed more often to Anthony or Tim for help or response over the meal than to her mother, sensing her mother's abstraction, Anthony guessed. She told them little about her stay in Krusograd, or about Jane, so Anthony, a polite man, felt compelled to make conversation, though he would have liked to stroke her and kiss her tired face. She had never looked so old, so taut: it frightened him. And he had never felt better. The irony was surely apparent to both. To be polite, he told her about life at the house, about the outings he had been on with Molly, and, more remotely, about Giles and the I.D. Company's affairs, about Len and Maureen, about the storm, but she did not seem to listen very closely. She said, Yes, No, Really, as politely as if she had been himself listening to Tim on that first evening. She's out of touch, he told himself, it's hard to get back into touch when one's been away, alone, for so long.

Lacking the television, Molly went to bed early: Alison let Tim take her. Anthony hoped that Tim would tactfully retire, but there was nowhere for him to retire to except a darkened bedroom, so the three of them sat together and listened to the radio news. As usual, it was all bad. The pound was sinking, more deaths in Northern Ireland, a new strike at Leyland, the storm damage throughout the country had destroyed millions of pounds' worth of property, the doctors were threatening to strike again over private beds, there would be a potato shortage, the Americans were still complaining about Concorde. It was so awful that Anthony began to find it quite funny, and when the final announcement was made, with equal solemnity, announcing the death of an eighty-eight-year-old former music hall star, he began to laugh, hoping to cheer Alison up with a few wisecracks about Britain's state. But she was in no mood for laughing; indeed, she actually said, "It's all very well for you to sit here laughing, Anthony, but what about the rest of the country?"

Anthony tried to defend himself, by saying that he was in no position to laugh either: he, like the nation, was living beyond his means, on borrowed time and borrowed money, and he, as the nation ought to be, was perfectly prepared to accept a lower standard of living, to live quietly, and work harder.

"You've got a completely artificial way of life," said Alison; and Tim, sensing trouble, withdrew, leaving Alison to speak. And she spoke. About the folly of Anthony's brand of escapism, about the dirt of St. Pancras Station, about the monstrous mess that the developers had made of Northam, about the wickedness of Len Wincobank and his like, and the naïve folly of Anthony's getting mixed up in such a money-grabbing immoral corrupt line of business. In part, it was like hearing Babs all over again, but more worrying, for before, Alison had always been so much on his side. She spoke of the state of the nation. "You wouldn't understand," she said. "When I was in Krusograd, I wanted so much to come home. But now I'm back, I don't like it. It's changed. It's not the same."

"You haven't been converted to Communism, have you?" he asked, perhaps too lightly. She shook her head. "No, it's not that. It was worse over there. They don't have bail, or proper trials, or Tampax, or anything civilized. But then it probably never was very nice there. And it used to be nice here."

"Oh, it's not so bad," said Anthony. "I know there are things wrong, but I like it here."

"Where?" said Alison. "Up the side of this hillside, in this nice seventeenth-century house? Oh yes, I grant you, it is quite nice up here. It wasn't here that I was talking about. I was talking about the news, and St. Pancras station. And what people like you have done to the face, to the very *face* of the country."

"It's not true," said Anthony. He did not want to argue, could not make himself do it. "There have been some good buildings built. You know there have. And clean air, and landscaping. It wasn't all so good in the past. You mustn't think that. You don't think that."

"I don't know what to think any more," said Alison forlornly. "I'm thoroughly confused."

"I'm sure we all are. There's nothing so wrong with that."

"And I'm so tired, too. I think I must go to bed, Anthony. I've not been feeling well." She rose to her feet. "But I do think it's a bit awful of you, Anthony, to knock other places down, and that nice Mr. Boot from the sweets factory, and drive them out, and put up all those great blocks, and then come and sit up here in this—this Ancient Monument, and say you like it. Of course you like it. But it just isn't consistent of you, is it?"

"I don't know, I'm sure a lot of developers are also escapists."

"Well, that just makes them all the worse." She picked up the coffee tray: he opened the door to the kitchen for her. "At least Len Wincobank was *consistent*, I suppose," she said, walking along the corridor. "He liked horrid places, built horrid places, and lived in one himself. And has ended up in one. That's consistency."

In the kitchen, she put down the tray on the table, and in the semidarkness stumbled over the little dog.

The little dog did not move. It was dead.

Anthony shone a light on it, but it was certainly dead. It had stiffened at last into the rusty corpse it had so long resembled.

Alison stood and stared at it. He told her where it had come from. "I'll bury it tomorrow," he said, covering it with a piece of old blanket, carrying it to the back door. "Molly will miss it, but I can't say I will. Much."

"Do you think I killed it, by kicking it like that?"

"No, of course not. It was on its last legs already when it got here, it's never been anything but half dead."

Alison did not tell Anthony about the dog she had seen on the road at Northam. She wondered if it too was by now dead.

In bed, where she had hoped she might thaw out a little and turn to him, she lay tense and rigid and trembling. He stroked her back, her face, her hair. "I'm not well," she kept repeating, and he could tell that she was not, but it was unlike her to say so, so often.

The next week was bad. Alison was so strange that he did not know how to deal with her; Molly grieved over the death of the dog, and refused to be comforted; it took six days to get the electricity and the television back; and Tim, offended by Alison's indifference to him, departed sourly, with many double-edged expressions of gratitude.

But it was Alison that worried him most. Indeed, he wondered if she were not perhaps suffering from a nervous breakdown, whatever that might be. As on her first evening she had sounded like Babs, so, over the days, she seemed to confuse him with her ex-husband, Donnell: she accused him of spoiling her career, of making her send Molly away to school when she would have been happier at home, of being careless with money. When he tried to defend himself, she would seem to listen, seem to agree, and then, a little later, begin again. Most of her accusations being so irrelevant, they did not worry him much, but there were two points on which she reached him. He did not like it when she called him an escapist, attacked him for his liking for the house, the garden, the view. She tried to spoil it for him, and he felt that it was all he had; the more she attacked it, the more he loved it, the more he wished to justify his need for it as a profound need rather than a passing one. She told him he was playing house in the country. He had thought this so often himself that he did not like to hear it from her.

The second direct hit was about Molly. She told him that he had deliberately stolen Molly's affections from her. And indeed, it did seem that Molly now turned to Anthony more than to her mother. "But I did it for you," he would say, to a drearily perplexed Alison. "No, you alienated her from me, after all those years, I gave myself to that child for all those years, and you walk in, you charm her, you take her from me. . . ."

"But you had to be away, for Jane's sake, what else could you do? I was only trying to help."

"I can't divide myself in two," Alison said, and from time to time repeated.

On the fifth day, he took Molly and Alison down to the pub, to see if a change of scene would cheer her up. It did not help much. Mrs. Bunney greeted Molly with enthusiasm, would have greeted Alison with like enthusiasm, but Alison took her drink with hardly a smile, and walked away, to sit in a corner, watching the game of darts. Anthony, leaning on the bar, chatting to make up for her taciturnity, glanced at her from time to time: there she sat, resolutely out of place, in her smart gray wool dress, with her smart shoes, and her smart ankles, and her expensive bag, alien, inassimilable, hopeless. It was all hopeless. The time was past, had never been, when he and Alison could have lived happily together ever after. It was not the death of love, for he still felt love for her. It was the hopelessness of time past that lay between them. The hopelessness of accident also had divided them. He glanced at Molly, ungainly, her nose running slightly in the indoor warmth, in her pleated check woolly skirt and her woolly jersey. Molly could not even sit tidily, let alone perform a tidy action. Her feet were always all over the place, she tripped others and tripped herself ten times a day. She dribbled when she drank. Even her head did not sit neatly on her neck. The contrast between the two of them was too poignant to contemplate. The one so perfectly, so delicately articulated, the other so inarticulate in every way. What was it for? A joke, a trial, a punishment? Too much had been asked of Alison. No wonder she sat like a tidy stone. And poor Jane, poor Jane, a great wash of sympathy for Jane, the first ever, overcame him, as he stood there and talked to Mrs. Bunney about the condition of the village call box; no wonder Jane had abstracted herself, confronted daily with so eloquent a vision of irredeemable injustice and irredeemable pain. That Alison, of all people, should have been called upon in this way; that Alison should have so denied herself; that she should so have undone and unknitted herself in all ways but one—it seemed too unkind to bear. And this unkindness she herself had borne for ten years now, and would forever.

It was true, of course, as he had read surreptitiously in a book on the handicapped child, during his first acquaintance with Alison, that it is not necessarily an advantage to the handicapped to be born into an advantaged family. There are some disabilities that money and privilege may lighten; others that it accentuates. Mrs. Lightfoot's fat boy, the child of her middle age, would run around the village with an I.Q. below 60, and nobody would much notice. Whereas one could hardly expect Jane and Alison not to notice Molly.

He wondered if it would be at all possible to persuade Alison to continue her career. Would anyone let her, now, after so long a gap? Perhaps he could put it to her that his own finances were so appalling and his prospects so poor that it was necessary that she should work again. She must do something, or she would get worse, he could see.

Christmas of that year was much the same as usual. Economically, the country was declared to be in acute decline, and yet, of course, record spending went on, accompanied by record moaning. There were no festive lights in Regent Street; some thought this a bad thing, some thought it a good thing, but most of the nation did not notice. (Most of the nation does not live in London, though this fact is not often mentioned by novelists and the national press.) Many households celebrated the event with their usual enthusiasm or lack of enthusiasm: children enjoyed themselves, mothers complained, and fathers sneaked off to pubs. Bitterly antagonistic families gathered together in order to quarrel bitterly, in the name of unity and love. Perhaps there was an attempt to economize on light, heat, and other forms of energy, but this seemed to have been counteracted by an ever-increasing expenditure on alcohol. Some families, of course, particularly those of the unemployed, suffered real hardship, or at least a real cutback in merrymaking, and the usual quota of poor feckless old folk died of cold. But, on average, most people in Britain were having a better time than they or their forebears would have had in the middle of the nineteen thirties. Indeed, immeasurably better. Naturally enough, few people thought about this at all. People have short memories. There was an unusually high sale of electric blankets in the pre-Christmas period, which sales analysts interpreted in different ways: as a fear of unheated bedrooms and nonelectric power cuts; as a fear of a very cold winter (the snails in the valley of the Po had been reported to be behaving oddly again); as a relatively cheap substitute for the more elaborate presents that otherwise might have been given, such as second cars, outboard motors, diamonds and fur coats, dishwashers, and so forth.

In the nineteen thirties there were no electric blankets, and only the rich or the ill thought of sleeping in heated bedrooms.

But, despite the national average, there were some for whom Christmas this year was an exceptional event. It was Len Wincobank's first Christmas in jail, and Kitty Friedmann's first without her husband. It was also Jane Murray's first Christmas in jail: her trial had been postponed until January, partly because the vanishing boyfriend had turned up and was willing to give evidence. It was Maureen Kirby's first Christmas without Len since she had first started to work for him, six years earlier. And it was Anthony Keating's first Christmas in the country.

It was not what he had imagined. On purchasing High Rook House, he had had visions of open fires, Christmas trees, snow, the Yule log, if not exactly of Mummers and carol singers. He got the snow, all right: it began to fall on Christmas Eve, a thin, fine powder, a white cold dust that settled everywhere, picking out the lines of the walls, the contours, the paths, and drifting icily across the top of the fell. But little else went to plan.

It was Anthony's first Christmas without Babs and the children. Like many a divorced, separated, or reluctant father, he had always before put in his time on this unholy festival: in the old days, he and Babs with one or two small children had gone up to his parents' in the Cathedral Close, but that ritual had lapsed with the birth of the third, and since then they had always had Christmas in London, with a visit from his parents for the New Year. Since his affair with Alison, he had always managed to spend either Christmas Eve or Boxing Day with her; this was the first year they had been together for the whole holiday. Though it was not so different from other times, except in the memories it evoked, for his normal life in Yorkshire was hardly marked by a strict work routine. Indeed, he was beginning to wonder whether, when the Riverside disaster sorted itself out, he would ever be able to work again. And, if so, what at.

He had to organize what there was of Christmas himself, for Alison remained worryingly listless and passive, it was uphill work, organizing presents, ordering a turkey (one had to do these things for Molly, he told himself), and remembering to provide Christmas boxes for people like the grossly underage paper boy. He thought of inviting Maureen over—to fill their rather empty house, and because she was the most cheering person he could think of—but when he rang her, she said thanks ever so, but she had to go to her mum's. He then thought of inviting some of his own children up: perhaps, he reasoned with himself, Babs would be glad to have one or two off her hands. So he rang them, in London, and made his offer. It was rejected. "No, thank *you*," said his eldest daughter, Mary, indignantly, "what on earth would I want to come up there for? You must be mad. I don't want to come up there miles from anywhere and *freeze*, thanks a lot."

"I just wanted to be helpful," said Anthony.

"Oh, we'll get on all right without you," said Mary, cuttingly. Or perhaps she meant to sound optimistic and cheerful. He spoke to Babs, to ask how everything was: she sounded as dotty as ever, and he could hear the noises of excitable living going on in the background—yelling, music, banging, doors slamming. Babs said she was fine, just a bit hectic, she had her new husband's parents coming to stay for Christmas and didn't know how on earth she was going to cope, she'd had a nice card from Anthony's mum, Peter had broken his leg on a school ski-party practice on a grass slope—"Not even in the real thing, damn it, and we don't get the deposit back, would you believe it?" said Babs, who was stirring (he could hear) something in a pan at her elbow at the same time. She just remembered to say, as she was about to ring off to put the stuff from the pan into the oven, that she'd had a phone call from the real estate agent to say he'd had an offer for the London house, and what should she do.

"What was the offer *for?*" asked Anthony, but Babs couldn't remember. The agent had tried to ring Anthony, but hadn't been able to get through. Why didn't Anthony ring him?

"Because it's after hours, there'll be no one there," said Anthony. "Do try to remember, Babs."

"Honestly, I haven't the faintest idea," said Babs, clattering around ostentatiously.

Irritation with Babs and all his family returned in its old strength. No wonder he hadn't been able to put up with that kind of thing.

"Well, you're a bloody fool not to remember," he yelled. "It's important to me, to get rid of that house. Why the hell couldn't you take a note of it?"

"Because I was busy, that's why," said Babs. "And thanks for the Christmas spirit." And she slammed the phone down.

He tried to ring the real estate agent, but he wasn't there. He could hardly believe that anyone actually wanted his old house, so little did he want it himself. But maybe it was a good omen. Maybe, if he sold the house, they would manage to sell the Riverside site too. And how could he have even momentarily doubted that a melancholic Alison was better than a euphoric Babs? At least Alison would never forget a message. He would go down to London, as soon as the holiday was over, and make some effort to sell the house, and bully Giles, and make his presence felt. He had had enough of keeping quiet, waiting for things to happen. He would go mad, if it went on much longer, or Alison would go mad, which at the moment seemed more likely.

Tim spent Christmas Eve in a pub in Drury Lane, with a crowd of actors (mostly out-of-work) and ballet dancers. He regaled those who would listen with stories about the extraordinary affairs of property magnate Anthony Keating, who had gone melancholy-mad and locked himself up in a great house in Yorkshire, where he ranted and tore his hair, like a latter-day Heathcliff.

Giles's ex-girlfriend Pamela spent Christmas Eve with her friends the Sinclair-Davieses, in Wiltshire. There were many other house guests, none of whom was quite sure who any of the others were, or to whom it was necessary to give presents, so many unallocated gifts drifted around the place, making their way from stranger to stranger, in an orgy of alcoholic exchange. Pamela ended up with a King Charles's spaniel, which was dead before Easter: she left it in her car one weekend in London by mistake, and by Monday morning it had expired.

Giles Peters spent it with his secretary, in bed. The intensity of speculation about the Riverside site had by now given him a very unpleasant skin disease, but his secretary was polite enough not to mention it, perhaps because she had noticed that Giles was temporarily unmarried, and had never been known to remain so for more than a year. The year was almost up. Also, she found Giles rather fascinating, spots and all, and for reasons other than his money. She was frightened of him, and sorry for him, at the same time, and the sensation of feeling sorry for so powerful a man gave her a quite peculiar sexual thrill.

Len Wincobank spent it watching a worthy group of left-wing actors performing a modern morality play about advertising, racism, and the unemployment problem. It made a change from the telly, but he found it inexpressibly naïve, and agreed with the general view that it was a scandal that they were offered that kind of crap, when they might have had a decent singer or a variety act.

Len was feeling rather bleak these days. He still had another six hundred days to go, at least, and there seemed little hope that Maureen would wait for him: he ought to have married her, he now realized, but there had somehow never been time. He was also oppressed by Tom Callander. Ever since his fateful overture of friendship on the night of the storm, Callander had persecuted him, boring his pants off with arguments about coincidence and ESP, treating him to the dullest and most embarrassing of confidences. He was as mad as a hatter, and Len often felt he ought to report him to the doc, but didn't. Nor did he like the train of thought that Callander's spineless evasions inspired in him. If Callander went to the lengths of going mad rather than think he had been justly convicted, what, thought Len, if I am doing the same? Len did not much like the company he was forced to keep.

Finally, he was haunted by the vision of Northam's derelict L.N.E.R. station. He had worked out in his head, for his memory was astonishing, who owned every foot of the land, who owned each inch of bordering land, and it did not seem to him possible that it would wait for him to get out. He felt that every speculator in the country must have his eye on the same site. How was it possible that nobody had thought of it till now? *Was* it possible that he, who knew Northam like the back of his hand (or so he had always claimed), had only just thought of it? And if he thought of it too much, and if that old drag Callander were right about ESP, might not his very thinking about it tip somebody the wink? He must put Northam station out of his mind, in case somebody read his mind. He felt like a research chemist, on the brink of some discovery at once so sensational and so simple that he feels scientists all over the world must get there first; or like a writer who invents a plot so spectacular that he cannot believe it has not been done before. A race against time, but what race could the disqualified Len now enter? For the first time he began to think that it might have been better to have gone down, gone bankrupt over the Porcaster deal. One can get out of bankruptcy quicker than out of jail.

These were Len Wincobank's thoughts as he watched a group

of actors trying to embody the Race Discrimination Act in a few meaningful tableaux. Poor sods, thought Len, sparing them too a thought, *they* can't have made much of a go of it, to find themselves in this sodding dump at Christmastime.

Maureen Kirby, who was by much the nicest of this perhaps unrepresentative group of British citizens, spent Christmas Eve, as she had told Anthony she would, with her mum, who still lived in Attercliffe, Sheffield. Maureen's mum was an old bag of the old style, with henna hair and a fag constantly stuck in the corner of her mouth: she had been a barmaid, but was now more or less retired, though she sometimes stood in for Enid at the Prince of Wales. She had a croaky voice, smoked forty a day at least, and spent most of her spare time laughing raucously about lung cancer and what a laugh it would be if she went and got it. She was not bad company, but limited. On Christmas Eve she assembled the entire family and crowded them into her tiny front room, where she gave everyone pork pies and tinned salmon sandwiches and trifle and kept the telly on all the time even though it was quite impossible, with twenty people in a room twelve feet by ten, for anyone to see it. But she liked a high noise level, and achieved it. Maureen was quite fond of her, and of our Dave and our Sid and our Mavis, and of their Darrens and Sharons and Marlenes, and the whole event was very undemanding: one could just sink into it and disappear, contributing, if one felt like it, a shout of mirth or even a song from time to time. But it really *was* overcrowded. Maureen had become accustomed, with Len, to better things and wider spaces. She felt at home, at home, but it certainly did provide a contrast with the carpeted expanses of the powder room in the Queen's Hotel, Leeds, or the Hallam Tower, Sheffield. No wonder, she thought, as she squeezed her way past ten bodies and along a crowded corridor to the much overused lav (Darren had piddled all over the floor *again*) that she had such a yen for large powder rooms. One couldn't even settle down in here for a minute without someone thumping on the door.

Kitty Friedmann also had a large family gathering, though of course she had more space to put them in. Her branch of the family had for years celebrated both Christian and Jewish festivals, indiscriminately, for she did not believe in letting an opportunity go to waste. But she was not feeling quite as cheerful as she managed to appear. The solicitors had been frightening her, with talk about death duties, and loans, and discrepancies in accounts. She could not understand a word of it, but knew it was not good news. Nor did she much like the look of Miriam. There was definitely something wrong with Miriam. She hardly ate a thing, and her collar bones stuck out shockingly. And the more Kitty pressed tempting little pieces of cake and biscuits on her, the more unpleasant Miriam got. Kitty could not understand it.

For Alison Murray, Christmas Eve was an ordeal. But then, it always had been, which was one of the reasons why it was so bad now, for it contained in it the grim recollections of an ever-receding chain of such celebrations. There must have been, in the dawn of time, she supposed, a few Christmases that she had enjoyed, but she could hardly recall them. Instead, she recalled the intense ill nature of her sister, Rosemary, who had grabbed her presents and quarreled over them and turned them into a misery; the year her grandfather had had a stroke and died in the bath; the year her aunt had been so miserable and cried all the time and said that nobody in the family ever paid her any attention all the year round, and did they think they could make up for it by asking her to stay for four days a year; the year Rosemary had invited her fiancé to stay, for the first time, and had been so extraordinarily unpleasant and self-satisfied and rude with him about Alison; the first year with Donnell, when Donnell had caused an outrage by going off to the pub with her father instead of sipping sherry at home, and they had both come back pissed; subsequent years with Donnell, trying to make things "proper" for Jane, crying herself into the tinsel, refusing to have Donnell's girl to stay for Christmas, finding Donnell in bed with the au pair; a long, long string of exacerbated failures. And now, when everything should be coming right, it was as bad as ever. How could one not think of Jane, in prison? And why was she herself behaving so appallingly badly to poor Anthony?

She did not know how to stop herself. She knew she was doing it, but she could not stop. She sat in a corner, her feet up in a large chair, alone, for Molly and Anthony had made their usual trip to the pub for juice and beer, and smoked, and worried. How could she so nag and sulk at him, and edge away from him in bed, when she had so longed to return, when she felt so tenderly toward him, with such love, such respect? And he put up with it with such patience. He had become so patient, the sight of it almost broke her heart. Mopping up Molly, bringing cups of tea to Alison in bed. I think I'll start running a rest home, he had begun to joke, from time to time. He was patient with her, as she had always been, until now, with Molly. Does that mean he loves me, or hates me, she wondered? She was too frightened to think about it much: her mind cut out, as at the approach of a sheer drop, whenever she tried. It was as though, in her rejection of Jane, she had wandered into some dangerous territory of the spirit, where any disaster might await her; what had seemed at the time logic, reason, proper dignity, had betrayed and undone her, had lost her, had left her at once hard and helpless and blind. She had hoped that her rejection of Jane (and she had meant it, had been momentarily relieved by it) would have released her for Molly, for Anthony, but bewilderingly the reverse seemed to have happened. There seemed to be nothing left for anyone. She did not really think that Anthony had stolen Molly from her: how could she think such a thing, for why could he have done it but through love of her? There is no end to the meanness of the spirit, to its jealousies.

She had had a card that morning, from her sister, Rosemary. Rosemary had virtuously invited their widowed mother for Christmas, and did not lose the opportunity of making her sense of superiority clear. Alison thought about Rosemary. Rosemary hated her, and she was not at all sure that she did not, by now, hate Rosemary in return. She hated Rosemary for the sheer unreason of having so resented her existence. What could I have done about existing? thought Alison. Could I have undone myself, unmade myself? As a child, when she had tried to gain Rosemary's affections, it had seemed to her bitterly unfair that she was so persistently and cruelly rejected; as a young woman, she had reasoned, had tried to understand, and had, in large measure, in the absorption of her own career, her own success, her baby, forgotten. Months had gone by during which she had not given Rosemary a thought. But then, with the birth of Molly, things had changed. The old nightmares returned; nightmares of confrontation, of answering back, dreams of slapping, kicking, screaming, from which she would wake shivering with guilt.

And so, then, she had tried to undo herself. She had stripped herself, leaving only her body, a clotheshorse, for that she could not relinquish. It had its own demands. I cannot split myself in two, she said nowadays, frequently. But she had done precisely that.

Maybe, but for Anthony's disasters, it would never have come to this. But for Jane's accident. But for Rosemary's lopped breast.

I don't know what to do, thought Alison, sitting there in the big chair in the old house, staring at the log fire. (Anthony had started to make a fire of an evening, with wood he chopped himself.) Why is it that when Anthony and Molly return, I won't be able to get up, to greet them, to be pleasant to them? I am held in some cold grip. Let me out, she prayed, let me go.

In the New Year, Jane Murray's trial was held. Her boyfriend, who had been picked up in Turkey and extradited to Wallacia, gave evidence. He said that Jane had been driving with proper care, and that the other car had seemed to swerve into their path. It was not very likely that he would say anything else, but in these days, Alison and Anthony felt, even so much was a relief. They had had fears, which neither had dared voice to the other, of a vindictive or brainwashed boy who would be quite willing to help to commit his ex-girlfriend to jail. Though she went to jail anyway. She was given a two-year sentence, a mandatory sentence, against which there was no appeal.

The consul wrote reassuringly to Alison, telling her that although there was no possibility of appeal, sentences were some-times reduced or canceled on compassionate grounds; the prosecutor had spoken to her in a kindly tone, he said, and had assured her and him that she would be well treated. "She still seems very subdued," wrote Clyde Barstow, "but that is hardly surpris-ing. She doesn't speak to me when I visit her, but I gather from the prison officers that she has asked for books from the library, and a grammar, and is trying to learn a little of the language. She looks in good health; the diet is not lavish, but it is perfectly adequate. Indeed, it is the kind of diet we would all be much healthier for, I imagine, though I daresay she finds it monotonous. I do assure you that I will visit her regularly, and pass on any requests she may make. She is young enough, and such an experience, terrible as it is, will not mark her for long, may one dare to hope."

Neither Alison nor Donnell went out for the trial. Alison did not want to, and Donnell could not obtain a visa. He had too many other visas in his passport, from hostile states.

The press did not give the outcome of the trial much cover-age. Alison's resolute avoidance of publicity had diminished their enthusiasm for Jane's cause. They tried to get a reaction from her, but she refused to speak on the telephone, and none of them had the energy to drive all the way up to West Gonnersall, on an off chance of a story. Now that they had had time to think, perhaps some of them had decided that a two-year jail sentence for fatal driving was not so shocking after all. One notoriously anti-Communist paper tried to stir up indignation over the way in which the trial had been conducted and Jane represented, but as they knew no facts, they could do little other than cast aspersions; and, as Clyde Barstow assured Alison, the trial had in fact been conducted with every appearance of fairness, Jane had never de-nied being the cause of the accident. She had simply maintained that it was not her fault, a remark she had refused to substantiate.

Anthony hoped that the outcome of the trial, predictably depressing though it was, would in some way cheer Alison up, or at least settle her thoughts. He still could not feel too sorry for Jane. Two years in prison was not the end of the world, and she might even make use of the time: she could probably learn more there than she would have done in her two years at art school. And, if she was the kind of person he thought she was, she would know how to get the last ounce of profit, sympathy, and publicity from her ordeal on her return. Alison might fight shy of the *Daily Express*, but Jane would show no such diffidence, if the *Daily Express* was still there on her release.

Alison, oddly, seemed not to be thinking much about Jane. She rarely spoke of her. She had been talking more about her sister, Rosemary, than about either Jane or Molly in the week since Christmas. "I don't see that I ever did her any *harm*," she would say, suddenly, over her breakfast. "After all, I did stop, didn't I?"

"Stop what?"

"Stop acting."

"What on earth has your acting got to do with that cow Rosemary?" said Anthony, on one of these occasions, to which she replied, "Well, it's all mixed up together, isn't it?"

As, of course, he supposed, it was. None of our decisions is taken in isolation—if decisions we can call them.

He had cause to think of this again when, in the second week of January, Alison's harping on Rosemary was followed by a telephone call from his mother, telling him that his father had had a stroke. She rang again, before he had packed his bags to drive down, to tell him that he had had another stroke and was dead. You needn't come, your brothers are coming, said his mother, bravely, over the phone. And indeed, his brothers rang him, one after the other, to confirm the ill news and their own intentions; both advised him that he need not bother to go. Which, of course, so advised, he resolved to do. It was so long since he had seen his mother or his brothers, and now he would never see his father alive again. He had told them nothing—of his heart attack or his business worries; as far as they knew, he was still wickedly prospering and gaily committing adultery. How could one possibly retrace one's steps so far? He felt he had no emotional capacity left to deal with this new shock, this new event. He had been bracing himself to go down to London, to have it out with Giles and Rory, to see his solicitor, to try to recapture the lost offer for the house which Babs had let slip through her fingers—in short, to get moving. But even that had presented problems, for he did not feel he ought to leave Alison and Molly alone together, in such isolation, with Alison so low. Perhaps he would not bother to visit his mother and attend his father's funeral after all. His father, dead or alive, was hardly his first priority.

He rang his mother again, to discuss the matter further. One brother was there already, the other on his way, so don't you bother, she said, as though their presence would obviate any need for his. At the tone of her voice, and the knowledge that she had informed him last of the family, a deep rage filled Anthony. "I won't set off now," he said, "but I'll be there in the morning," and he slammed down the phone, and went in search of Alison.

In the short journey from the phone to the kitchen, where Alison was making soup, he was assailed by a large black concrete vision of his two crowlike, pecking, dark-suited barrister brothers: she must have read it in his mind, for as he started to explain, incoherently, that he would have to go, she turned from the sink and the half-peeled onions, and put her arms around him, leaning on him in her damp apron. "Poor love, poor love," she said, as though all the sorrow had passed from her body to his, all the sorrow and all the anger. Her eyes were red from grief and onions, but she was smiling, as she released him.

"Don't you let them get you down," she said to him, sniffing, smiling. "You're a hundred times better than either of them. You tell them what's what, my love."

They agreed that she would stay alone. "I can't go with you, I'm not your wife," she said, when he asked her if she would rather accompany him.

"It's time we got married," said Anthony.

"Yes, it is, I suppose," said Alison. They smiled at one another.

He drove down to Crawford the next morning. It was not too far away: a hundred miles or so to the southeast. Around his mind, as he drove, walked three figures. His dead father was not among

them. His brother Paul, his brother Matthew, and his old friend
Giles walked round and round in his brain. What had he wanted to
prove to them, and why? His dead father he absolved. He had put
nothing over: he had been neutral, harmless, even helpful. He had
given him and Babs two hundred pounds, to marry on.

Two hundred pounds would not go far, these days.

Occasionally, Alison's sister, Rosemary, joined the sinister trio.
She was wearing, whenever he thought of her, a fluffy striped gray
and lemon-yellow jersey, which made her look fatter than she
was.

And we think we make decisions, choices.

He had not been to his parents' home for years. He had intended to go, often, but had never got around to it. Now he was
returning, the prodigal son, too late. He wondered what his father
had thought of his strange career. He would never know.

The cathedral, which dominated the small city, could be seen
from many miles away, for it was built on a hill, rising steeply out
of a flat plain. It was midafternoon as he approached, and the sky
was full of a peculiar radiance: the sun was shining from behind
banked clouds, glancing downward in those strange religious rays
beloved of landscape painters, and lighting the cathedral's roof and
spire with a golden light. It was a classic scene, and had indeed, in
such a light, been much painted, by Turner, by Prout, by Girtin,
and by innumerable lesser men. Under this shadow had Anthony
Keating been reared, in the circumference of these rays. Well, he
had got out. Had built his own cathedrals, bought his own close.
His pond, his brook, his trees, his rooks, his house. He would not
let them put him down. They had done well, his brothers: one a
prosperous Queen's Counsel on the northeastern circuit, the other
an equally prosperous junior in London. He had no wish whatsoever to see either of them ever again. But would, shortly, over tea.
He looked at himself in the driving mirror. How did he look?
Anxious, ill, hangdog, failed, or prosperous and thriving? On balance, he thought he looked rather well. The abstension from drink
and smoking, the fresh air had improved his appearance. I could at
least pass, he thought, for a man who is prospering.

When he set eyes on his brothers, over tea, he realized that he had had little cause to worry about his own appearance. Neither of them looked in enviable condition. Both of them had, astonishingly, grown fat, and both of them had grown exceedingly boring. Even his mother did not seem to be able to concentrate on their ponderous sentences. Poor judges, poor juries, poor bloody accused, thought Anthony, as he helped himself to another cup of tea. He recalled Len's remark that one of the worst trials of his own trial had been listening to the interminably monotonous delivery of the prosecuting counsel: bad enough being put away for four years, Len said, but to have to be bored to death for a fortnight as well, it was really too much. I kept falling asleep. They won't let you fall asleep in the dock, did you know that? You've got to stay awake and listen to everything being said fifty times over by fifty different people, and you're the only person there who knows the whole story already. I had a job propping my eyes open, I can tell you.

Anthony smiled, remembering Len, added milk to his tea. The thin china cups of childhood, how had they lasted so long? And there sat his mother, not much changed either.

He had always thought his mother beautiful; she was thin, dark, with a touch of the gypsy, which she liked to accentuate with bright scarves, dark dresses, wooden bangles. But since her heart operation ten years earlier, she had worn into an almost translucent thinness: her cheeks were softly hollowed, her legs and arms were so frail that one feared to knock against her, or to shake the floor she stood upon. There was no other word for it: she looked ethereal. Not quite flesh. She had been so near to death, so often, and there she sat, with her heart full of plastic, eating a scone, pertinacious, shadowy, skinnily alive. While his father lay dead. She seemed untroubled. He wondered if it was because her faith was great. She had been more of a Christian than his father, certainly, and had, she had said since her illness, no fear of death. She had always been good to Anthony, the little one. He wondered what she made of him now, how disappointed in him she had been, in the breakdown of his marriage, in the mess of his career. It reassured him, to see her restlessness at the dullness of his brothers' legal anecdotes. They looked bloated, both of them, he decided, particularly in comparison with his mother's frailty. And how self-absorbed they were. Almost as self-absorbed as himself.

As she cleared the tea things away, his mother said to him, in the kitchen, as he put down the silver tea pot, "Of course, the real problem is, I shall have to find somewhere else to live. We'd been expecting to look for somewhere, your father and I, when he retired, but now I shall have to look on my own. We must talk about it some time, Anthony. You ought to be able to advise me. You must know so much about that kind of thing, by now."

The thought of his mother being turned out of her house, like a farm laborer out of a tied cottage, was not very pleasant. They were doing something now about tied cottages: he doubted if anything would be done about boarding-school masters' widows.

"Now's a good time to buy," he said, feebly.

"The pension will be quite comfortable," his mother said, her back to him, sweeping crumbs off a plate into the wastebin. "You needn't worry about me, you know. And we had a little put away." She folded up the napkins, laid them in the drawer. "What a comfort it is to me," she said, with a distinct note of irony, "to see that you're all doing so very well."

In the early evening, just before evensong, Anthony went round to the cathedral next door. He was rather ashamed at the thought that his mother might have thought he was going to pray for his father, or whatever one did on such occasions, and almost started to explain to her that he was not—as he would certainly have done, offensively, punctiliously, in his adolescence. But it did not seem worth bothering. So he said, "I'm just slipping out to have a look at the old building, Mum," choosing a moment when neither of his brothers was listening. She nodded, unquestioning. Slipping into the cathedral, which she indeed used as a short cut on her way back from the shops down the hill, seemed to her a perfectly natural activity which required no explanation.

The cathedral was floodlit, in the cold January night. His mother had had all this view for free, laid on for her every night for the last fifteen years (there had been some talk of discontinuing the floodlighting, because of the energy crisis, but as yet nothing had been done). And now he had an uncomfortable feeling that she would end up in some dull little bungalow on the outskirts of Crawford—very handy it would be, with no stairs to strain her heart, easy to keep clean, he could hear all her justifications of it. Whereas if he was the tycoon he was supposed to be, he could buy her a nice little cottage in the Old Town. A nice little old cottage. With beams and uneven floors and windowboxes. A cottage of outstanding character and charm, amidst all her old clerical friends. He supposed that the church did do something for clergymen's widows, but it was doubtless not enough to buy a cottage of outstanding character, even in these slumping days.

He had seen the cathedral so often, from so early a date, that he found it impossible to see it as a whole, or as (which it was) a fine example, if not the finest, of eleventh- and twelfth-century architecture in Britain. The carving, the crocketed pinnacles, the great flying buttresses of the chapter house were and always had been too much for him. He paused, stared, then made his way to the door, and pushed through the heavy leathern flap. As a small boy, the leather flap had reminded him of bat wings and death; and did so now.

There was nobody in the dimly lit interior, as far as he could see. He wandered down the aisle, glancing into the Chapel of the Crucifix, where an old woman knelt, and up to the Choir of the Seraphs. The figures of stone, of heavenly beauty, seven centuries old, soared above him, pale gold. Impossible not to be moved, by the fact that men had made all this. For an illusion. And the whole

life of Crawford revolved around this ancient illusion: its snob-
beries, its social life, its power, its dismissals, its approvals.

Len Wincobank, Harry Hyams, Richard Seifert, they were
the modern builders. And London's Centre Point stood as empty as
Crawford Cathedral, an anachronism before it had even been occupied.

Anthony remembered expressing, recently, his admiration of
the Chrysler Building to an old friend. A friend from the old high-
minded days. And the friend had said, "But how can you admire
such buildings? They are built to the glory of commerce." It had
struck Anthony as such an extraordinarily quaint comment that he
had worried about it for days: which of them was off the rails?

Needless to say, the man who had uttered the comment had not
himself been a believer. Ozymandias, King of Kings. Look on my
works, ye mighty. Well, he hadn't been far wrong, Ozymandias,
he had lost his kingdom, perhaps, but at least part of his monument
remained. By their monuments ye shall know them. By the Pyra-
mids, the Parthenon, by Chartres and the Hancock Building, by St.
Pancras Station and the Eiffel Tower, by the Post Office Tower
and the World Trade Center. All large buildings express both piety
and pride: how could they not? Man's own achievement, they
point to the skies. His own gasometer had enmeshed the skies.
They witness at once man's sufficiency and his insufficiency.
When the I.D. Property Company's office block, Imperial House,
had been completed, a ceremony of piety had been held, on the
rooftop: the last stone was laid by the architect, and there had
been champagne—for the foreman, the architect, the three partners in greed, and the borough planner, who had accepted his glass
with a nervous laugh. The sun had beat down upon them, on the
high roof. On top of their own building, on top of the world. It
had been a curious thrill, an impious thrill. Whom had they celebrated up there? Themselves, or the mightier power which had
permitted them to play for a while?

The aisle was cold. A huge ironwork boiler, part of some
antiquated heating system, dispensed a little local warmth. An-

thony, pacing, reached the aisle which was lit from within, by a small light, to show the depth and richness of the carving. Roses and tendrils of stone curled, intricate, involuted, around a central boss. The undying rose. Craftsmanship, genius. He paused, walked on, watching the changing patterns in the wall. Diamonds, trefoils, toothing, a display of invention, fantasy, fancy—dedicated to what end? Of what had these men thought, as they nagged and whittled and chiseled at the solid blocks? Of the glory of God? It seemed somehow unlikely. Of employment, employer, wages, security of tenure. It had been a long job, the building of Crawford Cathedral. Imperial House had taken only two years. The craftsmen of Crawford had been secure for many decades in their work. Had they too asked for higher wages, boosted inflation by unreasonable demands? A historian would know. He paused again, by a strange little row of knobs of stone. They reminded him of something, some familiar pattern. He stared at them, intently, wondering, his mind empty, except for the fear of thinking about his father. There stood the row of little round knobs, each round but four-sided, each tapering into a funny little peak, as though the stone were not stone but some more liquid substance. What did they remind him of? Nipples? No, something softer, more clay-like. He touched one, felt its soft point. And suddenly it came to him: of course. They were like little icing decorations, little peaks, squeezed through a forcing bag and a rosette, onto a cake, a birthday cake, and with the realization, a whole scene, long forgotten, came back whole into his memory: his mother, in the kitchen where he had just half an hour ago left her, but younger, more than thirty years younger, himself a small child, and she skinny like a greyhound, her hair tied back in an orange and red scarf, cherry earrings in her ears, the bobbydazzler, the witch wife, and she had a cake on the table in front of her, his own birthday cake, and she was icing it, and he, a small boy, was watching her, and she was hardly aware of him, she was deep in her own thoughts, and sighing. The white icing squeezed through the little metal nozzle onto the pink cake, steadily, methodically, rose after rose, and his name was written on the middle of the cake, in darker pink. He had wanted pink, had asked for pink, had cried when his brothers told him pink was for girls, and his mother consoled him, and said—even her words came back to him—that pink was a good choice, because it was hard to get hold of anything for decorations, and she had half a bottle of cochineal. Crushed spiders, crushed spiders, his brothers had mocked, and she had driven them away, and he had stood there alone by the table, watching. It was wartime. Weeks of rationed sugar had gone into the icing. The cake was made from an angel food cake mix, sent by a friend in New York. And his mother sighed, as she iced the cake, because of the wartime, and the shortages, and because her husband was away, an army chaplain in the Middle East, and she was left with three boys, and the fear that the Germans would take their revenge and bomb the conspicuous cathedral, which no blackout, no camouflage could conceal. And yet who could leave its symbolic protection? In his memory, his mother sighed again, and spoke. She said, "I always made such lovely cakes, for your brothers. And look at this." He did not know what she could mean, he thought the cake beautiful, but she went on, "I'll make it up to you, my sweetie, when the war's over, I promise I will—" and he remembered that he had felt such a sense of being the chosen one, of being blessed and favored, with untold riches promised to him, and at the same time so bitter a flash of hitherto unexpected deprivation—who were his brothers, that they had had prewar cakes, prewar toys, cream, bananas, grapes, tomatoes? They had been born into the Land of Plenty. But he was the Chosen Son.

She had not made it up to him when the war was over. Instead, there had been years of whalemeat. And his father had come back, flapping his black gown like an old rook, like a frightening old crow. Interfering, intruding, pecking his way between Anthony and his mother, forming an evil Trinity with his brothers, forcing Anthony from the nest. God, families. He had not given his much thought for years. They had seemed not to matter. He had left, and made his own way, and done things that would displease them, on purpose to displease them, he had acquired a family of his own in Babs and the kids, a second family in Alison and Molly and Jane, the past was past, and well over. And yet. There it all was. A classic case. The spoiled youngest son, the jealous one, trying to outbid, failing, trying again. I have to win, thought Anthony, staring at the stone icing. In whatever terms I must win. I must choose the terms. They must be unmistakable.

Shivering, he began to make his way back. He could hear an echoing scuffling and a distant talking that preceded lonely evensong, that desolate ritual. He would not stay. He walked toward the leather door, and it came to him that he knew how it was that Alison felt, now, about Jane and Molly. She, Alison, fastidious, perfectionist, had been presented with the impossible. It is impossible in any sense to be a perfect parent, a perfect child. Jealousy, resentment, undying hatreds breed and thicken around an iced cake. Alison had aspired to perfection. How often had he himself heard people say to her, of her, "Oh, Alison is the perfect mother." But it was impossible. She was right, she could not divide herself in two. She could save Jane, or Molly, but not both. So she had committed herself to saving the one that could not be saved. No wonder poor Jane was embittered. To her, too, it had not been "made up." There was no way of making up to Jane. A great sorrow for her filled him. He was sorry that he had so disliked her. When she came home, he would make it up to her.

When he got back to the house, he found his family in a state of some excitement. On his account. It seemed that the phone had not stopped ringing since he had left for the cathedral. First Babs, then Giles Peters, then a man named Huntingdon, then his solicitor. There had been messages about houses, contracts, offers, but nobody had written them down: everyone would ring back. Action, thought Anthony to himself, feeling a familiar pulse beat and a strange lift, despite all, in his damaged heart tissue—and looked round his family and saw that they took it without question that he should have such calls, although they too were slightly fluttered by their frequency and urgency. This is my métier, he thought. His brothers did not think him a fraud: they took him on the terms he had created. He had convinced them.

He got on to Babs first: listened to condolences about his father, queries about his mother, inquired about Peter's broken leg, then was told that a firm offer of £35,000 had been made for the house in Notting Hill. It seemed too good to be true, but Babs said it was definite, and could he please come and sort it out, as soon as possible, after the funeral, before the funeral, before the buyer found somewhere he fancied more in this buyer's market, before more squatters broke in or more cats stank the place out. "I've been doing my best to keep an eye on it," said Babs, plaintively, "but I'm eight months gone, you know, and I'm absolutely whacked." Eight months gone: he had completely forgotten that Babs was pregnant. Good old Babs: the thought of her having another baby by another man filled him, to his own surprise, with an amused tenderness. He promised he would be down as soon as he could manage it. Perhaps I ought to come to your dad's funeral, said Babs, after all he did lend us two hundred quid when we really needed it, but it wouldn't look too good, would it? No, not really, said Anthony, thinking of the dean and the bishop and the choir boys and the clerics: a hugely pregnant Babs would hardly be appropriate. They both laughed. I'll see you soon, he said, and rang off, and rang Giles, who was engaged, then Rory, who gave him some garbled story about a proposed deal for the Riverside scheme: he was hedging so badly that Anthony got off the phone, tried his solicitor, who was also engaged, then got back to Giles.

Giles said: you must come down at once. We've had an offer, from the council.

Anthony was not as surprised as he might have been. How quickly one adjusts to a change of fortune. Ever since he had heard that Giles had been on the phone, Len Wincobank's words had been going through his head: Giles has got a trick or two up his sleeve, Len had said.

For an hour and a half, Giles tried to explain the complications of the council's offer, and Anthony tried to take it in. It sounded good, but there were drawbacks: of timing, principally. The sums involved were so complex that not even Giles and Rory, over days with the calculating machine, had been able to come up with anything like final figures, or so Giles said. Anthony, listening, felt himself returning to the ignorant, bewildered, hopeless confusion of his early days in the property business, but at least he knew better than to let Giles realize his confusion. He kept his end up. He had learned a thing or two, and one of the things he had learned was the art of bluffing, that most simple, useful of arts. He asked questions, stalled, mumbled. He even managed to imply, on the basis of his newfound confidence over the £35,000 for the house, that he had a trick or two up his own sleeve. He could hear Giles changing tack: the shift amused him. The conversation ended amiably: if it all pays off, said Giles, we'll celebrate. What if we only break even? said Anthony. Ah, Jesus, that'll be worth a celebration too, said Giles, with something like heartfelt sincerity. Anthony was pleased that he had been amiable enough to confess to strain. Perhaps he and Giles could get rid of their stretch of riverbank, and remain solvent, and remain friends after all, though at times it had seemed far, far too much to hope.

He returned from the hall telephone to the drawing room with a feeling of unseemly optimism. There sat his mother, knitting, his brothers watching an American detective series, like relicts from another, slower world. And his poor father, schoolmaster and clergyman, had slowed down to an eternal standstill. Anthony sat down and tried to calm down, and tried hard to fix his eyes politely upon the implausible antics of the television, but his own life seemed to him inexpressibly more romantic, more dramatic, than any fiction he had ever observed.

He had of course to stay on for the funeral, even at the risk of losing £35,000 or more; then he had to take the car back to Alison, at West Gonnersall, for she said she was lost without it. We'll get a second car, when I've made our fortune, he promised, on Leeds station, kissing her good-bye. Good luck, she said. You'll be all right for a few more days on your own, he asked her, and she nodded, and smiled, and said, "I like it, really, you know, I like the house. It's just that I haven't been able to tell you so." He thought it generous of her, to say she couldn't say.

On the train, he opened his daily paper and read about North Sea Oil, the black miracle, the Deus Ex Machina. It seemed that Britain might be saved at the last hour. What an unpredictable joke. Would the fortunes of the Imperial Delight Company take the same direction? That also would be a black joke. He wondered what kind of moral ought to be drawn from it. Sermons in stones. The words spoken over his father's coffin, by the bishop, had been far from original. There was not much help in those old quarters, these days. His mother had shocked him by remarking that the bishop was going dotty—"He's got a thing about exorcism, the poor old boy," she had whispered in his ear, over sherry and sandwiches. "I don't know what'll happen if he gets any worse, it's almost impossible to get rid of a bishop, you know."

A senile Britain, casting out its ghosts. Or a go-ahead Britain, with oil rig men toasting their mistresses in champagne in the pubs of Aberdeen. And himself where? A man of the past, the present, the future?

He had a lot to do in London. He had to see his solicitor about the house contract, he had to see Giles, he had to see his accountant, he had to see his doctor, he ought to go and see Babs, and have a look at the old house. But the train would get in too late for business: business would have to wait till the morning. So what, tonight? Giles, the house, Babs? He rang Giles from King's Cross, but there was no reply, nor was there from Rory, so he took a taxi, on impulse, to the old house that he and Babs had lived in for so long. They had bought it in 1966 for £10,000; it was now, even in a slump, worth nearly four times as much, it seemed. It had been uninhabited for months, ever since Anthony had been taken ill. Babs had said that on her last visit, it looked all right: she had got rid of one lot of squatters for him by the subtle method of suggesting to them a more convenient squat in a more lenient adjacent borough, where the authorities tried hard to accommodate the homeless, but who knows who might have moved in during the last twenty-four hours? The taxi slowed down outside the Victorian terrace: to his alarm, he thought he could see the flickering of a light in one of the front rooms. Perhaps it was only

Babs, or the house agent, or the prospective buyer, he told himself firmly, as he noisily inserted the key in the lock, and noisily made his way into the dark hall, hoping that any illicit intruder would have the grace to run off in terror at his approach. But he could, alas, unmistakably hear scuffling, in what had been the living room. Bravely, he shouted, "Hey, who's there?" but there was no reply, only a kind of strange moan, more disconcerting than any other response he could have imagined. It was dark: the electricity had of course been disconnected, and Anthony, now a nonsmoker, no longer carried lighter or matches. The thought of encountering an ill person in the blackness was not encouraging, but luckily a considerable amount of light fell from the street lamps into the house through the open door and the uncurtained windows, and as his eyes adjusted, he realized that he could see quite well. He pushed open the living room door. On the floor, in a heap of rags and newspapers, covered by an old coat, lay a person. The person was groaning, quietly and rhythmically. It was very cold. Two candles flickered. Bottles stood about.

"What is it, what's the matter?" said Anthony, approaching the heap, but he could tell already, from the peculiar quality of the groaning, which he had heard already several times in his life before. It was a woman in labor. Oh Christ, oh Christ, thought Anthony, and I bet the telephone's been cut off for months. The woman moaned. It did not sound too bad yet, not too near the time. He knelt down by her, picked up the candle, tried to see her. What kind of person, tramp, junkie, drop-out, simpleton? There was a bad smell, of spilled drink. He lifted the coat, looked at her face: she was young, a child, pale, spotty, sticky with sweat. She opened an eye at him: rolled drunkenly upward with pain, white, unseeing. "You hang on," he said, touching her damp cheek, "you just hang on, I'll get an ambulance." She moaned, and cried, No, no. "Why not?" he said. "You need to be in hospital."

"No, no," she shrieked, rolling her head from side to side. "No, no, no ambulance. Where's Bill?" she cried, and then began to groan again.

"Who's Bill?" asked Anthony, relieved that he was not alone

with his drama. "He went to get somebody," the girl said, and as she spoke, Anthony heard footsteps, fumbling up the stairs, into the hall, and there was Bill, filthy, tatty, grinning in the half light, pissed out of his mind, useless Bill, he had forgotten what he had gone out for, he collapsed on the floor, grabbed for an empty bottle, fell over, and passed out. That simplified the issue: Anthony went round to his ex-neighbor, rang the police, rang an ambulance, rang Babs, and went back, armed with a flashlight, to wait. His ex-neighbor, a graphics designer, came with him, and Anthony accepted from him the first cigarette he had smoked for months: down went the smoke into his lungs and up into his head, and it was so unpleasant and overpowering that he put it out after three inhalations. The girl groaned, and Bill revived, sat up, started to ramble on about the police and how they mustn't get him, but Anthony had taken an intense dislike to Bill and handed him over to the first copper that arrived. Bill was too far gone to resist, and allowed himself to be hauled off like a sandbag. Anthony felt no remorse at all; he hoped he got what was coming to him. But the girl, that was another matter. The ambulance was slower than the police, and while they waited the graphics designer tried to apologize for letting people into Anthony's house, which Anthony found excessively polite of him, and the girl managed, between moans, to mumble abuse about that bugger Bill, who had walked out on her, and how she never wanted to set eyes on the bleeder again. Anthony was glad that she was not a middle-class drop-out, eager to embark on a discussion of property rights and the rights of squatters; indeed, when she had established Anthony's identity, she even said she was sorry if she'd made a mess of his house, but it was that fucking cold out, and they'd been hosed out of their last squat, and anyway, look at the state she was in now, she really couldn't help it. Anthony found himself holding her hand. She hung on to it grimly, squeezing with astonishing force during contractions. Anthony and the graphics man found themselves timing the contractions, as each had done for their respective wives, and praying that the ambulance would get a move on. In the odd moment or two of lull, they exchanged news, unreal news, about the prospective buyer (architect, said the graphics man, whose wife was a friend of Babs), about property prices, about Anthony's heart and the graphics man's recent acute peritonitis. It struck them both, as they talked, that it was not really very surprising that young girls were reduced to having babies on other people's uncarpeted floors, for how could anyone without a wealthy father or an enormous income ever afford to buy a floor of his own, these days?

The ambulance took twenty minutes. It seemed a long time. Anthony could not disentangle his fingers from those of the girl, so he decided he had better go with her. Anyway, he wanted to have a proper look at her, in proper light. So he left his neighbor to lock up, and climbed into the ambulance with the girl, astonished, glancing at his watch, to see that it was only half past seven: it felt like midnight. The girl seemed to be getting calmer, rather than more agitated; perhaps it was partly fear that had been distressing her so much. She seemed resigned to ambulance, hospital, doctors. She was not, he guessed, even at the best of times a pretty girl: her skin was a terrible color, her features plain, and she was dressed, under the old army surplus coat, in a horrible collection of tat—a long shiny maroon skirt, a baggy flowered blouse, a gray cardigan, and green cardigan on top of that. She had no shoes, and was wearing brown knitted socks. No flower child this, though possibly a junkie. She smelt of drink, but her clothes were so stained that maybe Bill had spilled it on her. Under the grave eye of the ambulance man, Anthony tried to ask her if there was anyone she wanted him to get in touch with: mother, family, friends. She groaned at the thought. "Don't tell nobody," she said. "What's your name?" he asked her. "What's that to do with you," she said, automatically, still holding on to his hand convulsively. "I'll call and see how you are tomorrow," he said, as the ambulance drew up outside the hospital. "You know what hospitals are like, they'll never let me in now." Before they carried her off, he gave her a five-pound note and some silver, though he doubted that she would be able to hang on to it. He wondered where it would end up. "Good luck," he said, as she was carried off. She did not reply.

Good luck was the best she could ever hope for, he thought, and she wasn't likely to get much of that. Though perhaps it had been luck that he had found her, that Bill hadn't been left as solitary stoned midwife. The sooner his well-heeled architect buyer signed up and moved in the better. He would hardly appreciate a house littered with afterbirths or dead babies. Or not at £35,000.

Anthony took a taxi from the hospital to Babs's. He had never been to Babs's new place, or exchanged more than a civil nod with her new husband: all divorce and maintenance exchanges had been conducted on neutral territory. Babs lived in a large flat in Little Venice. It looked peculiarly inviting, from the outside, after his last grim visit: the lights glowed warm through striped curtains, and flowers grew in a windowbox, but he felt put in his place by the fact that he had to ring the doorbell—to ring at the door, for his own wife and children? But of course the enormous aproned Babs who opened the door with her hands full of cutlery was not his wife any more, she was the wife of this plump young man in a roll-necked pullover who was advancing after Babs along the corridor, and who was, yes, there he was, extending a hand. Anthony took it, shook it. "Hello," he said nervously. The young man smiled, also nervously, and Babs dropped a clump of spoons and forks: both Anthony and Stuart bent down to pick them up at once, and their heads knocked, and both apologized, each letting the other retrieve an object or two, straightening up, smiling again. "You'll have some supper, won't you?" said Babs, patting Anthony on the shoulder, then pottering off, calling behind her that she wanted to hear the story of the woman in labor immediately, but not until she'd put the rice on. Her place in the corridor was taken by Peter with his leg in plaster (not still, said Anthony, and was told with scorn that the cast would be on for another three weeks); by Stephen, on a skateboard, who looked as though determined to emulate his brother's misfortune; and finally, as they disentangled themselves, and battled their way past bicycles and cardboard boxes into the living room, they were joined by the youngest, Ruth, who threw herself hard at her father and spilled most of the tonic that Stuart had politely poured for him. Family life. They seemed very thick on the ground, his offspring, and the eldest was

missing, already back at college. Gone off early to get some peace
and quiet, Babs shouted through the kitchen door, as she held the
door open with one foot, stirred a panful of sauce with one hand,
and fed the cat with the other.

There was no time to protest about eating with the family, or
to feel uncomfortable about breaking bread and eating salt with
Stuart on Stuart's own territory. As ever in Babs's company, time
flew past, in a welter of gossip, some hard, some soft, and a spatter
of food and drink. Babs was feeling wonderful, she said, she was
due in three weeks, she was overweight and had high blood pressure but who cared, Anthony was looking wonderful, she said, had
never looked better—and Anthony, sneaking a glance at his reflec-
tion in the glass face of the kitchen clock while moving plates,
decided it was true. He did look exceptionally well. The drama of
Bill and the pregnant girl went down big, without too many inter-
ruptions from his audience, except a cry from Babs, who suddenly
remembered, out of the blue, that Giles had called, had left a
number, had said to ring after eight, had said he was expecting him
for the night—but you needn't go to Giles's, you can stay here,
said Babs, can't he, Stuart? Where, said Stuart, looking around
rather unhappily. Anthony assured Stuart that he would have to
go to Giles as arranged, and Babs said that was perhaps just as well,
they hadn't really got a spare room, and God knew where the
baby would sleep when it arrived. I'll leave home and go and live
with Anthony and Alison, shall I, said Ruth, sidling obsequiously
and treacherously over to Anthony and leaning heavily on him. He
put his arm around her. She was a tall girl, fourteen, grown up,
with feet sized 7 and long legs, and she was the only one of the
four that looked like him: his baby. And the only one whose
paternity, before birth, he had secretly doubted. Nature has random kindnesses: she was unmistakably his.

They talked of his father's funeral, of the sale of the old
house, of the problems of squatters, of property rights and the
property market, of inheritance, and wills, and money, and North
Sea Oil, of leaseholds and freeholds, of solicitors and stamp duty.
Anthony thought of his mother in a new bungalow, and the dirty

girl giving birth on a borrowed floor, and Babs and Stuart and all cramped into this overflowing flat, and of the new half-built council flats on the Riverside, and of Len in a Nissen hut, and of Alison and Molly alone in his spacious stately home. Babs inquired only once, in disparaging terms, about his new house: she was cross and dismissive, envious (reasonably so), so he placated her by describing his problems with the cesspool and the blocked drains and the tree roots, painting a black picture. And then, rising from a litter of cheese rinds, biscuits, crumbs, apple cores, orange peel, and nut shells, he went off to ring Giles.

Giles was high. It's all going to be all right, said Giles. Would you believe it? It's all right. Get a cab and come round here and then we've got to go to the theater. Whatever for, Anthony protested, it's too late, but Giles was insistent: they had to go and see a late-night one-man show presented by an old friend from the old days, Mike Morgan. You remember Mike, said Giles. We've got to go, I promised him we'd be there. Ring a cab and come round here. Where *are* you? asked Anthony, just in time, before Giles rang off: Giles was at his ex-mother-in-law's, in Regent's Park.

In the cab, Anthony remembered Mike Morgan. He had not thought of him for years, until recently, over the last eighteen months, his name had begun to appear more and more frequently in the papers. Mike Morgan, like Anthony, had had a peculiar career. He had, at university, been clown, wit, and intellectual, a working-class intellectual, son of a Welsh miner, grammar school boy from the green valley, clever, outrageous, camp, severe. He had also been extremely left-wing, even by university standards, but that, in view of his origins, had surprised nobody. A brilliant future was prophesied for him: talent spotters from London were on to him in his first year, agents were making offers and dangling contracts. "The funniest young man in Britain," the *Daily Express* had called him, after one revue that transferred for a short run to the Lyric, Hammersmith. But Mike Morgan, for reasons which he did not explain, decided that he did not want to be a funny man, but a straight actor, and had accepted a job with what is now the Royal Shakespeare Company. He was not a good straight actor, and not a good Shakespearean clown. He played bit parts, not well. Anthony, in the year or two before he forgot Mike Morgan's existence, saw him as a murderer in *Macbeth*, as Second Citizen in *Coriolanus*, and as a eunuch in *Antony and Cleopatra*; they were not roles that gave his talents scope, though he managed to impart an uneasy edge to the scenes in which he appeared. Perhaps for this reason, he did not flourish at Stratford, dragged on for another season or two, then disappeared. Looking back, with hindsight, Anthony wondered whether the problem with Mike's Shakespearean performances was that he exuded an ineradicable air of disapproval. Second Citizens are not supposed to disapprove of their betters.

After Stratford, Mike had disappeared from the scene. Anthony had assumed, without paying the matter much attention, that he had left the stage, discouraged, and turned his hand to something more obscure and more profitable. It seemed a waste of real talent, but Anthony was too busy to think about it much. They had been friends, but not close friends: Mike had no close friends. So no news of him filtered through into the general gossip. Until recently. At first Anthony, idly reading of the brilliant new American comic, assumed that it was some other Mike Morgan, until a photograph and an interview assured him that it was his very own, not American at all, but returned from several years in the States, with a one-man show that quickly became fashionable. So here was Anthony, in a cab on the way to see Giles and Giles's ex-mother-in-law, on their way to see Mike Morgan. It was all somewhat unexpected. It was rather sneaky of Mike, Anthony felt, to have returned so abruptly, after so long a silence. He did not much want to go and laugh at his jokes.

Giles's ex-mother-in-law was a shriveled, elegant woman, quite glazed with drink. She managed to join up with Anthony's hand, to shake it, but her pale china blue eyes rolled and wandered as crazily and with as little focus as the eyes of the girl in labor. She was wearing a pale blue silk jersey dress. Before he could say no, she had poured Anthony an enormous tumblerful of vodka martini: her manual control seemed restricted entirely to the area of the bottles and ice bucket, for she then started to grope quite helplessly for a cigarette in her bag, and Giles had to abstract one for her, and light it, and return it to her tremulous fingers. In comparison, Giles seemed quite sober. Anthony held his glass of icy gray venomous spirit, and wondered what to do with it. The sight of Mrs. Chalfont made him feel that he might as well down it and drop dead on the spot, as continue to strive, against the odds, to make some sense of life. But he resisted. Instead, he admired the floral decorations, which were, indeed, superb. Mrs. Chalfont agreed. "Yes," she said, "they *are* so pretty, aren't they?" She waved her cigarette at the great vases of lilies and narcissi and fluttery pink orchidlike butterfly blooms, so strikingly out of season. "I get them from . . . from . . ." and her voice trailed away, as though she had forgotten not merely the name of the florist, but also that she was speaking at all.

Giles's line with her was to ignore her. He made no conversational moves toward her during the entire evening—she was to accompany them to the theater—but contented himself with lighting her cigarettes, guiding her toward doors, dressing her in her coat, unwrapping her from her coat, and helping her into cabs. Meanwhile, over the drink, which grew warm in Anthony's hand, and in the cab on the way to the theater, Giles described the deal, elaborated on it. He was very pleased with himself. But it had been a near thing, Anthony could tell. Anthony could not quite believe the good news. Could it be true, that the anxiety was over, that he had been given a reprieve, and time to think again? He had become so accustomed to living with self-reproach that he did not think he would adjust very easily to self-congratulation. The denouement seemed so uncanny, so undeserved. Such a bad plot. In the cab, listening to Giles, Anthony realized how near he had come to accepting a scenario which had ended in defeat. Defeat would have been more artistic. With astonishment, watching the London streets pass, the traffic, the lurid posters of Charing Cross Road, he thought: I should feel relieved, but in some way I feel obscurely cheated.

He had no time to dwell on this odd response for long, as

they arrived at the theater and were ushered into the small, intimate, modern auditorium. It was a very long time since Anthony had been to the theater, or indeed to any public entertainment, and he found himself gazing like a stranger at the once familiar scene. For here were all the people he had gone into property to avoid: all the smart alecs, all the bitter trendies, all the snipers and laughers and jokers, all the people who spent their time laughing at what they had no hope of understanding, all the desperate comfortable lazy liberal folk. They were his friends. He was one of them. He recognized many faces: people waved at him, waved their programs at him, grinned and mouthed across rows at him. Some were dressed smartly, some were shabby, some had new wives and some had new lovers, but there they all were. Why did they fill him with such distaste? Was it simply that he had been out of touch for so long, alone for so long, with no companions but Molly, and Mrs. Bunney and Ned Buckton in the pub, and the renunciatory Alison? A countryman, shocked by town manners. Mrs. Chalfont sat upright, in a glazed silence, staring from right to left blindly. What did she see, with those blank eyes? He hoped she had found the oblivion she sought. It would be frightening, if she came around from the anesthesia, in the middle of the show, before she was safely home in her bed. He tried to look at the program, to concentrate on the summary of Mike's career, but could not help looking around at the menagerie of people: there was Chloe Vickers, waving at Giles, there was Hattie Baines, his first girlfriend, there was Gino Vignoli, there was his old director of programs, there was Austin Jones, there was Tim, and there, all the way from Oxfordshire, was Linton Hancox, classicist and purist and scholar and poet, Linton Hancox of all people. How strange they all looked. The theater-going élite of Britain. The scene seemed set for a Restoration comedy or a Weimar Republic drag show. He wondered what Mike Morgan would pull out of the magician's hat. And yet one could not say that each of these people, each individual, was in any way shocking, distasteful, unpleasant. They were not even overprivileged. There were the rich, it is true, like Chloe and Giles and Mrs. Chalfont; but there were also upstarts like Austin Jones, and those who were nothing at all, like poor Tim. Britain in the midseventies. Looking around him, Anthony felt in his heart a small confidence. I think, thought Anthony, I think I can really do without all this. I think I can manage on my own.

People should not get together. They are more attractive in smaller groups. Collectivity corrupts. Man is a social animal, but only at a great risk.

Mike Morgan, when he appeared upon the stage to enthusiastic applause, was very much alone. He had changed, aged, of course, but there was still that same white rat-clown face, impassive, cold, disdainful. The audience liked it. They liked it when he began to berate them for being what they were: drunk, idle, affluent, capitalist, élitist. They liked it when he told black jokes about blacks, queer jokes about queers, Irish jokes about the Irish, Arab jokes about the Arabs, then mocked them for laughing. He sang some songs, accompanying himself on the piano: the melodies were not very good, indeed Anthony thought one of them bore a sinister resemblance to an early work of his own, which was not much to its credit, but the lyrics were, he had to admit, brilliant, and the delivery electric. All in all, Anthony thought it a brilliant show. But it was not funny. So why was everybody laughing? Even Mrs. Chalfont was laughing. Anthony could not see the joke.

Mike Morgan spotted the fact that Anthony Keating could not see the joke, for at the end of the second part of the show, after he had used up his formal material, he came down to the footlights, squatted down, and said to Anthony, who was in the third row, "Well, Keating, aren't you enjoying yourself?" Anthony did not much like participatory theater, but he was not particularly afraid of it either, so he replied politely that he was enjoying himself, in his own manner, but was not much amused. This amused Mike Morgan no end. "Ha ha," he shrieked, leaping from his haunches to his feet in one athletic well-trained actorly movement, "Anthony Keating, like Queen Victoria, is not amused." Then he went into a strange little dance, with which from time to time he would punctuate his patter, then rounded on

Anthony, and shrieked again, "Who said that property is theft? Any answers?" He threw out his arms, embracing the audience, his mad white face gleaming. "Who said it? Come on, dumbbells. Who? What's the matter with you all? Left your dictionaries of quotations on top of the pile of French grammars in the *loo*, have you?"

Anthony knew perfectly well who had said that property was theft, and he was sure that some of the audience knew also, for they were not all stupid, but nobody replied. Mike Morgan continued to extemporize upon the theme. He quoted Locke, Hobbes, Marx. The man is mad, thought Anthony. Mike launched into Engels on the origin of the family and private property. The audience began to get restive. Feet shuffled, people coughed, one or two crept out. Anthony wondered if this was the way the show always ended, with some boring intellectual diatribe that finally drove the cattle, ashamed, from their stalls, full, one supposed, of a nasty self-recognition. Or was it a new departure, a new twist, leading up to a new punch line? After a few minutes it became clear that Mike Morgan was going to go on forever, unless stopped. One could not but admire such frenetic energy, coupled with such a good memory. Quotation after quotation poured forth, as in some final examination in political theory (had Mike read PPE at Oxford?—Anthony could not remember), and one by one the audience left, beginning to laugh again, comfortably, as they got the joke, as they received dismissal from their entertainer's increasingly hostile, averted manner, manipulated willingly into release, docile, responding to his tone and gesture, ceasing to listen to his frenzied outpourings—chatting, milling, thronging, determined not to be embarrassed, determined to have enjoyed themselves, they made their way into the dark streets, to waiting cars, to taxis, for the last tubes and buses had long ago departed. Technically, it was a bravura performance. Such perfect control of the audience, such timing of hostilities, such embodiment of attitudes. Anthony was much impressed.

Anthony sat it out. So did Giles and Mrs. Chalfont. Mrs. Chalfont had fallen asleep, fortunately, and was leaning on Giles's solid shoulder, snoring slightly. Her poor neck, at an uncomfortable angle, was thin and stretched. The tendons stood up in it. Mike continued his harangue until there were but the three of them left, isled, marooned, amongst the empty red seats, the red toothless gums of the theater. Then he collapsed, in midsentence. Theatrically, gracefully, he went limp and flopped to the floor. Anthony and Giles clapped. The sound of their clapping echoed thinly in the empty auditorium, like the last plaudits at the end of the world. It had been a good show.

"Well?" said Mike Morgan, sitting there, cross-legged, staring at his old friends. "Who was it that said that property is theft? I'm damned if I can remember. It went straight out of my head."

"Pierre Proudhon, of course," said Anthony.

"*Of course*," Mike echoed, with irony. "Of course. Well, one can't be expected to remember everything."

"Your brain seems pretty well stacked," said Giles.

"You nicked my tune," said Anthony. "That's theft, too. I'll report you to the Performing Rights Society."

"Your tunes were never much good," said Mike. "Which was the one I nicked? *My* tunes aren't much good either, I admit. Pap, that's what they are. But they serve, they serve."

Anthony climbed over the footlights, onto the stage, strummed the tune that Mike had played: Mike acknowledged the theft. They played a few more from the old days. Giles went off to put Mrs. Chalfont in a taxi. "Not that I care about theft," said Anthony. "I always thought it was something of a miracle that anybody recognized the concept of property in artistic copyright. 'The duration of labor is the just measure of value.' Who said that?"

"Pierre Proudhon?"

"You've got it in one. So how can one assess the value of a work of art? By the time it took to make it? By the years of training?"

"I work for my living," said Mike Morgan.

"You certainly do," agreed Anthony.

"I put in the hours," said Mike.

"Yes," said Anthony, for it was true.

"Whereas you and Giles, you sit around and exploit," said Mike.

Giles had by this time returned; he and Anthony looked at one another, and both laughed. Sitting around and exploiting did not seem to them an adequate explanation of the last few months, even of the last few years of intense sweat, anxiety, speculation, and terror. Now they could afford to laugh. Three months ago, thought Anthony, this encounter would have driven me mad. As it was, he proposed that they should go off and have a drink somewhere, as he could see a stage manager boy and a charwoman hanging around waiting to lock up and clean up, and Anthony Keating was ever considerate of the labor of others. The others agreed to move; Anthony wished the stage manager boy and the charwoman good night, but could not help noticing that Mike Morgan ignored the latter and dismissed the former with a reprimand and a prima donna flounce.

They ended up in a drinking club off Old Compton Street. They continued to talk, of this and that, old friends, politics, the state of Britain. Mike Morgan sketched in a little of his missing years, but they had guessed at them already: disillusion in England, escape to America, involvement in radical politics of the late sixties, disillusion with the same, return. "And where are you living, now?" asked Anthony.

"I live in a bed-sit in Kilburn," said Mike, grinning, baring his sharp teeth. "I don't approve of home ownership."

It was probably true. And if so, it showed at least consistency. But then, it was easy enough for a single man to live in a bed-sit, reflected Anthony. And Mike was very much the single man. He exuded solitude. It is the family unit, as Engels said, that inspires us with a need for a home of our own. Mike, Anthony guessed, was a sadist: his audience were all masochists. He had found a harmless enough way of exploiting for gain his own psychological bent. A solitary sadist with strong homosexual tendencies, probably unable to satisfy himself because of a mixture of narcissism and puritanism. He was better off employed amusing the idle theater-goers of

London than seeking to fulfill himself more privately. Better to seek to destroy the willing indestructible public than the willing or unwilling private person. And he was a professional: one could not but admire the skill. But, thought Anthony, finally, I am not a masochist, and I do not like to be chastised by a bent entertainer who is no better than myself and who, moreover, forgets the name of Pierre Proudhon. What is it, in the English, that makes them take it so meekly?

He asked the question of Mike. Mike replied at length, and with much feeling. The English are guilty, they are self-denigrating, they are masochistic, they love to be kicked, he said, because of their deeply engrained inalienable disgusting *certainty* of superiority. They are island xenophobes, shopkeepers, petty investors, tax evaders, proud of their sillinesses and their mistakes and their inconsistencies, and they love to be kicked because they know it does not hurt. It does not hurt, it tickles. They are rich bitches who like to be degraded.

Why then connive with them, asked Anthony, unkindly. And it was indeed an unkind question, for Mike Morgan looked at him with his hard, sad, insincere eyes, and said, "Because I can't resist it. I like to get the boot in. It amuses me. All right, I'm a victim too. A jester. What else could I be? They pay me to kick them. It's better than working in a brothel."

"*I* think," said Giles, rousing himself from his apparent stupor, "that the English are changing. I don't think they're going to go on finding life quite so funny. Because they've lost their superiority. I think you're the end of a line, Mike." He stubbed out a cigarette, to make his point. "Your act's out of date, Mike," he said. "They'll turn on you in the end. Or if they don't, they ought to."

Mike was offended, but too committed to the seriousness of the discussion to express personal pique, though it flooded like a dark stain into his eyes and face: how childish and vain we all are, thought Anthony, sadly.

"All right," said Mike, "so I'm out of date. So I've got an out-of-date audience. (I have *got* an audience, you noted?) So what next. What do you phophesy, Giles?"

A silence fell around the small round table, over the overflowing ash tray, descending like a pall on the threadbare carpet, settling with a faint sigh in the stained and emptied glasses. Anthony knew, in the silence, that Mike had worked in a brothel, that he had not been employing a figure of speech. To what an end we have come. It seemed indeed the end of the act. To the question, what next, nobody answered. But it seemed to Anthony, as he sat there listening to the silence in the room, and the creaking sounds of London, that there would be an answer, for the nation if not for himself, and he saw, as he sat there, some apparition: of this great and puissant nation, a country lying there surrounded by the gray seas, the land green and gray, well worn, long inhabited, not in chains, not in thrall, but a land passing through some strange metamorphosis, through the intense creative lethargy of profound self-contemplation, not idle, not defeated, but waiting still, assembling defenses against the noxious oily tides of fatigue and contempt that washed insistently against her shores. An aerial view, a helicopter view of this precious isle came into his head, and he saw the seas washing forever, or more or less forever, around the white and yellow and pink and gray sands and pebbles of the beaches, this semiprecious stone set in a leaden sea, our heritage, the miles of coast, as yet unenclosed, not yet roped and staked and parceled. What next? The roping, the selling, the plundering? The view shimmered, fragmented, dissolved like a cloud. The silence lasted.

It was broken by a gunshot in the street below. Because it was London and not New York or Detroit, they assumed it was the backfiring of a car rather than a gunshot, and did not much react. They agreed that the night was over, that it was time to go to bed. Mike Morgan's question remained unanswered. He went home to Kilburn in a cab.

In bed, at Giles's flat, Anthony thought of the girl in labor, and wondered whether she had produced a baby or not, and what would happen to her and it. Babs's new baby would be the same age, but with better prospects. Children of the midseventies. He was utterly unable to imagine their future. There was a future, but he could not force it to take shape in his mind. Shapes drifted, insubstantial, unconvincing. He knew that he had no reason, other than a congenital personal optimism, as arbitrary as Mike Morgan's spleen, for his posture of faith. Maybe there was no future. He fell asleep.

Linton Hancox, driving back from the theater to his wife and his cottage in Oxfordshire, after spending an hour in the bed of the wife of a colleague in Oxford en route, wondered what had happened to Mike Morgan in the intervening years since they had last met, and what was happening to his old friend Anthony Keating. He had glimpsed Anthony across the auditorium, and waved. Anthony looked gray and haggard and determined. His hair was graying. Mike had looked white and mad. And I am beginning to put on weight, thought Linton.

Linton's wife, Harriet, was having an affair with a local farmer. His own relationship with Harriet had become acrimonious beyond belief. Linton, in revenge, was having an affair with the wife of the bursar of the college: a double-edged revenge, for he did not like the bursar. The bursar was a nuclear physicist. Harriet's farmer was a stupid, slow, philistine boor of a man whose favorite diversions according to Harriet were fucking Harriet, playing darts, and watching mindless endless television serials like *Coronation Street*, *Crossroads*, and *Upstairs, Downstairs*. He thought they were all very true to life, Harriet reported, giggling to herself mindlessly at her own memories. The bursar's wife was a bad-tempered bitch in public, constantly lamenting her ruined career as a librarian, but in bed she was humble and amorous.

Oh Jesus, thought Linton, as the white road unrolled before him, how have we come to this? What has happened to all of us? It should have been so different.

He tried to summon up the good people that he knew, for he was desperate. But he could think of none. He no longer knew any good people. Mike Morgan was right: the people of Britain are selfish, mercenary, greedy, corrupt. It crossed his mind to drive his car hard into a tree. Harriet could have the insurance. The ancients considered suicide a noble act; or perhaps not noble: sensible, rather. One of his undergraduates had killed himself recently. Everybody had remarked piously that it was a tragic waste but Linton did not agree. He thought that the undergraduate, who had been suffering from what other dons described as "girl trouble," had taken a wise short cut. Much better to die young than to struggle through the process of aging and disillusion. Better to die young and beautiful, than to die fat and depressed. He thought of Antigone, descending into her living tomb, her bridal bower. The three fates.

On her the gray fates laid hard hands.

Choose death, before it chooses you. They were all dead, all the young men and maidens, Antigone, Hector, Penelope, Cressida, Achilles, Orestes, Clytemnestra. The faithful and the faithless, all dead. And what difference did it make? The solitary goose of classical learning flapped its scraggy wings and squawked. The bursar's wife slept soundly in a warm damp bed, gathering strength for the hectoring of the morrow. Harriet Hancox dreamed of owls and goats. Mike Morgan sat awake in a bed-sitter in Kilburn and tormented himself. Anthony Keating dreamed of balance sheets and bank statements.

A thin flattened stoat ran across the road in the headlights, gaining the safety of the far hedgerow.

Would it matter, at all, if the new dark ages rolled over the face of Europe? Linton Hancox was committed to believing that it was of importance to keep the tradition of scholarship alive. His own son, committed to admiring his father, could read Thucydides, Herodotus, Euripides, with apparent pleasure. But it might be true that he read Greek because he did not admire his father: it might be true that Linton tried to preserve the life of the classics because it was already fled. A scholastic stronghold, standing out against the barbarians, with the living flame within? Or an empty shrine, a pillaged tomb? How could one, any longer, tell? The ancient voice spoke to him no more. The muse was silent, though she had once teased him from every leaf and tried to catch his eye from every dusty textbook. Was she dead therefore, or dead to him alone? Would she ride back in triumph over the Eastern plains, clanking with armor, ferocious reborn matriarch, drinking blood?

There is no blood left in me, thought Linton Hancox. I am a dry husk, dry as parchment. There is no blood in my veins, but some strange woody sap. Xylem or phloem. A protective spirit has mercifully turned me into a tree, to spare me the rape of the mind.

The next day, Anthony Keating agreed to sell his old house for £35,000 and the Riverside scheme for half a million, did a few sums, and discovered to his surprise that, after all that excitement, he was going to break just about even. It seemed too neat to be true, but so it was. He was more or less back where he started, with a better house, in a less convenient place, no job, no income, and about four thousand pounds in the bank. And five years older. It seemed, somehow, conclusive proof that he, Anthony Keating, was not a serious person.

He forgot to ring the hospital about the girl in labor. Had he rung, he might or might not have been told that the girl had died, and that the baby was suffering from heroin addiction. On the other hand, he did remember to keep his appointment with his own doctor, who expressed surprise at his healthy appearance. It must be because I gave up smoking and drinking, said Anthony, that I look so well.

You don't mean to say you really gave them up? said his doctor, with surprise.

It was you that told me to, said Anthony.

Yes, but I didn't really think you'd manage it, said his doctor.

You mean I needn't have bothered? asked Anthony.

No, I don't mean that at all, said his doctor. Nor do I mean that you can take it up again now. Though I don't suppose you'll abstain forever.

Oh, I don't know, said Anthony. I'm a new man, now.

And he walked out, a new man. And walked straight into the nearest pub, and ordered himself a double Scotch. He felt deeply aggrieved. He had taken every step in his nature toward self-destruction: he had played with fire, he had gambled, he had tried to turn upside down his dearest principles, and by any law of justice, he, like Len Wincobank, should have ended up in prison, or, like Max Friedmann, dead. But fate had given him a second chance. Yet again, he was going to have to decide what to do with his life. It was too exhausting. It was too much of an effort. He wished that somebody would throw a bomb through the pub window and put him out of his misery. He did not know what he thought about anything: why should he be expected to go on making up his mind? The problems were too complex. He had neither the intelligence nor the perseverance to solve them. On the other hand, he was quite well aware that he had too much intelligence and too much perseverance to give up the struggle. He had no choice but to go on making choices. No guardian angel would put him quietly away in a cell where he could go quietly mad. He wished profoundly that he was where Len Wincobank was, out of harm's way. He felt deeply depressed. He was saved from ignominy and shame, from bankruptcy and self-reproach, and the prospect depressed him unimaginably. He ordered another double Scotch.

As Anthony Keating sat drinking double Scotches in a pub in West London, Maureen Kirby lay in bed in a hotel in Aberdeen with Derek Ashby, her architect employer. She had given up resistance and had succumbed. It was a relief, really, to get it over with. And she liked Derek: he was a nice fellow, considerate in bed as well as out of it, he had come too soon, as men tend to do the first time, but had licked her and sucked her afterward, and now they lay there, comfortably in one another's arms, watching Esther Rantzen on the television. Maureen approved of oral sex and thought it was a good invention. She was rather surprised that Derek was so good at it, because he must be at least forty-five.

Derek was pleased with himself. He had a contract to build a new house for an American oil man, in a village on the East Coast. No expense spared. Derek enjoyed the opportunity, rare enough, to indulge his flights of fancy. He was also pleased with himself for laying Maureen. He had never slept with any of his secretaries before; indeed, the only extramarital sex he had ever indulged in had been an affair with another architect, initiated at a conference in Bonn, and she hadn't been much fun, she had been far too serious and had threatened to tell his wife. Maureen was the kind of girl who would never tell anyone's wife. Derek respected her for that. Indeed, he had a great deal of respect for Maureen, who seemed a thoroughly sensible person, and who listened to his complaints about his wife with exactly the right degree of sympathy. She didn't imply that his wife must be an awful old bag—which, of course, she wasn't—and indeed was quite capable of criticizing Derek's version of events: "You *must* have done something worse than that," she would say indignantly, when Derek tried to suggest that his wife had run away to her sister's simply because Derek had forgotten to tell her he couldn't be home for supper. She was also sympathetic to Derek's wife's desire to better herself through evening classes, and told Derek off quite sharply when he complained about her messing about making jewelry and silk-screen printing: why on earth shouldn't she, she spent enough of her life looking after you and the kids, Maureen would retort, with a flounce of womanly solidarity. Derek approved of that, for the truth was that he was quite proud of his wife's ambitions, but convention, deeply rooted, and a fear that she might make herself ridiculous, forbade him to show much sympathy either to the wife or to Maureen.

Maureen was a sophisticated creature, in her own way, good at playing games. "My wife doesn't *understand* me," she would moan, whenever Derek started on that timeworn topic. Her mockery had made it easier to get into bed with her with some decent sense of equality. And now there she lay, propped up on his shoulder, a can of beer in one hand, and a cigarette in the other. She was

very soft and warm, and seemed in good humor, laughing at the
jokes on the television. There seemed no need for either of them to
suffer remorse. He would try not to think about his wife, Evelyn,
who was also, no doubt, sitting up in bed watching Esther Rantzen. He hoped she was sitting up in bed alone, but could hardly
share this anxiety with Maureen, who, being a modern young
woman, would not think twice before labeling him a male chauvin-
ist pig. Which, thought Derek—uneasily, thoughtfully, with
perplexity stroking Maureen's left breast—which undoubtedly I
am.

Maureen, for her part, had stopped thinking about Len. She
had given him up. It was finished, with Len. It had been good
while it lasted, but it was over, for Len would come out of prison a
different man, not her man. He had become a different man during
the trial. Now she could admit it. Now that there was no point in
her loyalty, she could let him go. She'd gone off him.

Maureen was not thinking much at all. She was feeling good.
It had been a cold day, tramping around a bleak site on the bleak
coast, with the wind howling and the waves breaking along desolate miles of shore; it was good to be back in the warm, good to
have had a warm meal, good to be in bed, with all one's body
melted away into intimate nothingness. How nice people are, she
thought, as Derek's hand caressed her breast and tried to make her
nipple stand up: her nipple refused, it was too warm and tired, it
had gone to sleep, and after a while he sensed this, and simply held
her, kissing her from time to time on the temple. He was a solid
man, a big man, with a big shoulder to lean on. A comfortable
man. The television program was amusing: it showed an elderly
lady in the East End sampling snails and delivering her views on
the matter. They both laughed. Maureen felt happy. The last year
with Len had been a nightmare. She would forget it, she would
meddle in such matters no longer, she would keep to her own
limits. Derek Ashby felt happy: he was pleased and moved by the
way Maureen had fluttered and dissolved against his mouth and
stroked his wet hair and said thank you, thank you; he was pleased
to have made her content. She was a good girl, too good to be a

secretary, and vague noble notions of recommending her to train for a course in management and a top job drifted pleasantly round his head, replacing the vision of the solitary austere Evelyn, perseveringly remaking her soul in this earthly vale; fantasies of promoting Maureen to better things mingled comfortably with his vision of the house he would build, gray by the gray sea and white breakers, the stone would tinge with pink in dawn and sunset, like the faint pink tinge of the sand, and from the blue-gray reflective glass windows his oil man could watch the endless roaring tides. The wood would be brown, and knotted like ship's timber; but the house would be white and gray, like the sea, like the gulls, like the Northern sky, and it would stand there like a lighthouse, a mark of a last sail, at night the oil man would switch on his lights and they would shine forth from the windows like signals. They would ward away wrecks. I am a lucky man, thought Derek Ashby. What more can a man want, than to work, with his mind and his spirit?

It was just as well that Maureen did not know that Len Wincobank had that evening lost remission for breaking the nose of a fellow prisoner. He too had reached breaking point, and had lashed out, not at the source of the trouble, which was old Callander, but at a relatively inoffensive whey-faced cardsharper, who had happened to say something crude about Len's Maureen. In a better mood, Len might have taken the remark as it was meant, as a joke, but the truth was that Len was being driven mad by Callander, who had attached himself to him like some old man of the sea, who followed him and pestered him with dull tales of parapsychology, with strange fantasies of mind-reading powers. It did not help that one of Callander's mind-reading feats had also featured Maureen Kirby. "I have inner knowledge of the new laws," Callander would tell him, from time to time. Len had joined a lot of evening classes, not, like Derek Ashby's wife, to shore up his identity, which needed dilution rather than reinforcement, but in order to get away from Callander. But Callander had joined up too, and sat at Len's elbow through lectures on astronomy, through lessons in art history, through demonstrations of upholstery, muttering and mumbling. Len could stand it no longer, but could hardly bash a poor old nutter, so when Bert Gifford had opened his big mouth once too often, Len had let him have it. Like Maureen, he was at first quite relieved by the fact that he had taken action, and action true to his character, even though he had lost remission thereby, and even though he had hit the wrong man. And the scene had also given him an opportunity to explain to the governor about Callander. The governor was quite sympathetic, said he would get a psychiatrist to see Callander, said that he fully understood the frustrations of prison life must be difficult for an active and independent man like Len Wincobank. He was a new-style governor, with a degree in sociology. Len left him feeling better, relieved to have spoken to somebody who took him seriously; but lay in bed awake, shocked that he had allowed himself to be soothed by promises, and by a bland tone. I must be low, thought Len, to be taken in by talk like that. Like a sick man in a hospital, believing idle encouragements from nurses, through a desperate need to believe.

And an image of Maureen, in bed with a man, flashed into Len's mind. Unlike Callander, he did not believe in ESP, but the image was real enough. There was nothing supernatural about its arrival. It was obvious that, by now, Maureen would be in bed with another man. One did not have to suppose an alteration in the laws of nature, a reversal of the natural order, to guess right about that. And what the fuck can I do about it? thought Len. Fuck all. Astronomy, upholstery. For the first time, he felt despair, he felt that he would never live to see the end of his sentence. The wise governor had warned him about such moods. All the men go through it, he had said, there's always a bad patch, often when you least expect it. But it doesn't last, you get over it.

A bad patch. All the men go through it. Men and women are machines, thought Len. He found the idea of going through a bad patch, like everyone else, inexpressibly dreary. He had thought himself different. He had made himself different. But they had unmade him, and here he was, just a man, lying on a bed. Like all the other men. No wonder Callander had gone mad rather than accept so depressing a reality.

When Anthony returned to High Rook House, he returned not as conquering hero, but with bloodshot eyes, two days' growth of beard, haggard, gray, and drunk. Relief had undone him. Alison, sizing up the situation in a glance, pulled herself together, as people do when they have no option, and took over. She shopped, cooked, cleaned, gardened, paid bills, answered phones and letters, unblocked the sewage pipes, got the builders for the leak in the roof, and listened, in the intervals, to Anthony's ramblings. They did not make much sense, for he was drunk most of the time. The principal themes seemed to be his own inadequacy, and an alternating admiration of and hatred for Giles Peters. Alison went through all his post, and rang Giles herself to see how the company's affairs stood: to her horror but not to her surprise, Giles, clearly undaunted by his narrow escape from disaster over the Riverside scheme, was eager to expand, was full of new ideas, was quite confident that he knew how to make another million. But you lost the last million you made, said Alison. Yes, but think how much we learned while we were doing it, said Giles.

Alison rang Anthony's solicitor, and her own, and inquired about the dissolving of partnerships. Anthony's behavior was so erratic that she could all too easily imagine him putting his signature to some vast new lunatic enterprise; and maybe this time no wealthy council would be there to bail him out. She was determined not to go through all that again; she had had enough. She could not tell what Anthony's intentions were: he seemed to swing from a violent and, in her eyes, quite healthy loathing of the world of speculation, to a crazy conviction that it was all child's play, that he and Giles and Rory were the greatest financiers of their generation, and that from now on they had only to lift their fingers and the golden apples would drop into their laps. When he was in the latter mood, she tried to point out to him that it was merely by chance that he was still able to call his own home his own, and that far from having made a fortune, he had merely managed to keep afloat. But Anthony did not want to listen to the voice of reason. Other voices were speaking to him. Watching him listen to them, she wondered if he were having a nervous breakdown, whether she could get him certified, and thereby prevent him from further ruinous speculation.

For the first time, she began to think about her own legal status. Maybe it was true, as Anthony had said when leaving for his father's funeral, that they should have married; maybe they had left marriage too late, as Anthony and Giles had left their most ambitious deal too late. Perhaps the moment was past. She had never been particularly eager to remarry, and had not given the matter much thought, but perhaps, after all, there was something to be said for the old forms of commitment. As a wife, she would be better placed to restrain Anthony from future follies, both morally and legally, though the picture of herself binding him to his study chair or hiding his checkbooks was neither attractive nor plausible. She would find it hard to be that kind of wife. But her knowledge that she could, simply, walk out on him, worried her. She watched him reach for the whisky bottle at eleven in the morning, and realized that there was nothing to bind her to him: she could clear off, and no one would blame her. She would not have left him during the past year, while ruin was hanging over him, nor would she have left him had ruin, bankruptcy, and disgrace overtaken him, but the present situation, with its delicate ambivalence, left her curiously free—to think again, to reconsider. It was as though they were back at the beginning. But the beginning, this time, of what? She could not face a repetition of the past years, but what else was there, if she stayed with Anthony? Like Anthony, she wished at times that she had not been presented with this sudden freedom of choice. It had felt safer, when they had been blinkered by sickening anxiety, walking the narrow path, unable to risk a glance to right or left. Now, they stood in a flat and featureless plain, older, wiser, but somehow diminished.

She knew how Anthony felt, she sympathized. He felt as she had felt when she abandoned Jane: that the struggle was over, that the struggle had solved nothing.

Reading the morning papers, trying to follow analyses of Britain's plight, she realized that she had no picture of the future, either her own, or the country's. I belong to the wrong generation, she thought, the generation that had its certainties when young. We worked hard when young, we had a conception. But instead of solidifying into attitudes, opinions, convictions, however bigoted, we have fragmented and dissolved into uncertainty. Lead and water. We are dull, without shape. We are too old, with all our knowledge, to begin again, for who would embark on such struggles, knowing as we know, from the completion of the first cycle, the sad end? Who could leap in, now, knowing what we know?

It had been a mistake, perhaps, to remove themselves from the scene of action. Had Anthony been in London, in daily contact with Giles, with Rory, with gossip and scandal and propositions, he might never have paused to reflect; he might, like Giles, have been prepared to jump in again at the deep end, simply for the thrill, for the shock, for the splash. But circumstances—the heart attack, the quiet house, the disaster with Jane—had sobered Anthony, had given him too much time to brood, to dwell on consequences, on the emptiness of his success. They had sobered him; though sober was hardly the word for Anthony, these days. There was, she had to admit, something impressive in the spectacle of his determined self-destruction. And there was nothing else to watch, for Molly had gone back to school for the spring term. So they were alone, in a desert of their own making, in their own fortress. Anthony Keating, man of leisure, in his country house, and Alison Murray, ex-actress, ex-mother, unemployed. It could not go on like this forever, but what next, what next, what next?

At times Anthony talked of selling the house, returning to London, buying a flat. At other times, he talked of buying a dog and of learning to shoot. He wanted to shoot rooks. Their noise was driving him mad, he said, and he would glower at them moodily from the bedroom window, he would yell at them and abuse them. Frightening though his moods were, and seriously as Alison knew she ought to take all this drinking and depression, Alison could not help finding his passions touching. They touched her heart. She loved him, after all, and should have predicted that it would turn this way, for had she not always known that Anthony was an emotional man, a man of spirit, who would not sit quietly beneath the blows or benefactions of fate? She had not the heart to nag at him too much about the drink and the smoking, so well did she understand his state of mind. It is hard work, weaning oneself off an addiction to violent stimulants, and, the stimulant of acute fear removed, what more natural than that he should replace it with alcohol and cigarettes?

One ought to be able to find a life, Alison Murray thought to herself, as she swept out the ashes from the huge grate, one ought to be able to find a life where violent stimulants are not necessary. A life where stimulants are not destructive. Where one can be satisfied with clouds, flowers, sky, water. Anthony had tried it, for those weeks on his own, while she had been away in Wallacia. She had admired his attempt, had been impressed, almost alarmed by his success. He had survived those weeks well, honorably, with his kindness to Tim and Molly, his quiet visits to the pub, his half pints of beer, his vegetable patch.

Mrs. Bunney in the pub could not make out what had happened to Anthony. His drinking pattern had changed beyond recognition. Instead of a half pint of an evening, he now drank at home most days, with occasional drunken forays when the bottle ran out, when he would down surprising quantities. He used to be such a nice quiet man, whispered Mrs. Bunney to her regulars, as Anthony raved about the tax system and the Land Act to startled customers, as Mrs. Bunney pocketed his fivers.

Which is the real Anthony, wondered Alison, as she listened to the wild drinker playing the piano and singing to himself, loudly and with agony, some songs of Schubert: "*Ich grolle nicht*," shouted Anthony, musically, making the old house echo—which is the real one, this maniac drinking speculating self-destructive gambler, or that quiet sensitive man who was quietly and tenderly and happily roping up a split elm tree when I got back from Krusograd? And which of the two do I prefer?

Alison had a nasty suspicion that she preferred the drinker. She had been upset by the quiet, kind Anthony, she had resented his success, his self-contained contentments. She had been frightened of him, excluded by him, she had felt inferior to him. Whereas this present Anthony was more manageable, in his way. One could do more for him, look after him better, protect him from himself, stop him setting the house on fire with cigarettes, pick up spilled glasses. Does that mean I want to destroy him? thought Alison, crouched in the ancient hearth, staring at the gray wood ash, the crumbled knotty joints, the charred fissured shining black stumps. Does that mean I can only like those that I manage, dominate, support? Like Molly?

Ich grolle nicht, cried Anthony. He had once had a good voice, and still sang well. Alison swept the ash into the pan. Sex was better, with the drinking Anthony. Indeed, it had been unusually interesting, of late. But then she had herself, she remembered, turned coldly away from the good sober Anthony. Also, Anthony had now decided that he did not care whether or not he died on the job, as he crudely put it. Let's kill ourselves with it, he would say, crunching her, biting her, grinding her, wearing her out: murder me, kill me, she would cry, assenting, moaning, unresisting. Kill me, she cried, she who of all people had to stay, for the sake of another, alive.

But in the light of day, over the gray ash, she thought: I do not want Anthony to kill himself. We must be able to work out some better way of living.

That evening, she rang Maureen. For advice, for sympathy. It was not in Alison's nature to ask advice, and she was not a woman with women friends of her own age; her proud defense of Molly had isolated her, as had her beauty. No other women could like me,

Alison had reasonably enough decided, at an early age: they would be sure to resent me. (As her sister, Rosemary, had done.) This was a realistic decision, for other women did resent Alison, but had not, in view of Molly's existence, and Alison's withdrawal from competition, been allowed the opportunity to express or formulate their resentment; therefore they had resented her all the more, though they had been obliged to call her a perfect mother, a saint, even, behind her back. It was not fair on them, or on her. But life is not fair.

So Alison had had no friends. Nevertheless, she got on well with those who would accept her for what she was, who were sufficiently removed by time or class to accept her without a threatened rivalry: with Kitty Friedmann, whose own lack of vanity and self-interest was so astonishing that Alison did not even feel the need to envy it, for Kitty was the real thing, Kitty was an innocent, a saint; with Maureen Kirby, the opposite of innocent—knowing, realistic, amiable. With Maureen, and with Maureen only, Alison had been able to play the game of being girls together, while the men talked, and the two of them had had many an interesting discussion, in powder rooms, in hotel bedrooms, left together over coffee in dining rooms while the men talked of other things. Maureen was a confidential talker, hard to resist. Her accounts of what went on in the business world were fascinating. And Maureen did not resent Alison, for she had no standards whereby to judge Alison's superiority; so unself-conscious was she that she would even compliment Alison upon her appearance, and comment approvingly on her clothes. Maureen was young, confident, shrewd, unthreatening and unthreatened. And during Len's downfall, Alison had come to admire her for other reasons: principally, for her loyalty. She was sure that she had seen in Maureen's face, in those dark months, the shadow of suspicion, an awareness, a wariness about Len; Anthony had found Len so plausible that he had accepted his arguments about his own actions, but Maureen had known more, suspected more. But had not let on. Perhaps she had thought that she could rescue Len, by love and faith. As Alison now might rescue Anthony?

Maureen was at home, in her little Sheffield flat. She already knew the news about the Riverside deal, for she had read it in the papers, but wanted to know more: was it as good as it looked, what were the catches, how was Anthony feeling? "Anthony's started to drink like a *fish*," said Alison, using a figure of speech she would certainly not have used to others. "You'd think he'd lost a fortune, or been given a prison sentence, the way he's carrying on. I just don't understand it," said Alison, who did, but who wanted to have an outside opinion on the matter.

"It's the relief," said Maureen, "after all that strain. Perhaps he'll calm down, in a week or two. After all, he's had a terrible lot of strain this past year."

"So have you, but it hasn't driven you to drink."

Maureen agreed that she hadn't been driven to drink, but that she had broken out in spots, and been driven into sleeping with her boss; also, she pointed out that for her the strain wasn't exactly over, so she would hardly tell how she'd respond when relieved from it. "The test will be," she said, "when Len gets out. I'd take a bet that he'll drink himself into a blind fit for a month, then sober up and get back to work. That's my bet, but I don't know if I'll be around to watch it. No yellow ribbons for Len, I'm afraid."

They discussed the behavior under stress of Len and Anthony, its differences and similarities, and agreed that both had expressed it, bizarrely, by a search for fiercer and fiercer condiments. "You should have *seen* the amount of mustard he used to shove on his steak by the end, and whenever it was curry, it had to be Vindaloo," said Maureen. Alison revealed that Giles, like Maureen, had suffered from spots. They both laughed a good deal over these eccentricities of the body's reactions and requirements.

"Actually," said Maureen after a while, "I think perhaps I am relieved. And that's why I'm sleeping with Derek. I was thinking about Len, the other day, and Anthony, and the horrible responsibility of having all that unsold, unlet property weighing on one like a load of bricks—well, damn it, it *is* a load of bricks, a load of concrete anyway—and I thought how glad I was I'd never let Len make me a director, and how glad I was it wasn't *my* responsibility any more, and how could I ever think it had been fun—and how could I ever think it was funny when Len used to go on with all that big talk about how he didn't give a fuck about the share-holders—I suppose he was being honest, but honesty isn't every-thing, is it? and I thought how glad I was that there was only me, on my own, just me in this flat that I pay for myself, out of my own earnings, and I don't own a thing, not even a Mini any more, and I don't have to worry about the interest rate and the flaming Land Act, and if I want a new pair of shoes I can go and buy one and if I want to complain about the price of spuds I can, and how simple it is, just being me, and when Derek offers me money or presents I can say, 'No thanks, keep your money, I do it for fun.' I know now how much I hated all that weight of everything lying on me. Len liked it, and I thought it was fun to begin with, but by the end I hated it. You know what I mean? Of course you know what I mean. You know, Alison, I used to think when they were preparing the case that if I loved Len *enough*, if I willed *enough* for it to be all right, then it would be, but even at the time I knew that wasn't true—but I went on willing, because I had to, for Len's sake—but I didn't believe it. It is a relief, not to have to pretend any more.

"But it's different, with you and Anthony. It'll be all right for you, because Anthony isn't as hard a case as Len, he isn't as hooked, and he'd never have done what Len did, he'd have had more sense. Len's a bit mad, you know. He let it get out of hand. He really did commit massive fraud, you know, however honorable his intentions may have been. Anthony's affairs are different. He hasn't got any shareholders to worry about, for a start. I can't tell you how sick I got of hearing Len yelling about shareholders sitting on their backsides."

Alison, curled up in a chair in the drafty hall, listening to the distant sounds of Anthony watching an American thriller on tele-vision, said, "But I think Anthony may be a bit mad too."

"I don't think so," said Maureen. "Well, a *bit* mad, perhaps, or he wouldn't have got mixed up in this property business in the first place. Particularly at a time like that. But he's not *very* mad. And anyway, he's an educated man. There are all kinds of other things he could do."

"Such as what?"

Maureen considered.

"I don't know. But you must get him out of this business. You'll have to think of something else to keep him busy, or he'll be lured back. They're like addicts, you know, some of them."

"There isn't any work. There's large-scale unemployment. Redundancies everywhere."

"Yes, I know. Still, a man with Anthony's background and qualifications . . ."

They both paused, contemplating the fact that a man like Anthony might, precisely, find himself deeply unemployable.

"I could always go back to work myself, and keep him," said Alison, as a joke. "But I don't suppose he'd like to be kept."

"No, you've got to keep him occupied," said Maureen, and they both laughed again, amused by having slipped into the female attitude that men are children who need to be kept busy, to keep them out of mischief.

After Alison had rung off, comforted by a sharing of views, though disturbed by Maureen's perhaps inevitable desertion of the impotent Len, Maureen sat down to a supper of cheese on toast with egg in it, and thought about Len. Perhaps, she felt, if she had willed *enough*, she would have got him off. Love is a force that will move mountains, and a good woman can even get a man out of jail, if she protests enough. And to love on, despite the evidence, despite common sense, is as stubborn as to pile debt on debt, fraud on fraud, hoping to be saved by a miracle. Obstinacy is no virtue. A wise person knows when to quit.

Yet there remained a nagging doubt: had she quit too early? Why had Len not confided in her, during those last months, when he had made all the mistakes? Had he sensed that she was withdrawing support, and was that perhaps the reason why he had behaved so foolishly?

She would never know. She cut neatly into the slice of toast. Cheese on toast was her favorite supper, but Len had not been fond of it, he said it gave him indigestion and kept him awake at night. Cheese was a shocking price these days, but it was still cheaper than most things. She'd heard a dispute on the radio that very morning between a Milk Marketing Board man and a doctor: the doctor said cheese was very, very bad for you, the milk spokesman said it was very, very good for you. One had to admit that the doctor's views were probably more disinterested. Still, who cared? It wasn't so bad, sitting alone in one's flat, having one's favorite supper, in fact it was quite good fun. It was, as she had told Alison, a relief. Most people eat too much, particularly businessmen on expense accounts. The only way one can have cheese on toast in a posh restaurant is to eat it as a savory, after a whole meal. Maureen remembered with amusement her shock at some of her discoveries about the expense-account life, the life of good living. How her mum had laughed, at the story of the seven-course dinner with a whole separate fish course. She'd often wondered how it was that people managed to stay roughly the same size— well, the same size within ten stones or so—when some of them eat four or five times as much as others.

Her mum had always been partial to cheese on toast too, but she liked it different. She liked it done under the grill, in hard slabs, browned on top and hardly melted underneath. Maureen thought that was the lazy way. She liked hers grated in milk. Sloppy.

Maureen thought about money, and what Len had wanted all that money for, when people's real needs don't really differ all that much. It wasn't so much what you got for your money that appealed to him (and that appealed, she admitted it, to her), it was the *idea* of it. Like traveling first-class on a boat and hearing the loud-speaker tell second-class passengers to get out of the first-class accommodation. When the difference between the two was hardly worth paying for anyway. Like saying to your mum or Auntie Evie or Marlene or even old Stan, oh, we're staying in the Dorchester, of course. Like getting into that Rolls and being stared at, when the Mini had been just as good really, and a damn sight easier to park. She sighed, picked up her fork, picked at the tablecloth. Oh well, it had been fun while it lasted. Seeing how the other half lives. She'd got ideas above her station, as her mum told her at Christmas, laughing raucously at Maureen's pernickety emptying of ash trays. The idea of having a station was a laugh in itself. But she'd certainly ended up in a station further along the line than poor old Auntie Evie, and poor Marlene with all those kids. At least I can pay my own rent, and buy my own piece of cheese, and shut my own door on myself, thought Maureen Kirby.

Part Three

It ought now to be necessary to imagine a future for Anthony Keating. There is no need to worry about the other characters, for the present. Len Wincobank is safe in prison: when he emerges, he will assess the situation, which will by then have changed, and he will begin again. He will make no more such mistakes. He will take risks, but he will not make mistakes. As he will say to the prison governor on the day of his release, I have learned my lesson. Max Friedmann has been, throughout, dead; Kitty Friedmann will not alter where she finds alteration, but will continue as before, so determined is she to ignore the implications of reality, so adept is she at translating into her own terms the messages she receives from the outside world. Like Tom Callander, she is protected, but by a wiser angel.

Len has lost Maureen Kirby. She is happy with Derek Ashby, who has persuaded her that she is wasting her talents working for him: she is doing a course in business management, and in 1980, somewhat unpredictably, she will marry Derek. A sociologist will write a report upon their successful combination of careers, and she will have to give many interviews, in her little spare time, as a representative of the new world of businesswomen. She will think of Len, and at times regret the wild good times, and the children she never had, but she will know she has been a lucky woman. Evelyn Ashby, who has not been allowed to appear, will not re-marry; she will grow eccentric and solitary, and refuse to see her own children: I prefer to be alone, she will say. And she will mean it.

But what of Anthony Keating and Alison Murray? What will they do? Return to London and the vicissitudes of the market? Farm trout or watercress? Donate High Rook House to the Youth Hostel Association, or transform it into a home for the handi-capped? Will Alison resume her long abandoned career, will Anthony drink himself to death?

They thought of all these things, but did not have time to choose between them.

After two months of heavy drinking, Anthony sobered up, and rang Giles and Rory, and told them that he wanted to release himself from their partnership. They had been expecting this, and agreed, gladly, for they had for some time viewed Anthony as a liability. They themselves had all sorts of plans afoot, and when Anthony departed, they merged with another group of enterprising and not wholly honest real estate agents, and made some clever purchases. There was still money to be made, even in those dark days; the Pension Funds, the new rich, swollen with capital, were buying property and Picassos like cakes.

Spring came, and Anthony and Alison walked, across the hills, by the river, up the valley; they took with them books to identify flowers, trees, fungi, birds. They took possession. It was a good time: it was, almost, what they had planned.

Anthony wrote some songs, and sold one to Mike Morgan, another to a record company. Alison took up poultry and embroidery, and in the evenings poured over the small stitches in her well-illustrated embroidery book. They talked and speculated. They would be all right, they said to themselves. They toyed with notions of trout and watercress. They even thought of running a pub together. They had time to think, as the snowdrops gave way to primroses, violets, daffodils, butter burr, as the rooks built noisily in the remaining elms, as the lambs scattered across the hillsides.

Babs had a girl, safely, despite the high blood pressure. Anthony was pleased, and sent flowers, telegrams, gifts. At Easter, the three younger of his own children came to stay, to give Babs a rest. It was as they had planned. The children liked the house, seemed to like Alison, were helpful and polite. There appeared to be no enmity among them. We have not done so badly, thought Anthony, watching them on their last evening as they mopped up their chicken stew with hunks of bread and talked about potholes and limestone scenery: the clints and grykes on the hilltop had actually interested their urban spirits, though perhaps only because one of them was doing geography O Level. Their faces were healthy and open, their teeth were good, they munched and smiled, the next generation. Would they survive? How could one tell? He wondered whether they would be capable of earning the enormous incomes that they would doubtless find necessary to support themselves if capitalism and inflation continued to govern the land; whether they would have the wits and resources to survive in a totalitarian state, should things turn that way. There was no point in worrying too much about them. Theirs was the future, not his. Babs had been a good mother to them. He had not been too bad a father. One can do no better than hope.

In the morning, he and Alison drove them off to Leeds station, settled them on the train, saw them off, waved them good-bye. Come again soon, they cried, and all three cried that they would love to, it had been great, could Babs and Stuart and the new baby come too next time? I don't see why not, said Anthony, as the train drew out.

They went shopping in Leeds that afternoon, and bought various dull household objects, then went back to the house and went to bed for half an hour, before supper. They talked about whether or not to buy a dog for Molly, who was with Donnell; they had decided not to risk having the two families together, just yet. There would be plenty of time, plenty of other holidays, so they thought. Molly was returning the next day: Alison was going to fetch her. It would be a nice surprise for her, said Anthony. We'd have to train it not to chase the lambs and not to eat the chickens, said Alison. But yes, they agreed, a puppy would be fun. Contentment filled them, in their safe and private place, and both were old enough to feel its rarity. Perhaps this is the only way, thought Anthony, that a man can remove himself from destruction. By removing himself. But peace is so expensive, love so fitful, destruction so relentless. A thrush sang in the apple tree in the garden, despite this.

When they got up, they walked down to the village, in the early evening. It was clear, soft and bright, and the evening star hung luminous, dilating, in the water-color sky, large like a promise. They passed a newborn lamb in a ditch: it was struggling to its feet, the mother was standing already, the afterbirth at her feet.

They went down and stood on the bridge over the river: boys were fishing, with a saucepan, and small birds with dipping tails skimmed the surface of the water. The boys had caught two min-nows and a bullhead: they showed Anthony. The fish swam around the shiny confines of the pan. "What will you do with them?" asked Alison. "Put them back," said the boys.

They held hands, and gazed at the fast clear flowing brown water. Their hands rested on the old packhorse bridge, on the gray lichen-encrusted stone. If one could so stand forever, they thought. A lamb bleated, nearby. If they were careful, if they avoided every risk, was there a chance that they might stand there on other evenings, for years of evenings? It seemed possible, but not, they thought, probable. They were not a confident couple: they had had no cause to be so. And as they started back up the hill to the house, Anthony thought he could feel, for the first time for months, an ominous sensation in chest and heart. It reminded him that he had decided to remake his will: he had made one many years earlier, leaving all he had or had not to Babs and the children, but did not now see why they should inherit everything. He would leave the house to Alison, and make some provision for his children. Babs's husband could look after Babs. He was, after all, earning a safe £12,000 a year, although he did not look a man of such mettle.

The evening star shone on Anthony and Alison, as they walked slowly up the lane. Alison was thinking of supper. She would make a flan. Their leeks were doing well: an egg and leek flan. Tomorrow, she would have to go to London to collect Molly on the train. Anthony had offered to go with her, but she had said she would go alone; fares were so expensive these days, she said, as a reason, but she guessed that Anthony did not want to go to London. He was afraid of disturbing himself. There is only the tiniest area, thought Alison, in which one can stay peacefully, without hurting, without being hurt. The smallest space, the small-est cell. Let us stay in it a little longer, please God, she prayed, gazing at the enigmatic star. Let us fend off for a little longer the incursions.

They fended them off for one whole evening. Both were to look back on it often, wondering what remote sense of fair play in heaven had allowed such remission. Alison, recalling the intense precarious silent happiness, the egg and leek flan, the music on the radio, the ashen logs falling like flakes of snow through the bars of the grate, was to evolve a theory of time as bizarre as Tom Callander's views on the laws of averages. Time, she came to think, is not consequential: it occurs simultaneously, and distributed through it in meaningless chronology are spots of sorrow, spots of joy. We combine them as we will, as we can best bear them. We make our own ordering. An undue concentration of sorrow is due to bad selection, or undue fortitude. And calm before the storm is chosen by the spirit, for its own sustenance. Or as a warning, like the pink sky before the darkness: who can say?

She did not believe her own theory. Facts belied it. There is no comfort, no sustenance. But who can be surprised that one so subject to the blows of circumstance should attempt to see in them a possibility of self-will, freedom, choice?

It was an exceptional evening, without event. Alison cooked, Anthony chopped wood and painted the new outhouse door with creosote. He liked the smell of creosote. Alison fed her chickens, and looked at a poultry catalogue. They ate the flan. Anthony washed up their plates, while Alison finished the novel she was reading, and wondered what to read next; they made coffee, went to sit in the drawing room. They talked about fancy poultry, whether to embark on a few exotics, whether or not to get geese. Both claimed they were frightened of geese. Anthony played the piano. At nine, they listened to Mozart on the radio: Alison, who was not musical, did not understand music, sat by Anthony and he showed her how to follow the score, and tried to tell her about what it was that he so liked in it. When the music ended, they sat and stared at the fire, dying in its ash. It seemed to them both that some secret was about to be revealed, was perhaps even there with them: the secret of living without ambition, agitation, hope. Intense silence flooded the house. They had stilled themselves to nothingness. It lasted: there it was. Neither moved, neither spoke. The fire faded. No sound from the world could reach them. Time paused: they heard its heart stop, they heard its breath hold, they heard the lapse of thudding and rustling and pumping and beating. They listened to the silence.

In the morning, Anthony drove Alison to Leeds to catch the train, then drove himself back to the house. As he parked the car, he could hear the telephone ringing: it will stop, he thought, and did not hurry himself. But it continued to ring, on and on, and when he had let himself into the house, and picked up the post, and hung his jacket on a hook, he answered it.

It was a man he did not know, a voice he did not know. It spoke urbanely, urgently, from London. It wanted to know if it was speaking to Mr. Anthony Keating. Assured, it introduced itself, as the voice of Humphrey Clegg, of the Foreign and Commonwealth Office. Premonition of disaster leaped along the wires and crackled into Anthony's head.

Humphrey Clegg wanted to speak to Anthony about Jane Murray. He was very pleased that Anthony was there, rather than Alison, as he did not wish to distress Mrs. Murray and would like Anthony's co-operation and advice. Could Anthony come to London? It was difficult to outline the problem on the telephone. No, Jane was all right, as far as anybody knew: she had been on hunger strike, but was reported, by the consul, to have abandoned the attempt. "We have here the monthly report from the consul," said Humphrey Clegg. "He saw your stepdaughter eight days ago. He says here that he was about to write to Mrs. Murray, but I'm afraid I don't know whether he did so or not. Unfortunately, Mr. Barstow died yesterday."

Anthony was finding it difficult to breathe normally; his ears were singing, and his chest seemed to refuse to expand properly.

"You want me to come to London," he said, flatly, stating the obvious. Humphrey Clegg agreed that it would be advisable. "It may, after all, be good news," said Clegg cautiously. "There are indications that the Wallacian authorities may be prepared to release your stepdaughter shortly. But the situation is somewhat delicate. I would prefer to discuss it with you in person, if you could spare the time."

"What should I tell Alison?" asked Anthony.

"I wouldn't mention the matter to Mrs. Murray until we have talked further," said Humphrey Clegg. "Nor, if I may suggest, to Mr. Murray. In fact, perhaps it would be better not to mention my call until we have met." He paused. "How soon do you think you could get here? I note that there are trains leaving Leeds at two p.m. and three p.m. Or there is a flight from Leeds airport at three. Or maybe you would prefer to drive."

Anthony thought for a moment, and said that he would catch the two o'clock, leaving the car at the station for Alison on her return. They arranged a meeting. "I really am most grateful," said Humphrey Clegg calmly.

As soon as Anthony put the phone down, it rang again. It was a man from Reuters, wanting to know what Anthony knew about the situation in Wallacia and the assassination of the British consul, Clyde Barstow; wanting to know what news Anthony and Alison had from Jane.

"I'm afraid Mrs. Murray isn't here," said Anthony, in tones that imitated well the discretion of the Foreign and Commonwealth Office. "And I don't know anything about the news from Wallacia. I haven't even read today's paper yet. So I'm afraid I can't help you."

On the train, Anthony reflected that if Reuters had got in before the Foreign Office, he would undoubtedly have co-operated with them and asked them a lot of questions. As it was, here he was, rushing off to London, ignorant of what claimed him, his passport in his pocket, already committed to Humphrey Clegg. On the official side of the fence, for once. On such details of chronology, affiliations and ideologies hang. He wondered who had assassinated Barstow, and why; Alison had liked him, his letters about Jane had been kind and considerate. He tried to remember everything he had ever read about Wallacia, everything Alison had told him; since Jane's accident, his eye had been so sensitized to reports from Wallacia that they had leaped from the page at him. But there had not been many. A couple of weeks ago, there had been a Reuters report on an internal power struggle: one or two ministers had been demoted, but nobody knew why. Apart from that, nothing. A small earthquake which was thought to have killed six people; a trade agreement with some Arab country, he forgot which; a suggestion that the country might for the first time be represented at the Olympic games. Hardly a comprehensive view of a country of several million people. He hoped that Humphrey Clegg might inform him.

But Humphrey Clegg, in his quiet office in Whitehall, claimed not to know much either. Of course, he might have been lying. It was true, as the Reuters man had claimed, that Barstow had been assassinated: it seemed that there was also a degree of civil disturbance. "Not exactly an uprising," said Clegg, gazing meditatively at Anthony, the tips of his fingers carefully placed together, neatly balanced in a small spire, his elbows on his large polished desk. "Not exactly an uprising, yet. But there is certainly a fair amount of unrest." He closed his eyes, opened them again. "Sniping. Roadblocks. That kind of thing."

"Who is sniping at whom?" asked Anthony.

"The situation is rather obscure," said Clegg, smiling briefly at his own understatement. "As you and Mrs. Murray have good reason to know, lines of communication between Wallacia and the West are not exactly clear. There are probably several factions involved—the Central Party, which has traditionally preserved its independence from the Soviet Union, but which has been experiencing some difficulty in maintaining its authority recently—and another group, led by the Minister of Trade, who wishes for closer ties with the U.S.S.R. Then there are the Christian Nationalists.

And the Maoists. And various other suppressed groups, which might make their presence known, if widescale trouble ensues."

"Are you implying that there's likely to be a civil war?"

"I'm not implying anything. Like you, I am in the dark. We have only the most unsatisfactory eyewitness reports. And this."

He handed Anthony a large telegram. It had that morning's date. It was from the Minister of Public and Social Order, and it agreed to release Jane Murray from Kresni camp on compassionate grounds, as her health was poor. It gave a date: a fortnight away. Anthony stared at it. It looked official enough. "Is this true?" he asked. "And if so, whatever for?"

"It's true enough," said Clegg. "And it will doubtless remain true, if Konec remains Minister. We must hope, for your step-daughter's sake, that he remains Minister for the next fortnight. You ask what for, which is a very sensible question." He did not try to answer it.

"What do you suggest we do about it? Do we just wait for her to come home?"

Humphrey Clegg explained that that was another very sensible question. On balance, he thought it would be somewhat un-wise to wait for her to be put on a plane home. The situation was fluid: Jane was not well; there was a certain urgency. Diplomatic regret over the assassination of poor Barstow might not last long enough to get Jane out of the country, Konec might be replaced by someone with very different views on Britain, and Jane Mur-ray. "Unfortunately," said Clegg, "as you know, we have not many representatives in Wallacia. The embassy staff is very lim-ited, and at the moment their activities are somewhat restricted by a close surveillance. . . ."

Anthony wondered if that were an F.O. euphemism for being under lock and key. Or already dead, like Barstow. He stared at Clegg's highly polished shoes under the desk, he looked around the walls at a portrait of the Queen and an oil painting of camels at an oasis, he stared up at the small glass chandelier. He wondered what was motivating Clegg. Concern for Jane, duty, or something quite different?

"Perhaps," said Anthony, "I'd better go and collect Jane myself."

Clegg's reaction was so smooth that Anthony could not tell whether he were trying to feign concealing surprise, or whether he was genuinely surprised. It quickly became clear that even if he was surprised by the fact that Anthony had made the suggestion first, the suggestion itself had been considered already. Yes, Clegg agreed, it would certainly be more satisfactory if somebody could look after the situation personally: at a time like this, so much depended on prompt and decisive action; he himself, as representative of HMG, would feel much happier to have all British nationals removed as soon as possible from a potentially unstable situation; how important it was to have somebody on the spot. . . .

"But I'd never get a visa," said Anthony, thinking fast, remembering the weeks it had taken Alison, in calmer times, to get hers.

But Clegg had thought of that. He was rummaging in his desk. He had taken the liberty of applying, he said; here were the papers, if Anthony could sign on pages four and five.

"You see," said Clegg, "it would have been impossible to get papers for Mr. or Mrs. Murray. Mrs. Murray has a visa already, issued by the last Foreign Minister, and it expired too recently to be renewed easily. And Mr. Murray, even if he had been willing, has unfortunately been refused a visa already. May I ask you where you have your current passport, Mr. Keating?"

"Here," said Anthony. He fished in his pocket, produced it. Clegg smiled.

"You have a good deal of foresight, Mr. Keating," he said.

"Yes," said Anthony. "Sometimes I can see whole strips of time unrolling, like reels of film. Speeded-up reels."

Clegg was leafing through Anthony's passport. "I see you have visas for Rumania, Czechoslovakia, Hungary, and Egypt," he said. "And an expired one for Bulgaria."

"Yes. I was filming there. Current affairs. Is that good, or bad?"

Clegg looked up, with a fairly human expression of uncer-

tainty on his pale, cultured face. "All right, I should think. But I
don't honestly know," he said, and laughed. "At least," he said, "if
things turn nasty, there'll be a few borders you can escape over."
Visions of blasted airports, derailed trains, and rolling tanks
filled Anthony's mind. Clegg seemed to see them too, for he has-
tened to add, "Not that there's any indication that things will
deteriorate so rapidly. Not in the next few weeks."

"I'll have time to get out there and back again?"

"Of course. We wouldn't consider it, otherwise." Humphrey
Clegg looked at his watch.

"If you would have the time, we could dine together, and
discuss the situation further," he said.

"Of course," said Anthony Keating.

And that was how Anthony Keating became a British spy.

Over dinner, which was served in a private room in a private club,
Humphrey Clegg told Anthony Keating more about the situation
in Wallacia: more, but nevertheless not much. He also gave him
several documents, and folders with names and addresses of people
to contact. He seemed to know more about Anthony than Anthony would have thought possible, and less about Wallacia than
Anthony would have thought possible, but maybe he was bluffing
on both fronts. Anthony was quite clear in his own mind that he
was not being properly informed, but he assumed that Clegg knew
what he was doing. All the films he had seen and all the thrillers he
had read had led him to expect a high degree of deviousness from
the Foreign Office, so he did not really expect to be told much. His
own role was all that concerned him, and that seemed quite simple.
He had to catch the plane to Krusograd, where he would be met
by Mr. Kammell, then proceed to his hotel, whence he would ring
the Ministry of Public and Social Order about Jane Murray. They
would no doubt arrange a meeting, and a time for her release.
"There should be no difficulties at all," Humphrey Clegg repeated.
It flashed across Anthony's mind, in a moment of wild surmise,
that the whole affair was a gigantic fake, that Humphrey Clegg

was some kind of double agent, that nobody had ever had the slightest intention of releasing Jane Murray. But he dismissed the surmise, over the claret. Clegg was too plausible to be a fake. Anthony knew too many people like Clegg. He had been at Oxford with them. Sincerity and authenticity dwelled side by side in Clegg's symmetrical features, in his long fingers, in his gray suit.

And anyway, Anthony Keating did not mind if the whole thing was a fake. He was too curious to turn back. His own eccentric career wound back behind him: songwriter, television producer, property man, man of enforced leisure. He had been idly casting around for action, and here it was, it had presented itself to him, it had picked him out. He could hardly refuse so mysterious a solicitation. The prospect was, after all, more exciting than a watercress farm. And he could buy the watercress farm, or one like it, if he got back.

They decided that Alison should be told that Anthony was going to collect Jane, as indeed he was. "You could ring her now," said Clegg, indicating the private phone in the private room. "She's at Donnell Murray's, isn't she?"

Anthony found Clegg's appearance of omniscience reassuring. It was as though, at last, somebody else had taken charge. He was slightly nervous at the prospect of ringing Alison, for he feared both her gratitude for his quixotic intentions, and her inevitable anxiety on his and Jane's behalf, but he obeyed Clegg, and rang. Clegg's omniscience, however, had failed. Tim answered the phone: he was babysitting with Molly, Donnell and Alison had gone out to dinner. They would be back later, could Tim take a message? And how was Anthony? Tim wanted to know. He, Tim, was fine, thank you, he had a small speaking part in a new science fiction film about a hijacked space ship. The Chinese hijack it, said Tim, and then they invade India. He would have told Anthony more of this ludicrous plot, but Anthony said good-bye, firmly, and rang off.

He returned to the table, where Humphrey Clegg was cracking a walnut with a meditative expression. Anthony assumed he was pondering the Balkan problem, but when he spoke it was to invite Anthony to stay the night. "In my flat," he said. "There was plenty of room, he said, for his wife had recently left him, taking the two children. Unless, of course, Anthony wanted to stay with his ex-wife, or with Donnell and Alison.

Anthony accepted the offer of a bed. "I think that would be wisest," said Clegg, and sighed. "I could teach you a little Wallacian, over breakfast. You'd be amazed, how few people speak Wallacian."

"Do you?"

"Not really. A few words. There's a girl in the office who does, she's quite a linguist."

Clegg rang for a brandy. Anthony declined one. Clegg sipped his, and sighed again. Then he began to tell Anthony about his wife, and the reasons why she had left him. It was an interesting story. She was fifteen years younger than Clegg, who was himself forty-five; they had been married for five years, and had two children, aged three and two. Clegg said: "It wasn't her fault, really. She could never get over the idea that I married her because I ought to have a wife, for professional purposes. Which was true, of course. It's hard to get on, in my line, without a wife." His pale fingers picked at the nut. He had a large signet ring on one finger, with a carnelian. Anthony felt he had known him all his life. "You were wise, Keating," said Clegg. "You got married at the first opportunity. You didn't hang around waiting. The longer you wait, the harder it is to take the leap."

"I got married far too young," said Anthony. "I just didn't think. It was very irresponsible."

"But you don't regret it."

"No, I don't suppose I regret it." Anthony paused. "No, I don't regret anything."

"My wife," said Humphrey Clegg, "is a very good-looking woman. She'd have no problems, in finding another husband."

"She must have cared for you in the first place," said Anthony.

"I don't know. She was impressed by me. I bullied her. She was very young."

And Clegg proceeded to tell Anthony about his search for a wife, his troubles with predatory and unsuitable and unreliable

women, his fear of attractive and eligible women, his fastidious-
ness, his inability to involve himself or commit himself, his preference for divorced women with past histories unacceptable to the
Foreign Office; he did not speak of his preference for men, though
Anthony, himself from a minor public school, did not need to hear
him describe his predicament. It was too common to need description. We are, thought Anthony, moving into a time when homo-
sexuality will be so acceptable that it will no longer constitute a
security risk, but it is too late for Humphrey Clegg. Though, as
Clegg implied, he was not a natural homosexual anyway, for when
he had met his wife, Sylvia, at a reception for the Belgian ambassador, he had in his own view fallen in love with her, and had
wooed and courted her until she succumbed, and agreed to marry
him.

To begin with, Sylvia had been the ideal wife. She enjoyed
company, enjoyed entertaining, obliged by producing a son and a
daughter. She was intelligent, vivacious, tactful, discreet. But the
life of discretion had begun to overburden her. She complained
that she could never let her hair down, could never talk freely.

"And it's true," said Clegg, "being married to a man in my
position is a strain."

On the way to his flat, in the taxi, Anthony wondered if Clegg
was so indiscreet about his marriage because of the necessity for
discretion in all other directions. Or was it merely the immediacy
of her desertion that had impelled him to these confidences? Or
the sense that in Anthony, a woman's man and an adventurer, he
would find a sympathetic, an uncritical audience? A confessor who
was, anyway, about to depart the country, perhaps forever, with
his secrets?

But even Anthony could not guess at the secret that Humphrey Clegg kept locked in his heart, the secret guilt over which,
endlessly, he brooded. Anthony's guesses were near enough, rea-
sonable enough, but Clegg had never been, in fact, a homosexual:
he had been, both better and worse, a solitary transvestite. More
eccentric, but, in security terms, could he have made anyone
understand, less of a risk. He had never confessed to anyone, until,

after marrying Sylvia, he had confessed to her. She had taken it badly. She had tried, gallantly, to rescue him, had pretended not to mind, had employed all her energy to divert and please him, and had succeeded, from his point of view, for he had loved her and admired her; but the secret of his locked suitcase of women's clothes, hidden in a secret locked cupboard, had weighed upon her mind, had corroded her spirits and sapped her optimism. Bluebeard's cupboard, she had called it, laughingly, patting his arm, smiling at him bravely; and he had given her the key. I have locked it up, now I have you I will never open the cupboard again, he said. And she had taken the key from him, turning quiet and subdued with the sinister gift. But the knowledge that she alone knew this thing had tormented Sylvia Clegg, as his temptations had tormented her husband. He knew that he should never have told her. There are some things one cannot tell. But once told, they cannot be untold.

So she had left him, the light-hearted Sylvia, carrying off the two little ones, to her father's house in Sussex. She had written to him: *I do not trust myself with you any more. I feel these wild impulses to talk, to tell people things I should not tell. I am afraid of hurting you, dear Humphrey, and I must go before I do you any harm. We should never have married, though I suppose I am glad we did, because of the babies.* She enclosed, in the letter, the key to the suitcase.

In terms of Humphrey Clegg's career, her desertion might not prove too serious. It is better to have had a wife and lost her, than never to have had a wife at all. But he wanted her back. He missed her.

Her ghost haunted the flat in South Kensington. She smiled brightly from silver frames.

Anthony and Humphrey Clegg sat up for half an hour, over a pot of tea. They talked of marriage, and children, and public schools, and state education, and whether or not Anthony had ever contemplated the Foreign Office or the Civil Service. Anthony described the way in which he had drifted into his own various activities. Clegg said that he envied his flexibility.

"And now I'm about to drift off to Wallacia," said Anthony. "I do hope I manage to drift back again alive."

Clegg smiled. "There is no danger," he said.

Humphrey Clegg's life had been ruined not by Eton but by a maid who had dressed him up in her frilly blouses and silk underwear, and painted his little boy's face with lipstick and rouge, and dabbed his throat with Californian Poppy. He had been imprisoned by this misfortune in a jail from which there would be no release.

Jane Murray, hoped Humphrey Clegg, would be home within the week. "Don't be surprised if she doesn't look too well," Clegg reminded him in a more somber tone, as he found Anthony a hot water bottle, a John le Carré to read in bed. "She's been starving herself, you know. I wouldn't comment on it to anyone, if I were you. She'll recover quickly enough, at her age."

In bed, with his book and his bottle, Anthony stared around and wondered what on earth he had stumbled into. The guest room in Humphrey Clegg's flat was profoundly comfortable, in an old-fashioned, solid, reliable style. The bed was high, wide, and soft, the carpet a patterned Victorian Indian, the wardrobe solid mahogany, the adjoining bathroom modern and well-fitted. Most of the furniture looked as though it had been inherited from parents or grandparents: it was heavy and dark, but perfectly good. It would last forever. Framed prints of the nineteenth century hung on the walls: there was one of Chelsea before the Embankment had been built, one of the Great Exhibition, one of Windsor Castle, a prospect of Eton College, a prospect from Westminster Bridge. A framed embroidered Oriental bird struck a more recent exotic imperial note, as did a Javanese shadow puppet in a glass box on the mantelpiece: relics, no doubt, of past postings. Anthony, lying and gazing around him, thought: this is some kind of trap. Life is not like this at all. It is another mirage, for all that its accouterments are so substantial.

He was not looking forward to ringing Alison in the morning, to tell her of his imminent departure. She would be sure to protest. But what can I do? thought Anthony. I have to go.

The room was a room of the past. Nothing in it spoke of a future. Victorian England surrounded him, as it had hung on Clegg's office wall, in the shape of camels and an oasis, and dangled from his office ceiling, in the shape of a crystal chandelier. So that was it, that had been England. Anthony stirred, restlessly. Surely, even as a boy, he and his clever friends had mocked the notion of empire? Surely they had all known the past was dead, that it was time for a new age? But nothing had arisen to fill the gap. He and his clever friends had been reared as surely, conditioned as firmly, as those like Humphrey Clegg, who had entered the old progression, learned the old rules, played the old games. Oh yes, they had dabbled and trifled and cracked irreverent jokes; they had thrown out the mahogany and bought cheap stripped pine, they had slept with one another's wives, and divorced their own, they had sent their children to state schools, they had acquired indeterminate accents, they had made friends from unthinkable quarters, they had encouraged upstarts like Mike Morgan, they had worn themselves out and contorted themselves trying to understand a new system, a new egalitarian culture, the new illiterate visual television age. They had tried: they had made efforts. They had learned to help their working wives to cook and care for the children; they had learned to live without servants, to give elaborate dinner parties without the white cloths and cut glass and silver cutlery of their grandparents, they had learned to survive broken nights with screaming babies, broken nights with weeping, angry, emancipated, emaciated wives. They had learned—academics, teachers, and parents alike—to condemn the examination system that had elevated them and brought them security: they had tried to learn new tricks. But where were the new tricks? They had produced no new images, no new style, merely a cheap strained exhausted imitation of the old one. Nothing had changed. Where was the new bright classless enterprising future of Great Britain? In jail with Len Wincobank, mortgaged to the hilt with North Sea Oil.

Well, I give in, thought Anthony. There is no point in struggling against the tide of one's time. I will go where Humphrey Clegg pushes me. I might as well accept that I belong to the world that has gone, reared in the shelter of a cathedral built to a faith that I have sometimes wished I could share, educated in ideals of public service which I have sometimes wished I could fulfill, a child of a lost empire, disinherited, gambler, drinker, hypocrite: and who am I to resist an appeal to a chivalric spirit that was condemned as archaic by Cervantes? I will let myself be pushed. I am nothing but weed on the tide of history.

He found the notion of being weed on the tide of history oddly reassuring, rather than depressing: amusing, even. He smiled to himself. I always feel all right, he thought, in a moment of acute self-knowledge, when I have found some grandiose way of explaining and justifying to myself what I am too weak to resist doing anyway. There had been no possibility of resisting Clegg. He had to go, for Jane, for Alison, for himself.

He wondered how Jane Murray would look, after more than half a year in a foreign prison, after weeks on hunger strike. Over dinner, Clegg had showed him the report from dead Clyde Barstow: she had abandoned the hunger strike after she had started to bleed from the esophagus each time the prison officer introduced the pipe for forced feeding. But, Barstow insisted, she had not been ill treated. As far as he could tell, all she needed was attention. She had been seeking attention, like any lonely teenage girl.

They would have to try to make it up to Jane, if they got her safely home.

He was three days in Krusograd before he was able to see Jane, but there seemed no cause for anxiety over the delay. Everything worked smoothly: the visa was fixed, the flight was on time, Kammell met the plane and received the documents. Anthony found messages waiting for him at his hotel, which he duly conveyed to appropriate quarters, in exchange for other packages. The Ministry of Social and Public Order was polite and helpful, and arranged an appointment for Anthony to see Jane and the governor of the prison; Mr. Barstow's successor, a man called Hopkins, took

Anthony out to a dinner of goose and dumplings covered in what seemed remarkably like Heinz tomato ketchup. Everything seemed very normal, too good to be true, except for the unnerving way in which Hopkins kept lowering his voice and looking around him whenever any new person entered the restaurant. Nor were the piles of sandbags around the restaurant windows, and across the foyer of the hotel, entirely reassuring; but then, sandbags had become a commonplace of the London scene also recently. If the restaurant where Max and Kitty Friedmann had celebrated their Ruby wedding anniversary had been barricaded with this new fashionable decor—which looked, in fact, not unlike the kind of modern sculpture on which the Tate had recently been spending vast sums—perhaps Max might not have been dead, nor Kitty without a foot.

At night, however, one could hear shooting. At least, Anthony thought it might be shooting. He had never heard shooting before. And the horizon had a faint red glow.

There were a few English-speaking people in the hotel: they were foreign correspondents, waiting for something to happen. They greeted Anthony warmly, a welcome addition to their small circle. Clegg had warned Anthony not to talk to them much, but he had not said he could not drink with them and play poker with them. The journalists were bored: there was less action at the capital, a hundred miles farther east, but more diversion. They were full of unreliable-sounding gossip about the political state of the country. It did not seem worth listening too closely to their contradictory accounts, but he was glad of their company to pass the time, for he found, as Alison had found before him, that there was not much to do in Wallacia. The mixture of boredom and anxiety was not pleasant, and Anthony could not help worrying lest the papers that Kammell had given him, in exchange for those he had delivered, might be stolen from his hotel room. They could not be particularly secret, Anthony decided, for surely Clegg would not have trusted him with anything secret; and if he had done, he would have issued much more strict instructions about what to do with them while waiting for Jane's release. But he did not want to lose them. Nor did he want to lose his passport, or his money, or his return ticket, or Jane's return ticket, so he took to carrying rather a lot of papers around on his person, and thumbing nervously through them from time to time to check that nothing was missing.

On the third day, he was summoned to the Department of the Ministry. It was a modern building, on the banks of the river: the town had been more or less flattened during the Second World War, and most of the buildings were new. Anthony had to wait an hour before being summoned into the presence of the Minister's deputy, but when he reached the presence, the deputy, through a fair-haired girl interpreter, was very civil. He was a large, stocky man, with short hair and a red complexion; he looked not unlike a Slavonic version of Giles Peters, thought Anthony. He conveyed, through the interpreter, the Minister's thanks to Anthony for coming to collect Jane, and the Minister's regret that Jane had so unwisely endangered her own health. Anthony politely apologized on Jane's behalf, and thought to himself that it would be hard to imagine any scene less reminiscent of the savage and brutal bureaucracy invoked by the *Daily Express*. The decor of the office was bright and bourgeois, of the midfifties, with shining clinical surfaces and orange and black geometric curtains. The deputy gave Anthony some papers relating to Jane's release and asked if he would sign them. Anthony said he could hardly sign papers he could not understand, so could he have an English version, please; the interpreter was sent off to produce a translation, and the deputy minister offered Anthony a small glass of vodka while waiting. As they could no longer converse, without the fair-haired girl as intermediary, they sipped and smiled at one another, and tried out a few experimental words of each other's language: Anthony managed, Please, Good morning, Good evening, and counted up to ten, and the deputy did rather better with various phrases such as, To be or not to be, or Down by the Riverside, and finally, triumphantly, if not wholly comprehensibly, Lucy in the Sky with Diamonds. Stones and Beatles had clearly been passing through diplomatic bags, and international relations seemed momentarily simple. Though there was a moment of panic when the girl returned with the English documents, and Anthony realized that he had no means of knowing whether or not they were faithful renderings of the originals. They looked innocuous enough, but he felt obliged to explain that he felt he could sign only the English version. The deputy and the interpreter looked hurt, and said the English versions were not official, for see, they had no seals on them; and, sweating slightly, for he did not want to initiate any further delays, Anthony signed for he knew not what. It will all be over soon, he said to himself.

They told him he could go and see Jane that afternoon, if he wished: she would be released, provided that the minister in Beravograd ratified the papers, the next day. "So you can arrange your flight home," said the deputy. "Mrs. Murray will be pleased to have her daughter home."

Then they explained to him how to get to the prison, gave him yet more papers to present to obtain admission, shook his hand warmly, and dismissed him.

He walked out into the bright sunlight. It was late morning. There was a strange air of expectancy in the dull little town: of stasis, of pause before movement. There were more people than usual on the streets, standing in knots, talking; for the first time Anthony looked at them, had time to look at them. Had the Reuters men looked at them at all? Some, perhaps. There were all ages, both sexes: hard-faced brown old peasants, fat women with baskets, students in the local approximation to jeans. They were standing and talking, with an air of interest, hope, lively concern, slight menace. The Wallacian people. Blond Slavic broad faces, nutcracker brown ones, and student faces such as one can see in any city in the world: only in middle and old age do the more extreme characteristics take their final form. What were they up to, what were they hoping for? I am an ignorant fool, thought Anthony; here is history, and I can't understand a word anyone is saying, and my only aim is to get out of it as quickly as possible.

The sun shone down on the square modern blocks, and on the

odd little Oriental remnants of fluted and tiled roofs of little tur-
rets and domes and dovecotes. The sun redeemed it into a moment
of beauty, and the red stone hills glittered on the horizon. Anthony gazed: it was not for him. It was utterly foreign. In no way
could he ever understand such a place, such a life. He walked back
to the hotel: he would ring the consul, to report.

But the line to the consulate was dead. The hotel operator
apologized: he could not get through. He went down to the bar, to
see if there were any journalists hanging around who could tell
him what was going on. There was one Reuters man, who informed Anthony of the blowing up, by landmine, of a busload of
thirty-five workers from the eastern province. Who was responsible? Nobody knew, but it meant trouble. All the other journalists
were on their telephones, blocking the lines. Anthony decided to
walk around to the consulate, as it was only a quarter of an hour's
walk away; he could not really believe that there was shooting in
the streets. But the main road leading toward the consulate was
cordoned off. Guards in blue uniform stood with guns. Beyond, he
could see a crater in the road and a wrecked car. He turned back.

The prison lay out in the other direction, luckily. He ate an
abrasive sandwich in the bar with the Reuters man, then set off,
again on foot. For some reason he did not wish to risk taking a
taxi: he felt safer on foot, more independent. He fingered the
papers in his pocket as he walked along. The road to the prison
wound upward, out of the town center, through a shabby fringe
district, of badly made roads, past high abattoir walls and haphazard factories. For the first time since his plane had landed,
Anthony felt and smelled that he was abroad, noticed the vegeta-
tion, the twisted gnarled evergreen oaks, the dusty olives, the
patches full of tomatoes, the little corners of vines. This had been a
country of peasants, subdued peasants, now freed by the protective powers of Eastern Europe. The land had been distributed and
redistributed, in many a conflict. Anthony remembered holidays in
Greece, Turkey, Yugoslavia. Nobody ever came for a holiday to
Wallacia. But one could see that the town had once been attractive: the road rose, toward the outskirts, toward a strange red

sandstone outcrop, and if one looked back downward, the roofs nestled together, in a harmony much broken by new square blocks. He could see the roof of a building that looked like a mosque. But religion was not permitted in this modern state. Perhaps the mosque was preserved as a museum? A museum, a memorial to the past credulity of mankind.

Walking up the path toward the high, white, wire-topped walls of the prison, Anthony Keating found himself thinking, I do not know how man can do without God.

It was such an interesting concept that he stopped in the roadway, like Paul on the way to Damascus: not exactly felled by realization, for alas, faith had not accompanied the concept. But it stopped him in his tracks, nevertheless. He stood there for a moment or two, and thought of all those who accept so readily the nonexistence of God, who find such persuasive substitutes, such convincing alternative sanctions for their own efforts. Anthony had never been able to accept the humanist argument that man can behave well through his own manhood. Man clearly does not do so: that is that.

But now was hardly the time to ask for a revelation from his creator. It was hot: the late spring sun beat down fiercely on his bare head. Mad dogs and Englishmen, reflected Anthony Keating, and began to wish he had tried to commandeer a taxi; not that he was tired, but that he feared that to arrive on foot might prove his lack of seriousness and authenticity. He might, he feared, be dismissed as a madman. He felt for the papers in his pocket. Everything was still there. A man without God and without his papers would be truly lost, thought Anthony.

The prison wall was enormously high. Jane had been transferred back to it from the camp in the mountains a month ago, the consul had said. He rang the bell, and wondered if he would really have the opportunity to discuss, the next day, in a civilized manner, with his stepdaughter-to-be, the conditions in a Wallacian prison. It seemed highly unreal, like so much of life.

A porter answered the door. Anthony presented his papers, wishing he had been able to get hold of the consul to accompany him, helplessly aware of his inability to answer back, if refused admission. But the porter accepted his papers, and ushered him into a waiting room. There, Anthony waited.

In half an hour, another official of higher standing arrived, and beckoned to Anthony. Anthony followed him, down a long tiled corridor, to another waiting room. Here, Anthony was asked to sign a paper: he asked for an interpreter, but none was forthcoming, so he signed recklessly, realizing he would get no further if he did not. The higher official disappeared with the paper, and came back in quarter of an hour with a young woman, who offered to escort Anthony to the women's section. She spoke a little English. As in England, women appeared to be better at languages than men, he noted. As they walked down another long corridor, and through a double locked vestibule, and into another corridor, he asked her if all Wallacian prisons contained both men and women. Yes, she said, of course. The camps, not, but the prisons, yes. He asked if she was taking him to see Jane. No, she said, not yet: she was taking him to the governor. Ah, said Anthony.

The governor turned out to be a woman too. She was a small, heavy, elderly woman, with very short black cropped hair, and a cream nylon blouse and a dark navy skirt. She gripped his hand with both of hers, somewhat emotionally, he thought. She spoke English.

"Mr. Keating," she said, "how pleased to meet you. What pleasure. Such anxiety." She was sweating slightly, not wholly from the heat. She shook his hand again, waved to him, with authority, to seat himself. He sat. She fanned herself with a sheaf of papers. "What pleasure," she repeated. She proceeded to tell him that she had once been to England, to study. Before the war. She talked about England. British Museum. Marchmont Street. Museum Street. Collet's bookshop. *New Statesman*. George Orwell.

She was another generation from the deputy minister, with his Beatles and his Rolling Stones.

He listened to her. She asked him questions from time to time, but they could not converse, for although he could understand most of her English, she could not understand his. She asked him about London, about the site of the new British Library, about Emanuel Shinwell, about the British response to Solzhenitzyn. He did not have to worry about compromising himself or Clegg in his answers, for she did not wait for them. After half an hour, she ran down, paused, and said, "But you will want to see Miss Murray."

Anthony nodded, politely, as though to indicate that he would much rather listen to her reminiscences, but knew he ought not to trespass on her time.

"Come," she said, rising to her feet, beckoning. Her manner was very abrupt, in contrast with her words. He found her alarming. He followed her. The young woman who also spoke English followed them.

Jane Murray was sitting in a small windowless room on a hard chair, at a table. There was another chair at the table, for Anthony, and one in the corner, for the interpreter. Jane looked up, as Anthony entered the room. She gazed at him. She did not speak. She began to cry.

"Jane," said Anthony. "Jane. Don't cry, it's all over."

She buried her face in her hands, but he had already seen her swollen lips, her puffy eyes, her dark bruised face. She was as thin as a scarecrow: her clothes hung. Her hunched shoulders stuck out of her cotton jersey. Her hands, covering her face, were taut and oddly spotted, like the hands of an old woman. She sobbed and sobbed. Anthony sat down and reached out and patted her: she reached for his hand, and squeezed it. Then she looked up at him. It was Alison's face, haggard, distraught, sick. "Never mind," said Anthony, "never mind. It's all right, I've come to get you, we're going home tomorrow."

It was clear that she had not been expecting this. She stared at him, disbelieving, then croaked, "Home? To England?"

"Tomorrow," he said. Her voice sounded terrible: whatever had they done to her?

He did not know what to say to her; he told her Alison was well, told her of his flight, of the hotel, of his walk up to the prison. She could not speak, so he talked, patiently. He was still talking when the governor arrived, with another batch of papers. She seemed agitated. He feared bad news, some setback, some delay, but instead she beckoned him out on the door and said, "Mr. Keating, you go now. Take her now."

"But I thought—" began Anthony, then stopped himself. This was no time for fair play; it was time to get out, while the going was good.

"I have telephone communication, from Minister," said the governor. "You go, now." She seemed in a hurry.

"All right," said Anthony.

And an hour later, in an official car, with Jane's few things packed up in a bag, they went. They went back to the hotel: Anthony tried to ring the consulate, again without success, then tried the embassy in Beravograd, also without success. Then he rang the airport, to see if he could change the tickets for the plane that evening but they were having their lengthy siesta, and answered him in Wallacian on answerphone. He rang the hotel desk, and inquired about planes: there was nothing, anyway, until the next morning, they told him.

Jane, meanwhile, lay on the bed. He wanted to ring Alison to tell her he had got her, but there was clearly no hope of getting an outside line, least of all to West Gonnersall, whither he presumed Alison had gone. West Gonnersall seemed a thousand miles away. And was.

Jane slept. He unpacked her bag. There were the things she had had with her eight months ago, carefully preserved and labeled, a pathetic collection. A pair of sandals. A Marks and Spencer's bra and three pairs of knickers. An Indian cotton skirt, a sweatshirt labeled University of Neasden, two packets of Tampax, unopened, a packet of contraceptive pills, half used, some postcards of Istanbul, her passport, a pack of cards, a diary, a purse, a pair of Levi's, laundered but bloodstained, and two books: a paperback of the Theban plays of Sophocles, and a copy of *Zen and the Art of Motorcycle Maintenance*. A ballpoint, some travel sickness pills, a toothbrush, a hairbrush, and, strangest of all, a plastic Phillips Planisphere. He thought of himself and Alison, discussing the difference between dippers and gray wagtails, the common rowan and the Hupeh rowan. Her mother's daughter. His.

There she lay, crumpled, shriveled, asleep. He thought of the girl in labor, who now lay, beyond his knowledge, dead. He thought of waking Jane, making love to her. It was the only way to comfort a woman that he knew. She would accept it: he could tell from her earlier tears, from her grip on his hand, from her whispering, that she would accept it. She wheezed and stirred and mumbled in her sleep. He gazed at her dark face. Had she not so, in her loss of adolescent weight, resembled Alison, he would have done it, he later thought, and it might not have been the wrong thing to do. In the past, such things had sometimes turned out well, sometimes badly: one could never tell. But she was so skinny; one ought not to force one's way into so brittle a frame. It might, for all he knew, have been as painful as the tube down the esophagus. And she was so profoundly asleep, though restless: through shock, he supposed. He decided that she needed sleep more.

He wondered what to do with her. She looked as though she must certainly need medical, if not sexual attention, but this was certainly no time or place to seek it: she would have to wait till next day, in London. He wondered what he would need most if just released from prison. Food? A bath? A drink? Someone to tell? It was hard to imagine. Jane was wearing a worn and shapeless green skirt, not, he thought, her own, and coarse stockings, and laced canvas shoes, and a white cotton jersey, baggy around the neck. He looked at her, and looked at his watch. It was seven in the evening. It had been a long day. There was a flight out at midday. He wondered if he ought to try to get a room in the hotel for Jane, but some instinct warned him that it would be better to advertise her presence as little as possible: she could have his bed, he would sleep on the floor. Or perhaps he could borrow a bed off one of the journalists? The man from *Le Monde* had a twin-bedded room, he said. Jane began to sit up: at the sight of her face, he thought no, I will stay with her, and keep an eye on her, I'd better not leave her on her own.

"How are you feeling?" he asked. Jane attempted a smile.

"Not too bad," she said. Her voice croaked, agonizingly, and she clutched at her throat. "Sore throat," she said. "You haven't got anything for a sore throat, have you?"

"I don't know if you ought to have anything, without seeing a doctor," he said. What on earth could one give a girl with a scraped esophagus? Lemon and honey pastilles? Tablets designed for the English influenza?

"You could have some Disprin," he said. He had some in one of the zip pockets of his travel bag: they had been there for years, but he supposed they were still potent. He took them out: there they were, in their rather crushed cardboard pack, each wrapped in its little silver foil case. He took two out and went to get a glass of water from the bathroom, and when he came back, he found Jane examining the pack with a kind of wonder. She drank the water with the dissolved pills, swallowing hard.

"How long is it, since you had a meal?" he asked her, wondering if he ought to try to find soup, or coffee.

"Oh, I've been eating for days," she said. "They made me eat. That's why it hasn't got better, I think."

"I could find you something liquid. Some soup, perhaps? You probably ought to have something."

She shook her head. "I don't want to be a nuisance," she said.

He wondered whether to point out that she had already been the most astonishing nuisance, and that fetching her a bowl of soup would be neither here nor there in the international scale of nuisance she had caused, but he refrained.

"I really think you'd better have something," he said. "I don't want you collapsing on my hands. You sit here quietly, and wait for me to get back. I won't be long. Look, here are your things," and he handed her the bag. "Or, if you've read those books already, here's mine."

He was still reading the John le Carré lent to him by Humphrey Clegg: he had made little progress with it, and could not follow the obscure plot. He laid it on the bed by her, along with her own possessions, and made his way downstairs. It had occurred to him that it would be cheering to speak to the journalists, though he had better not admit that he had already got Jane, or they might want to interview her. But a quick drink and a quick briefing would do no harm, surely. Then he could get some soup, direct from the kitchen. He knew better than to try the nonexistent room service: it was always quicker to get things oneself. There was a man in the kitchen who was quite helpful.

There were two journalists in the bar. He joined them, bought them each a vodka, and one for himself. They told him that there had been several explosions during the day, all in the Vratsik quarter to the east: the military were out in force. There had been a demonstration of some sort in Beravograd, so far peaceful. It was rumored that the President was about to sack the Minister of the Interior. Tomato growers in the southern region were sending a delegation to Beravograd to protest about rising food prices. Telephone links with the British consulate had been restored. The Krusograd evening paper claimed that a member of an extreme religious sect, illegal of course, had claimed responsibility for the assassination of the British consul, Clyde Barstow, and had been apprehended. "If something more interesting doesn't happen soon, I'll get recalled," said the man from the *Examiner*. He had already written his in-depth report on life in Wallacia, based on a few chats with the barman and a taxi driver or two, an interview with a man in the Housing Department, and a visit to a nursery school. "Something will happen tomorrow," said the man from *Le Monde*. "I'll be gone by tomorrow, I hope," said Anthony. They asked him how his interview with the deputy Minister of Social and Public Order had gone; he replied, cagily, thinking of Jane sitting upstairs in his bedroom. It had been stupid of him to remind them that he was hoping to get her out and away tomorrow; they would be sure to want to speak to her, and she was hardly a good advertisement for life in a Balkan prison. Not that Anthony cared about the reputation of Balkan prisons, but he did not wish to be reapprehended at the airport for spreading malicious gossip about the state. The more he thought about it, the more surprised he was that they had released Jane at all, looking as she did. How could they have been so certain that he would be too nervous to display her before returning home? What did they expect, what did they want him to do? Or had they got more important things to worry about than Jane Murray?

It was not his affair. His affair was to get Jane out of the country, on the next possible plane.

When he returned to his room, with a jugful of chicken soup for Jane and a plateful of tepid meatball and rice for himself, Jane was in the bath. It cheered him that she was taking a bath. Perhaps it would make her look more presentable, too. While she was still in there, the phone rang: it was Hopkins on the line, from the consulate. Hopkins, seemingly regardless of the possibility that his line or Anthony's line might be tapped, said that he heard Jane had already been released, and what a relief that was. He would send a car in the morning, to take Jane and Anthony to the airport. If the car didn't turn up, Anthony should make his own way. He would have come to see Anthony off, in normal circumstances, but a lot of work had accumulated during the day, because the telephone lines and indeed the water supply to the consulate had been sev-ered during the day by incompetent roadworkers re-laying sewage pipes, and there were a lot of things to straighten out. Might he wish Anthony a good journey, and how glad he was that the affair had been settled so satisfactorily.

Anthony sat on the bed, and ate a mouthful of Oriental meat-ball. He tried to inspect the picture of the road to the consulate in his mind. It showed a bomb crater, untidy, jagged, surrounded by anxious men in uniform, and an overturned car. He tried to turn it into a peaceful scene of roadworks and sewage pipes. Perhaps a gas main had blown up?

Jane emerged from the bathroom. She was wrapped up in a towel, and she looked marginally better. She collected her own clothes, and came back in a moment wearing her Levi's and the Neasden sweatshirt. They hung on her. "I've lost weight," she whispered hoarsely. It was a joke.

She drank most of the soup, slowly and carefully, while An-thony munched his way through the rice. Then she began to talk, to whisper. She told him how extraordinary it was to use soap that made proper lather: the soap in the camp had been huge great yellow blocks that produced nothing but a harsh yellow scum. Anthony's Palmolive was fantastic, she said. And to find lavatory paper that didn't scrape. Anthony, who had thought the hotel lavatory paper, by Western European standards, extremely rough, began to get a good picture of her past few months. She told him more: of the cabbage soup, of the bitter cold and the beautiful trees up in the mountains, of the camp workshop where she had made cardboard boxes. "You wouldn't believe," she whispered intensely, "how difficult it was to get the hang of making those boxes. I felt so stupid. And there were all these women around me, assembling them so quickly, and I was messing about; I simply couldn't get the idea. I felt such a fool." She paused. "Everything made me feel such a fool," she said.

The worst thing, she said, had been the fear that she was pregnant. She seemed afraid of embarrassing him by telling him, but unable to desist. He found her own embarrassment the most endearing feature he had so far encountered in her. Perhaps it would be possible to like Jane, after all. She'd been on the pill, she said, but she had to admit that she sometimes forgot to take it, and anyway she'd heard that even the pill wasn't a hundred percent reliable. And then, after the accident, she just never had another period. I was dead scared, she said. I didn't dare tell anyone. I kept hoping that it was the shock, I know shock can do funny things to you, but I've never had that before, I've always been like clockwork, so for three months, I thought that was it, and I didn't know what to do. I couldn't tell anyone in the camp—they'd have made me have an abortion, and they might have killed me, I know. I used to sign on for these revolting sanitary towels—sorry, Anthony, what a horrible story for you to have to listen to—and then throw them away unused, because I thought if I didn't sign on they'd spot something was up, and examine me. It was pretty risky anyway, because there were no doors on the lavs. I wanted to tell Mr. Barstow, but he was so—well, you know what Mr. Barstow's like, he's so serious and old-fashioned and sweet, I just didn't dare tell him.

Jane clearly did not know that Clyde Barstow was dead.

So, Jane went on, I kept it to myself, and I kept prodding myself and feeling myself, and I didn't seem to get any fatter, and I didn't feel sick, or faint, or any of the other things people are supposed to feel. And after Christmas, I decided I couldn't be pregnant after all, that it must be something else wrong.

"You didn't tell anyone then, even?"

"No. What would have been the use? Nobody would have cared, anyway. There were girls there suffering from the most awful things, and nobody did anything about it." She paused. "You don't suppose there is anything seriously wrong with me, do you?"

"No, I don't suppose so for a moment. I'm sure it was just shock. Or the change of climate, and diet. All that kind of thing," said Anthony vaguely. "Though I'm sure you didn't do yourself much good by going on hunger strike," he added, after a moment. "Whatever gave you that idea?"

An incomprehensible, mystical, fatuous, infuriating expression spread itself, at the question, over the features of Jane Murray, transforming her from a reasonably normal, sensible, coherent person back to the idle and irresponsible teenager he had always thought her to be. He seemed to remember that one of Alison's complaints about her had been that she used to indulge herself in strange self-inflicted consciousness-raising practices: egg and grapefruit diets, milk diets, rice highs. Barstow and Clegg had guessed that she was starving herself for attention, to make herself exceptional; Anthony had hitherto assumed that she had done it because she thought it regardless of its aim both fashionable and heroic; but he could see from her face that her reasons had been yet more perverse. "I did it to see what it would feel like," she said.

It seemed an answer from the dead end of the world.

"And what did it feel like?" said Anthony bitterly.

Jane smiled, to herself. "I couldn't describe it," she said.

So it was for this that he had come all this way: the radiant future, the next generation.

It was his own fault, for asking so stupid a question. His own children's aspirations were probably no better.

Nor, for that matter, were his own.

Jane slept in the bed, Anthony on the floor. He slept badly, and woke from time to time: in the distance, he thought he could hear noises, and his fitful patches of sleep were filled with dreams of airplanes and mines and explosions. At one point he got up and went to the window: the horizon was again lit by a strange pink glow, which might or might not have been the dawn. Jane slept. Anthony heard her even breathing, and was sorry that he had felt angry with her the night before: she was a child of her time, as he of his, and if she wanted to starve herself nearly to death, just for fun, just to see what it felt like, when three quarters of the world was starving reluctantly and in earnest, then that was her affair. Just as it was his affair that he had traveled out here to collect her, and would have done so whether or not he had considered her worth collecting.

He was glad when it became light; he had to admit to himself that he was intensely anxious, and could not wait to get out of Wallacia. The consul had ordered the car for ten. Breakfast arrived, the only meal that room service recognized, and Jane and Anthony shared it. He checked his papers ten times, making sure that everything was in order. He went down to settle the bill, was told that the hotel had been instructed to send the account to the consulate. He went back again, and he and Jane played Twenty-one, to calm their nerves, while waiting for the car. "In eight hours we'll be in London," he said, but somehow he did not believe it: images of possible hitches drifted in front of his eyes—canceled exit visas, searches at the customs, delayed flights.

The car did not turn up at ten. At quarter past, Anthony tried to ring through to the consulate, but was told that the line was dead, again. He asked the hotel to order a taxi. They said that they would. Ten minutes later they rang back and said that all the taxis were engaged, Anthony would have to wait. Anthony looked at his watch. His heart was beating strangely, he was breaking out in sweat. It was as though he were experiencing the concentrated essence of the panic of all missed flights, all delayed taxis, all missed trains. The airport was only twenty minutes' drive away, but however could one get there, without a car? Jane also was looking sick with anxiety: we could go down and stand on the street and hitch a lift, she suggested, somebody must be driving that way. It seemed a not impossible suggestion: better, anyway, than sitting in their room, impotent. They made their way down to the foyer, with their two small bags, and there, an answer to their prayers, was the man from Reuters. He had a hired car. Anthony threw himself on his mercy: we have to get to the airport, he said, quickly, could you take us? The man from Reuters looked as harassed and uncertain as they were, but he got his car and told them to hop in; on the way, he interrogated Anthony about Jane's release. "I hope to God your flight's there," he said, as they made their way out of town. "Fighting's broken out in Beravograd. I think I'd better get off there, when I've dropped you. It looks as though you'll just get out in time."

"I feel sick," said Jane.

"No time to be sick now," said the man from Reuters. "Wait till you get on the plane. They provide paper bags on the plane."

He pulled up outside the terminal building at eleven: officially, they were five minutes late for checking in. "There's your plane," said the man from Reuters. It was standing on the airfield. "Don't worry, they'll let you on. But you'd better get moving."

Anthony and Jane jumped out, with their bags. They made their way to the airport building, which seemed to be bustling with more activity than one flight would warrant. A lot of large trucks and armored cars stood about. Anthony did not know which door to approach, at which desk to present himself: the notices were in German and Wallacian and Bulgarian only. There were too many men in uniform about. Anthony had never felt so anxious in his life. Something was wrong: what should he do? He looked about: there, after all, was the right desk for checking in, with the flight time and number announced. He ran over to it, and quickly uncrumpled the air tickets from his pocket, and flung them down in front of the steward, who was on the telephone. "Please," said Anthony. "*Pelquej.*" It was one of the only twelve words of Wallacian he knew: Humphrey Clegg had taught it to him over breakfast. It attracted the steward's attention, but did not detach him from the phone. Still talking fast in Wallacian, he looked at Anthony, looked at his watch, shook his head at Anthony, pointed to the clock. "*Pelquej,*" said Anthony again, with desperate urgency, and pointed to the forlorn Jane three yards behind him, hoping to God that she looked more like an ill child than a criminal driver prematurely released from jail. Anthony could see the airport bus, full of lucky checked-in passengers, ready to taxi across the runway to the silver plane: it was only twenty yards away. The steward continued his urgent conversation; even the distraught Anthony managed to take in that it did sound urgent, rather than desultory. Finally, he slammed down the receiver, and turned to Anthony. Anthony pushed the tickets once more under his nose. He gesticulated, wildly, at the plane, at Jane. In despair, he heard the airport bus driver switch on the ignition: to his relief, the steward, glancing at Jane, at Anthony, at the tickets, at the passports, made a signal to the driver. He switched off the ignition. He would wait. Jane burst into tears of relief. The steward stamped their tickets, waved them on: they still had to go through the customs, through passport control. Delays here, Anthony could see, would be the end. The customs man seemed satisfied that they could have nothing to declare, in view of the small quantity of their hand baggage, and even made some joke about hidden vodka. Anthony, fretting, impatient, managed to praise the local brand yet again; as he had praised it to the hotel barman, to the taxi driver, to the friendly woman in the hotel kitchen, to the deputy Minister of Social and Public Order. His ears were straining for the sound of the passenger bus's ignition: he could no longer see it or the airfield, for they had entered one of those long, low, insubstantial sheds that litter airports. The customs man waved them on, around the corner, to the passport office. From here, they could see the airfield: the bus was still waiting, but its driver was looking at his watch. So were some of the passengers. They were as eager to get out of Wallacia as Anthony himself.

Anthony could not have explained why he was so afraid of the passport inspector. It was irrational: they had let him in on his Foreign Office visa, why should they not let him out? But he could tell, from the expression on the inspector's face, that there was trouble. He stamped Jane's, but when he opened Anthony's he stared at it in perplexity, and scratched his ear. Then he beckoned to another official, and they stared at Anthony's passport together, and together shook their heads. Jane glanced at Anthony with an expression of such terror on her face that his stomach turned; she had been through enough, worse than she had told him. She was a brave girl: she had survived well. He was trying to think of some way of asking, through gesture, if Jane could go through and catch the plane without him, when he heard, from the long hall out of sight around the corner behind him, a lot of shouting and commotion, which promised yet more delay, for it distracted the passport official entirely from the task of vetting Anthony Keating: he made off toward the inner hall, leaving Anthony and Jane alone together in the small, final office, the last step.

He took Anthony Keating's passport with him. Jane's lay, stamped, on the desk.

The driver of the bus had his eye on them. He beckoned. Anthony waved, begging him to wait. The driver shrugged. Across the airfield, the plane shimmered in the morning sun. The driver switched on the engine again. Anthony picked up Jane's passport from the desk, thrust her passport and ticket into her hands (and with extraordinary presence of mind, the papers for Clegg). The bus set off. "Run," said Anthony. "Run."

Jane ran. On thin sticklike legs she ran after the bus, in a spurt of energy he would not have thought left in her, waving, shouting: the bus slowed down for her, and he saw her clamber on to it, and look back toward him. "I'll catch the next plane out," he shouted after her, waving, smiling, though he doubted if she could hear. The bus speeded up, toward the runway. Anthony turned back to the flimsy, featureless, empty little office, still hoping that perhaps the official would return in time for him to follow Jane, telling himself that there was no reason why Jane should not travel safely by herself, telling himself that at the worst, he would indeed catch the next flight out.

But there was no next flight. As Anthony walked toward the door that separated the passport control from the main hallway, there was an explosion. Bursts of gunfire followed it. Anthony flung himself on the floor, behind the passport official's desk. Jane, as the plane moved off, saw smoke rising from the terminal and heard shooting. She was too frightened even to scream. The other passengers also were glued to the windows: the plane gathered speed. The pilot, a Turk from Istanbul, had no intention of hanging around to see what was the matter; the air hostess made soothing announcements about seat belts and cigarettes, in several languages, including English. The plane lurched horribly upward. There, below, was a scattered scene of confusion: trucks and cars were converging on the airport, tiny figures were running in all directions, smoke continued to pour upward. The plane rose relentlessly, leaving Anthony Keating to his fate. Everyone on board it, except for Jane, heaved a sigh of relief. It had been a near thing. Air travel was so risky these days: hijacks, civil wars, guerrilla attacks. They relapsed into chatter, those who were innocently passing through from Istanbul to Zurich: solid businessmen relaxed, bankers stretched their legs and thought of ordering drinks. A CIA man pretending to be a travel agent decided, too late, that he should have stayed behind, and several Wallacians, some with all their worldly wealth concealed on their persons, congratulated themselves on having utilized their privileged exit visas just in time. Where they would go, what they would do there, they hardly knew. But anywhere would be better than Wallacia, their home, their native land. Life in Wallacia, they guessed, would not be particularly pleasant for anybody, in the near future, least of all for those who had backed the wrong horses. Though, as one or two considered, remembering the history of Czechoslovakia, of

Hungary, of Cyprus, of Lebanon, maybe this was a race that no horse would win.

Life in the immediate future was extremely unpleasant for Anthony Keating. He lay on the floor under the desk, and waited. He could smell fire. His one consolation was the sound of the departing airplane: run, he had said to Jane Murray, and she had run, perhaps for her life. She was on board, on her way back to the West, to Alison, to doctors, to Palmolive soap and Tampax. And here was he, stuck under a desk, without his passport.

He waited there for quite a while. The noises increased, then diminished. He had plenty of time to speculate about the nature of the activity, but could arrive at no conclusions. Humphrey Clegg had not briefed him for this possibility. He wished he knew more of the history of the Balkans. The history of the Balkans was so confusing that he had always chosen other options, at school, at university. But now there was no other option. He tried to recall a few facts. Was it in the fourteenth century that the Ottomans had invaded? He thought hard: in 1453, Constantinople fell. To whom? He had forgotten: 1829, Greek independence acknowledged; 1830, Serbian independence acknowledged. In 1913 the Balkan League—ah yes, this was rather nearer home—the Balkan League defeated Turkey, in a series of battles so complex, and fought on so many fronts, that no one had ever been able to memorize them. He was sure it had been 1913. Then there had been the First World War, and the Second World War. Electoral victories for the Communists in most of the states. Peace treaties between Hungary, Bulgaria, Rumania and the Allies in 1947. Tito in Yugoslavia, Hoxha in Albania, Tetov in Wallacia, three independents. Warsaw Pact, 1955. Both Albania and Wallacia had subsequently withdrawn from the Warsaw Pact, though for different ideological reasons. When? He could not remember. Why? He had never known.

As a boy, thought Anthony, this is how I spent the time at the dentist's. Trying to remember dates, to stop thinking about the pain. He was out of practice, as most Western civilians are. Anthony Keating had never thought of himself as physically courageous. On the contrary, he had always assumed that if put to any kind of test, he would prove a coward. But after a quarter of an hour lying on a dusty floor under a desk, he began to think that his old enemy, boredom, was rather worse than fear. He would certainly not like to be stuck there forever. The shooting had died down. He decided to go out and investigate.

He stood up, and dusted himself down. He decided that the best thing to do would be to look as calm and normal as possible, as though he had every right to be there. As long as nobody spoke to him in Wallacian, who knows, he might be able to walk away unharmed, unobserved. He was alarmed, as he stood up, to find that he was shaking and trembling: that would be a giveaway. He did not wish to be shot down as a shaker and trembler. He practiced controlling his muscles. I must put a good face on it, he thought. Emulate Michael Caine, Sean Connery. He made himself think of Jane, by now well over the mountains. He could see why the poor child had gone on a hunger strike. It was a free act, not to eat. Anthony walked to the door leading out of the little hardboard office and quietly opened it.

The scene before his eyes was unpleasant. Various officials lay dead on the ground, watched by various other officials. Most of the dead people had been not very adequately covered with sheets of newspaper, a small mercy. There was clearly no possibility of crossing this particular arena unquestioned and unmolested, however little one trembled, so Anthony quietly shut the door again, unobserved. He would leave the other way.

He went out onto the airfield. There was nobody in sight. Well, there was nothing else for it. He would have to try to get away. This was a dangerous place to loiter, even though the building itself was no longer on fire.

The airport bus was standing, abandoned, a few yards away. He wondered whether it would be worth making a dash for it, hoping that the ignition key was still in place. He decided not. He would look conspicuous in an airport bus: he did not at all resemble the blond Wallacian driver. In fact, he did not resemble in coloring or physique any Wallacian he had yet seen. He looked what he was, an English gentleman of the middle classes. He had no hope of disguising himself in this flat terrain. Krusograd itself was not particularly flat; he thought with longing of all the little nooks and crannies and kitchen gardens he had passed on the way to the prison yesterday morning. But the airport, like all airports, was as bare and level and exposed a place as the engineers had been able to find. Naturally.

He began to think it might be wiser to wait until nightfall, before doing anything at all. But the prospect filled him with despair. It was still only midday. Should he go and present himself —haughtily demand protection, asylum, repatriation—to the British consul? He thought of Clyde Barstow. Better not. He leaned against the whitewashed wall, and blew his nose firmly in his handkerchief. Then he went back into the passport control office, sat down at the passport control desk, and started to finish the John le Carré, which was waiting for him in his bag.

He finished the John le Carré in a couple of hours, still not quite sure what had happened in the course of its plot. Then he embarked on the Theban plays of Sophocles, which he had also packed in his bag. It was a new translation: after a while it occurred to him to look for the name of the translator whose version struck him as excellent and saw that, by God, it was Linton Hancox. The discovery cheered him. He looked around the office with more curiosity and less terror: the walls were bare, except for some red and green notices in Wallacian, and a highly tinted portrait of President Tetov. The furniture was standard cheap office furniture: pale splintery wood. He pulled away a few splinters. Daring, he opened the drawer of the desk. Inside were some multilingual documents about visas, some descriptions of currency regulations, a few cheap ballpoints, some paper clips, a pair of spectacles, a postcard of a ski resort, and an apple. He wondered whether he might eat the apple, but refrained. There was no point in being wantonly provocative.

The airport had gone very quiet. It was almost as though everybody had gone away. It was not a busy spot at the best of times: only two planes a day from the outside world, one going east, one west, and a few internal trips to the capital. These did not seem to be taking place.

Anthony rehearsed his lines, should anyone come and discover him. It was a pity that he could not speak Wallacian: he was forced to fall back on various old-world possibilities, such as, "Ah, I see you have come to return me my passport." He wondered why any course of action seemed to suggest behavior more suited to a Victorian gentleman than to a modern operator; it was as though the spirit of Humphrey Clegg and his bedroom had subtly filled Anthony Keating's submissive body. Here he was, a hostage, prepared to represent Queen and Country with the polite and honorable codes of the English public school. He had not even eaten the Wallacian apple.

I don't suppose these codes will last long, if anyone starts shooting at me, thought Anthony.

He reopened *Antigone*. Antigone had gone out and died for a completely meaningless code. She had buried her brother, although her brother was a no-good traitor. He noted that Linton, inevitably, made some interesting anthropological kinship commentary, in his introduction, on Antigone's extraordinarily unconvincing explanation for her behavior: I would not have done this for husband and child, said Antigone, for I could get another husband or another child, but where will I find another brother? Linton explained this in terms of endogamy and exogamy; even Linton, old world as he was, had become a reluctant structuralist. Anthony was prepared to believe it, while reflecting that his own society was so different that he would willingly, could he have found the courage, have died for Babs or Alison, or for any of their various children, but that nothing on earth would persuade him that it was worth dying for either of his two disagreeable brothers.

Although, in a way, it was the pointlessness of Antigone's sacrifice that was so significant. Linton Hancox recognized this. "While accepting the force of the anthropological argument," he wrote, "we nevertheless today continue to be moved by the abstract nature of the sacrifice. . . . Maybe our society, so lacking in rigid codes of behavior, so influenced by the rationalism of the eighteenth century, turns all the more strongly toward the apparently irrational. It is interesting that Anouilh, during the German Occupation, turned to the same myth. . . ."

Yes, thought Anthony. That weekend at the Hancoxes' flashed back into his memory with a horrible clarity: the cold, the sloping bed, the wet fields. He knew, in his bones, that he, Anthony Keating, was in for worse than discomfort, that shortly he would look back to Linton's cottage as though it were the height of physical luxury.

The airport had gone silent. There was not a sound. At about four, he could hear trucks moving away; he was thinking he might risk opening his door when he heard sounds, shuffling, banging, voices, then again silence. It would be wiser, after all, to wait for dark; though then, where should he go? Perhaps it would be worth trying the consulate: there was no reason to suppose that everyone was dead.

It began to grow dark. Jane, by now, would be in England. A lemon moon hung low in the sky. The airport buildings were, as far as he could see, in darkness, which implied that there was nobody around at all. It was uncanny. If the Wallacians had an air force, why was it not doing something? Had it already been wiped out by the Russians, the Chinese? Or were there other, military airfields scattered all over the country? Yes, that was clearly the explanation. This was nothing but a small commercial provincial airport, which handled only a few flights a day. It had closed down for the night. Perhaps nothing much is happening at all, thought Anthony to himself: perhaps the whole thing was a mere skirmish, a false alarm.

A false alarm, in which I unfortunately lost my passport and missed my plane.

He decided to walk back into town.

.   .   .

No news of Anthony Keating reached England for four months. He was presumed dead, by Babs and Alison, by his own children, by his mother and brothers, by Giles Peters and Rory Leggett, and his solicitor. Even Humphrey Clegg began to think he was dead. Humphrey Clegg had been responsible for a not inconsiderable number of deaths over the Wallacian crisis, but he could not really blame himself: he had done his best and his best was better than most people's. It could have been much worse. It had been better than the Albanian fiasco, anyway. Moreover, Jane Murray was alive, well, and free, and Anthony Keating would surely have been pleased about that, as an English gentleman.

Only Jane insisted that Anthony must still be alive. She had become a passionate admirer and advocate of Anthony. Alison, listening to her breathless emotional panegyrics, found herself wishing dumbly and bitterly from time to time that perverse Jane had realized what a wonderful man Anthony was a little earlier, and allowed him and Alison a little happy married life together, before this disaster.

Anthony Keating certainly looked heroic, in the British press. His photograph adorned many editions. The Foreign Office did not suppress the publicity, for the image of Anthony as Scarlet Pimpernel, flying out to rescue stepdaughter in distress, was the least damaging image that the Wallacian factions could receive, assuming that Anthony might still be alive. And Alison let Jane talk to the papers and on the television as much as she wanted: poor child, she had deserved a brief hour of notoriety and glory. In her better moments, Alison had to admit that Jane was behaving, at last, rather well: she took entire responsibility for the car accident, no longer saying that it was not her fault; she took responsibility for her own shocking appearance, explaining that the hunger strike had been her own idea, and a silly one at that; she praised the Wallacian prison authorities, who had treated her quite fairly, in all, she said. The governor in particular, she said, had been kind, and had lent her books to read. She hoped, she said, she hoped and prayed that Anthony Keating would be treated as well as she had been.

Alison always shut her ears and eyes at that bit, for she knew Anthony was dead. She tried hard to avoid the violent pictures that filled her mind—bombs, guns, snipers, grenades exploded endlessly in her dreams and her waking hours. There are worse fates than death, she tried to tell herself. But she knew that that was not true.

The Wallacian crisis seemed to Alison to last a long time. News was uncertain. An alleged pro-Chinese conspiracy was alleged to have been suppressed, the elderly Tetov was accused of neo-Stalinism, and his Minister of the Interior was accused of Revisionism. Both were shot. There were many executions, some orderly, some disorderly. International opinion protested about the death of Tetov, but there was not much that international opinion could do. The Russian tanks did not roll; the Warsaw Pact countries had shuffled off Wallacia, as she had shuffled off them. At one time it looked as though neighboring states, despite Russia's disapproval, might involve themselves, but they did not move; neither did the Americans, the Cubans, the distant Chinese. The Arab world shifted uneasily and made uneasy pronouncements, in the time it could spare from its own troubles, for ubiquitous Palestinian guerrillas were said to have been involved in training anti-Tetov insurrectionists. Various experts in international affairs wondered if some new shift of power in the Near and Middle East might be about to take place: was this the beginning of the flow of Eastern power across Europe? It appeared not. Law and order were restored. Wallacia remained what it had always been, a small, independent Communist republic, though it became less isolationist in its policies: it reopened diplomatic relations with the Soviet Union, which had been severed in 1964. The new President, Clejani, declared himself in favor of detente and the Helsinki agreement. Despite fears on all sides, the struggle had been contained, and compared with the death toll in Lebanon or Angola, the fighting had been modest in scale.

Nevertheless, Alison remained convinced that Anthony had been one of its innocent and accidental casualties, until news reached the new ambassador in Beravograd that a man who said he was called Keating was being held in the Plevesti camp. He had been sentenced to six years' strict regime in a labor colony, for anti-Wallacian activities and espionage.

The ambassador immediately requested to visit Anthony Keating. Permission was refused. Protests ensued. Finally, a letter from Anthony Keating, satisfactorily establishing his identity, arrived. It said that he was in good health, that he fully accepted the justice of his conviction, that he was in the process of subjecting his past life to an intense and thorough analysis, and was reviewing the ideological basis of his past attitude toward the Wallacian people and their heroic history. He was being treated well, receiving an adequate diet, and wished to send his affectionate respects to his family, to whom he hoped, in the course of time, and at the discretion of the governor, to be allowed to write.

The ambassador stared at this communication with interest. He wondered how Keating had managed to survive without being shot. He had certainly learned the right vocabulary quickly. As far as the ambassador knew, Keating had no past attitude whatsoever to the heroic Wallacian people, and there was an ironic clumsiness in his wielding of the usual instruments of apology that suggested he was keeping his head well screwed on. He would apply for permission to visit in another month. They would surely let him see him in the end. He recalled a story, told him by a man in Hungary at the time of the Revolution, of a prisoner who had emerged after more than ten years in jail, a British citizen, released when the jails were opened by the revolutionaries; she had languished unknown, utterly lost from all records. Keating was comparatively lucky.

He reread the letter. Clegg had made a balls-up of the whole thing in some ways, but perhaps he had been right about Anthony Keating. Perhaps Keating ought to have entered the Foreign Office, been a diplomat. Perhaps he had missed his vocation. He had, after all, managed to get that tiresome teenager to deliver some useful goods in London. Or goods that might have been useful, had things taken a different course. Poor old Keating.

There was little hope, in the circumstances, of getting him released, but at least one could go and have a look at him.

As Anthony Keating had politely and respectfully hoped, in the course of time he was allowed to write to Alison and to his children. Unfortunately, not much information could be gleaned from his monthly letters. There was, of course, no account of what had happened between the time that Jane had last seen him on Krusograd airfield and the time that he had emerged in the Plevesti camp. Nor were there many graphic details of conditions in the camp, beyond the information that, as Alison would be relieved to hear, the food was luckily remarkably low in cholesterol content; in fact, wrote Anthony, "ideal for a man in my state of health." Alison, pondering this sentence, decided that either Anthony had gone mad, or that he was in a better frame of mind than she had dared to hope.

He had at first had little contact with his fellow prisoners, he wrote in his third letter, but now was permitted to mingle freely and share their duties. He made it sound quite a treat.

The mountainous scenery of Upper Wallacia was particularly splendid, as Jane would remember, he wrote, and the climate bracing.

He hoped that they were all well. He wanted Alison to know that she should consider the house as her own. He had intended to make a will, leaving it to her, but had not got round to it. She should do what she wished with it. God would advise her.

This last sentence perplexed Alison extremely. God would advise her? Who was God? Was it a code name for Giles Peters or Len Wincobank? She knew that God was illegal in Wallacia, and had never known Anthony to refer to him before, except when he called upon him and took his name in vain.

She did not know what to do. She explained to the ambassador and to Humphrey Clegg and to Amnesty that Anthony had a weak heart, and ought not to be subjected to the rigors he was clearly undergoing. She got his doctor to write to the ambassador. The ambassador continued to protest about the refusal of the authorities to allow him to see Anthony Keating, though his private opinion remained that Anthony Keating was lucky to be alive, and that if he had survived so far, he would probably continue to do so. Plevesti camp was not famed for its humanitarian outlook, but it did not torture its inmates or starve them to death on purpose. On the other hand, some of its inmates died from time to time from natural causes. If it was true that Keating had a bad heart, then something ought to be done about him. The ambassador went on writing letters. He suspected the bad heart. All prisoners' wives claimed them for their husbands.

Anthony continued to write letters about the trees, and the camp cat, and the sunsets. He continued to assert that he was well. Alison wrote back, with innocent details of the same nature; it occurred to her once, as she tried to think of something else innocuous and interesting to say, that writing to Anthony in labor camp was not unlike writing to Molly at the Margaret Gaskill School.

Toward the end of the first year of Anthony's detention, the ambassador, now familiar with the new regime and a little more certain of the regime's reluctance to offend the outside world, worked out that the Wallacians must know that Keating was innocent of espionage, in any serious sense of the word. If he had been guilty, they would have shot him. If they had even thought him guilty, they would have shot him. The fact that he was still alive meant that they knew he was of no importance. The ambassador decided to risk making more fuss, and as a reward, was granted an interview with Anthony Keating, in the presence of two camp officers.

The interview took place in Mjesti, a small mountain town fifty kilometers from Plevesti. The Wallacians did not want the ambassador to see the camp. He did not make an issue of this point.

As the ambassador had never seen Anthony Keating as a free man, he was in no position to compare the new one with the old one. But he thought that Anthony looked not too bad. He had grown a beard: the razor blades, he said, did not encourage shaving. He was thin, but by no means emaciated; he did not look as though he had been knocked about. His skin looked weathered, a condition due no doubt to open air life. When the ambassador inquired about his health, Anthony said that the worst he could complain of these days was dermatitis, and displayed his hands, which were swollen and indeed peeling rather badly. "It's the so-called soap," said Anthony. "But then, I always had a delicate skin." The ambassador asked if the camp medical authorities were aware of the problem. Anthony smiled, a smile much in keeping with the tone of his correspondence. "Oh yes, I think so," he said.

They were allowed to talk for half an hour. The ambassador conveyed messages from Anthony's family: his mother had moved to a bungalow in a village ten miles outside Newcastle, where his elder brother practiced; his children were doing well at their various places of education; Jane had decided to leave art college and train as a nurse. Alison had let High Rook House for the year to some Americans, and was living in London, as she had no doubt informed him in her letter. "You do get her letters, don't you?" he asked. Anthony nodded.

Anthony had not much information to impart in exchange, and every time he spoke, the two prison officers moved imperceptibly nearer. He managed to convey that he had spent the first two months of his sentence in solitary confinement, and that he had found it an unnerving experience. "Then they decided I had nothing to say," he said, "so they let me out."

He added, "It wasn't very pleasant, waiting for them to decide that I had nothing to say."

The ambassador pricked up his ears. "You weren't actually ill treated, were you?"

Anthony shrugged. "Well, it was a state of emergency, you know. And when I was picked up, I was found associating with people of the wrong persuasion."

The prison officers moved in and said that the time was nearly up. The ambassador offered them and Anthony cigarettes. Anthony accepted one, inhaled, and started to cough and splutter.

"Out of practice," he wheezed. "I don't buy them in the camp. I spend my money on paper and pens."

The ambassador was interested in the people of the wrong persuasion with whom Anthony had been found, but could not think of any clever way of phrasing his questions so that the observers would not understand; perhaps, after all, Anthony had been involved in Wallacian politics, other than as a carrier of Humphrey Clegg's messages? Anthony, for his part, would have liked to explain that his association with these ideologically confused people had not been exactly a free one: he had simply exchanged one set of captors for another. He had had a run for his money, in Krusograd, but it had not been a very long one. He was surprised, like the ambassador, that he had not been shot, all the more so as he had committed several real offenses, as well as unreal ones: he had stolen a car, broken into a deserted farmhouse, and shot a barking Alsatian with a farmer's shotgun, before being stopped. Somebody else had shot the farmer, but Anthony did not expect anyone to believe him, especially as he was not able to explain himself in Wallacian. The shooting of the Alsatian had been so horrifying that he had realized at once that he was not cut out to shoot human beings, and he had surrendered to the first comers. It did not seem worth going back over this old history, even if the officers had permitted him, which they clearly would not. He had had plenty of time to come to terms with his memories, in those two months of solitude.

The ambassador puffed meditatively at his American cigarette. He returned to the subject of ill treatment. Anthony explained that he had been obliged to undergo certain rather uncomfortable forms of medical treatment that he was sure would be considered archaic in the West, except perhaps in some very run-down mental hospitals, but that he had survived them without lasting ill effects. The other unpleasant aspect had been the behavior of certain of his fellow prisoners, who had taken against him on account of his nationality; other inmates, however, had defended him, and now he found he rubbed along quite easily. There were two other fellows who spoke English, of a sort, some who spoke German, and Anthony himself was learning Wallacian. He found he had more time for study, now: he was so exhausted, in the first months, that he'd been unable to concentrate in the evenings, but now he'd adapted, and they'd put him on lighter duties since the ambassador had written about his bad heart. For which he was grateful to the ambassador.

"Is there anything I can get you?" asked the ambassador. "I could try to get books sent through. Or writing paper."

Anthony hesitated, then laughed. "There *are* some books in the camp," he said. "There are even some English books. There's a detective story by John Dickson Carr, which I've read fourteen times. I know the plot rather well by now. And there's a copy of the *Pickwick Papers*, which is rather more satisfying. And an annotated Boethius. I don't know what to ask you for, really, there are so many things I'd like. I wouldn't mind a book on Eastern European birds. There must be one, surely? We see quite a lot of birds. Passing through." He paused, embarrassed. "But what I'd really like," he said, "would be a Wallacian tampura. It's a sort of guitar, you know? Do you think they'd let me have one? One of the other chaps has got one, he's been teaching me to play. We sing, in the evenings."

"I'll try," said the ambassador. "I'd forgotten you were something of a musician."

They were both silent. The time was up. The guards rose to their feet. The ambassador reached out, shook Anthony's hand as warmly as he could.

"Tell them not to worry about me," said Anthony. "As you can see, I'm all right. In fact," said Anthony, "you could say that I'm making good use of my time. We should all be obliged to spend a few years of enforced contemplation. There's something rather consoling about the lack of options. Freedom is a mixed blessing, don't you sometimes think?"

The ambassador smiled wanly. "I'll send you the bird book," he said. "And a guitar, if I can get hold of one. And I'll try to visit again. I suppose it's possible that they might let Mrs. Murray visit you, in the autumn. I'll try to fix it."

"I wouldn't bother Mrs. Murray, if I were you," said Anthony. "I shouldn't think she wants to visit Wallacia again."

And they shook hands again, and parted.

The ambassador, driving back in the diplomatic car, down the winding road to the flat alluvial plains of the East, reflected that Keating had not asked him a single question about the outside world, about English politics, about world affairs, even about Wallacian affairs. He was not much surprised. Prisoners, like long-term hospital patients, lose interest in everything beyond the confines of their own institution. Keating's state of mind seemed good, all things considered. He had been the victim of the most appalling bad luck, but he seemed to be taking it well. Not bearing grudges. What he would be like in two or three years' time, who could say?

The ambassador did not feel too worried about Anthony Keating. He had himself spent the last two years of the war in a Japanese prisoner of war camp, without a copy of the *Pickwick Papers* for company.

Anthony Keating is writing a book, while he is in prison. He is not the first prisoner to spend his time in this way, and will not be the last. His book is about the nature of God and the possibility of religious faith, and he suspects that if he lives to finish it, and if ever he returns to England, and that if he is allowed to take it with him, nobody will want to publish it. He realizes that his memoirs of prison life would be of more general interest, but thinks it would be unwise to write them while still captive on Wallacian territory, and anyway, he is more interested himself in the problem of God. He is not too perturbed by lack of reference books: Boethius's *Consolation of Philosophy* has influenced him more than it should have done, perhaps, or would have done in other circumstances, but he cannot help that. He admires Boethius. He too was a prisoner, and Anthony is interested in the fact that he found consolation more in philosophy than in faith, in those last terrible years. Anthony's book is not very well written because he is not a very good writer. But he writes for himself. He has lost interest in any market.

He recognizes that his interest in God may be due solely to his peculiar situation, and the number of times he has escaped death, unusual for a Briton in the nineteen seventies. He cannot evade the idea that God has given him the chance to work out the first causes and the last causes, and that he must not reject it. Those long winter days alone at High Rook House were a warning and a preparation. He should have concentrated harder then, but was too distracted by the memories of the living, by the immediate future, by Alison, Jane, Molly, Tim, Len Wincobank, Maureen, Babs, Giles Peters. Also, he was not then sufficiently uncomfortable. Now he is often bitterly cold, usually hungry, and frequently afraid. Unpleasant things happen to his fellow inmates from time to time: they fall ill, disappear without warning, one or two try to escape into the inhospitable surrounding wastes, and are shot. The absence of drink, sex, warmth, and human affection has concentrated his mind wonderfully. If God did not appoint this trial for me, then how could it be that I should be asked to endure it, he asks. He cannot bring himself to believe in the random malice of the fates, those three gray sisters. He is determined, alone, to justify the ways of God to man.

Religion was illegal in Wallacia, until the Tetov regime was overthrown, although now some forms of it are tolerated. Some sects are still proscribed. Several of his fellow prisoners are prisoners of conscience, clinging pertinaciously to obscure beliefs. There are two Latter Day Bogomils, one Jehovah's Witness. Anthony does not get on with them at all well. He thinks they are crazy. He cannot see how anyone can voluntarily endure years in Plevesti camp for principles so unlikely. They worry him, however. For maybe he is equally mad. But he feels that if God exists, he would not care either way in what way men confessed him, what strange rites they undertook for him. The question is: is he there, or is he not? And when will he greet Anthony Keating?

He takes time off, of course, for other matters. He has learned to play his guitar quite well, has learned some fine Balkan ballads, and is in demand for evening musical entertainments. He has made some friends, of sorts, and learned much of the sufferings of others, and of their courage. This is natural, in a prison. He thinks more of them now than he thinks of the shadows from the past. He has ceased to dwell on the empty private dream that he and Alison once shared, of peace and love.

This book too, like Anthony's, could have been about life in that camp. But one cannot enter the camp, with Anthony Keating. It is not for us, it is not, anyway, now, yet, for us. But we must acknowledge, we must pay our respects, within our limitations. Into some of Anthony's experience, we can enter.

We can appreciate, for instance, his interest in birds. The ambassador, true to his promise, sent him not only the guitar, but also a well-illustrated bird book. Anthony takes pleasure in observing, identifying. They are free, they fly in and out freely, unalarmed by the sight of human imprisonment. He resents them less than those in Scratby resented the soaring jets of the RAF. The birds are innocent slight spirits.

Toward the end of his second year, as Anthony is sitting in a half hour's break from sawing wood, he sees a rare bird, a wonder, a bird that, as he knows from his book, rarely visits below the snow line, rarely visits the haunts of men, a secret beauty. It is a tree creeper. It perches, for a while, as Anthony watches, on the barbed wire of the high fence. It sits, and waits, then off it flies, its rounded little wings a brilliant red, beautiful, rare, dipping and leaping up, fluttering like a butterfly, for him alone. Off it will go, back to its rocky crevasses, up, high up in the mountains. But it has visited him. And it is alive. His heart rises. Perhaps it will come again. It is, he thinks, a messenger from God, an angel, a promise. I think these things because I am high on suffering, he tells himself, but nevertheless his heart rises, he experiences hope. He experiences joy. The bird will fly off, fluttering away its tiny life. There, we leave Anthony.

Alison there is no leaving. Alison can neither live nor die. Alison has Molly. Her life is beyond imagining. It will not be imagined. Britain will recover, but not Alison Murray.

A NOTE ON THE TYPE

This book was set on the Linotype in Janson, a recutting
made direct from type cast from matrices long thought
to have been made by the Dutchman Anton Janson, who
was a practicing type founder in Leipzig during the
years 1668–87. However, it has been conclusively demonstrated that these types are actually the work of Nicholas
Kis (1650–1702), a Hungarian, who most probably
learned his trade from the master Dutch type founder
Dirk Voskens. The type is an excellent example of the
influential and sturdy Dutch types that prevailed in
England up to the time William Caslon developed his
own incomparable designs from them.

Composed by The Maryland Linotype Composition
Company, Inc., Baltimore, Maryland. Printed and bound
by The Haddon Craftsmen, Inc., Scranton, Pennsylvania.

Typography and binding design based on a design
by Virginia Tan.